Jo
may u
 Be wise ones
 and your pathway
       Rosy.

    Sally Kerr-Kelly

     YRTCMNDYFi.

Jun
my fair Choice
of all the
and fair authors
Book

Jeremiah

Books by Sally Kerr-Kelly

Up From The Boggy Bottom

Beyond The Scope of Reason

Up From The Boggy Bottom

By Sally Kerr-Kelly

Up From The Boggy Bottom

A NOVEL

Sally Kerr-Kelly

Pacohi Publishing

UP FROM THE BOGGY BOTTOM
An *original* publication of Rapport Books.

 Rapport Books imprint of Pacohi Publishing, a division of Pacohi, Inc.
1525 Aviation Boulevard – Suite 442, Redondo Beach, CA 90278

Visit our website at www.PacohiPublishing.com about special discounts for bulk purchase information.

Copyright © 2010 by Sally Kerr-Kelly.

The characters and events in this book are fictitious. Any similarity to real persons, living or dead, is coincidental and not intended by the author.

Rapport Books Paperback Trade Edition Printed September 2011

All rights reserved. No part of this book may be reproduced in any manner whatsoever, including information storage and retrieval systems, without permission in writing from the publisher, except by a reviewer who may quote brief passages in critical articles and reviews.

Library of Congress Cataloging-in-Publication Data
Kerr-Kelly, Sally
  Up From The Boggy Bottom: a novel / Sally Kerr-Kelly – 1st ed.
  p. cm.
  ISBN 978-1-937319-02-1   (hardcover)
1. Life change events - Fiction. 2. Family secrets – Fiction. 3. Religious aspects - Fiction.
           Printed in the United States of America

This Paperback Edition: ISBN 978-1-937319-00-7
eBook Edition: ISBN 978-1-937319-01-4

Printed in the United States of America
10 9 8 7 6 5 4 3 2 1

*Dedicated to my loving and devoted parents,
Hubert and Agnes Kerr*

Acknowledgments

To my family and extended family who have encouraged me every step of the way, thank you.

Thank you to my excellent editors, Dennis and Shane, who have shown great diligence in perfecting the final product.

Many thanks for the useful suggestions from my readers: Karen, Judy, Beck, Pat, Kitty, Carolyn, Larry, Roblyn, and Barbara, some of whom suffered through the early stages of the book. Special thanks to my mom who, even though legally blind, listened as I read each version to her.

And thanks to the Women's Scholarship Committee of Allegheny College, and the dedicated individuals there: Nancy, Jan, Beth, and, most especially, Dr. M. Jeanne Braham, poet, writer, publisher and gifted teacher.

Foreword

Some people follow a path their whole lives bound on either side by hedgerows of normalcy; a restrictive road, that one, but also a safe one if you forget the intersections. Whether by a toss of a coin or a look at a map, intersections require that we choose. And in choosing, how many turns, how many straight-ahead choices do we make before we realize that turning back is not an option?

Like many others, this is a story about choices: Wrong ones, to be sure; primal ones; considered, right ones; and ones that seem predetermined, trickling down from the choices that others made long before.

Up From The Boggy Bottom

1   Emmaus, Virginia
Summer 1951

On a morning when the heat from the day before still hovered over the street in front of their house, they took her away.

The little tar bubbles that had boiled up and burst open the day before had settled back, smoothed over and sealed off once again. The sun hinted at its presence along the eastern horizon, shooting up little shards of light as though it hid there, just below the trees spaced along the edge of the church parking lot across the street. Soon, perhaps while their heads were turned, the sun would steal into the sky and burn its way through early morning mist and, once again, seek out the little tar bubbles.

But they were out of the driveway, onto Walnut Street and approaching the corner of Main Street before the sun peeked over even the shortest of the trees.

He stood at the study window unaware of the sun's progression or of the smudges in the corners of the upper windowpanes.

He stood there long after the taillights of the Studebaker faded to pinpoints off in the distance and then to nothing at all.

2 — Teddy – Emmaus, Virginia
November 1976 – Fall 1977 (25 Years later)

The Reverend Doctor Theodore Teeple found the ledger, documents, and letters while cleaning out some boxes in the attic of the church where he served as senior pastor. Sealed in a legal-sized envelope, the documents, originals with raised seals intact, had yellowed with age. The leather-bound ledger held pages of meticulously written entries.

The letters had been opened and flattened with their individual envelopes attached. Twenty of them in chronological order, they were all dated between August 1, 1951 and March 2, 1952. Considering the dates on the envelopes, Teddy Teeple could only assume that his father, the late Reverend Amos Teeple had put them there. His father had been pastor from 1940 until his death in 1962 of this same church in which Teddy served. All were addressed to Teddy's sister, Neena, with the return address: Will McClure, c/o Frederick County Jail, Winchester, Virginia. Teddy noticed they had three-cent stamps on them. He felt safe in assuming the letters had never been delivered to Neena.

He began reading the first one. It was short, like the writer had been interrupted or had run out of words. But Teddy found the fourth letter, dated three days later, more compelling.

August 4, 1951   *8:30 Sat nite*
Dear Neena,
    I guess I can't understand why you don't write to me. Are you getting my letters? I wish you were here

with me right now. I am so scared about what is going to happen to me. My nerves are shot. I'm in solitary confinement because I ran away and tried to talk to you. I wanted to explain. To you and your dad but I couldn't get the words out. I didn't mean to hurt him. I have a hearing and that scares me. Like I said in the first letter I'm so sorry for what I did to you. I love you and always will. Please don't worry about anything. I will get out of here and make things right. I wish I knew my own mind but I'm all mixed up. Not about you. About me. About why I do wrong things. Wouldn't it be fun to roller skate to Please Send Me Someone to Love?

Do you feel okay? Are you scared, too? Write to me. Please, please write to me. I'm so alone.
Love, Will

The letters raised in Teddy an empathy that surprised him. The Will of the letters seemed a much different person than the boy whom Teddy had so disliked when they were young together. He wanted to know what kind of man Will had become.

As was his custom, he started thinking of parallels between these letters and scripture text for upcoming sermons.

He thought of David, a boy, out in the open air, a tender of sheep, who, when confronted by Goliath, picked up from a stream a smooth stone for his slingshot and aimed. Just like that, with little aforethought, he became a giant-slayer. Later, while in exile, David wrote the beautifully plaintive words to some of the Psalms. A man by then, a man with grown-up indiscretions, to be sure, David's words were no more heartrending than Will's. They were just two boys, this David who would be King; this Will who would be just a man, a man like Teddy, like those men in his congregation, men who made mistakes that no doubt affected those around them. Just a boy; just a man ... ..

Then, just one month after finding the letters, he unexpectedly became reacquainted with Will. Teddy made no mention of his possession of Will's letters. Rather, still using the letters as inspiration for sermons, Teddy kept the letters for months, arguing with himself about whether he should give them to his sister, Neena, and in doing so cause her to revisit a painful and confused time in her life, or just destroy them.

Then, more than six months after discovering the letters, documents, and ledger, he photocopied them, keeping the copies ostensibly in case the originals became lost but, in truth, because he could not part with them. He left the original documents in their manila envelope and placed the originals of the letters and ledger into another, larger manila envelope and, timing their receipt to just prior to Neena's departure on an ocean-going cruise, mailed both envelopes to her. Perhaps onboard ship she would have leisure time in which to read and digest them.

3

Aboard the Southern Sun Cruise Liner
Fall 1977

He caught no glimpse of them as he boarded the cruise ship, but he hadn't really wanted to, at least not then. He had wakened that morning with a severely sore throat and a headache, and later, as the afternoon wore on, he had begun to feel feverish.

Despite the warmth of the Floridian afternoon sun, his chills had driven him immediately to his cabin where he had taken no time to settle in, had merely poured a glass of water from the pitcher on the vanity, shed his outer clothes, donned a bathrobe, put his wallet into the safe, and then crawled between the sheets. He turned on his television and, hoping that it would help him fall asleep, decreased the volume so he had to strain to hear it.

But the television voice droned on, and even though the bed felt good, he slept fitfully, waking to the cabin steward's delivery of his suitcases, stirring when the ship began its turn and then slow departure out to sea. He got up once to turn off the receiver in his room blaring out the captain's service announcements. He fell into a deeper sleep then, waking momentarily when the steward started to enter, apologized, and hastily left.

He woke with a start. The clock read two o'clock, and he assumed it was two a.m. His damp t-shirt and underwear clung to his body. Rising on wobbly legs, he went into the bathroom and showered. The chills began again, but the warm water helped. Stepping from the shower, he toweled off, felt dizzy, but regained his equilibrium. As he stood there he looked at himself in the full-length mirror. Viewing himself through blue eyes much like his old man's, he hoped his were brighter, not depthless nor flat as his father's had been. At age forty the muscles on his six-foot frame remained hard, toned, yet he had developed a very small paunch in recent months; little love handles that no amount of exercise could eradicate. His hair had grayed in spots making his dark blonde hair sparkle in the light. Curls were still evident on his wet head despite keeping his hair close-cropped. As he dried his face, he had to admit that the freckles he thought he had left behind in his youth still popped out on his nose and across his cheeks after any prolonged sun exposure.

Another bout of dizziness and nausea hit him. He went into the bedroom and wilted onto the bed. He slept, waking only long enough to put the *Do Not Disturb* sign on the door.

He slept.

4
Neena – Aboard Ship
Fall 1977

A stout breeze swept back Neena's hair as she stood alone on the ship's forward deck. She watched as the sun lingered on the horizon, splaying light across the choppy sea. She expected to see others join her on deck, but most people were still inside finishing their dinner or readying for it.

She closed her eyes, pat images of what land over the horizon would look like playing behind her eyelids: Palm-lined shores, coconuts littering the ground, white sand, volcanic outcropping. Her hands resting lightly on the rail, her eyes still closed, she let the movement of the ship lull her. The tension and anger she had experienced for so long stayed lodged there in her stomach like a heavy lump of food that her system wouldn't, or perhaps couldn't, digest. Yet in this moment it was quiet, that lump, not roiling about, not threatening to expose her by bringing on one of her little snit fits. Letting the rhythm of the sea take her, she let her body sway slightly, then dramatically, until she wondered how much time had passed.

She opened her eyes again and, hanging tightly to the rail, peered over the side. The waves were huge, the sinking sun making their tops mirror-like, if a little red. But the big ship cut through them, pushing water out of its way, piling it up to the side almost, in the wake it left.

For some reason the ship's progression through water made her think of how each of us progresses through her own history. And just as the ship carries a salt residue from the waters through which it moves, so each of us carries forward some residue from the past.

Her recent afflictions had numbed her, yet a deep sadness kept seeping through, as though through a lesion left by some old, old fester.

She looked down at the waves and thought again of each person's progression through history, and then of history, mere history itself.

Teaching at the University of Virginia, her alma mater, had been satisfying. Having taught there for the past twelve years and recently tenured, she was now a full professor. She had been approved for sabbatical leave this coming year, starting December first. Despite the fact that her pay scale was nothing to brag about, her summers were free, and she still enjoyed her subject: History.

Each year the format for the course she taught changed somewhat, but her lecture on the first day of class varied only slightly from term to term:

This is a history course. History in textbooks confines itself to established, significant dates, primary leaders or particular sequences of events. More specifically, recorded textbook history places events on a timeline by referencing wars, stock market crashes, poor leadership, or weather phenomena; in other words, disastrous cataclysms and negative events.

We must remember that current events of today become tomorrow's history. Yet life comes at us so fast in our busy everyday existence that we rarely document any of it. Instead, we remember events in recent history relative to what we may have been doing at any given moment.

I might remember, for example, that when I heard the announcement over the public address system that President Kennedy had been shot, I was meeting with a student in my new office at the university. I was teaching American History that fall, and I had just begun my first year of study for my PhD so that I could assume a full-time position. Ah, yes, I will never forget that year, that month. And even though most of you were less than six years old at the time, we can be sure of one thing. The year was 1963; November of 1963, in fact. We have heard that date repeated so many times it's pretty difficult to miss getting the correct year of that event on a trivia test.

Of other events, spoken of less, we are less sure. We may recall, for example, that major power outages – blackouts and brownouts – occurred along the eastern seaboard in, when was it, 1973 or 1974? Not so long ago anyway.

We would be close with that guess because major brownouts did occur during Nixon's administration, and he was President from 1969 to 1974. And to narrow down the time even more, I can remember that when a major brownout occurred in New York City, I owned a 1966 Chevelle. I remember hearing the announcement on my car radio. But I sold that car in the fall of 1972, so 1973 or 1974 could not be correct. So, if we were to look up the specific month of major brownouts along the eastern seaboard of the United States, we would find that the actual year was 1970 - September of 1970 to be more specific. Memory is then fallible, even perfidious, when not backed by some data. So, to some extent at least, we need a structured record of history.

Sometimes history is better understood if we look at the way things were in a certain era – the sensibilities, the fads, the taboos, or even what was acceptable behavior and dress.

At this point, her students' eyes began to glaze over, or they doodled or gazed out the window – her cue to cut short the first day's lecture.

In this course we will study history, not through chronicles or history textbooks, but through memoirs. A memoir, as you may know, is a record of events written by a person who has observed or actually experienced certain events.

Let's be aware, however, that all memoirs are subject to distortions, such as the preconceived ideals of the author, his or her biases, values, acuity of observation, objectivity, or even his/her set agenda, to name several. Some are based on diaries that make dates and moments in time more memorable, even more plausible.

You will find common threads in the books I have chosen for this course that will give you insight into accepted customs or social standing within a certain group, or decade, or in a specific area of the country.

So in this class dates are important to the extent that you can place events in time - much as I did in my brownout example - during an emperor's reign, during a decade, or during a U.S. President's term of office. But what I really want you to look for are patterns that tend to repeat themselves, for parallels between something occurring now and an event from the past.

Perhaps, as I have, you will see that history does, indeed, repeat itself.

Even as she finished her lecture and gave the first assignment, she thought again how the same things she had mentioned to her students were things she looked for when she wrote reviews of books. What had often fascinated her were those things obvious by their mere absence: Mr. Hollywood Mega-Star had been, for instance, married three times but makes little or no mention of any of his spouses in his memoir.

Yet how much could be surmised of facts left out, characters not mentioned, or painful memories perhaps brushed aside. The unsaid things are often more important than the spoken if we are able to unearth them.

Despite having a book reviewer's talent for ferreting out such things in her scrutiny of others' lives, she floundered when examining her own. No reviewer's talent was required to see that her concept of her own personal history was only partly true. There were big holes in it. Still she had to admit there were probably three versions of her own history: What she remembered, what other major players in her life remembered, and, in all fairness, what really had occurred.

5

Aboard Ship
Fall 1977

Patrice *Reecie* Teeple Marvin wasn't stupid. After all, she had grown up in a parsonage where parishioners frequented her father's study. And even though no one in that house discussed another's business, some of those parishioners wore their troubles as conspicuously as red paint globs on a white choir robe.

Ever since Reecie and her older sister, Neena, had boarded the cruise ship, Reecie had noticed tell-tale signs, a leaching of color, as though those big red globs had seeped right through Neena's quiet façade. But in Neena's case it was almost too subtle to spot. Reecie's husband would tell her he didn't know how she came up with this stuff, but she knew people, and she knew she was right.

That was not to say that Reecie was brilliant or anything, or even overly astute. The whole family knew that Neena had faced some real struggles lately, what with her illness, and putting up with her ex-husband's shenanigans. But Reecie saw more there in her sister. Not only that Neena was ticked off at the world and downright bewildered by it but, more so, that her soul was wilting, sagging down to her ankles. She looked fragile and in need of rest.

Well, that's why they came on this cruise, wasn't it? They came to relax, to enjoy each other, and to see Neena safely to European shores where she would spend the next five months doing what Neena loved best: Acquiring more knowledge.

But the part that Reecie hadn't signed on for was Aunt Toot, their mother's little sister. She didn't even know Toot all that well. Reecie wondered how old her aunt was. Reecie's mother was, what, seventy-two years of age? That would make Toot sixty-eight, or so; but she seemed old, older than that. Maybe she, Reecie, at twenty-four, lumped them all together, all those people over fifty. She had been known to do things like that.

Now that they had been onboard ship for a couple of days, it looked like Reecie would be in charge of Toot since Neena seemed otherwise-occupied. Still, Teddy should be entertaining their aunt since he invited her. And not only had he invited Toot, but he had brought along his wife, Margot, and their three-year-old daughter, Angie. On top of that they even brought a babysitter, Twila Reckinwald.

What a grand event it had turned into. What had started out as Reecie's quiet accompaniment of Neena to Europe had turned into an extended family reunion. If it really was a family reunion, Reecie now felt a twinge of guilt that she had not encouraged her husband, Danny, and their four-year-old son to come along. But Danny and his mother would watch him well while she was gone. No worries. *Que sera, sera*, she thought.

Getting Toot onboard had been an experience in itself. First, the group's ride from their hotel to the dock required three vehicles since Toot's luggage, alone, took up the whole trunk of one of the taxis. Upon arriving at the Miami dock, Toot paid the porter twenty bucks extra if he would wheel only her luggage on the giant luggage cart, straight into the ship. The porter took the twenty and her luggage, and wheeled off, straight over to another group of people. He then tossed their luggage on top of Toot's and had moved on before Toot could chase him down.

But that wasn't the end of it. Toot recounted the whole scene to Reecie, Neena, Teddy, Margot, Twila, and to anyone who came within ten feet of her. She finally changed subjects once they had checked in and actually boarded the ship. Then she started fussing about finding their room.

When they passed through the welcome lounge, and Toot saw the champagne, she lit up. She took a flute, flirted coyly with a steward one-third her age, threw her dangling scarf another loop around her neck, and became *Party Girl Toot*. Reecie saw a whole new Toot, a young and impish Toot. Those bubbles in her champagne popped up to her eyeballs, climbed right on and did a little dance while her family looked on. At that point Reecie had decided that the cruise could be fun after all.

Finally finding their room that first day, the three women discovered their balcony butted up against a lifeboat. The lifeboat hung so close to their railing that they could, with a little effort, board the thing. Inside, a set of bunk beds snuggled one wall, while a small cot had been jammed against the opposite wall. Out of consideration for her, Reecie assumed, Neena had taken the top bunk, leaving the bottom for Reecie. Toot slept on the small cot. Compact and attractive, the room could accommodate Toot's wardrobe and toiletries with ease. Reecie and Neena's clothes, with a few exceptions, had to remain tightly packed and snugly tucked under the lower bunk bed.

6	**Will - Aboard Ship**
	Fall 1977

Feeling the movement of the ship, Will wakened. He felt disoriented, having no idea what time it was. Still feeling a bit dizzy, he stood and walked into the bathroom. His stomach growled from hunger, and he needed a shower. His throat still felt full and a bit sore. He searched through his ditty bag until he found some aspirin. Coming out into his stateroom, he noticed the clock read 8:30, but he wasn't sure whether it was a.m. or p.m. Sipping from his glass of water, he swallowed an aspirin tablet and washed it down.

Opening the draperies, he unlocked the sliding door and stepped out onto his small deck. The moon up, light shone on the tops of the choppy waves six or seven decks below. Not quite tropical, the breeze blew softly into his face, ruffling his hair. He thought about lying on his deck recliner but remembered the time and realized he had already missed the early seating in the dining room. If he hurried, he could grab a bite to eat from the buffet and still make it to the evening live-theater performance.

Within twenty minutes he had showered and dressed in a tropical shirt and light slacks. Making sure he had his passkey with him, he hurried from the room, heard the door slam behind him, walked down the narrow hall, and then stopped.

He retraced his steps and, hurrying back into his stateroom, used his key to unlock the safe. While grabbing some cash from his wallet, he knocked something onto the floor. When he bent to pick it up, he noticed two items, both pictures; both were pictures of Neena.

The top picture he had tucked into his wallet before leaving for the cruise. He ran across it from time to time when it fell from his pocket calendar or from a file. He had finally placed it into a manila folder in which he kept postage stamps and envelopes. Since then, over the years, her picture popped out at unexpected times. He was always caught a bit off guard when he found the picture since, despite his growing older, she remained fixed in time. He couldn't help but remember that, even at age fourteen, she had seen in him something special when many others merely kicked him aside.

When they were young, he had often watched her, wondering what made her so happy. Her mission, it seemed at least then, was to bring a smile to the faces of those she met. She had been big on hugging: Her family, her friends, the elderly ladies in the church, and, especially, after a time, him. She often found something about him to comment on, to let him know she noticed him even if she mocked him like a brother or complimented him like a girlfriend.

He had been many things to many people since then — husband, father, lawyer, mentor, employer, lover. He put the picture into his shirt breast pocket.

The other picture, a snapshot Teddy had recently given to Will, showed Neena with her arm around a younger woman, Reecie. They stood in front of a big-trunked tree on what looked like someone's lawn. Both were dressed in t-shirts, shorts and sandals. Both were smiling broadly, their heads tipped toward each other, their hair touching, even though Reecie stood a bit taller than Neena. Neena's auburn hair framed her delicate, fair-skinned face. Her eyes squinted against the sun. Reecie, with her rare combination of light blonde hair and olive skin, smiled at something or someone beyond the camera's eye. Her lids open, even against the sun's glare, showed her eyes' dark depths. Two little children played in the background, off to one side. Neena looked older, her face a bit thinner, her body a little fuller, but there was no mistaking her. He remembered her straight teeth and her luminous eyes. Her hair seemed lighter, perhaps graying, perhaps highlighted, he couldn't tell. Reecie's smile held nothing back.

He added the second picture to his pocket, stuffed his passkey and cash into his trouser's pocket, and then entered the hall, slamming the door behind him.

He hurried up to the cafeteria.

After eating enough to settle his stomach, he headed forward, toward the auditorium. As he neared the showroom, he heard music and worried that he might be late for the performance.

Hurrying onto what proved to be the balcony, he found a seat at the end of the front row by the stairs going down to the stage. This vantage point gave him a full view of half of the auditorium seating on the starboard side of the ship. He hunched forward in his seat a bit, leaning his arms on the cool brass railing in front of him.

The lights were still up in the auditorium while the stage crew dismantled apparatus from the bingo drawing that had preceded the musical revue due to begin soon. After scanning row after row, starting on the aisle and working in, he spotted them. They were close enough that he could see them quite clearly. Neena sat mid-row with Reecie on her left and an older lady on her right. Beside the older lady sat Teddy and Margot. Neena and Reecie both wore shawls over their bare shoulders. Even though he could easily recognize her from her photograph, Neena now seemed somber by comparison. Perhaps it was the lighting. He rested his head on his forearm and studied them for some time. At one point, Neena looked around and up and appeared to be looking directly at him. He drew back into his seat just as the lights dimmed and the curtain came up.

* * * * *

Will thought he heard his phone ringing as he walked up the hall. Fumbling with the lock, he opened the door and finally entered the room.

"Hello."

"Hi, Will. Hope I didn't wake you. I didn't realize it was so late when I dialed. I haven't seen you at all since we boarded ship. Wondered if you made it. We looked for you to join us at dinner last night but decided you may still be settling in."

"I have been a little under the weather. I didn't make it to the dining room, yet, but I saw the show tonight. I'm not sure this trip was such a good idea."

"Sure it was. Come to dinner tomorrow night. We don't have plans much before that, or you could join us earlier."

"I may wait another day. I'm not sure, yet. But thanks for the call."

"Goodnight, Will."

"Goodnight, Teddy."

7   Neena and Reecie - Aboard Ship
Fall 1977

Neena Teeple Shaw and her younger sister, Reecie, sat in deck chairs on board the Southern Sun cruise liner. On a southern Atlantic crossing they had expected more warm sunny days, but this was their first deck day.

"I think I'm going in," Neena said, as she started gathering her towel and bag.

Reecie turned to look at the deck clock. "It's eleven o'clock. You have been here all of fifteen minutes." She lifted her sunglasses and gave Neena a wilting look.

"I don't have your skin tone. I don't want freckles or age spots," she said, making a face. "And I don't like to burn my skin." Smiling, she added, "Besides that, I haven't eaten in two hours."

"Right. Just sit back down. Watch that guy - the handsome one, graying hair, athletic build, aviator glasses - at ten o'clock, at a table over by the ping pong tables. He's been watching us for most of the time we have been out here. I'd say he has an eye for you, or on you, whichever the case may be. And he's about your age. Maybe you should go for it. You need a little excitement in your life."

Neena had noticed him today in the casino, and last night in the balcony of the showroom. He did seem to be watching them. "There's something familiar about him. It's like I know him or have met him at one time or another," Neena said. "Or maybe he just looks like somebody else. I can't put my finger on it. Something about the way he moves or maybe the way he holds his head, a little tilted to the side, like he's shy or something."

She sat back down on the lounge chair and nudged Reecie. "You don't know him, do you?" When Reecie didn't respond, she nudged her again. "Reecie, are you awake? Quit joking around. Do you know him or something?"

Finally Reecie sat upright, put lotion on her shoulders and then flopped over onto her stomach. "Think about it. Do you ever *really* know anyone?" Then she lay her head down on her forearms.

Neena stood looking at her. There was something Reecie wasn't telling her. Reecie just lay there, soaking up the sun as though she hadn't a care in the world. Nothing fazed her. She looked to Neena at the moment like one of those fuzzy ewes on the farm adjoining Aunt V's. One ewe would lie down for a rest after grazing for hours, and her lambs, usually two per ewe, cavorted around, spring-boarding off their mother's back, stumbling over her head, and she just lay there, contentedly gazing around as if she were enjoying a normal, uneventful day in the life of one valium-snarfing fuzzy ewe. Egad!

8 | Teddy - Onboard Ship and in Emmaus, Virginia
Fall 1977 back to Spring 1977

Teddy Teeple dangled his feet in the water of the pool while his daughter, Angie, played with a family of rubber ducks at pool's edge. He was happy for the warm air and water on a late fall day.

He realized now that his decision to accompany Neena and Reecie on this Atlantic crossing had been a good one. It gave him some much-needed time with his wife and his daughter as well as with his sisters and aunt. He still pondered whether he had made a wise decision in inviting Will to join them. Yet he still thought it was a good idea despite his worry that Will's presence might make both Will and Neena unnecessarily uncomfortable.

Margot had reprimanded him in her gentle, yet direct way. "Are you playing matchmaker again, my husband?"

Truthfully, he was indeed playing matchmaker but, then again, he really wasn't. He thought of his actions as merely aiding two people in healing a painful past. It didn't mean that they had to get together.

And he liked Will McClure. Since becoming reacquainted in the spring of that year, Will's story had slowly unfolded so that Teddy understood so much more than he could even have surmised from his own memory of the past. The two men had become really good friends, playing tennis and golf together, and joining a men's prayer fellowship.

He recalled now the Sunday when they renewed their acquaintance. During the offertory that Sunday, Teddy had noticed a newcomer who had been in the Sunday morning service several times before, who sat toward the back of the church, and who usually slipped out during the closing hymn. But that Sunday morning, Teddy noticed that the newcomer stayed through the closing hymn and benediction. At the close of the service, Teddy proceeded as usual to the back of the church to greet parishioners at the door. Greeting his people remained a highlight of his week. As he looked down the line between handshakes, he noticed the man but still could not see his face clearly enough to recognize him. As the man walked out where the sunlight reached him through the doorway, Teddy tried to place him. His walk was so familiar.

"Good morning, Reverend," the man said.

Teddy would have recognized that deep voice anywhere. "Will, it *is* you. I noticed you two weeks ago, couldn't quite place you, and then you slipped out the side door before I could get to the back of the church." Will smiled and shook Teddy's hand. He had never been a talker.

"Could you stop by and have some lunch with my family and me?" Teddy asked. "I'd love a chance to catch up with you."

Will hesitated and then accepted. They would meet at 1:00 p.m.

Teddy pointed across the street at a white, clapboard house. "I walk to work," he said, smiling.

"I assumed you would live in the parsonage, the same house you lived in when you were a kid," Will said.

When Will arrived at 12:45 p.m., Teddy introduced him to his wife, Margot, and daughter, Angie.

"Dinner will be ready in about forty-five minutes," Margot said. "I hope you two can entertain yourselves that long."

They assured her they could.

"Come out and see my latest woodworking project," Teddy said. "I'm making a bookcase with glass doors for my antique Bible collection, a collection my father started." He ran his hand reverently over the sanded wood. "I shouldn't do that, shouldn't rub my hands over the wood like that. It gets oil from my hands onto the wood and I have to sand it all over again."

Will checked out the door joints. "Nice job on the joints," he said.

They chatted at length, catching up on the past twenty-five years.

"I've heard your name mentioned professionally, know some of your friends, always expected at some point to bump into you, but never did. It seems so strange in a relatively small town."

"I know," Will said. "I have always traveled a lot for my law firm, so that has kept me away. Our main office is still in Arlington, but five years ago we opened a satellite office here in Emmaus so I'm in town much more than ever before. I don't know what took me so long to come hear you speak. I did, come to think of it, hear you speak at my stepson's baccalaureate, several years back."

Teddy sensed that Will wanted to say more, so he remained silent, giving him a chance to find the words.

After what seemed like a long silence, Will said, "I hoped, coming to your church two weeks ago and today . . ., that, perhaps . . ., Neena might be in town."

"I," he hesitated, "I would like to speak with her some time. There are some things I need to say after all these years."

"Go talk to her." Teddy said.

"I don't even know her."

"You will," Teddy said.

9   Aboard Ship
Fall 1977

Seeing that an art auction was in progress, Will slipped through a side door so he could bypass the crowd by way of the promenade deck.

A slight breeze blew in from the water so that, at first, he thought he had imagined hearing his name.

"Will?"

He turned.

Neena stood there, statue-like, her arms down at her sides, palms forward, her hair riffled in a breeze, a puzzled look on her face.

Caught off guard despite his imagining scenarios much like this, he said, only, "Neena."

He thought for a moment he was having a heart attack, but then he started breathing normally again.

"Did you follow us on this trip?" Recognizing the sharpness of her words and tone, she added, "I recognized you somehow after all these years – your walk, maybe, or the way you move your hands or tilt your head. I don't know. Something." She seemed nonplussed or very angry, he couldn't tell which.

Dumbstruck, he couldn't speak even though he had practiced over and over what he would say when he saw her.

"Neena," he said again, and added, almost mechanically, "it is so good to see you. I have thought of this moment for so long."

"What is this about, Will? After all these years, what? What do you want?"

He recovered somewhat then and began his rehearsed speech. "Neena, I need to apologize to you. I am sorry. I have come to ask your forgiveness. I know I complicated your life. I know I hurt you . . . .."

She interrupted him, speaking so softly that he hardly heard her. "That was a lifetime ago, Will."

He stepped closer to her and reached out to take her hand. It felt soft and cool, and she curled her fingers around his for an instant before abruptly withdrawing her hand.

Continuing his rehearsed speech, he said, "I have never forgotten you, Neena." He had thought of her almost constantly at first, but gradually thoughts of her had tapered off. Sometimes whole years had passed when he did not actively think of her, but she had always occupied a special niche in his heart. "I tried for so long to find you. I wrote to you. Then I decided you didn't want me to find you, didn't want anything to do with me. Part of me didn't blame you. I was no prize." He smiled, tipping his head a little to the side in that shy way of his. "Then I let life just suck me in." He trailed off.

She shifted her body slightly so that her back blocked the breeze. Her eyes were large in her face, larger than he remembered. Dark circles surrounded them, and he wondered again if she had been ill. Her hair spiked a bit on the crown of her head, but medium strands feather-framed her face. She seemed to gather herself, her face reddening, but said nothing. He began to wonder if she would ever say anything but she finally spoke, her voice louder; her tone sharper.

"You what? You wrote to me?" She turned to look out-to-sea, and then abruptly turned back, adding, "Oh, forget it. Forget it. I refuse to have this conversation."

She waved, her hand by her check, as though shooing a fly - or him - away, but continued looking at him, puzzlement creasing her brow, her eyes moving over him as though he held some secret, just under his skin.

"You're lovely," he said, inanely filling the silence.

Putting her hand up to her forehead she started to laugh, but no mirth reached her eyes. Then she drew in her breath, cleared her throat, and spoke. "Okay, I get it now. Teddy put you up to this, didn't he?"

She turned around, walked over to the railing, placed one hand on it, and then turned toward him again. "That's why this turned into an entourage instead of a quiet, just Reecie and me, trip. That bugger cooked this up, didn't he?"

"Yes. No. It's a bit simpler than that or maybe a bit more complicated. Teddy and I have become reacquainted over the past six months, and I asked how you were and, and . . ."

He felt inadequate, tongue-tied, and almost desperate to convey his point like he had his first day arguing a case in court, back when he was twenty-five. He walked closer to her. "I haven't pried, haven't asked any questions at all. It's not what you think."

"Well, doesn't it feel a bit bizarre to you that I have never seen you in all these years and *poof,* here you are, on my family trip? And out in the middle of an ocean, no less." She put her hand up to her hair and stroked some strands near her ear, as though taming her hair could help her gain control of their encounter.

"It's true," Will said. "I wanted to see you. I wanted to ask your forgiveness. I even went so far as to think we could be friends. Then Teddy spontaneously suggested that I come along on this cruise. He and I have become friends even though, as a kid, I could never have imagined it. I had mentioned that I was going to Paris in the next month for a deposition, and he said that you were going there as well. Then he called me a few weeks later and suggested I come along on this cruise instead of flying since he and his family had decided to go. I guess I didn't give it enough thought, didn't think it through. Getting the ticket was so spur-of-the-moment. I didn't mean to upset you."

"It's okay. It's okay, Will," she said, placing her hand momentarily on his forearm as though quieting a flighty foal. "It's good you came," she said, mechanically, formally. "How nice that you and Teddy are friends. It has been good talking with you. Perhaps we can chat again some time. I don't even know what you chose to do for a living. In fact, I know nothing about you."

Before he could say anything, she added, "I'm pleased to have bumped into you." She knew she sounded just like her mother, Dessie, so equanimous, so polished, so very, very polite. She hated her reserve, despised her inbred reluctance to just rip into him, give him a piece of her mind, tell him just how perturbed she remained, still, after all these years. But, instead, sounding just like Dessie, pastor's wife extraordinaire, and with carefully modulated tones, she added, "This ship is small enough that I'm sure we will see each other again."

She turned forward, looking, he presumed, for a doorway back into the interior of the ship and an escape from him. "I have to skip off, Will. My Aunt Toot and Reecie will be wondering what happened to me. Good to see you," she said giving a little wave over her shoulder as she walked hurriedly away.

Kicking himself for how he had handled the conversation, Will watched her go. He wanted to run after her, take her into his arms the way they did in movies, pick her up like Rhett had Scarlett, and whisk her away. After she went inside, he walked over to the railing instead, felt an increasingly brisk breeze on his face and stared down at the undulating waves.

* * * * *

As Neena walked away, she felt awash with emotion. Part of her had been thrilled to see Will. Like any old friend who turns up after years away, she wanted to know everything about him: Whom he married; how many children, if any, he had; and what he did for a living. But the other part of her seethed with anger. How dare he approach her like this? How insensitive of Teddy to thrust this on her, this, this rehash of a devastating time in her life. How dare he invite Will on a family trip as if Will had never cut the very legs from under her? She wanted to scream and curse and slap someone or some thing. But no, she couldn't vent her anger; not calm, capable Christina; not *affable Neena*. Her family would think her unstable or, worse yet, pity her. What was wrong with them, anyway? Didn't her family realize that this was a particularly bad time for her? Too much had happened lately. She felt inundated; and ticked off. She wanted to ask Will, with her nose an inch from his, she wanted to ask him, "Do you realize how presumptuous you sound, parachuting into my life, asking for forgiveness and even friendship, and reclaiming me, in a way, like laundry you dropped off all those years ago and forgot? I went to a new owner in your absence, you egotistical turnip."

She let the wind slam the door behind her as she entered the ship. But she couldn't shut the conversation of the past few minutes out of her mind.

She walked through a lounge where a young man sang the Chicago tune, *If You Leave Me Now*, while a piano and even a violin accompanied him. She continued on, entering a hallway that serviced the staterooms.

She realized now that over the years, on the rare occasions when she thought of Will at all, it had been with hatred, sometimes searing hatred but with a certain longing, as well. Then, when her mind once again overcame her emotions, she puzzled as to why she would allow him to pop into her mind at all, let alone command such feelings. As a teenager he had responded to her attention – and kindness – with a grateful tenderness. That was true enough. But intellectually she now suspected that much of his youthful emotion had derived from his forlorn circumstances. When she met him, he had been removed from his home for whatever mysterious reason - she never felt she had received more than a sketchy version, at best, of what had really happened to him. That alone – being removed from his home and family – she now knew from her own experience, had to have made him vulnerable to anyone.

As an adult, she knew that youth and newness of experience can potently charge memory. She suspected what she longed for was not Will, but she as she had been: So fresh, so innocent, so playful, and so brand spanking new, compared to the jaded and angry woman she had become. She wished over and over for that girl she had barely gotten to know. She longed for experiences that she merely sampled on one or two occasions, or had missed altogether, simple little things like going to a movie with friends, going skating, to the prom, to a sock hop, or just going out with some giggling friends for a banana split.

Yet, in spite of her thoughtful parsing, in spite of the anger that made her slam doors and want to pitch little old ladies and small children over the railing into the sea, part of her still wanted to be loved in the way that young Will had loved her; part of her still believed it had been real.

And that night on the ship the man for whom she had cultivated a long-term hatred had stood before her. Despite that and his graying hair, she saw a boy she had once loved, a wary, freckle-faced child so scared words stuck in his throat, a fleet-footed boy posed to run.

Will remained on deck for a while, reprimanding himself for having come on this trip at all, yet trying to recall the tone and every word of his conversation with Neena.

She had seemed at least vaguely interested in his life. Maybe if they ran into each other again they could talk about their lives over the past twenty-six years. In any event, he planned to avoid her for at least another day.

He proceeded along the deck until he reached the door Neena had entered. He went in. He could hear music coming from the lounge near the center stairway. He continued forward to the auditorium, having planned to attend a lecture given by a former Scotland Yard detective, an expert on the real *007,* the real James Bond.

He sat down in the back row removed somewhat from a cluster of people.

Funny, but even at his age he often saw himself that way: Part of a group but somewhat removed from it. He felt that way, as well, while attending Teddy's church for the past six months. Will noticed that Teddy's sermons resonated with a certain familiarity for him. Yet Teddy spoke of men who were put upon by God, in a sense, men who must endure affliction before God would again bless them; victims, per se. But Will did not see himself a victim; in fact, he had a certain disdain for those who assumed that role. For most of his life he had seen himself instead as a perpetrator of ill-advised acts, not the victim of them. He wanted to have done with this introspection of his. "God requires us to be happy," Teddy had said. Happy. Will, nevertheless, looked back too much.

Lately he had begun each morning in wonder. He noticed little individual tufts of grass or the way a robin strutted across the lawn then gracefully soared off into the air, or even the way his fingernails grew faster the more caffeine he ingested.

For the first time in his life he knew the meaning of *marvelous*.

Still, sometimes, he wished he could share this newly found peace, this joy, intimately with someone. Whether he had glorified her because they were young together, or whether she was yet another indication of his looking back, Neena often came first to his mind.

She had always looked for the good in him and in others, brushing aside, not noticing at all, or deeming unimportant, the bad. He had loved that about her more than her physical beauty, more than her humor.

Yet, having seen her just now, and after their brief conversation, he feared that the Neena he remembered had left or been buried so deep it would take a miracle to bring her back, at least to him. But he had come back in a sense. He had begun to feel like a better version of himself. Teddy said she had suffered. Will had not asked for details; he wanted to hear them from her, if the chance ever arose. He knew he had hurt her all those years ago, but he hoped he had not caused the pain to which Teddy referred.

When he spoke with her, she had seemed, what . . . vulnerable, for sure, jaded, perhaps, but definitely sad, and angry? A lack of light in her eyes told him that something or someone had gobbled up her sweet innocence, maybe in increments or in one big gulp, he couldn't know. He had wanted to enfold her in his arms, but that would have been hugely presumptuous and, he suspected, she would not have permitted it anyway.

When he had taken her hand, he had felt her respond, if only momentarily. When he had looked into her eyes, he couldn't help that tears pooled in his, while hers had remained bone dry.

Time. She needed time to digest new information, time to find herself at this stage in her life before she could consider anything with him or anyone else.

Time. That's all. Just a little time.

10 — Will - Onboard Ship — Fall 1977

Not wanting to appear too eager or, for that matter, too nonchalant, Will did not want to be the first one to arrive at the dinner table that evening nor did he want to be the last. As it turned out, he was among the first to arrive at the dining room entrance, waiting in line until the *maître d'* opened the doors. Having difficulty finding his table, Will approached a waiter and asked for help. Five days into the cruise, the waiter seemed neither puzzled nor, for that matter, interested as to why this was Will's first time at the dinner table but merely ushered him to his seat.

Having arrived first to the table, Will felt relief that he could sit wherever he wanted, so he sat in a neutral position, along one side, neither directly facing the rest of the dining room nor the water. When the others arrived, anyone who wanted to sit beside him could do so. As it turned out, Teddy and his wife, Margot, were the first to arrive, Margot spotting Will first. She let out a delighted cry, trotted over and, when he stood, kissed him hard on the cheek. Right behind her, Teddy hugged him and then seated his wife between him and Will.

"Glad you finally made it," Teddy said, winking as he leaned over Margot.

"Happy to be here, I think."

Will sat back down.

"Where is Angie?" he asked. "Where's that adorable little magpie?"

"We brought Twila Reckinwald with us. You know her from church. Her husband died last year, so we thought this would be therapeutic for her and would help us out as well. She has time to herself while Angie is with us or busy participating in activities for kids. Then Twila eats dinner with Angie and spends the evenings with her while we are out. It has worked really well for all of us. This is Twila's first cruise, and she is delighted."

Teddy sat down and took the menu from the hovering waiter.

While the three of them considered menu choices, Will watched the doorway. Soon Reecie entered the dining room, trailed by the older lady he had seen with her two nights ago, and Neena, although he could not get a good view of Neena. Reecie walked in a half turn so that she could continue talking with the older lady. The lady talked at the same time. Neither of the women seemed to notice that she did not have the attention of the other.

When they got closer, Will recognized the older woman as Neena and Teddy's Aunt Toot. She wore black-and-white-checkered reading glasses and mauve-colored silky jeans with a t-shirt with lettering across her chest that read: *You're so vain you probably think this shirt is about you.* Over that she wore a silver mink stole. Three wide yet tasteful gold chains hung from her neck. But, as he remembered her from years before, she was laughing and upbeat, if a little too talkative.

"That's what I'm trying to tell you," Toot said to Reecie. "Up on the eighth floor, where the suites are. I transferred us up there. I have been badgering them every day, and they finally arranged to move us tomorrow morning. Then you and Neena will be more comfortable."

Neena trailed behind them and, in the process of seating Toot, seated herself directly across from Will not appearing to notice that he sat there. Not acknowledging anyone at the table, she seemed preoccupied.

Reecie pulled out her chair and sat down across from Teddy.

"But why didn't you even mention it to us?" Reecie asked Toot before turning toward Neena. "Did she tell you she made arrangements for us to move?"

Neena seemed not to hear her.

"Who do we have here?" Toot asked, looking at Will.

Neena turned to hang her evening bag on the back of her chair, leaned back as the waiter placed her napkin on her lap, and accepted the menu from him. Then she drew the menu up to her chest and began, stiffly it seemed to Will, greeting the others. When she saw Will, she was so taken aback that he regretted even being there.

"Hello . . . again," she said, a deep blush creeping up her face. Will wondered if she was embarrassed or very angry.

"Hello, Neena. I . . ." he trailed off as Teddy interrupted him.

"I have been calling him daily and bugging him to join us."

By then, everyone's attention had turned to Will. Reecie and Toot had even ceased talking.

"And who is this handsome man?" Toot said, looking at Will. "I had noticed that we had an empty chair at our table the past few nights. I guess I thought it was Angie's chair – their daughter," Toot added in explanation to Will. She stroked one of her necklaces and smiled. "So now we have a new tablemate. How lovely."

Teddy stood. "I would like to introduce you to our friend, Will McClure," he said while tapping Will on the back.

Will rose to be introduced.

"Will, this is our Aunt Toot whom you may or may not have met at one time or another."

"And you already know our sister, Reecie, our little baby sister," he smiled as he looked at her. He turned to Toot and said in explanation, "Will attends our church, so he knows Reecie, her husband, Danny, and their son."

Neena shot an intense glance at Reecie, but the younger woman seemed not to notice.

"And, of course, you know Neena and my lovely wife." He smiled down lovingly at Margot.

Will acknowledged them all in turn. Toot seemed a bit puzzled but welcomed him to the table.

Toot peered at him over her glasses. "You're that . . . I remember. Yes. Yes. Yes."

Teddy sat back down. "Let's order and take the heat off the poor man," he said, indicating Will, who sat as well.

Neena sat quietly, concentrating on her menu and not chatting with anyone.

Reecie and Toot seemed to have forgotten their previous discussion and began discussing the menu items.

"I wanted veal. Do you see any on the menu?"

"Tomorrow night is Italian night, remember, Toot? The waiter told us last night."

Looking at the menu, Reecie continued, "Tonight looks like island food: Jerk chicken, grilled items, pineapple, and coconut. Yum. The grilled shrimp looks good. Key lime sauce, mango."

"That's what I want, the shrimp. Or maybe the fish. What is the fish? Snapper? I don't know. We ate those burgers at, what time was that? Two?"

"We're dancing tonight. You need to eat, Tootie Babe. You need energy."

While Neena placed her order with the waiter, Will surreptitiously studied her. She looked lovely; her hair soft on her face and much lighter than it had been when they were young. She wore no wedding ring, but then Teddy had said she was no longer married. For a moment he wished he had allowed Teddy to share more details about her, but he had wanted to glean whatever information he could directly. He noticed again the deep circles under her eyes. Perhaps she was just tired.

The waiter came then and took their orders. Toot held him the longest, asking questions about menu items, making specific requests for cooking and garnishment. Before he could leave the table, she said, "What's for dessert, Ingmar?"

"He brings that later, Toot. Remember, he brings a tray with samples of what is available?" Then, addressing and thereby dismissing the waiter, Reecie added, "She'll wait until you bring the dessert tray."

"Teddy . . . *psst* . . . Teddy, did you know we are changing cabins?" Toot struggled to put her stole over the back of her chair and then continued. "From the seventh to the eighth floor. I arranged for a suite. It is wonderful up there. They have a lounge available twenty-four hours. Pastries, coffee, tea, and a cocktail hour before dinner. They bring fresh fruit and fresh flowers to the suite every afternoon."

Neena turned in her seat. "When did you arrange that, Toot?" Her words sounded sharp but her aunt seemed not to notice.

"This afternoon while you two were out there cooking your skin. I can't take that. You two will look like old prunes if you keep that up."

Toot rummaged through her evening bag.

"Here's your key, Dearie. We are now in Room 8116. Well, our belongings haven't been moved yet but we can go in and look around. Not hard to find, not hard at all. Go up the main elevator, the glass one by the central staircase. The suite is right there, three doors down on the starboard, no, on the port side. Oh, I can't remember. You'll find it. And you'll love it," she said, smiling.

Then she turned to Reecie.

"And here's your key. Don't lose it."

"Why do you think I'll lose it and that Neena won't? You think I'm irresponsible?" Reecie asked, smiling.

"A little."

"Did you hang up my clothes?"

"Not yet, of course. They'll deliver everything in the morning. Then we can put things where we like."

But everyone else had dismissed Toot's topic by then as they discussed their day's activities.

"I played ping pong today, Will," Teddy said. "I tried to call you so you could join me. Maybe tomorrow. I usually go about four while Margot gets all dolled up for dinner."

The chatter continued as their several courses were served and enjoyed. Everyone commented on their entrees and, especially, the dessert each had chosen.

Then Reecie announced, "Listen, guys, I'm going to the casino after dinner and before the show. Anyone want to come?"

"What is the show tonight? Anyone know?" Toot asked.

"The show's that Sylvia Silverstein who played piano themes for old movie soundtracks. She's phenomenal, I hear. And yes, Reecie, we'll come to the casino," Teddy said. "In fact, let's all go. Margot and I will go dancing later tonight. What do you say Neena, Toot, Will? Come join us?"

So after lingering over their coffee, they left the dining room, *en masse*. The ladies took an interminable restroom break, and then they all proceeded to mid-ship where the casino flashed welcoming lights.

Reecie hustled over to the roulette table and soon began placing chips on significant – to her at least – numbers. The wheel spun, the marble danced and finally picked a spot to settle in. The group watched her, each of them *oohing* and *aahing* when she won or lost a round. Neena wandered off after a few minutes and settled into a recently vacated chair at a blackjack table. Will positioned himself so he could watch both her and Reecie. Neena appeared to be a proficient blackjack player although she played extremely conservatively.

After about forty-five minutes, Toot, who had tired of being a spectator to a game she did not really understand, announced that it was time to go to the auditorium if they were to get good seats.

After both Neena and Reecie settled with their dealers, the group moved forward once more to the auditorium. When they arrived at the auditorium, they discovered that only seats in the front row were still available.

"See, we should have come earlier. This is terrible. I can't sit in the front row. I'll get a kink in my neck. What can we do?"

"Toot, settle down. We can sit together, or, if you prefer, we can split up."

"No, no. I'll sit up there. Maybe we'll get selected to go on stage or something. I'm okay. Okay, okay," she said, leading the way.

The last to enter the row, Will ended up seated on Toot's right. He noticed that both Toot and Reecie separated him from Neena.

Careful not to be observed, he watched Neena, how still she sat with her legs crossed and her hands folded decorously in her lap. Once or twice she reached up to pull her shawl closely around her as though she were cold. She applauded vigorously in the right places, but otherwise she remained very still. He wanted to be there beside her, to lend his jacket if she were cold, or merely to hold her hand.

* * * * *

After the show he declined Teddy's invitation to continue on with him and Margot. He did not want them to tire of him. "I think I have had a big day and evening. I'll go back and read a little before turning in." He thanked everyone for including him in their evenings and then wished them all a good night.

When he reached his room he discovered that the room steward had turned down his bed and had put a well-used, handwritten note on his pillow. It read: *Please turn your timepieces one hour ahead tonight. Thank you.*

Still weary from having been ill, Will, still fully dressed, flopped down onto the bed.

He kept thinking about Neena, how vulnerable she had seemed tonight, and for some reason his thoughts strayed from Neena to his mother. He thought about his mother, Lilly, then as he often had over the years since her death. Groggy now, he tried to fix a clear picture of her in his mind. In a dream-like state he found himself drifting toward a memory that momentarily eluded him. Finally the memory played litany-like in his head like a child reciting something committed to memory:

In my first memory of my mother, her face is in stark profile. It is night. She is driving our new car as light from street lamps drifts across her face in spaced intervals. My little brother, Binky, sits beside me, slumped and sleeping against the baby sitter, Dixie. We are taking Dixie home. Our father, big-shouldered, bare-chested, his hair moving slightly in the breeze, sits precariously on the hood of the car, straddling the Plymouth hood ornament , his feet resting on the front bumper. My mother does not drive fast enough for him so he rocks back and forth - forward and back, forward and back - waves one hand in the air, urging her on, and rides the car like a bucking steed. It has become my fixed image of them: My father - outrageous, unpredictable, a real-life buckaroo; my mother - tentative, emotionless, and unable by that point to smile.

Will stirred, coming a bit awake. He realized again that he had not saved his mother nor, more to the point, had he brought her back from her emotional inertia. He mulled on that for a moment and then began again to drift, in and out, down, down. His mother's lovely yet saddened face floated behind his closed lids, part memory and part dream, like those disjointed images that come and go as we begin a slow descent into peaceful sleep. But before falling into a deep, dreamless sleep he remembered thinking that he wanted to keep Neena from his mother's fate. He wanted to see on her face a smile as wide as the horizon of a sun-filled dawn.

11

Neena - Aboard Ship
Fall 1977

As Toot, Reecie, Teddy and Margot discussed which lounge to visit, Neena excused herself saying that a good book awaited back in their room, that she was tired, cold and wanted to get into something warmer.

She passed the elevator, taking, instead, the stairs that wound up through the ship, until she reached their new cabin three floors above. She let herself in with the passkey Toot had given her at dinner, and walked over to roughly open the sliding door leading out onto their small deck.

Alone now, finally alone, after a day she did not want to repeat, she sharply thrust her foot toward the railing, as though kicking away a dog that slurped open her barely scabbed-over scars, or booting a cat that wound around her ankles, its soft fur stirring up feeling and emotions she didn't welcome. What was he doing here, anyway? What did he want from her after all this time? Why would Teddy be so insensitive as to invite him without asking her first? She was tired, tired of swallowing her rage. She was weary of pushing it, pushing her anger down under the surface of a falsely calm demeanor. She dare not feel; feeling was too costly. Feeling made her go back to questioning why? Why? Why? Why had Will . . .? Why had her father . . .? Why had her mother . . . ? Why had Teddy . . .? Why? Why? Why?

The moon had come up and, in the distance, glistened off the tops of the waves. She wanted to calm herself before returning to their original room and long enough to enjoy the tropical breeze. Deciding to go inside to look around, she took a deep, calming breath, and entered the suite.

Looking around the suite, she found it lovely with a master bedroom, another with twin beds, a full bath with tub and shower, and a sitting room. Checking the drawers and closet, she found them to be spacious and more than adequate.

She walked back out onto the deck and sat in one of the lounge chairs. Calm now and still full from dinner she let her head fall back against the cushion.

So Reecie was in on it, too. Just like Teddy. Reecie had known Will planned to join them on the cruise. And just how well did he know Reecie, her husband and their son? And Will; Willis Jacob McClure was here, on this ship, in the flesh, no less.

Her thoughts drifted to him but then continued on to the little town where everyone seated at their table that evening — except Reecie, of course — had been born; where all of them had been raised.

Despite all the years that had intervened since she had lived there, Emmaus, Virginia, still called to her, as home and the past so often, eventually, at least, do.

12

Emmaus, Virginia
Summer 1940 and before

Situated twelve miles upstream from the confluence of Vespers Creek and the Potomac River, the Borough of Emmaus, Commonwealth of Virginia, population five thousand and eighty-two "and one old grouch" as the locals joked, had been settled by a devout Anglican, Josiah Vespers.

Vespers had lived for one year and three months in a mud-chinked hut a mile up the little stream before he went back to Alexandria, Virginia, to retrieve his wife and six children. She had stopped hoping that her husband would return so, planning to remarry, she was stitching a wedding dress when Josiah walked through the door. He put a stop to any marriage, loaded the belongings he deemed necessary into an oxcart and he, his wife, the oxen, and his children set out to walk across the wilderness. All eight Vespers arrived safely in Vespers Creek, as some passers-through referred to the area. When he found the mud hut too cramped for his family, Josiah moved inland half a day's walk where he built a bigger dwelling dwarfed by the virgin timber that surrounded it.

"The river swells come spring," he gave as explanation for moving inland. "But come winter it's so narrow," he was known to say, "you could spit into Mary Land if you had a mind to."

When by 1736 six other families, including three of his sons, had built dwellings there, Josiah decided to give the cluster of houses a real name, calling it Emmaus after the place where Jesus had appeared following his resurrection. Unknown to them, Thomas Fairfax, the Sixth Lord of Fairfax, had arrived in Virginia the year before to claim a grant he had received from King Charles II which included the area between the Potomac and the Rappahannock Rivers. Whether the Emmaus settlers ever knew the land on which they had squatted had already been claimed by another is not known. Nor is there mention in either written or oral history of the town recording that, as a young man, George Washington himself had surveyed for Lord Fairfax the area that included Emmaus. And when, during the Revolutionary War, the Hessians occupied areas west of the town, they must have passed by and somehow missed the little village nestled in the trees just half a day south of the river.

But the town had survived the near-passing of blood-thirsty Hessians, the occupation by both the Union Blue Boys and the Southern gray-clad Rebels during the War Between the States, the loss of some of its citizens during three subsequent wars, and yet had grown and by 1940 offered anything you might want from a small southern town.

The grist mill remained a bustling enterprise as farmers outside the borough limits brought their grain in once a week to be ground and mixed. And within a two block stretch on the south side of Main Street, one could find the Vesper Building which housed a little one-teller bank, a bakery, and Semple's Hardware. Also on that side of the street sat Lindstrom's General Store, a small U.S. Post Office, and Earl's Meat Market. Located beyond that, stood the Voting/Social/Grange Hall, an all-purpose gathering place for meetings, public dinners, weddings, the quarterly secret meeting of the Grange and, in winter, its monthly dances.

Since July of that year, talk around town predicted trouble for the meat market and the grocery section of the general store since the upstart Broxterman's Grocery and Dry Goods had built its new store on Widow Ingham's vacant lot on East Main Street.

The two restaurants in town perched like bookends on either end of the business district: An Italian café owned by Luigi Cafini, open for lunch and dinner; and a simple fare eating establishment called Harry's Diner, open from five a.m. until any influx of customers petered off to nothing.

The W&OD (Washington and Old Dominion Railroad) train station still sat on the corner of Walnut and Main Streets. The railroad in that part of Virginia had changed its name many times over the years but most everyone still referred to it as the old W&OD. The Great Depression had hit the railroad an economic blow from which many feared it would never recover. The rail line had, in fact, discontinued all but freight service to Emmaus the year before, in 1939, having abandoned the western end of its line, altogether. Yet most everyone in Emmaus hoped passenger service would soon resume once again providing transportation east to Arlington or even Alexandria.

Situated on the north side of Main Street, across from the post office, the barber shop with its candy cane pole had on any given day except Sunday one in the chair and at least three or four waiting. Vesta's Beauty Shop, located next door to the barber shop and operated by the barber's wife, remained the meeting place for many of the ladies of Emmaus who had their hair washed and styled once a week, come rain or shine.

Whether at the market, the barber shop, at church or merely passing on the street, by late June of 1940, most residents of Emmaus were talking daily of the war in Europe. In May, the new English Prime Minister, Winston Churchill, had been sworn in to replace bungling Neville Chamberlain. Having announced to the House of Commons that he had "nothing to offer but blood, toil, tears and sweat," Churchill was, nevertheless, championed as the hope of the English people. That same month, Germany had invaded France; and Rommel had pushed his way north as far as the English Channel. Then earlier in the current month, June, the Luftwaffe bombing of Paris had begun. And Canada, following Mussolini's March alliance with Adolf Hitler, had declared war on Italy. Most of Europe writhed in turmoil, and England had only the Channel between it and some of the heaviest of fighting. In America, news had begun to trickle in of the disappearance of loved ones amid the conflict. Most everyone in town had an opinion on when the United States would enter the fray, especially since FDR had asked for money to produce more planes. Most felt that the United States stood just an announcement away from going into battle.

If the Emmaus residents weren't talking about the war, they were discussing the fact that the electric company had extended home electric power beyond the South Side and out of town for six miles along Oxen Hill Road. And in addition to that, outhouses had begun to disappear in the areas beyond the borough limits; people were beginning to piddle indoors, in modern bathrooms.

Within the borough limits of Emmaus, however, most everyone in town knew everyone else or at least someone once-removed like a cousin, an uncle, a co-worker, or a neighbor.

Named after a place where Jesus walked, it was no surprise there were more churches in town than bars. In fact, except for Cafini's which served table wine, Shorty's, situated east of the center of town was the only bar in the borough.

The number of churches totaled three if you didn't count the tent tabernacle that had sprung up in April of that year on the eastern borough limits and was still going strong in July.

The Anglican Church, as the old-timers still referred to it, occupied the southeast corner of Washington Avenue and Oak Street, where the Presbyterians worshipped in their quaint little wooden structure halfway up Oak Street toward Adams Avenue.

The Reformed Evangelical Baptist Church on Elm Street sat across the street from its parsonage. *The manse*, as Mrs. Teeple, a former Presbyterian herself and the wife of the current minister, incorrectly referred to the house, sat back from the street and was fronted by a large yard through which a sidewalk wound, bordered on either side by flower beds. Extending along the entire front of the old Victorian house and wrapping around its east corner, the verandah had two chain-hung swings, one on either end.

Since Catholicism was not very prevalent in the area, the only Catholic parish sat on the south side of town, on Brook Street, just west of where Finney Bridge, commonly called the rickety-rackety bridge, crossed Vespers Creek. A small community which townspeople referred to as *The South Side* had sprung up where a group of Irish immigrants, a handful of Slovaks, and a few token Italians had settled. Many of this group still worked the surviving coal fields over in Mineral County, West Virginia, formerly Hampshire County, Virginia.

In that year, 1940, and in years to come, a Friday night custom was observed by many of the townspeople and even by those in the outlying areas. They either drove into town or merely walked to town center. Not in their Sunday best, but not in their gardening clothes either, they congregated and visited with their neighbors in the *downtown* area. Some came for dinner at one of the restaurants or, in warm weather, at Ma's Hot Dog Stand over by the railroad station, although most residents didn't eat out that often. Many of the women who had bought their dresses and even their shoes from the Sears and Roebuck Catalog walked over to the general store to buy hosiery or a new purse, some dusting or face powder, or even some canning lids. Husbands and sons lounged against the buildings at the two main corners reminiscing, one-upping, and generally enjoying their neighbors.

By eight o'clock on any given Friday night the women had returned to collect the male members of their households. Once collected, the men joined the women as they walked to the grocery store or the meat market to stock up for the week.

After they had packed the groceries into the trunks of their sedans or the beds of their pickup trucks or perched them in the crooks of their arms, they congregated at Harry's for a hot chocolate or coffee if the weather had turned cold or for a soda or sundae if it was warm.

On Saturday afternoons in summer many came for baseball games; in the fall for high school football games. During any season, many others came for the movie showing at the Odeon, a little building shoved in between the meat market and the post office. So far that year movie-goers had seen the Walt Disney film, *Pinocchio*, the Steinbeck account of the Great Depression, *The Grapes of Wrath*, starring Henry Fonda, Hitchcock's thriller, *Rebecca,* and the Mae West and W. C. Fields spoof, *My Little Chickadee.*

On Sunday mornings Emmaus women and children and most of the town's male citizens attended their respective churches. Smelling of breakfast cinnamon rolls, and seared roast beef already in the oven for Sunday dinner, The Reverend Amos Teeple, pastor of the Reformed Evangelical Baptist Church, his wife, Dessie, son, Theodore, and daughter, Christina, known as Neena, needed merely to cross the street to reach their place of worship.

The Evangelical Church, as it was commonly referred to, butted up close to old man Llewellyn's pillared mansion. One of the oldest houses in town and certainly the most impressive, the mansion belonged to Lloyd Llewellyn, a superintendent of the railroad, long-since retired, who, at eighty years old, had suffered a stroke and remained housebound. He had complained on occasion that the Evangelicals' joyous singing and Dessie Teeple's vigorous piano-playing drowned out his private Anglican meditations, but since it proved hard for people who had been moved by the Spirit to tone things down over-much, Mr. Llewellyn had eventually given up complaining and merely closed his windows on the Evangelical side of his house.

The Reverend Amos Teeple claimed that a chasm of difference lay between the Evangelicals, Anglicans - like old man Llewellyn - and even the enigmatic Roman Catholics. And it was true that the mantilla-clad Catholics in their everyday dress, and the stark, Puritanical dress of the Anglicans seemed drab next to the primped and plumed Evangelical congregation. But some of the townspeople believed that, besides appearance and a subtle differing in approach to worship, there stood merely a figurative hedgerow between the churches and the people who attended them.

Towing a string of sleepy children, the Roman Catholics strolled happily, if a little piously, into their South Side church on Sunday, having ridded themselves in a Saturday confessional of their sins of the previous week. Yet a few walked tentatively into the church narthex, a stellar Saturday night already under their belts.

The thin, well-prepared Anglicans walked to church in time for a chat and, in the old tradition, tea and a biscuit before Sunday school commenced.

But the Evangelicals, sparkling, coiffed, and dressed well for the dressing-down Amos gave them every Sunday, trudged into their church just in time for Sunday school. Once the sermon began, they heard what pathetic little selves they had become, how the struggle between godliness and pathetic-ness persisted, how the devil in his many forms sat there on their shoulders, making them lie to their parents and to each other, tempting them to fight with their neighbors, to ogle their brothers' wives, and encouraging little fat ladies to want fudge instead of peas.

When the doors of all three churches flung open at high noon (or thereabouts for the long-winded Anglican priest), the people of all faiths burst forth in a half run, either from fear or relief or, perhaps, both. Smiles broke out on parishioners' faces since they knew that the alms for the poor, the struggle for more, and the clearing of the door were all under wraps for another week.

Yet it seemed to some that God, who no doubt observed their willy-nilly retreat, occupied a spot in the heart of at least one person who sat in a pew somewhere in each of those structures.

13 — Neena, age 5 - Emmaus, Virginia
1942

The Reverend Amos Teeple sat at the head of his dining room table, his head bowed, well into his usually long-winded blessing of the food before him. Neena peeked from under her lashes, first looking at her father, then her mother, and avoiding Teddy who often made faces at her, causing her to laugh aloud.

Daddy's blessings went on and on so that plenty of time remained to look at the others at the table. This was a special occasion with Mama's family present for Teddy's birthday. There were Mama and Daddy, of course, and Teddy. Grandma Lowry sat beside Neena and then beside her, Grandpa Lowry. They were Mama's parents. Also at the table were Grandma and Grandpa's other daughters, Verina whom everyone called *V*, her husband, Monroe, then Toot, the youngest daughter, and her husband, Jimmy. That made Mama the oldest of Grandma's daughters.

Aunt V and Uncle Monroe only came for special things, not that often, and mostly, Neena figured, to see Grandma and Grandpa. V and Monroe always said "Hi" to Neena, sometimes patting her on the head and telling her how she had grown; but not Toot and Jimmy. Jimmy picked Neena up into the air, swung her around, and Toot kissed her and fluffed her hair and said she was "just the prettiest thing she had ever laid eyes on." They were like Grandma, always kissing and hugging, not like Mama who acted more like V. Mama just hugged at bedtime and once in a while during the day.

Neena looked around the table again and realized that Toot peeked, too. Toot winked at her and they both closed their eyes just as Daddy said, "Amen."

Mama had made ham and sweet potatoes, two of Teddy's favorites, and chocolate cake for dessert. Grandma said that Teddy was a real *sweet tooth*. She didn't know that three times that morning Neena had stuck her finger into the penuche frosting and licked it off like the little *sweet tooth* she was. If Grandma knew, she would shake her finger at Neena and say, "you little stinker," but she would never get angry. She would just wink and her eyes would twinkle, like Old St. Nick himself.

* * * * *

The next morning, Neena walked toward the French doors leading into her father's study. The Venetian blind had been drawn up, her signal that she had permission to enter. She knocked anyway.

"Come in. Come in," he said, his tone jovial.

"Hi, Daddy," she said, entering the room, skirting the desk, and walking toward him where he sat in his plush chair.

"Well, if it isn't Maid Marian," he said, a smile in his voice, as he reached for her. Lifting her, he placed her ceremoniously onto the desk.

"Why do you call me Maid Marian, Daddy?"

"Because she was a comely lassie."

"I'm not a dog, Daddy."

"A dog?"

"You know Lassie, Daddy. You know Lassie from that Saturday book. You read it to me," she said, accusation in her tone.

"The Saturday book?"

"Yes, Daddy, you read the story to me about Lassie the dog that travels a long ways. You said it was in the Saturday book, Daddy. Don't you remember?"

"Oh yes, yes I do remember. It was a story I had saved; I saved the magazine, the *Saturday Evening Post*. It's a magazine, a periodical, not a book. Periodicals come once a week or once a month or several times a year. But you are correct. Lassie was the dog in *Lassie Come Home*, yes, she was. But in this case, when I call you a lassie, a lassie is actually a young girl, not a dog. And Lassie the dog in the story I read to you, is a female dog, a girl dog, so that is probably why they call her *Lassie*. You are my comely lassie."

"Is comely like homely? Teddy says I'm so homely I have to sneak up on my food, or it would crawl away."

"No, not at all; in fact, comely is just the opposite of homely," he said as he tied her shoe. "Comely is very nice to look at. Pretty, I'd say. Pretty. Of course, sometimes the word was used to describe males, too. I have always thought of Joseph as comely. You know, Joseph in the Bible. You remember. His brothers sold him into slavery, but he forgave them. Think of him as comely. In that case it means handsome or good-looking, like me," he said, with a chuckle and a wink.

"Did he have pink hair like you, Daddy?"

"Red hair; my hair is red even though it looks kind of pink; yours also, even though you're more what they call auburn. My hair was like yours when I was a small boy." He adjusted her sock tops, folding them down and straightening them. "From what I have read, I don't think there were many fair people like you and me living near Joseph and his family. I believe that people in that part of the world at that time mostly had brown hair, hair like Mommy's. They lived in Israel. You have heard me speak of Israel?"

She nodded that she had.

"In fact, my comely Maid, you may have given me an idea for a sermon. So I must get back to work now."

He stood and lifted her down, swooping her around in an airborne circle as he did so. He placed her on her feet and sat back down.

"Off you go," he said. "Off you go, my Maid Marian, to the Sherwood Forest."

Daddy was always shooing her off when he had ideas for sermons, and she didn't really know what he was talking about; where was Sherwood Forest anyway? But she thought she liked being Maid Marian, whoever she was. And maybe the porch swing on which she had propped up her twin dolls, Pete and Repete, could be her pretend Sherwood Forest.

"Off you go," he had said again; as he often said.

So, off she went, softly closing the door behind her.

14

Neena, age 8 - Emmaus, Virginia
Spring 1946

The young girl sat on the hard pew, leaning heavily against her grandmother. The old lady's fingers stroked the child's face, traveled over its contours, skimmed lightly over the baby skin of her cheeks, and then stopped to gently tickle the lobes of her ears. The child's father spoke from the pulpit, his golden voice casting out toward his audience, bringing them to attention, but by the time his words reached the little girl, relaxed as she was, they curled around her head like smoke. Finally she shifted in her seat until her head rested in the older woman's lap. She slept.

When her mother, the church pianist, began playing the closing hymn, the little girl, Neena, sat upright and lightly rubbed her eyes.

The year was 1946 and in one month Christina "Neena" Pearl Teeple would turn nine. On her birthday Grandpap and Grandma Lowry would come to the Teeple's for dinner, and Grandma would tell the same story she had been telling for as long as Neena could remember:

You were born on the hard-backed pew traditionally reserved for latecomers and back-sliders. The church had barely cleared of people after Sunday evening service when, Wonder of Wonders, there you were!

Then she would hug Neena and everyone would applaud.

Neena never really knew how she had acquired her nickname. Her teachers and at least the older people of the church called her Christina, but her family and extended family, with the exception of her Grandma Lowry and her Aunt Toot, called her Neena. Toot called her by her given name more often than by her nickname and that seemed odd to Neena since Toot had to be a nickname. Grandma Lowry still called Toot by her real name, Pansy, so someone else must have nicknamed her Toot.

Her brother, Teddy, called her Nines because, he somehow rationalized, she and her maternal grandmother and grandfather Lowry habitually sat in row nine of the church sanctuary, and Nines sounded something like Neena. He sometimes called her the *half-way girl* since, he argued, row nine was a little less than halfway forward in a twenty pew church, and because, he said, she was often *half-way there, half-way up-to-speed*, or *half-way* with it. At some point he extrapolated his half-way nomenclature to calling her a *half-wit*, a term he had merged into his vocabulary that year at age eleven.

But Grandma Lowry said that none of that was true at all, that Christina sounded too grownup for a pretty little girl so they had shortened it first to Tina, and then, for some unremembered reason, she had become simply Neena.

15
Will, age 9 - Emmaus, Virginia
1946

At age nine, Willis Jacob McClure, like most southern children, answered adults with *Yes, Ma'am or No, Sir*, yet he appeared, somehow, even more respectful than most. Will hung back, seemed to reflect before responding but, like all children, really wanted approval most of all. Gentle with his mother, he had cultivated a shy tenderness toward other females, as well, most children, and animals. He had learned much about respect (or a certain semblance of it) at the parochial school he had attended when he and his family lived in Fairfax County, Virginia, before coming to Emmaus.

In second grade when Sister Mary Edith called upon him, she would say, "Willis, do you know the answer to problem number three?"

When asked any question by any of the nuns or the priest himself, he and the other students had been instructed to stand, say, *Yes, Ma'am,* or *Yes, Father*, if he or she knew the answer, and then to answer the question. Usually ready with an answer, young Willis rose quickly to his feet, observed the respectful protocol, and answered the question before taking his seat once again. With Sister Mary Edith it was easy because she praised the boys and girls for not only correct answers but for the effort put forth even in answering questions incorrectly. And at one time or another during a day she would compliment each of them for some little thing they had done.

"I caught you," she would say. "I caught you being kind when you opened the door for Gladys Oberlin." Or, "I saw you, Willis McClure, when you tied the shoe of that little first grader so he wouldn't trip and fall." And in her little bird voice she would add: "I caught you being kind!"

But by third grade he learned that all nuns were not as loving as Sister Mary Edith because that year, before he and his family moved to Emmaus, he had advanced to Sister Mary Margaret's class. Sister Mary Margaret was *cut from a different cloth*, Will's mother liked to say. Will thought she had a nose like a pig's snout, short, broad, and kind of mashed up against her face. She was always wiggling it like it itched or like she smelled something nasty. She criticized the children, nipping at them with her witchy voice, reminding them that they had erased one too many times on homework papers, or smacking their hands when they wrote sloppily. She walked silently about the room as the boys and girls worked, her rubber soles making no noise at all. Moving in and out and back and forth among the desks, she swooped in out of nowhere to catch them at something, anything.

Will learned quickly that year that being overly polite and just melting into the whole, doing nothing to draw attention, kept him out of harm's way.

He was a quick learner, finishing his workbook sometimes long before the others. So he had time to kill. During the afternoon class session, Sister M & M (what he called her even though she wasn't sweet like the little color-coated chocolate candies Uncle Norm had brought to Will and his sister from New York City that summer) hovered less and, sometimes, sat at her desk either reading or correcting papers. Will guardedly observed her then. She picked her teeth with the one long pinky fingernail she kept, ostensibly, just for that purpose since all her other nails were clipped short. Often she pushed her headpiece back, revealing crew cut-like stubble on her head, and scratched with all her might. Will thought it must be hot under her hat and veil, or maybe it fit tight and made her itch; he wasn't sure which. Or maybe she had cooties.

She was hard on all the children, favoring only one or two pandering girls; and, especially, she picked on the boys.

When Corky Murphy laughed at a gesture Lou Ponte made, Sister grabbed him by his hair and whomped him up and down in his seat, like she was dribbling a ball. Or when Georgie McDonald forgot and chewed on his thumbnail while he was concentrating on his arithmetic workbook, Sister swooped in and rapped his knuckles with her ruler. And when short little Pattie Peters passed a note to Betty McCandrew, Sister made her stand before the class and read aloud how Corky had tried to kiss her cheek on the playground and how she and Betty should stop by the market on the way home for a popsicle.

So it was that during the short time Will attended parochial school, he learned, in all environments, to keep his head down, as Gramps referred to keeping a low profile.

"That's what I did in The Great War, son," he'd say. "Those *Heinies* never put a bullet in me because I kept my head down."

So Will took Gramps' advice. He kept his head down in parochial school, in the public school after his family moved to Emmaus, and he especially kept it down when his father was at home. But when he was outside, playing kickball in the convent yard, or even up on the rickety-rackety bridge near his new house throwing stones into the water, he relaxed and brought his head up high, high 'til his head touched the sky, almost, big as life itself.

16 — Neena, age 9 - Emmaus, Virginia
Orndorff's Funeral Home - 1946

After her Grandpap died, Neena went with her family to Orndorff's Funeral Home for his calling hours and funeral. She was nine. She remembered people crying, but mostly she remembered the heavy smell of cut flowers like on Easter Sunday at church.

On Easter Sundays, Aunt Toot and Uncle Jimmy usually drove up to Emmaus to attend church with the Teeples, and Neena. Grandpap and Grandma Lowry sat with them.

"Don't sit up front, Baby Girl," Toot would say. "That flower dust gets up my nose, I start sneezing and wheezing and pretty soon I can't sing. Can't raise my voice *or* raise Jesus from the grave."

So Orndorff's smelled like flowers. They seemed to be everywhere and most of them had little cards attached. Some of them Neena could read, depending on the handwriting. *Our thoughts and prayers are with you during your time of loss.* Or, *Extending our deepest sympathy.*

But some of the cards she couldn't read at all. Those people, she knew, judging by their chicken scratches would get a *D* in cursive writing.

People spoke to her mother and grandmother in hushed voices, church voices, almost whispers.

"He looks good," old Mrs. Wentworth, a lady from their church, said as she held Grandma's hand.

Neena tipped up onto her toes for a better view of Grandpap. He didn't look good to her. He was pale, and his mouth was a straight line like he was mad or something. And Grandpap usually smiled a lot, at least when Neena – and sometimes Teddy – were around. And it looked like he had lipstick on or something. It didn't even look like him except he had on his scratchy blue suit with those folded-back wide things in the front, above the buttons, and the bowtie with the dots on it that he always wore on Sundays.

She walked over toward the fireplace where her mother stood talking with Mrs. Wainwright.

"He looks so peaceful," Mrs. Wainwright whispered.

"Yes, yes. It's a blessing he went the way he did instead of lingering. But we will surely miss him."

Neena wandered over toward the door where padded folding chairs were lined up along the wall and in the middle of the room.

She went over to one of the chairs situated between a window and a table with a lamp and sat down.

The light was dim like up in their attic when the only light came from a window high in the roof peak. But the lamp on the table had glass shades with little pieces of colored glass made into flowers and grapes or something. They were pretty the way the light came through them. But the bulbs weren't very bright; maybe they were those little Christmas tree bulbs or something.

She looked down at her skinny legs protruding from her skirt. If she slid backward until her shoulders touched the chair back, her legs stuck straight out. If she scooched forward, her feet in her Mary Janes touched the floor. She slid back and forth several times.

Finally, bored with sliding back and forth, she slid back in the chair and rested her head in the spot between the table edge and the chair back.

Light fell softly from the Tiffany lamps onto the marble-topped table, spilled silently onto the Persian rug and flowed over to be absorbed into the dark, dark boards of the floor. The window on Neena's left was draped in folds of fabric and tied off decorously with a cord draped around a brass knob. A tiny shaft of light from the window where the fabric had shifted to one side caught her eye.

She watched dust particles swirl around like bees that hovered over and around Grandpap's hives, the ones at the farm in the old apple orchard on the hill. Swirling, the dust particles mesmerized her and the hushed voices floated over and gently looped around her face and ears.

She closed her eyes and drifted off into a little girl's delicious sleep.

17 Will, age 11 - Emmaus, Virginia
Summer 1948

While on the north side of town, Neena Teeple played librarian with her neighbor, Georgette, Will McClure languished on the bank of Vespers Creek, on the south side of town. Whether by forced removal or by choice, the few Roman Catholics in town, a mix of Irish, Slavish and Italian families, had opted for this side of the creek. Will and his family lived in one of fifteen houses lined up on either side of Brook Street, a street aptly named since it ran parallel to the stream. Also on this side of the stream, three chicken farmers lived on their little two-acre farmettes which were neatly arranged perpendicular to the stream and along Oxen Hill Road which ran south out of town. Five Negro families lived in a little cluster of houses on this side of the creek as well, only east two miles of the Roman Catholic community. And one dairy farmer, Carl Ingstrom, owned one hundred acres or so along the southern borough limits of the town with a gore strip of land that extended across the borough line and reached to the center of the creek.

Will lay on his back in the grass in a dry spot on a high creek bank in Ingstrom's pasture. To get there he and his friend, Peto, had had to dodge cow pies and keep one eye out for the Brahma bull that the locals called Ferdinand. But now, as he lay there, the grass tickled his ears and he imagined he could hear bugs crawling through the grass toward his head although, in truth, the trickle of creek water drowned out most other noises. Wet to his knees, he had rolled up the pant legs of his jeans and the sun now warmed his skin as it peeked through the high puffy clouds.

He held his arm straight up from his shoulder and focused on his thumb as though he were aiming at something. He kept focusing on his thumb, first with one eye and then the other, one and the other, until he decided that his right eye was his dominant one.

After a while he sat up, looked around again for the bull, and thought about how hungry he was. He had picked and eaten some teaberries and some mint leaves earlier, but they had only made him hungrier. He kicked the head off a toadstool and then lay back down again.

The day had started off warm and sunny when, early that morning, Will and his best friend, Peto, had come to the creek. They poked sticks into crusted-over cow pies, threatening to fling dung at each other, and then climbed an old oak tree, scaling so high they felt on a level with the Anglican Church steeple on the other side of the creek. Noise came up to them, first from the eight o'clock freight train and then from the cars that putted around town. About eight-thirty, Farmer Ingstrom turned out to pasture his freshly-milked cows. They trudged down the lane that led to the stream, a single-file flow of black and white, their hides light-struck like spots in your vision that linger after a camera bulb flash.

Still high in the tree, the boys lounged in the crook of two branches, one each, not saying much, just picking leaves and watching them float down toward the backs of the cows. Ferninand hadn't come down to the creek that morning, so when the cows began to trickle back up the lane to spread out into the larger pasture for grazing, the boys descended and then jumped to the ground. They walked and slid down the embankment to the water's edge, avoiding when they could any manure the cows had left behind. Once near the water, Peto shoved Will who took two steps to keep from falling. His feet sank into the mud of the stream, his shoes filled with water, and his pants got wet.

Dodging Will's grasp, Peto moved along the water's edge where he spotted a snapping turtle in the grass. Will joined him then, and they headed off the turtle, keeping him away from the water and working him up toward the bank. They poked twigs at him and laughed as he snapped them in two. They tossed small stones, aiming them so they dropped just in front of him. He pulled his head in, withdrawing into the dark depths of his shell. Peto reached out with his toe and tipped the turtle over onto his back, which exposed armor-like plates along the underside of his tail. Then they watched and laughed as the turtle's legs worked, pedaling air, as he tried to right himself, tried to get back to his feet. After a while Will tired of watching the turtle struggle, even began to feel sorry for it, so he reached down to turn him over. The turtle's head poked out, his beady little eyes fixed on Will, his musky smell coming at them, and his prehistoric-looking jaw open. Then he nailed Will with a painful chomp, sinking his teeth into Will's index finger, and hanging on as though for survival.

Will jerked his hand back, shaking it, trying to free his finger from the jaws of the turtle as he kicked at its shell.

"Get him off me," Will screamed at Peto. "Get the son-of-a-bitch off me before he bites my finger clean off!"

Peto kicked, missed, then kicked again, landing a powerful blow to the turtle's out-stretched neck. The turtle let go but tore flesh from Will's finger so that blood ran down into the palm of his hand and then onto his arm.

"Oh, man," he moaned. "Oh, man, that monster bit almost clean through."

Peto kicked the turtle then, a square, center-shell blow that sent it spiraling into the water.

Will dropped onto the grass, holding his bleeding hand with his other one.

"What if he's got rabies or something?"

"I don't think turtles get rabies. I think that's just skunks." Peto paused, looking puzzled. "Or maybe dogs, sometimes, like my uncle's old dog, Ranger. I dunno. I know you get the typhoid or something if you eat them. Turtles, not dogs. Something like that. My grandpa said something like that."

Will waved his good arm impatiently. "You got your jackknife, Dog Breath? Did you bring it?"

"Yeah, yeah, right here. What do you need?"

"Here, cut the top off of my sock. A strip. Yeah, like that."

Peto hacked away at the sock, and Will grabbed the cloth strip from Peto.

"I'll tie it around my finger, maybe stop the bleeding. Oh, man. Oh, man, it hurts."

After Will crudely tied the strip of cloth, he looked out into the water. "I hope you hurt him, hurt him bad", he said as he cradled his hand. "And I was just trying to get him back on his feet." He shook his head. Despite his eleven years and his tall, broad-shouldered build, his face looked childish and innocent, big freckles standing out on his nose.

"How'm I gonna explain this to my mom? Huh? How?" he asked, while he cradled his bandaged finger. "You know how she hates it when I come home bleeding or in trouble."

They crawled up the bank, walked over to where the sun shown on an area of grass as though spotlighting it.

"I'm gonna sit here," Will said, as he dropped down to the grass.

Peto dropped to his knees, swiveled on them, and settled onto his butt.

"What ya wanna do now, Jerkwater?" he asked, elbowing Will in the ribs.

"I'm gonna sit here, I said. You deaf or something? It hurts. Go on," he added. "Just go on home. I'm gonna sit here just like I said."

"Jeesh," Peto said, getting to his feet. "You'd think I was the one that bit ya."

He shuffled off, and Will didn't even turn to watch him go.

He placed his aching hand onto his chest and lay back into the grass and let the sun warm him. Eventually he thought of nothing else except how hungry he was.

He must have slept for he began noticing birds' chirps, the croak of a frog, and the sound of moving water, soft at first and then louder and louder as though someone were manually increasing volume. And then he heard movement, footsteps that were not really footsteps and then hot breath on his face. He opened his eyes just in time to see taste buds in a swirl of greenish drool extending toward his face. A tongue, a cow tongue roughly slurped him leaving goo on his cheek. But then he was partway up, crab-crawling away toward the tree, jumping to his feet, sprinting for the lowest branch. He kept expecting to feel horns on his behind, sharp, thrusting, stabbing horns, but he felt nothing, and he had no notion of looking back – it would only slow him down. His feet hit bark three feet up as he jumped, grasped a limb and swung up.

He looked down expecting to see Ferdinand charging the tree, trying to shake him down like he'd seen in movies, but he saw instead a sole cow. She was grazing, munching her way in random patterns, seeming to think of nothing except her next blade of grass. Finally she brought her head up, chewed and chewed, looking around her yet seeming to have forgotten him, seemingly oblivious of him or his position in the tree.

He decided to come down and go home. A while ago he had heard three bells from the church tower, but now he had no idea what time it was. He did know it was Thursday, and

Thursday was a day when his dad worked double shifts, or so he referred to them. On Wednesdays and Thursdays his father stayed with his elderly mother who still lived west of them, over nearer the mines where his father worked, where his grandfather had worked, and maybe where Will and his brothers would one day work. Will liked Thursdays in particular because his mother came home early from her housecleaning job; they often skipped a usual supper on that day, and she would make pancakes with wet pecan syrup or maybe homemade potato chips, warm, with a light, soft bubble in the middle and crisp brown edges with the sweet taste of oil and salt coating them. They would play board games, or, if her friend Irma came over with her three kids, they would play hide-n-seek or leap frog or even hopscotch on the driveway. But since he was the oldest, he sometimes lingered on the porch steps while the women sat on the old porch swing and talked. They were guarded at first, aware of his presence. But if he kept really still, they seemed to forget he was there, and then they relaxed and began talking about personal things.

They talked about who was getting married, about who was having marital problems, who was pregnant, who got a new job, who got fired from an old one, and whether they liked their kids' schoolteachers, the hairdresser, or the meat market clerk. Sometimes his father's name came up, not by name really, but in capitalized form like *He* and *Him* said with discernible scorn. Irma usually spoke of him while his mother remained quiet, except when she said, "He'll be home tomorrow," or "I'll see what He has in mind." It was as though he deserved no name.

Will's father's drinking buddies and the man he rode with to work called him Mick. Will remembered asking his grandfather why guys called his dad Mick.

"Oh, I'd say because he *is* a Mick. That's an Irish Catholic, Will. You're a Mick, I'm a Mick, all our friends are Mick-Micks," he said in a sing-song voice, chuckling. "That's what they've called us Irishers for years, probably because so many of us have names that start with Mc. But that's just a guess because I never figured why they called Italian (he pronounced it *Eyetalian*) folks *guinea*s or *wop*s or *dagos*, either, or German's *hienies*. They just do."

Will's father's real name was John Jacob McClure - even though Will's grandmother called him Sean or *boyo* - but he preferred to be called Jake.

It was hard for Will to think of Him as a boyo, a lad, an innocent. To Will he was a trickster, always to be avoided. Sometimes at the dinner table on Friday night Will's father would lightly punch him on the shoulder, playful little taps, really. He asked all the children a question, like, "How old was your grandfather McClure when he came to this country?" and then he would say, "You're the oldest, Will. What's the answer?"

At the first shoulder tap Will became nervous, his uneasiness and apprehension building until he could not remember even his own birth date let alone the date of his grandfather's arrival in America. The more he hesitated, the harder his father tapped his shoulder. And if he got the wrong answer or did not answer at all, the arm taps turned into a face slap or a real punch to the arm, to be repeated over and over again while he was asked the question again and again.

Tipping back in his chair, a snide smile on his face, a triumphant luster in his eyes, Jake would then turn back to him. "You stupid kid. You can't remember a damned thing I have told you. You can't even remember your dead grandpa."

He harassed Will further then, asking more questions or forcing him to arm wrestle or repeat something he had learned in school that day. No matter what Will said, no matter what he did, he fell into His trap until his father began screaming, calling him stupid and, his favorite, a *worthless little bastard*.

Sometimes Will's mother intervened and was slapped for her effort, but usually Will begged her with his eyes to stay put, to not ruffle Jake's feathers further, to let the turmoil just die down.

Often little Vonnie began to cry, distracting Jake long enough for Will to escape and stay gone until long after Jake had drunk himself into a stupor.

On weekends as Will grew older, he became a furtive, darting shadow, slipping in and out of the house, stealing a sandwich or some cookies and a slug of milk straight out of the jug. Some nights he went to Peto's, but usually he waited in the garage until his father fell asleep while listening to the radio. Then Will stole upstairs and left the window ajar in case he needed a fast escape. A couple of times he slept under the bed so it would take his father longer to find him and give him, Will, a better chance of waking in time to jump out of the window.

Now he must escape old man Ingstrom's cow pasture before Ferdinand, that imposing Jake-like creature, came and gored him through. So he rose to his feet, walked through the thistles and forget-me-nots and the short-chewed grass until he reached a barbed-wire fence. He placed his good hand on a fence post and, still holding on, stepped back a couple of steps and then with his height and developing strength vaulted over the fence. He straightened his back, missing the barbs of the fence altogether, and landed squarely on his feet. Then he trudged through Widow Murphy's back yard, past the dog coop where old Shep lay panting even in the shade. Will stopped and bent to pat the old dog's head. Shep wagged his tail and nuzzled

Will's hand a bit. Then Will drifted off, random and carefree as airborne dandelion fuzz, until he reached Brook Street.

After walking a couple of blocks he saw Hank Martin walking toward him. A gawky, shy kid who was three years older than Will, Hank lived two doors down from the McClures.

"Hey, Hank, you got the time?"

"For what?"

"The time, you know, as in time of day? What time is it?"

"Oh, four. Well, almost four."

"Thanks," Will said, and then muttered under his breath, "What a dope."

Since it was only four o'clock, and his mother wouldn't be home until four-thirty, Will turned east on the sidewalk instead of west and walked up the street, past Mr. Tedesca's's market and the little shoe repair shop he kept next door. He walked on to the old rickety-rackety bridge over the stream, gathered a few pebbles that accumulated between the planks, and then went over to the railing and threw them one-by-one into the water. Little ripples moved out from where each stone had landed like echoes must look if you could see them. He thought about his father and wondered if Grandpa McClure had smacked him around, had taunted him, had made his whole house live in dread of his arrival home from the mines each day. Will wondered if he – Willis Jacob McClure - would drink himself stupid, if he would taunt his children and dominate his wife, ordering her around like some worthless *gofer*.

Oddly, even at his age Will wanted kids. He liked little baby things: Puppies with their drooling little pink tongues hanging out, wee birds peeping for their mouths to be filled, and stinky little skunks, even, as they followed their stinky mothers through Callahan's swampy yard. Of course, the first real baby he had ever noticed was his baby sister, little Vonnie, when they brought her home from Reiter's Memorial Hospital. She had been wrapped up real tight in a little white blanket with pink posies on it. He remembered wanting to touch the skin on her little face and that when he did she had turned her head with a jerky motion and opened her mouth like she wanted to eat his finger. He had been fascinated by her, holding her while his mother made dinner, watching her wrap her tiny, tiny finger around one of his. He liked the little snickeling noises she made into his neck when he held her upright or how she kicked if he freed her legs from the blanket.

And when wonderful food smells started wafting from the kitchen and his stomach began to gurgle like he couldn't wait to eat for even one more minute, that's when she would often cry. The food smells must have made her hungry as well. Then he'd pick her up and walk with her around the living room, up the hall toward his parents' room, back down the hall to the front door, all the while bouncing her and whispering secrets into her ear. He remembered his mother's words: "She's not a jug that you shake to mix the cream with the milk. She's not an egg you're scrambling, Will. You shake her with all your might, and you'll scramble her brain, sure enough. Just move her gently to distract her but make her feel secure."

He had learned the movements then: Walking, whispering, and ever-so-slightly moving her forward and back, forward and back, like when he had finally mastered patting his head and rubbing his stomach at the same time. Soon she would quit crying, and her eyes would widen like she listened to every word he whispered into her ear. Often he told her about his goofy friends or his dotty old science teacher who would surely one day blow them all up. But mostly he told her she was pretty like their mom with golden highlights in her hair and an outline on the edge of her eyelids like someone had drawn a line there. And her skin; he told her that her skin was this pretty pale pink like strawberry juice and cream mixed together in the bottom of your bowl after the biscuit and the berries had been eaten, pretty pink, pretty, pretty pink. And soft, she was soft, soft like the skin on the undersides of his mother's arms when she had rocked him as a little boy.

Will had been eight and one-half years old when Vonnie, Veronica Lake McClure, had been born. And now she was two and one-half and talked more than Binky who was four. Except at night; at night Binky chattered non-stop in his little bed. Next in age to Binky, skinny little Roycie was now seven years old. He suffered from asthma which worsened in cold weather and hung on him during hot summer months. Will's father didn't bother him much since he had almost died the year before during one of Jake's tirades. Now when his father's rantings began, little Royce, following his father's instructions, quietly got up from the table, went into the living room, shut the door behind him, and played with his toys. And Jefferson, "named after our third president and a prominent resident of this Commonwealth," Grampy used to say, would be nine and one-half now but had died when he was two years old from some childhood thing, some fever, or something. Will never could remember what had taken him.

So that was their family: His dad, his mother, him, the kids, Grandmom McClure over nearer the mountains, and Granny and Grampy Mosier, his mother's parents. Jake didn't like the Mosiers, nor they him, so Lilly and the children saw them only on occasional Wednesdays when his grandparents drove their shiny black Packard over to their daughter's house. But in the past year, since Gramps could no longer drive, his mother drove them in their Willys to the north side of town to visit Granny and Gramps. Riding with his mother was an experience. She let the clutch out too fast and stalled the car, or she let it out too slowly and drifted back against the curb and once into a ditch. But they made the trip numerous times.

Now that he was older, Will sometimes skipped school or part of a school day, at least, so that he could visit Granny and Gramps. He hung out in the garage with Gramps or sat on a stool in the kitchen while Granny baked him cookies. Their house was a quiet refuge from the turmoil of his. But they were old and sick. Gramps had lost part of one foot and now had big oozing sores on his shin. He often sat with his foot stub propped up on a stack of pillows atop the ottoman in front of his parlor room chair. He said his toes ached even though he didn't have them anymore. "Phantom pain, they call it," Gramps said on more than one occasion.

And Granny seemed tired.

"I have dropsy and heart trouble, Dear," she would say, tousling his hair. "I drop down and don't have the heart to get back up."

18 — Will, age 11 - Emmaus, Virginia
Fall 1948

He was gaining on him. Will glanced once more over his shoulder. Cripes. He couldn't believe it. The old man had never chased him before; had only come out onto the sidewalk and screamed at him in broken Italian.

"You taka mi banan, you taka mi fruits no more. No more, I say to you. You heara me? Huh?"

But this time when he took a pear the old *dago* tore out the door and chased after him. Will was running flat out, almost to the Murphy house next to the store and still old Mr. Tedesca was gaining on him. He must be fifty years old. He's short as my Grandma, skinny as a rail, and he's catching me.

He thought for a second about stopping. He hadn't run all that far, yet. The old guy might have a heart attack over one little pear if he kept chasing Will. Instead Will kept running.

He darted between old man Murphy's house and garage, dodged bed sheets hanging in the back yard, sprinted to his right, past an old tire swing, and headed back out to the sidewalk. He doubled back to his right, heading toward the store once again, still looking behind him. Mr. T lagged a little now. He might lose him yet.

Suddenly someone stepped from behind Mr. Murphy's hedge, hit him with a shoulder block, and knocked him off his feet.

Cripes. Will landed hard and bumped his head on the sidewalk. He looked up, dazed. With the sun in his eyes he couldn't tell who had hit him. He shook his head and got to his feet just as Mr. Tedesca came walking up, stopped, bent over, placed his hands on his knees and gasped for breath.

"Thanka you, Coach. He taka mi fruits again. Thanka you so mucha."

"You're welcome, Mr. T. Glad I happened to be here."

Coach Bowen stood before him, his huge biceps bulging from his short sleeves, his chest muscles stretching taut his t-shirt.

"So, you so hungry, McClure, you have to steal from Mr. Tedesca here?"

Will said nothing.

"I asked you a question, son."

"Yes . . ., No."

"Which is it, yes or no?"

"Yes, I was hungry, but no, I didn't need to steal. I coulda gone home."

Coach Bowen reached into his pocket, took out a nickel, and flipped it to Mr. Tedesca, who caught it. "Hope that covers the pear, Mr. T. Will, here, wants to apologize to you. He's not a bad kid. He just runs with the wrong kind of kids, like that Peto kid, and he doesn't have enough to do to keep him out of trouble. Too much energy."

"Will," he said, nudging Will in the ribs. "What do you have to say for yourself?"

Will was too ashamed to look at Mr. Tedesca. "I am sorry." There was nothing else to say.

"You do lotsa times. Lotsa fruits. Whatsamatta with you?"

"I'm sorry. I promise I will never steal from you again. I promise."

"I tell you what. You deliver grocery for me, one week you deliver. No pay. Then you do good job, no taka stuff, I pay you. You deliver grocery to old ladies this side of town. Be nice to them, bringa paper in froma sidewalk, taka grocery; learn what it's like to be good boy."

"Okay," Will said. "Okay."

"When do you hava go home?"

"Four-thirty."

"Okay, you start today. Right now. You taka grocery to Widow Tracy. Show her respect, then you bringa money right back here. You hear? Right back."

Mr. T turned, and went into the store to get the grocery bags.

"Your head okay, Will? I really didn't mean for you to hit your head, you know."

"It's okay."

"Will, I know you're basically a good boy. This'll be good for you. I hate to see you run with that Peto. He and his whole family are bad news. I suspect you got problems at home; you don't need more. In two more years you can go out for junior high football and track. You'd be good. You're fast."

Will didn't reply but merely kept his eyes averted.

"You come by on Sunday afternoons when I'm playing football with my boys. They are younger than you, but it'd be fun for you. Ask your mom, maybe when your dad's not around. Ask her then. I'll see you in Sunday mass anyway. You can just walk home with us after mass, have some Sunday dinner, and then spend the afternoon. What do you say?"

His head still down, Will said, "Okay."

When Mr. T emerged from the store, Will took the bags, careful not to squish the eggs, and then ambled down the sidewalk toward Widow Tracy's.

His head hurt, he felt ashamed because Mr. Tedesca had always been nice to him, *nica* to him.

As he walked along the sidewalk, he struggled again with something he had pondered many times. He realized again that no matter how hard he tried, he could not pinpoint when he had changed from a polite boy into a pear thief, a petty thief caught red-handed. The old Will, the polite boy, showed respect for girls, women, and any person in authority; that boy loved baby humans and baby animals, and would have done nothing to disappoint either his mother or his grandmother. And now he was a pear thief? When he thought about it, he realized it must have been his attitude that changed, perhaps ever so gradually, and then his behavior change had followed; it had to be in that order.

His father consistently singled him out for blame. He called Will names and had always, at least for as long as Will could remember, cursed him. He believed only partially the things his father said to him because his grandmother, grandfather, and mother, if merely by their behavior towards him, made him feel good, appreciated and even loved.

Still, in spite of their love, Will began resenting that he had to live in a house where he was afraid. He plotted in his thoughts and in his dreams how he would rid himself and those he loved of the man who tormented and terrorized them. Then Will started sneaking around, finding ways to get into and out of the house, either through the doorway or out the window and down the trellis, often totally undetected. He had become sneaky, sneaky.

At some point, like when he knew his dad was there, he didn't bother going home at all; he merely grabbed an apple or a peach from the stand outside Mr. Tedesca's store, or he helped himself at Peto's house, or, on at least two occasions, a candy bar at the Broxterman Store, on the north side of town.

Still he didn't want to deliver groceries to some dried up old lady. Widow Tracey had nose hairs, big, white, wiry ones, for cripes sake. And she had those crinkles around her mouth so that you couldn't tell if she was sneering at you or trying to move her lips into a smile. She was just witch-scary. He didn't need this nonsense. He kicked a stone that lay on the edge of the sidewalk, scuffing the toe of his shoe. He didn't want to take in her paper, collect her money and then run all the way back, in the wrong direction from his house, to give the cash to Mr. T. Cripes. He didn't like Coach Bowen talking about Peto like he was a bad kid just 'cause he didn't have a dad. Will liked Peto. They had been friends ever since Will moved to Emmaus. He wanted to continue doing all the fun stuff he and Peto did. He still wanted to throw rocks off the bridge, to climb trees, to sneak into the freight train cars and ride downstream, jumping off at the old thirty-foot railroad bridge. He wouldn't turn his back on Peto. But now he was stuck. Cripes. Yet, playing football with Coach Bowen, that didn't sound so bad unless he gave him another body block like the one he gave him today. He'd just have to run faster, that's all there was to it. If he didn't, his whole life he'd have people breathing down his neck; people like his old man, Mr. T and Coach Bowen. Like a circus seal, they'd have him flapping his seal flippers, barking for bites, and asking what silly-arsed job needed done next.

No, he'd have to run faster. That's all there was to it. Cripes.

19
Neena, age 12 - Emmaus, Virginia
Spring 1949

For as long as she could remember, Neena had sat in church with Grandpap and Grandma Lowry. But since Grandpap's death in 1946 when Neena was nine, Grandma Lowry and she sat together in church; usually just the two of them. That arrangement worked well for Neena's mother who played the piano during church services. And when Aunt Toot and Uncle Jimmy visited on average once a month, they sat with Neena and Grandma Lowry as well. But on most Sundays, Neena and Grandma Lowry sat behind the Piazzas, a Roman Catholic family converted to Protestantism. John Piazza whose old country name was Giancarlo and his wife, Rosa, were the first to pray aloud on prayer meeting night, like good reformed Baptists, but Aunt Toot said that "they still go weak in one knee as they enter the pew."

"Genuflecting died hard in them," Neena's father, the Reverend Amos Teeple, liked to say, although, for a long time Neena didn't even know what genuflecting meant. It seemed that lots of people had things to say about the Piazzas.

John and Rosie had four girls and five boys, one each year from the time Neena was six and old enough to notice. Mr. P seemed old, or at least tired, drifting off in the early part of morning worship, his bald head bobbing or jerking from side to side during the hymns, but once Reverend Teeple began preaching, Mr. P fell into a deep sleep with his chin resting firmly on his chest. Nothing made him stir, not wiggling children, nor pulpit pounding, nor even *amens* echoing around the room; nothing that is until Dessie Teeple hit the first chord of the closing hymn. Like some boot camp reveille, that first note brought him to his straight-spined, attentive self.

Neena's brother, Teddy, almost three years older than she and who had less restrictions, sat with Neena and his grandmother on occasion. Grandma Lowry's side vision was a little off, so the two youngsters got away with a lot of mischief as long as The Reverend didn't spot them. The Reverend watched his children quite closely in church, making sure they did not get out of hand. He did not tolerate giggling. If Teddy and Neena got silly, Reverend Teeple stopped the service, and, with his big voice, commanded them to move forward, either to the front pew or, if they had aggrieved him too sorely, up onto the platform with him.

Teddy smugly stepped onto the platform when told to do so, but Neena, embarrassed beyond belief, would rather have weeded Farmer Ingstrom's entire tomato patch than sit up there where everyone could see her. Teddy's discomfort was like the midday express train that passed through town: Here and gone. Neena's was like the mail train: Lingering in the station.

Despite occasional mischief, and despite rarely listening much at all to her father's sermons, Neena behaved well while in church. Seated as she was mid-church and with her grandmother, and because she was younger, Neena never developed a bond with Teddy's cool friends in the back pew, nor could she identify with the little white-haired ladies in the front pew who were, as Aunt Toot loved to say, "one step from Glory." The old saints *amen-ed* her father through his sermons even though their timing seemed a little off sometimes.

One of the white-haired saints was Betsy Moran's grandmother. And Betsy had been Neena's best friend since they met in first grade.

Neena invited Betsy to come to church on those Sundays when Betsy's grandma could bring her, but the old lady didn't drive as much as she once did, and even though other parishioners took turns giving Mrs. Moran a ride to church, Betsy could not come that often. Sometimes Neena invited Betsy to stay overnight on Saturday night so she could attend Sunday services with Neena but, since Betsy was a Roman Catholic girl, she was seldom permitted to do so. When they were together, they tended to giggle a lot, whether in church, at each other's homes, or in school. But knowing that her father was watching them closely, Neena tried to keep herself and Betsy under control while they were in the sanctuary.

But now they were almost thirteen – or would be before school let out for the summer. They were becoming young ladies, and their worlds were about to change.

20 — Neena, age 13 – Rural Area, Emmaus, Virginia
Summer 1950

Betsy and I are coasting downhill to her neighbor's horse farm as we usually do on the summer afternoons when I visit her. I pedal my Schwinn bike. She sits on my handlebars. I ride the brake and ask her to quit trying to steer. She wiggles and waves at the mailman. We're mercurial. We vibrate. We crack our chewing gum, a recent accomplishment, acquired after long practice.

We are thirteen.

With the sun straight overhead, the day is getting hot. We wear cotton blouses, white to look alike. She wears shorts and canvas sneakers with no socks. My jeans rub my knees. She squirms as she puts on lipstick from a tube she took from her mother's vanity.

We have no style, or at least have not found one on which to settle. We only know our eyelashes are not full enough, our fingernails are not long enough, and our breasts puzzle us; we are not sure just what to do with them. Our hairstyles, permanent-waved and drawn into ponytails, are convenient and still within our mothers' jurisdiction.

Sometimes we sit on the hill above her neighbor's farm, watching the woman who visits him. She is blonde, full-bodied, and wears all white – white blouse, white shorts, and a wide, tie belt. She swings her hips and doesn't get dirty, even when she rides on the tractor with the farmer man.

"That's what I will be like," says Betsy. "Only I'll drive a red convertible and I'll have more than one boyfriend."

"I'm not sure," I say. I'm never as sure as Betsy. "I don't think I could wear white. I'd get all dirty, for sure."

What I don't tell Betsy is that white reminds me of angels and weddings. I want more color. I sometimes think I'll be like my great Aunt Claudia from Scranton, Pennsylvania, the one with crooked lipstick and neck wrinkles. She wears red. She used to visit Grandma Lowry, her sister, out at the apple farm, but now she visits her at our house. Grandma lives with us since Grandpa died. Snappy behind her glass lenses, Aunt Claudia's brown eyes fix on me but with some detachment as though I'm not quite interesting. She wears a tinkling bracelet of charms from places she has been: A Washington Monument, an Empire State Building, a Liberty Bell, even a tire from Akron, Ohio. She calls me *child*, because she can't seem to remember my name. She smokes cigarettes only when Mother and Daddy are not at home, hovering over a tin can half-filled with water in case she has to quickly extinguish one. She says *damn* when she drops ashes from her cigarette onto her dress. She presses fifty-cent pieces into my palm and winks. She wanders the lawn looking for four leaf clovers, coughs a lot, and laughs at things that cause other people to suck in their breath. And she never wears white, not even in summer.

But I don't tell Betsy I prefer color. She will try too hard to convince me about the white, tight shorts she likes. She'll work on me until I agree with her, and then I will be mad at myself for giving in. Still we do agree on a few things. We agree we will never get old and crabby like the lady at the corner store, and we will not pick our teeth or grunt when we bend over, like her father's hired man. We will never wear aprons. And we will never eat leftovers.

When we have finished spying on the handsome neighbor man, we ride across the dirt road to visit Bernadette, another of Betsy's neighbors. She often suns herself on a chaise longue in the front yard, so we sit there and talk to her. Our brothers tell us that she sunbathes with no top, and we check this out. It's true. One time when we were there somebody drove by and honked the car horn at her, and it scared her so bad she jumped up and sure enough her bathing suit top stayed right there on the lounge while her big breasts hung out bare as can be. But it didn't seem to bother her a bit.

Bernie talks about sex as though we understand, but we only pretend to. At least I do. Betsy's mother says that Bernie works really hard every day at looking good. That's why she has a handsome husband.

Bernie's husband, Stitch, goes out of town a lot on business trips. When he's out of town, another man visits, a younger, rougher-looking man. He comes smack in the middle of the day. We can always tell when he's there even if he parks his truck around the back of the house because on his visiting days her kids are outside and have been outside sometimes since early morning. She puts a jug of water out on the stoop for them and tells them if they have to go to the bathroom they can just go next door to old lady Upton's outhouse.

On those days we play with the kids for a little bit. We play hide 'n seek and hold their baby bunnies. But they are younger than we are so we get bored quickly and move on somewhere else.

"Bye," we say. "See you next time," we yell over our shoulders as we pedal away.

Our hair blows in the breeze we make pedaling so fast. We are best friends.

When Betsy visits me, we are instructed to stay in the neighborhood which, to my mother, consists of a couple of blocks. On rainy days we visit Elsie, the lady across the street. Wearing a kerchief tied around her head like Rosie the Riveter, she scrubs her kitchen floor every day but doesn't do much of anything else regularly. When she gets ready to mop the floor, she puts us and her children out onto the porch. When the floor dries, she puts down newspapers so that no one will track on her clean floor. Then, after getting my mother's permission, she loads us all into her *woody* station wagon for a trip to the ice cream store.

When we get back, we are permitted to play anywhere in the house. She doesn't care. The radio is usually tuned to some drama with advertisements for soap or toothpaste while she reads and drinks Pepsi out of a big tumbler full of ice cubes she makes in a silver tray in her freezer. She gives tubes of lipstick and pennies to her kids to play with. She talks baby talk to everyone. She has many afternoon women visitors who play cards, drink soda pop, laugh or listen to the radio together. Her older kids are free to come and go, telling her when they will be back. But mostly they stay at home. Her house is certainly more fun than either of ours. There are piles of dirty clothes and stacks of clean ones on the couches and on the floor.

We want to be like her when we grow up. She smiles more than anyone else we know. She doesn't seem to care that our mothers are dusting while she is reading a book.

"I want to look like Bernie and act like Elsie," Betsy says while we ride my bicycle back to her house.

"I thought you wanted to be like the lady in white."

"Yeah, that's right. I forgot."

21   Will, age 14 – South Side of Emmaus, Virginia
Early March 1951

His face beet-red, Jake McClure roared through the doorway, a shot gun in his hand, the stock resting in the crook of his elbow.

"I'm gonna fix that little bastard," he said, "once and for all."

He stopped, pointing the barrel at his wife. "And then I'm coming back down here to deal with you."

Upstairs, having heard his father's threat, Will hung from the center of the clothes bar in his parent's closet, hidden among dresses, jackets and coats, hoping his hands were concealed as well. It was hard holding his feet up for so long, but he was afraid to put them down in case he didn't hear his father enter the room. The window his father had nailed shut was no longer an escape hatch for him. The other windows in the upstairs had been painted shut for years. So he was trapped in the closet.

He could hear his father's breathing as he entered the room and feel the clothes stir as his father moved them slightly to look for feet on the floor of the closet. Will held his breath, terrified that even his breathing could be detected. Sweating, he held his eyes tightly shut. He heard his father leave the room, heard the banging of the other upstairs bedroom doors. Hysterical crying came from the little ones; Will felt like he was being stuck with something sharp when they cried like that. From the sound of things, his father back-handed one of them and told them to shut up.

"Where's that little bastard," he yelled.

"He's gone, Daddy," Vonnie cried. "I don't know where."

When his father began descending the stairs, Will heard his mother's cry. It sounded like she had fled to the bathroom at the foot of the stairs. She slammed the door, clicking the lock. Tiptoeing out of the closet and peeking out into the hall, Will could see the back of his father's head as he stomped down the stairs.

"Open the door, Woman, or I'll kick it in," his father said as he neared the bottom of the stairs. Setting the gun against the door frame, he tried the knob. When the door wouldn't open, he stepped back, put one foot up, and kicked near the knob. The molding splintered, and the door gave way, pitching him forward into the room. Then Will's mother, who had obviously been standing on the toilet seat, hit Jake over the head with an old crock they kept in the bathroom to hold miscellaneous items.

Jake fell, hard, seemed dazed, then got up and rubbed his head. She pushed by him, running out into the hall, screaming, "Will, Will, get out of the house, now!"

Will darted down the stairs just as his father got to his feet and ran back out into the hall after Will's mother. Will's feet touched the hallway just as his daddy reached his mama and grabbed her by the hair.

Will picked up the gun.

22
Emmaus, Virginia
March 1951

The last mountain snow of winter drove the spring rains of 1951 down from the mountain toward the town like a herd of confused cows. The Town of Emmaus, Virginia, and the outlying areas, weren't ready for it. Still clad in their winter long drawers, farmers outside of, or bordering on, the little town had not yet planted their oats. In town, the rainwater overflowed the gutters and gushed toward the sewer drains already clogged by limbs and leaves. Runoff flowed down the middle of Walnut Street, some of it jumping curbs and seeping into lawns. Following its downward flow, the remaining runoff curled around the sewer drain debris, continued on to the intersection of Walnut and First Streets, swirled there momentarily, and then poured on down to cause a traffic problem on Main Street. Cars stalled. Walkers clung to their umbrellas despite the water climbing up them like oil up a wick.

On Saturday, Herbie, the janitor at the Evangelical Reformed Baptist Church washed the windows inside and let God take care of the outside. When the rains continued on to Sunday morning, people slipped into their over-the-shoe rubber boots usually reserved for winter wear, tucked in their pants or raised their skirts, grabbed their Bibles and slogged on through the gulley washer to Sunday worship.

Reverend Teeple prayed that the farmers would get a break to sow their crops, that the water damage at Gorman's Hardware store would be minimal, and that God would bless the faithful. He didn't pray for sun; that would be asking for too much, but it came out intermittently later that afternoon anyway.

By the middle of the following week the rain stopped completely and jonquils popped up just as the crocuses shriveled down to stubs.

Spring was there to stay just in time for Easter.

23 Will, age 14 – South Side of Emmaus, Virginia
Early Spring 1951

Will hadn't given his father any warning. He hadn't even raised the gun properly to his shoulder. He just pulled the trigger. The roar inside the hallway stunned him. The kick from the gun knocked him off his feet. He couldn't hear. He thought he had shot himself until he saw his father list to one side and then drop like a fallen tree. Motion slowed. Free from her husband's grasp, Will's mother turned, looked at Will, and then inched backward, crab-style, toward the wall. Will just sat there, slumped against the wall. The other children spilled down the stairs, running to their mother. Will heard only a run-together murmur, like voices from a far-off playground.

His father still did not move. Will continued leaning against the wall, looking at the scene as though it were a dream. After a time, his father rolled slowly over onto his butt, glared at Will, a roar bursting through his teeth. The sound came to Will no louder than a drawn-out burp.

Will's father grasped the back of his knee where blood steadily dripped through his fingers. In spite of his injury, he grabbed at the door frame with his free hand, trying to lunge at his son. But he fell back again, grimacing.

Burp. The muffled sound came out of his father's mouth again.

Will raised his hand to check his ear and was surprised to see that he still held the gun. It lay in his hand, still warm, a thing of burnished wood and shiny steel. He dropped it then. Without really knowing why, he went into the bathroom, picked up a towel, and drew a glass of water. He came back into the hall and, keeping his distance, handed the towel to his father. Then he walked over to his mother and, kneeling, offered her the glass of water. He didn't know why. It was all he could think to do for her.

Soon he heard a soft, keening sound and realized it was sirens, off in the distance.

Two police officers entered the hallway. One went directly to retrieve the shotgun and the other began examining Jake and questioning Will's mother.

Will tried to decipher their words, but his head seemed fuzzy and his ears still rang from the report of the shotgun in such close quarters. Then two men in white entered the hallway. One went directly to Jake and began examining his wound, and one came over to where the woman sat huddled with her children. Two more men entered the hallway carrying a stretcher. When the ambulance aids put Jake onto the gurney, his head rolled to one side and stayed there. He was gray-white, and Will wondered if he had fainted or if he was dead.

Will stood up then, walked over to the open door, and watched as they loaded his father into the ambulance.

A black sedan pulled up to the curb and a big-built woman with gray hair climbed out, hurried up the sidewalk, brushed past Will and entered the hallway. She spoke with Will's mother and, in a very loud voice, asked the little ones questions, but they would not answer, just looked at her dumbly. She explained that she would take the children to their grandmother's house. Within moments she had rushed the younger children from the house to the car. They were gone. Standing now, his mother, who still appeared stunned, was led almost tenderly by a tall officer to a nearby police cruiser.

Another officer from another police cruiser came over to Will, and said something at length. Will could see his lips moving, could hear the words, but their meanings registered haltingly, as though the man took long pauses between words. When he realized that what he was saying wasn't registering with Will, the policeman motioned him toward the car and touched his shoulder indicating that he should get in.

Will entered the cruiser and, looking at the back of the uniformed man's head, realized he was in trouble. The only thing he could think was that he wanted his mother.

24

Neena, age 13 – Emmaus, Virginia
Easter 1951

On Easter Sunday, March 25, 1951, Neena, thirteen, would turn fourteen in two weeks, and her best friend, Betsy, would turn fourteen in one month. Attending church together that day, they felt grownup. Their mothers had bought them new outfits. Too old for crinolines and taffeta, they wore suits. Neena's had a mid-calf heavy cotton skirt and a round-necked jacket that matched. The jacket had two rows of buttons although the second row was just for decoration. She had stuffed her hair into a wide-brimmed hat that matched her shoes. Like most girls her age, she wore white gloves with little lacy cuffs. Her right glove still had a tan stain in the palm from when she had worn them while sliding down the banister at *the manse*.

As on most Easter Sundays, Aunt Toot and Uncle Jimmy would be arriving soon to attend church with the Teeples and Grandma Lowry, who lived with the Teeples, and to eat Easter dinner with all of them.

On that day her mother let Neena wear her pearls, but Teddy told her she looked like Grandma Lowry.

Yet Neena knew whenever Teddy wanted to bug her about her looks, he said she looked like Grandma or one of the other old ladies in the church. Sometimes he said that Neena chewed like Grandma who had false teeth she kept in a glass at night on the bathroom sink. He said Neena snored like Grandma although Neena could never figure out how he knew what either Neena or her grandmother did in their bedrooms at night.

But on that Easter Sunday, according to Teddy, Neena looked like Grandma. In spite of him and his opinion, she was proud of how she looked. Betsy and Neena weren't allowed to wear mascara, so they had heated a spoon over the kitchen range burner and then held it against their eyelashes with a thumb. They discovered that if they held it there even for a minute or two, it curled their lashes. So after they had successfully curled their lashes, they put petroleum jelly on them to make them sparkle. It worked great unless they forgot and rubbed their eyes.

In the past year they had begun noticing changes in their bodies. Neena was taller than Betsy. Their breasts were growing and firming. Mrs. Teeple said it was time for Neena to wear a brassiere. Caught unaware, both girls had started their periods the month before, or as Betsy announced it, "Aunt Lucy had come to call." Betsy was anxious to shave the blonde peach fuzz from her legs, but her mother told her to wait a couple of years. Neither girl was permitted to wear lipstick either, so they bit their lips at strategic times like Scarlett O'Hara had in *Gone With The Wind*.

Neena washed her hair on Saturday evening and set it in curlers. She slept fitfully on them that night. In the morning she removed them and brushed her hair. It looked wavy and shiny, just the way she liked it.

So on Easter Sunday, 1951, when Neena and Betsy entered the sanctuary of The Evangelical Reformed Baptist Church of Emmaus, Virginia, they were the *cat's meow*.

Neena's father must have thought they looked like nice young ladies because he asked that they come forward to collect the offering. They strutted up there, accepted the plates, each took a side of the church, and then they collected the money. They felt like starlets, with everyone smiling at them as they moved down the aisle in their lovely outfits.

When the girls had finished, they waited at the back of the church until Reverend Teeple motioned them forward. When they reached the front, Neena somehow tripped, fell flat and, still holding the plate, watched as loose change rolled in most directions. Some landed under her mother's feet as she sat at the piano, some rolled forward to the altar, and some came to rest under the pews. People were scurrying around picking up pennies, nickels, dimes, quarters, maybe even fifty-cent pieces, who could remember.

From the back of the church Teddy said, "Way to go, Nines."

Neena wanted to cry or hit Teddy or just be somewhere else altogether. Mortified, she began collecting the spilled change.

After Betsy and Neena crawled around in their finest clothes, making sure most of the change had been located, they stood up, walked back and sat down. But after the last hymn, while Reverend Teeple gave the closing prayer, they ran out of the church, across the street, and shut themselves into Neena's bedroom. By that time it was funny. They laughed and laughed. Surprisingly, the Reverend didn't even mention it at dinner, even in his prayer.

Neena remembered that Sunday in particular because that evening Will McClure came to stay at the Teeple residence.

25 Teddy recalls Will – Emmaus, Virginia
Summer 1976 – back to 1951

Swiveling a bit, Teddy sat at his desk chewing on the end of a pen. One of his parishioners was due in one hour to talk, presumably, about her daughter. The girl was in the habit of crawling out of her window at night to meet her older boyfriend, and Sandy was beside herself. Teddy wanted to help but was almost out of ideas.

He kept trying to keep his mind on track, but it kept wandering to the file with the letters from Will to Neena. Worried that he might be obsessing about the letters, he had tried to go on to other matters but knew himself too well for that. He knew he had unresolved business so he might as well get on with working things through in his mind.

He tried to remember when he had first noticed Will. Teddy must have been fourteen, Will, eleven, or maybe even twelve, he couldn't remember. Will hung out with a tough kid named Peto whose father had died in a car accident. Teddy and Will had both gone out for recreation football that year. Tall and muscular for his age, Will was a natural, but the coach yelled at him for his lack of aggression. Slight of build and shorter than most boys his age, Teddy was all effort and not much skill. He resented that Will could play so well, yet winning didn't matter to him like it mattered to Teddy.

Teddy had always regarded him as a kid from the wrong side of the tracks yet he lived in a nice house, on the south side of town. His parents drove a nice car. His dad had a decent job, he thought, but Teddy wasn't sure where. His mom was really pretty, and so was his sister. He had other siblings, but they were enough younger that Teddy hardly remembered them despite the smallness of the school, and the town. Will's family went to the Catholic church on the south side of town. The truth was, Roman Catholics and Protestants didn't mingle much in those days; they each kept to their own. Will seemed personable enough but remote and unfriendly, almost watchful, or so Teddy remembered from this remove.

The kicker was that on Easter Sunday in the spring of 1951, when Teddy, Neena, Grandma Lowry, his parents, Aunt Toot, Uncle Jimmy and Betsy, Neena's friend, gathered for dinner, his father, addressing Teddy and Neena, had made an announcement:

"There's a boy you both know, I'm sure, who will be coming this evening to stay here for a while. His name is Willis McClure. I have been asked by the coach at the school to help this boy. He is a good boy, I'm told, and a good student, but his home circumstances make it necessary for him to stay somewhere else for a while. I don't want to embarrass him. Let's all try to make him feel welcome."

"Will McClure," Teddy said, color rising to his face. "What do you mean; his home circumstances?"

"I am not sure of everything," Reverend Teeple said, his tone dismissive.

Clearly agitated, Teddy shifted in his chair. "What do you mean you're not sure of everything? Is he moving in with us? Where will he sleep? How long will he be here? Can't we at least know why he has to come at all?" Teddy sounded exasperated.

"It is better that only he and I know that for now. I'm sure it will be hard for him to be separated from his family, so I will expect you to be kind to him."

So like my father, Teddy thought. So like him to announce something that could potentially change their home life yet give them no explanation why some kid Teddy didn't even like had to come live with them. So like him, he thought, resentfully.

Will had, indeed, arrived that same evening and had acted like a scared puppy, not talking, eating little, and withdrawing to the parlor to do homework as soon as dinner was finished.

At first Teddy had tried to include him, asking him to play touch football after dinner, or go bike riding. Will had politely declined.

Because their grandmother lived with them in the guest room, Will had to sleep on the davenport in the parlor. He went to sleep early, and was the first one dressed and ready for school each morning. Most Saturdays he worked down at the car lot, washing cars, and doing odd jobs. On Sunday mornings Coach Bowen picked him up for early Mass, and Will usually did not return until after Teddy's family had returned from their own evening church services. Teddy had no idea where Will went after church on those days. He wondered if he went home to see his family.

Not understanding why his father would not give the details of Will's need to live with the Teeples, Teddy resented Will a bit. He began spying on him. Teddy slipped downstairs after everyone had gone to bed to see if Will was sneaking out. Twice he found him crying. He wondered what really bad thing he had done that he'd have to leave his family. Teddy fought feeling sorry for him and spent a lot of time thinking Will was just a big baby. But Teddy had heard things at school, really bad things, especially on the Monday after Easter when the kids at school had speculated that Will had killed somebody.

Jimmy Evans took Teddy aside after algebra class that day. "I saw the cop cars at McClure's house. I heard Will killed somebody. There were three cop cars, an ambulance, a black car that could have been a meat wagon, and I saw them put

Will into a police cruiser. I saw it myself. You got a murderer living under the same roof as you? Man," he said, shaking his head. "I'd be scared to go to sleep at night."

But Teddy had heard nothing more about Will after that first week. No one knew for sure what had happened. Will couldn't be a murderer if they let him go live at a local parsonage with an innocent family.

The truth was that after two days Teddy got bored with Will. His secret was probably no big deal. Teddy got sick of waiting for Will to open up and start acting like a normal kid, so he just ignored him.

Neena did not. Neena seemed to think it was her job to make everyone laugh, even if she had to act silly to do so. Behind his dark and watchful eyes, Will seemed to warm to her a bit. They were the same age and shared some of the same classes. He walked to school with her as she chatted nonstop. Teddy thought Will liked her because when he was with her he didn't need to talk. Neena didn't give him a chance. She never gave much of anybody a chance to talk.

After a few weeks, the coach quit coming for Will on Sundays, so he began going to their church. Before Sunday School, Neena found Will and dragged him over to sit with her and her friends. And he usually sat with Neena and Grandma Lowry during the worship service.

Over a short time, Neena and Will became close, yet Teddy was so busy trying to impress his pals he hardly noticed.

Then a little less than six weeks after his arrival, Will was gone.

26 | Neena – Emmaus, Virginia
Spring 1951

Will was strange at first, but my mother said he was just sad and a little shy. Nobody told us why Will was sad or even why he was there. I thought he must have done something really bad that he'd have to leave his family. Teddy asked him to do things like play catch or ride bikes, but Will refused. After he had been there a while, I decided I was going to make him laugh or at least smile like when I did goofy things to make little babies smile. It took a while, but he started to warm up. He started walking to school with me. He went to the Catholic church for the first month and then started going to our church. He sat with me and Grandma Lowry or with Betsy and me. I felt like he was my best friend even though he didn't talk much, and he still looked sad when he didn't know anyone was looking. He was kind of my project.

In those days my mother kept me pretty busy. While Mother finished dinner, I set the table, and if Will was around, I made him help me. Will was gone a lot with his coach or maybe visiting his family. We never knew for sure what he did when he was gone from the house.

I worked two nights each week at the church, dusting, sorting, and assembling bulletins. I did homework and practiced piano. On Friday and Saturday nights Betsy was allowed to go to movies and visit friends, but I was not permitted to go out except with my parents. So I read a lot. And I still listened to the radio. Sometimes Mother and Teddy played board games with me. And once in a while Will was there but he held back unless we were alone.

One night after everyone was asleep, I went downstairs to get some milk and cookies. My mother always told me not to eat before going to bed because it would make me have bad nightmares, so I just waited until she went to sleep and had cookies anyway. I don't think she ever knew because I always cleaned up after myself.

That night I decided to see if Will might like some, too, so I peeked into the parlor where he slept on the davenport. I could hear him crying, more like sniffling. I started to go away so I wouldn't embarrass him but went in instead, and he was real uncomfortable. He wiped his nose on his pajama sleeve and pretended he hadn't been crying. I tried to make him laugh, but nothing worked. So I went out and got us cookies and milk, went back in, and told him to move his feet so I could sit down. We ate our cookies then, with me chattering about anything that came into my head. And it was hard for me to speak softly since I usually get excited when I talk, getting louder and louder.

When we finished our snack, Will thanked me and offered to help me take the glasses and plate out to the kitchen. We tiptoed out to the kitchen and quietly washed and dried the glasses and plate so we wouldn't leave any evidence.

Then he hugged me so hard I thought he would break my ribs.

"Nite, Neena," he whispered.

"Nite, Will."

Three nights later I went down again just out of curiosity. He asked me to stay with him a while. I sat down on the couch, and he scooched over, turning me so that my back was against his chest with his arms around me. He didn't seem to want me looking at him. We sat that way, and he told me stuff about his family, about stuff he had done. He seemed to want me to know so that I could decide if I still wanted him for a friend. Most nights when I was certain everyone was asleep, I went downstairs. At first Will and I had our usual cookies and milk and conversation, but after a week of that we began hugging and got into the habit of sitting with our arms around each other. He whispered to me the things near to his heart. He told me about his dad, but he acted scared, and I wondered what he had left out.

He often touched my face tenderly with his fingertips, like he had never felt anything like it before, and almost like he was memorizing me. He kissed me tenderly at times, but sometimes so forcefully my lips pulsated long after I went back up to bed.

One night I was shivering from the excitement of his touch and from the cold, so I crawled under the blanket with him. Soon, I just naturally crawled beneath the covers when I went downstairs. Our kissing had become more urgent and, strange to me, left me breathless. Most nights after we had kissed awhile and whispered our secrets, I lay with his arm around me and with my cheek on his bare, hairless chest.

I worried a lot that I might fall asleep downstairs.

At some point, Will began touching more than my face while he kissed me. He reached up under my pajama top, tenderly touching my skin, marveling at its softness. His touch, so strange to me, made me suck in my breath. When he kissed me, I kissed back.

The next night he touched my breasts and then rolled over onto me while we were fully dressed. He felt hard against my crotch. I was puzzled. He kissed me and moved against me, his breath coming in gasps. I didn't know what was happening. I liked his kisses; I liked the sensations. But I pushed against his chest, indicating that he should stop.

"Am I too heavy?"

"Yeah," I said, even though he wasn't.

"I'm sorry, Neena." He sounded short of breath, like he had been running.

He rolled off me.

"You better go on up."

I thought he was mad at me, so I went upstairs.

The next morning we walked to school as usual.

That night when I peeked out into the hall, Teddy's light was on. I went back into bed and fell asleep waiting for the house to quiet.

The next morning Will seemed agitated. After we had gotten some distance from the house, he asked, "Why didn't you come down last night? You mad at me?"

"No, I fell asleep."

I was puzzled but afraid, too. It was like my conscience was saying I was doing something wrong, but my heart - and maybe my body as well, I didn't know for sure - was urging me on.

"I'm sorry, Neena." His face reddened. "I don't know what's wrong with me. It's like my stomach is jiggling with worms or butterflies or something. I don't know if I'm happy or scared."

That night when I went down, he gave me one of the spikes off his football shoes. He had strung it on a rawhide shoe lace. "Wear this where your mom can't see it," he said.

He told me that he wanted us to go steady.

He told me he loved me and always would.

* * * * *

I loved Will more than anything. While I hung out the laundry for my mother, I fantasized about being his wife. As I put the clothespins on the wet shirts and socks, I pretended that the washing was his and mine. I thought about how he would come home sounding like Jim Anderson in the radio show,

Father Knows Best. And I would be more like Mrs. Anderson than Betty, their older daughter, even though Betty was more my age. Betty was just too boy-crazy to be like me. But Will, much like Mr. Anderson, might call me Princess, like he did Betty. I might even act more like Kathy, Mr. Anderson's younger daughter, the one he called Kitten. But I hoped Will would not be as sarcastic as Mr. Anderson.

I continued the fantasy while in class at school. I tried to act grown up and more sophisticated. In my fantasy, I saw Will and me playing catch and swimming and going to movies. It would be so much fun.

But I kept my fantasies to myself, then. I had begun to think before I spoke so I wouldn't give away my late night activity and get myself into trouble. Truthfully, I had become pretty sneaky.

That night when I went down to Will, he started kissing and touching me right away. He had me touch him down below. I had seen Teddy naked when we were little and later when he forgot to shut his door while getting dressed or something. But this was different. He asked if he could feel my skin against his skin, so I took off my pajamas. He held me against him, looking at, touching, and kissing my breasts.

He touched me down below, too, putting his finger into me. I can still remember how it felt. I couldn't believe how good it felt. I was so busy thinking about how good it felt that I was surprised when he rolled over onto me like he had that other time and stuck his hard thing into me. It hurt a lot and made me think of how my dad talked about pushing a camel through the eye of a needle or something like that.

But almost as soon as he had started, he stopped. I was kind of glad at that point. Then he grabbed a hanky from the end table and wiped me down below. And he wiped himself. Then he just held me and whispered into my hair how he was sorry if he hurt me and that he didn't know what he would have done if he had never met me.

I went up to bed feeling happy, a little strange, and more than a little puzzled. I needed to talk to Betsy if she came over on Saturday. I was a little afraid to tell her because I figured this was a pretty big sin I was committing.

When I went to the bathroom I was surprised to see blood on the tissue. But I was pretty sure it wasn't quite time for Aunt Lucy to come calling.

* * * * *

The next night and the next and for the rest of that week or more, I realize now that I was really having sexual relations. I was fourteen and should have known more than I did. But no one had ever talked to me about sex except Betsy who spent more time wondering what a boy's thing looked like and what a condom was than what it was like to have sex. In fact, after she had seen what she thought was a condom on the ground out behind the Meat Market, we had searched for one in our homes. I had looked in my parent's medicine cabinet; she had looked in hers. The only thing we ever found was a finger guard. Of course we didn't know that then. We thought we had found the real thing.

But I went back down to Will the next night, and it hurt again but not nearly as much. After that it just felt right, and we just kept doing it and doing it and liking it so much. Sometimes we would just get done, and we would do it again. I felt guilty, but Will said he felt like I was already his wife. I always wondered how he knew what to do. I guess it just comes natural.

I never did tell Betsy. She didn't come over that Saturday anyway. I felt like this was Will's and my secret. It didn't stay that way for long.

On May 8 – I remember because it was Grandma's birthday – Will and I were lying naked under the covers when we heard a noise. I jumped up, trying to get my pajamas back on before someone came in. Teddy walked in before I had my top buttoned. He just looked at me, and then glared at Will.

Then he turned and went upstairs and woke Mama and Daddy.

* * * * *

Neena's mother took her upstairs and just sat with her, saying nothing. Neena's father stayed in the den, talking softly to Will. After a while Amos came upstairs by himself and told his wife and Neena to kneel. The three knelt by the bed, and he asked Neena if she wanted to pray. She shook her head no; she was so scared she couldn't talk. Then she started to cry, softly at first, and then in big gulping sobs.

The Reverend Amos Teeple prayed that Neena would find the words to ask for forgiveness. He told her to think about what she had done. Then he said he would talk with her again the following morning.

After Neena's parents went back down to the main floor of the house, Neena crawled into bed and felt like something was keeping her from breathing freely. She didn't know if she formed a prayer, but she was remorseful.

She just kept wishing over and over that she had never done what she had done. If only, if only, if only she hadn't done what she had done. That night she learned that remorse is something that crawls into your belly, takes up residence there, stays on and on, and invites its relatives for a long visit.

* * * * *

The next morning at eight a.m., there was a light tap on Neena's door. Her grandmother peeked around the door and entered. She walked to the bed, bent and kissed Neena, stood erect again, and then stroked Neena's hair.

"Your Papa wants you downstairs, Honey; in his office, before his appointments."

She turned and walked toward the door.

"When you are finished, come on into the kitchen. I'll fix you some breakfast and eat some with you. Okay?"

Neena got up, went out into the hall and down to the bathroom, entered, ran the water until it warmed and washed her face, her swollen eyes itching. Then she went back to her room, dressed in a skirt and cotton blouse, brushed her hair, and descended the stairs to her father's office.

The door blind was down and closed.

She knocked on the door, and he told her to come in.

She entered. He motioned her to come over to a side table that was usually covered with piles of papers, but this morning it was bare on one end.

"Here, Christina, sit up here on this table."

She backed up then lifted herself up onto the table.

He walked over and stood before her.

"Now lift me up," he said, "onto the table."

She didn't even try to lift him but merely said, "I can't."

He moved closer to her, putting his hands on her sides.

"Ah, but see how easily I can bring you down?" he asked, as he lowered her to the floor, settling her on her feet.

He peered at her gravely for a moment, turned, and walked out of his office toward the stairs.

She knew he wanted her to chew on his words, chew them up and really taste them, of course, like he expected when he quizzed her about his sermons. He wanted her to get the point that Will, an undesirable, had brought her down to his level; and any lofty attempt to lift him up, would prove futile.

"We must feel sorry for heathens," her father was, in essence, saying, had said before, in so many words, "especially Roman Catholic ones whom we meet outside our church doors."

Was he saying that she was not a strong enough person? Oh, she had proven that, all right. But why, then, had her father brought Will into their home? Why had he preached to his family about how they were "required through charity to bring others to the love and comfort of the Lord who taught us to love in the first place?" Hadn't those been his very words?

She had loved Will. How could she have foreseen where that would lead? How could she have been so weak? She had failed. She had failed, and now her father had turned his back on her.

She heard doors opening and closing within the house and family members moving about, but the sounds faded so that she felt like she had entered a silent chamber, and had become aware only of her feet and how she must pick one up and put it down again, and pick one up — until she could close the distance between that table and the hall that led to her grandmother.

27

Neena, age 14 – Emmaus, Virginia

Spring - Summer 1951

Will was sent away in the early morning hours of May 9, 1951.

In July, after two months of what amounted to house arrest, Neena was taken to old Dr. Lupher. He examined her, seemingly sensitive to her embarrassment. He patted her shoulder, a grave look on his face, and asked her to wait out in the reception room with another patient, old Mr. Grail, who coughed and wheezed. When her mother came out of the examining room to join her, Neena got up, and they both walked the six blocks home. Dessie remained so silent as they walked that Neena began counting steps to distract herself.

When they arrived at the parsonage, she was told to go to her room.

After about fifteen minutes, Neena's parents came into her room and told her that she was pregnant and that she would be going to live with Aunt Verina, her mother's sister, down in southern Virginia. They would leave early in the morning.

Neena stayed in her room all afternoon.

Late the same afternoon, around 4:00 p.m., Neena heard a terrible pounding on the door. Her mother was at a meeting at the church with Grandma, and Neena's father was in the study, talking on the telephone, so she descended the stairs and answered the door.

Will stood there, crying so hard he couldn't talk so that she could understand him.

Neena's father came up behind her almost instantly and told her to go upstairs.

Neena couldn't see from the window, but the screens were in so she heard Will trying to say something through his tears.

Finally, Amos Teeple raised his voice and told him to "GO!"

Then there was more noise and then everything went quiet until Neena heard a police car siren. The police hauled Will away. An ambulance took Amos to the hospital, but he came home early that evening.

About six o'clock her grandma brought her a tuna fish sandwich, some cookies and some root beer she had made. She sat with Neena while she ate the food and then hugged her, told her to get a good night's sleep, and left.

The next day, before daylight, Neena's mother and grandmother woke her for the drive to Aunt Verina's.

28 — Will, age 14 – Emmaus, Virginia
Spring - Summer 1951

Will remembered the day they took him away to detention. He felt desperate. He didn't feel like the other boys around him, the tough guys who picked fights just so they could hit someone. Yet he survived for almost two months before, one hot afternoon in July, while the other detainees played kickball, he just walked off the field, then ran as fast as he could, darting in and out of alleys, through fields, and across a stream until he finally reached Neena's house.

Forbidden to go there, he nevertheless rang the bell and then pounded as hard as he could on the door. He was crying so hard he could barely breathe. When she finally opened the door, he couldn't read the look on her face. But then her father walked up behind her, loomed there, and then moved her aside.

"Go to your room, Christina," he said.

He turned back to Will and walked out onto the porch, closing the screen door behind him. Small of stature and slightly built, Reverend Teeple appeared kindly yet serious.

"Now, you go, too, Will. Now. Go ahead. And don't come back."

Will tried to say he was sorry but tears kept running down his face. He kept slapping them away, growing more and more frustrated that his voice wouldn't project. He kept struggling, turning in circles on the porch.

Finally he croaked, "Please, please."

He slapped at his tears, begging, crying, and trying to find voice and words beyond his repeated, "Please."

Reverend Teeple moved closer to him. His voice sterner, he said. "You can't come here anymore. You can't ever see her again. Never. Now go, Will. Go!"

Will wept hard, seeing Reverend Teeple in watery focus.

Struggle as he might, words wouldn't come past the throat lump that choked him. When Neena's father touched his shoulder, Will began punching wildly, blindly, feeling first something hard, then something soft and softer still, until his mind went blank.

He had tried many times to remember what happened after that. He had been told that the blows continued, that Neena's father had never struck back nor tried very hard to defend himself.

Will spun down to a dark place that day, in that moment. He wondered now if that was where his father went when he drank, when he threw blows at his wife and children. Had the bottle been his dad's direct path to oblivion? Did he ride that bottle like the hood of their old car, looking for that moment of nothingness? And if he did, what was behind him, driving him forward?

29   Teddy – Emmaus, Virginia
1951 - 1953

Two months after Teddy discovered Neena and Will together and reported it to his parents, Neena was shipped off to Aunt Verina's house in another part of the state.

It was true: Neena had been putting her pajama top back on when Teddy walked in. He could understand why they would ship Will off, but he couldn't figure out why they'd ship her off, too. It wasn't until Teddy overheard two conversations between his parents that he put two and two together. Realizing that Neena must be pregnant, Teddy began to hate Will with a slow burn. He hated him in large part because he, Teddy the cool kid, had been so slow to catch on.

By the time school started the next fall, Will was back in school. He lived way out in the boonies and came to school in a beat-up truck driven by a man who worked at the hardware store. He became the star athlete, lettering in football, and track. He dated one cheerleader, an outgoing but homely girl, from tenth grade on, although he showed no more warmth toward her than to anyone else.

Then Teddy's mother showed increasing signs of pregnancy but discussion on that and most other sensitive subjects was discouraged in the Teeple household.

In late December, Teddy's parents left him with his grandmother for two days. When they returned, they announced to him and to the congregation that their baby girl, Patrice, whom they nicknamed Reecie, had been born. Just like that.

Almost a year passed before Teddy saw Neena again when he, his mother and father, Grandma Lowry, and baby Reecie went to Aunt V's for a long Easter weekend. Neena had changed. She was still talkative with him but seemed angry, shamed and, he realized now, withdrawn, almost secretive. After that first weekend, their father's last visit with Neena, they saw her only on rare trips to his aunt's on holidays and for four days once during summer break. During those visits Neena gradually warmed to him. When permitted to be off by themselves, they had a good time. Still, they talked of nothing personal.

On those visits, as Reecie grew to a toddler, she seemed drawn to Neena, wanting to sit in her lap, or trying to engage her in play. But Dessie quickly intervened, keeping the two girls separate. "What a jerk," Teddy thought. But Neena tacitly gave in to her mother while studiously avoiding little Reecie. Teddy's sister acted like a whipped dog.

Then, at night, when it was time to go to bed, Teddy sulked as he puzzled over Neena. He didn't understand her. How could she let this happen, especially with a jerk like McClure? And his parents, what kind of parents would send their kid away without a second thought?

But over time Neena slowly relaxed with him, and they developed a friendship, guarded at first and then close as they began a weekly correspondence in which they talked of everything but Willis McClure.

In June of 1953 his appendix burst, preventing him from attending his high school graduation ceremony. He remained in the hospital for two weeks and required a three week recovery. After working at a soda fountain for the remainder of the summer, he went off to the University of Virginia.

Over all that time and the visits he and Neena shared, Teddy never quit blaming Will for taking his sister from him. But after a time he didn't permit himself to think about it anymore, because, by then, he had become re-acquainted with Margot Miller.

30 | Neena, age 14 – Albemarle County, Burl, Virginia
Early Fall 1951

Neena sat on what felt like a padded seat. It was quiet, too quiet. She heard someone crying while a man's voice drifted softly toward her as though he were in another room. She must be in church, but the seat was all wrong. She felt tears on her own cheeks but couldn't remember why she was crying. Her neck felt wrong. It hurt. Something was hurting her neck. What was it? She was choking. She couldn't breathe.

When Neena opened her eyes, she saw that she sat on a Chippendale sofa with her head tipped back against the armrest, at an uncomfortable angle. Funeral parlor quiet except for the steady ticking of the mantle clock, her Aunt Verina's house smelled of late summer flowers, maybe mums or gladiolas, she could never keep those straight. The odor was not a fragrance, really, just a fresh cut smell that kind of got up your nose.

Neena was now fourteen. She was four months pregnant.

Awake now, she realized she must have been dreaming, but it had been more like calling forth an old, accurate memory. Her grandma had been in the dream, stroking her cheeks and singing to her as she sometimes did when Neena was little. They had been sitting on the padded front porch swing at the farm house at Grandpap's apple orchard. Hung by chains from the porch ceiling, the swing creaked, a special sound for forward motion, a different one for backward movement.

Grandma's feet were on the floor, ever so gently keeping the swing in motion while Neena's head rested on the older lady's lap.

A lawnmower hummed off in the distance, and a dog barked at irritatingly irregular intervals a couple of houses down.

She rubbed her swollen eyes.

Having realized where she was, she felt tears begin again. They trickled down her face. She had cried so much since coming here she imagined furrows running down her cheeks to her chin from the steady flow of tears. She cried a lot, really, when she was alone, at night or when Aunt V took her afternoon catnaps.

Crying made Neena sleepy, but she would have slept anyway. She felt tired all the time despite sleeping well at night and despite these afternoon naps. She felt like something heavy had settled onto the tops of her feet so that going upstairs left her feeling drained of energy.

At least the morning sickness had eased.

Aunt Toot, who lived in nearby Burl, Virginia, visited once a week most weeks bringing Neena the oatmeal cookies she craved, with chocolate chunks and big pieces of walnut. Sometimes she brought the banana bread Neena loved, moist and studded with pecans.

"Eat, Sweet Neena Girl. You're eating for two now," she'd say, while Aunt V shifted in her chair and grunted as though wanting to speak and holding it back.

Finally Aunt V would say, "Take it easy, Toot. You don't need to fatten her up."

After Aunt Toot left, a single cookie appeared on Neena's dessert plate at lunchtime, or a slice of bread was presented at dinner. But where Aunt V kept the baked goods in the meantime, Neena had not yet discovered.

They had fallen into a routine now that she was beginning to feel better.

Mondays were wash days. Unlike Aunt Toot, Aunt V had neither maid nor cleaning lady. She washed in an old Bendix agitator washer with a rinse vat and an attached wringer. When V lifted the clothes out of the rinse vat, Neena ran them through the wringer – twice – to get all of the water out. Then she put them into a basket to carry out to the yard to be hung on the line.

The clothes line was on a large reel attached to the side of the house. Neena grasped one end of the line and then walked across to a pole where she looped the line around a hook. Then she proceeded to another pole where she did the same thing, before she stretched it back to the side of the house where she secured the line once more.

The rectangle made by the strung line seemed more than adequate for anyone's laundry, but by the time they stretched the sheets and hung up all of Uncle Monroe's socks, it was barely long enough.

Neena enjoyed hanging the wash. A mundane activity, it distracted her from her problems and allowed her to be out-of-doors. She wore Aunt V's pocketed apron. One pocket held the clothespin type with a spring that clipped onto the line. Those were best for socks, but they would not hold the weight of a sheet, especially on a windy day. For sheets and most other laundry items Neena used the pins you pushed over the line. They looked to her like little armless men with no facial features. They stood above the line like little soldiers, their crotches holding tight to a fold of sheet or the waistband of a pair of jeans.

On a warm day, Neena loved hanging clothes and feeling the sun on her back as she bent and on her face as she reached up for the line.

She wondered sometimes how the line could stretch so much, just like the skin of her belly. When she strung the line she made it as taut as possible. Yet after hanging a few items on it, she always needed the clothes props Uncle Monroe kept on a rack on the side of the house. They were hewn poles with a little vee in the top that slipped up under the line and raised it so the sheets wouldn't drag on the ground as they whipped about in a breeze.

In the afternoon, she collected the clothes and sheets, folding them as she removed them from the line and placing them into a basket to be carried back into the house.

On Tuesdays they ironed while listening to the radio. Sometimes they listened to Arthur Godfrey. Sometimes they listened to baseball games. The radio gave Neena an excuse not to talk. Since Aunt V had two irons and two ironing boards, they both ironed at the same time. Aunt V ironed the clothing, even Uncle Monroe's underpants. Neena ironed the flat pieces: Sheets, pillowcases, handkerchiefs, napkins and table cloths.

Neena liked ironing, something she had never done at home. The laundry always smelled so fresh and clean, and the starch had a fresh aroma as well. Before she started ironing, she sprinkled the clothes with water. After sprinkling them, she rolled them up and laid them on the end of the ironing board, and then ironed them one by one.

On Wednesdays they went to the Ladies' Aid Dinner at the little country church near V's house. Usually held once a month, the dinners had become so popular that they had expanded to twice a month and then to every week. Since theirs was a farming community, the women cooked their specialty dishes, and the men came in from the fields to join them for noon-time dinner. Except for preschool children, the gathering was mostly adult during the school year. After the dinner everyone lingered a while, and then the men went back to work, and the women cleaned up for the women's social group meeting held on alternating Wednesdays. Also, once a month they met for WCTU ("WCTU stands for Women's Christian Temperance Union," Uncle Monroe had clarified, but Neena never told him that she had to look up the word *temperance*). Except for Wednesdays when she helped in simple food preparation, Neena was never invited to help her aunt cook. Once in a while she baked a pie, in the way Aunt V had taught her, for the Wednesday dinner, but for the most part she either served beverages or helped do dishes afterwards.

She felt very out-of-place at the Wednesday dinners since most of the women were well-acquainted with each other, and none of them were pregnant girls with no husbands. Although two of the older ladies were very sweet to her, asking her how she felt, whether she felt any movement yet or if her energy was coming back; but the rest of them treated her as though she were invisible. So she sat on the edge of the group, learned their recited prayer, their in-unison creed, and overheard them discussing canning, knitting, sewing, embroidering, health issues, children, and, in a few cases, grandchildren.

On Thursdays V and Neena did whatever mending needed done, preserved some of the garden vegetables, visited shut-ins, and, while Aunt V took a longer-than-usual nap, Neena wrote letters to either her mother, her grandmother, or Teddy. She had never heard from either Will or Betsy. They had forgotten her, no doubt. At those times, in the privacy of her room, she cried. But that had begun to change. Sick of crying, she often worked herself up to an angry tantrum to avoid more tears.

One day, unable to stop weeping, she took out a sheet of blank paper and, with a pencil, began frantically multiplying large numbers together. But tears kept plopping down on the sheet. She worked herself into frenzy, repeating over and over, "I will multiply, I will divide, I will subtract," all the while pushing harder and harder with her pencil. When tears fell onto the sheet, obliterating the numbers, she hated, hated, hated with all of her might as she stabbed at the sheet over and over, to pound back the tears, palpable evidence of weakness, her weakness. That is what she hated; her weakness, her stupid, stupid weakness, her stupid, stupid ignorance. No wonder they didn't want her anymore. She wanted to curse like the dirty boys at school or like the bad girls who smoked in the washroom, but she couldn't think of the right words, and when she did they felt foreign to her tongue and, therefore, void of power. She mentally cursed her tears as she poked holes through the sheet of paper until she had ripped it to shreds. Then she began with a new one. But tears kept coming, falling in big blobs. Trying to wipe one away she discovered that another had replaced it. The tear blobs were spots, spots like that lady, what was her name, the lady in the story Uncle Monroe and she had read, that lady, that lady, Lady MacBeth, that was it, Lady MacBeth. Her tears were like Lady MacBeth's damned spot.

"Out damned spot," she stage-whispered. "Out damned spot!"

She repeated it over and over until she wilted down onto her bed and fell into an exhausted, chest-heaving sleep.

When she awoke, she went into her bathroom and ran cold water onto a washcloth and held it to her face. Then she went downstairs to greet Uncle Monroe who, even though retired, managed to stay busy and out of the house until dinner time.

Neena was pretty sure they had noticed her especially puffy eyes, but nothing was said. That night she went to bed early and fell immediately asleep.

On Fridays they went to town where Aunt V had her hair done. Neena and Uncle Monroe went to the hardware store, they bought groceries at the market, and then they all went to the diner for lunch.

On Saturdays she studied her Sunday school lesson. After a couple of months, she saw a little more of Aunt Toot and Uncle Jimmy in nearby Burl.

On Sundays she went to church, came home for Sunday dinner (whether at V's or Toot's), took a long walk, ate supper, and then went back to church on Sunday evening.

What a sad, sorry life she led. She was the fourteen-year-old niece of the perfect, upstanding Verina, who had gotten herself into a little difficulty. Like the Immaculate Conception or something - all by herself. In V's version, Will hadn't even been there when Neena got herself into trouble, got pregnant. Nor was he there then, as Neena sauntered down the dusty road kicking rocks.

Rather, Neena envisioned Will, athletic as he had always been, she envisioned him back home, running the football down the field, sprinting to cheers from the stands. No matter to them that he had never contacted Neena except for his one attempt at her front door. Unlike Neena, there had been no whisking out-of-town in shame for him, Emmaus High School's all-American football hero. His stomach never bulged to bursting. No big red Hester Prynne letter on his jersey.

Neena's opinion was solidly entrenched, despite never having shown remorse, he was the sorry one.

31 — Will remembers – Aboard Ship, Frederick County
Fall 1977 back to Summer 1951

Seeing Neena, Will felt he had come full circle. Admittedly, he was not the innocent he once was, although he had often marveled at the differences in his childhood when he compared it to that of others. He had never been as innocent as his classmates.

His father's cruel hands, his mother's fear and lethargy, Will's own inability to protect those he loved, his detrimental behavior toward those he purportedly loved, and his unpremeditated violence had somehow thrown him into a dark category. Even his easy success seemed to mock him. Yet, life as he knew it as a child had seemed normal to him because he saw no other life, at least up close.

What he saw as his violent sins had earned him detention. Then, piling sin upon sin, he had landed in solitary confinement at the county jail.

"We just want to get your attention, Son," the Sheriff had said. "Reform school didn't work for you so we brought you here for two or three weeks, or so. We wanted to get you away from some of those bad boys. Your coach assures me that you are a good lad, so we'll put you in here alone for your own protection, not as part of your punishment. We just want you to think about some things." Then the hefty sheriff patted him on the back.

Will might have lost his mind had he not been able to write to Neena. But solitary confinement had given Will time to think without much distraction. He had felt safe, at least. And on Wednesdays most weeks, a priest came in to talk with him. But Will did not trust him. The priest was quiet, his eyes kindly, but Will was afraid he would carry whatever Will told him back to whomever had put him there in the first place. So they talked about sports and fishing and God.

Though the priest could undoubtedly tell when Will had been crying, he never let on. Will occasionally asked about his mother, his brothers and sister. But he couldn't bring himself to ask about Neena although she remained the burning concern in his mind.

Then one day the priest told Will that Neena's father, Reverend Amos Teeple, had asked about him. When Will made no response, the priest had asked him if he had any comment, anything to say to Reverend Teeple.

"Is he okay?"

"Yes, Will. Yes, he is well. He is a good and understanding man."

"Will you tell him I'm sorry?" Tears had welled up in his eyes, then, and he slapped them away with the back of his hand.

"Of course I will. He does not plan to bring any charges against you. He understands the pressures you were feeling at the time you . . ." He had not finished the sentence.

Will made no reply.

"Is there anyone else you would like to ask about, anything else?"

"I guess not." But he had many things he wanted to ask. In addition to wanting to know about Neena, he had wanted to ask what would happen to him, but he didn't. He was too afraid of the answer.

On the weekend evening shift, during his stay in solitary confinement, an older lady named Dorothy brought him his supper and an evening snack. She usually offered him cookies that she had made. They were delicious, with nuts and coconut and chocolate chips. Maybe oatmeal, he wasn't sure. She'd tell him her feet hurt, and maybe, since she wasn't too busy, she'd sit down and chat with him a bit.

She was unusually tall and skinny, and her hands were veiny, her fingers long. They often talked about music or her grown children, and sometimes she asked how he was doing.

"I see you write lots of letters." She rubbed her thumbnail with her index finger, over and over, as though the smoothness of it soothed her.

"Yes. I like to write letters. It makes me feel better." He tried for a smile.

"You writing to a girlfriend?"

Will struggled for something to say, when she asked that, so he said nothing.

Was Neena a girlfriend? Yes, of course, she was, or had been. But she was his friend, the one he could act goofy with or serious with or could even cry and not feel like she would tell or make fun. He wanted to hold her hands and see her big blue eyes and that smile that made them sparkle. He wanted to know she loved him still, hadn't gone on to some other boy. So, one night, when Dorothy asked again if he was writing to his girlfriend, he just said, "Yes." Then pausing, he said, "She doesn't write back, but my aunt writes to me, sends me stamps and envelopes, even though she isn't allowed to visit."

Then not long after that he had cried one night in front of Dorothy, and she had taken him into her arms, hugged him to her bony chest, while his tears drenched the shoulder of her blouse. She hadn't seemed to care that liquid ran not only from his eyes, but from his nose and mouth as well. He felt like his whole body cried that night. He had no idea how long it went on.

He only remembered that she kept rubbing his back and saying over and over, "Let it out, Honey. Just let it out."

The next evening, a Saturday night, when Dorothy came in, he felt embarrassed, but she remained cheerful, as usual, and made no mention of his tears of the night before. They just chatted about the usual stuff.

He missed her during the week.

Then slowly, over time, he began talking more with her, little bits at a time. Reticent as he was, he shared only the bare bones about his father, what Will had done that awful night, about Neena's dad, and, finally, about Neena.

Then as quickly as he had been placed in solitary confinement, he was removed to a foster home way out in the country where he would attend a different school – not Emmaus' McKinley High.

The caseworker had come for him on Wednesday, so he had no chance to say goodbye to Dorothy. He missed her — would miss her. So he wrote a hasty note to her and asked the day warden to give it to her.

Dear Dorothy,

I'm going to the Shaffer farm, out in the township. I don't know the address. Please try to write to me if you can find out the address. I will miss you. I'll miss you a lot. Thank you for the cookies.

Love, Will

32   Neena, age 14 – Albemarle County, Burl, Virginia
Late Summer - Early Fall 1951

Five weeks after she arrived at her Aunt V's, Uncle Monroe, V's husband, started her school lessons. His enthusiasm made her want to learn anything he put in front of her. Of course, if she was studying with Uncle Monroe, she did not have to be with Aunt V, doing chores or, worse, alone and crying. And once Aunt V realized Neena's aptitude for learning, she drastically reduced Neena's household duties.

What started out as assigned reading of classic literature, math and algebra, basic science and biology, her uncle expanded into areas of his own interest. He seemed surprised at her eager interest and her level of comprehension. Before six months had passed, he had begun teaching her economics, what he called teaching her from the bottom up and then from the top down. On the sly, they did an overview of world religions, giving her the basic tenets of Islam, Judaism, Hinduism, and Buddhism.

As the months – and, eventually, years – went by, they studied Existentialism, as Uncle Monroe put it, asking fundamental questions of individual responsibility, morality, and personal freedom. They delved into philosophy, looking at Socrates, Plato, Newton, Darwin and Marx.

He assigned Hawthorne's *Scarlet Letter*, an appropriate tale of Hester Prynne and her scarlet *A*, and a book that covered Roman emperors from Claudius to Constantine. They read about a Babylonian emperor, Hammurabi, and Neena was surprised to learn that laws covering adultery, murder and divorce were in place even back then. She read about Marcus Aurelius, a field general and Emperor of Rome whose meditations addressed four virtues: Moderation, wisdom, justice, and fortitude. They read Shakespeare's *Hamlet*, *King Lear*, and *Othello*. They read from Plutarch's *Lives* and Caesar's *Commentaries*. Moved by the beauty of the words, she read the Brownings, both Robert and Elizabeth Barrett.

They studied the history of England from the Tudors to the Stuarts on down to King George himself, and a little on Princess Elizabeth, the next in line to assume the royal crown.

They read a little about British Parliamentary procedure and about the United States Supreme Court. They read extensively about the Civil War as seen from both perspectives.

They delved into the Early Middle Ages, the High Middle Ages, and the Italian Renaissance. They studied the foundations of western civilization.

Some of the information she ingested stuck, but because they had time for mere overviews, much of it passed over her head, despite her retaining at least a gist of trends, patterns, and ideals. By the time she was sixteen, she realized she wanted to be a historian. In addition to wanting to learn more about European and American history, she wanted to understand the history of the English language, the progression of language in general, how mythology informed modern thinking, and how theology found expression in art and music.

At some point Neena realized that her hunger for learning had given Uncle Monroe much joy. He was a demanding teacher who would give as much effort to the task as his student. None of what he shared seemed stale to him. It was if he were learning right along with her. His dedication continued through her high school years.

She found the cultures of other countries fascinating, yet she knew early on that her aptitude for foreign language was lacking. Still, after a lot of study and hard work, she learned to speak passable French. She attacked her studies, even foreign language, with an angry fervor as though by learning she could also conquer, conquer once and for all her weakness and ignorance. Then she would be whole once again.

33 — Will, age 14 – Frederick County, Virginia
Early Fall 1951

That afternoon Will was introduced to Mrs. Shaffer. She was a big, muscular lady. She milked cows and fed calves while her husband, a mousy little man named Bud, worked in town, in Emmaus, at the hardware store.

Will had never met a woman like Beulah Shaffer before. She was strong, not just physically, but she had opinions, did what she chose, and nobody messed with her. Her older son lived on the next farm over and came at planting and harvesting time to help out. Her younger son served somewhere in the military and wanted no part of farm life, or so she said. Her daughter had what seemed like a dozen kids who were wild, but they came around infrequently. She had as many opinions as her mother, it seemed. The two women clashed.

After the caseworker left that first day, Beulah had said, "Take your stuff up to your bedroom, second door on the left, top of the stairs. Come back down after you settle your stuff 'cause we need to talk."

His room was large and high ceilinged and clean, if a little worn. The two beds suggested that this had been her sons' room.

After putting his few things away, he hid the picture of Neena in the back pocket of his best jeans and placed them in the dresser drawer.

Then he went down to talk to Beulah Shaffer.

"We know your history, Will." She looked right at him when she said it. "Sit down; we'll go over the rules."

She handed him a typed sheet of paper that listed required chores, meal times, a $1.50 per week allowance, time allotment for homework, curfew time, but, save for Sunday afternoons, very little free time.

"You're Catholic, we're Protestant, but we'll work around that," she said, shifting around in her seat a bit. "School starts next week. We expect you to keep your nose clean." Then she stretched her hands forward and placed her palms flat out on the tabletop. "Study, play sports, work, that'll keep you out of trouble." She stood then as if to emphasize her words. "And if you're gonna live here, you gotta stay out of trouble."

Then she asked, "You hungry?" She made them each a huge sandwich with ham, fresh lettuce and tomatoes, and then sat down with him to eat.

After finishing her food and lemonade, she got up from the table and placed her plate and glass into the sink. "You get done, come on out to the barn."

He ate slowly, feeling apprehensive and a little angry that he had no choices. When he had finished, he placed his plate and glass into the sink beside hers.

Then he walked slowly out to the barn.

His schedule started the next day, to prepare him for school the next week. He had to be up by five to feed all the calves and chickens and get ensilage down from the silo before he went in to shower before school.

"You don't get up when that alarm goes off, there will be no time for a shower, and you'll have to go to school smellin' like barn," Beulah said.

Then, two days after his arrival, on the Friday before school was to start, Coach Bowen came out to the farm and asked to talk with Mrs. Shaffer and Will.

"I have permission from your caseworker to come and talk with you," he said, lowering himself to a kitchen chair. "She'll call you tomorrow. We want you to come play ball for us at your old school, Will. That is, if you could feel comfortable doing so." Coach Bowen, stood then, nervously pacing back and forth behind his chair. "You can do it, Son. It will be good to be back in your home school. Everyone has confidence in your athletic ability, and we need you, really need you, on the junior high team. We want to be conference champs, if not this year, then next."

Then he turned to Beulah and said, "What do you say, Mrs. Shaffer? If we provide transportation, can we do this?"

Mrs. Shaffer looked at Will only momentarily then turned to Coach Bowen and said, "Sounds good to me. Truth is, he could probably ride in with Bud. He goes in everyday to the hardware store. He works there."

It wasn't until after Coach Bowen had shook his and Beulah's hands, gotten into his pickup truck, and left that Will realized he had never answered one way or another either the coach or Beulah. Apparently, his consent was neither required nor wanted. And despite his apprehension, he was hopeful that, even if he didn't get to see Neena, he might hear something about her. And with any luck at all, he could see his brothers and sister.

Several days later he received a letter from Dorothy:

Dear Will,

My weekends are lonely without you.

I'm so happy for you that you have gone to a good family. I hear you will be playing football back in your hometown. Good for you, Will. Look forward to a good life; don't look back.

You have learned some of life's hard lessons. Now get some education and be happy. I will remember you always.

Love, Dorothy

He was delighted to get her letter, but how had she known, even before the coach had come to the farm to talk with them, that Will would be playing for his hometown school. Could she have had something to do with it? No, he decided, probably not. She had just heard about it.

He was so happy to hear from her. But she gave no return address, and he surmised that she was a part of the past from which she had advised him to turn.

34   Neena, age 14 – Albemarle County, Burl, Virginia
Early Fall 1951

Sometimes she loved the little bubble that floated in there; the little amoeba that had sprouted legs and stretched itself up under her rib cage, kicking its little heels against her sides.

Never having known much about sex and reproduction, it was difficult for her to believe that she housed a baby in there with a nose like hers and little itty bitty fingernails.

Sometimes she touched her stomach as Will had so long ago touched her face. Once in a while she hummed in her bed at night and wondered if the little bubble could hear her.

But sometimes she wanted only to be rid of it, that thing that protruded from her, like an ugly symbol of her weakness, like a growth that had gone out of control and would one day eat her alive.

So she loved and hated the little bubble, the little thing that grew larger every day, hiding evidence of it under too-big clothes, clothes so ugly she blended in with the kitchen window curtains.

35   Will, age 14 – Rural Frederick County, Virginia
Early Fall 1951

Will sat in bed, feeling tired but not all that sleepy. Looking for a piece of paper, he lifted his notebook from the floor beside his bed. A piece of paper slipped from the notebook and floated down onto his lap. He saw that it was a letter he had somehow failed to mail:

August 13, 1951
Dear Neena,
I have no idea whether you are getting these letters because I don't hear from you. I suppose your dad is taking them from the mailbox before you can see them. My letters I mean. And I guess I wouldn't blame him. It's just that I miss you. I went to a hearing today about my dad and your dad and running away and stuff. I was just one of the people there. Some of them were scary looking with greasy hair and big mouths. I just sat there scared to death of the judge and what he might say to me. I was glad my mom hadn't come because I didn't want her to see me like that. I told the judge my story. He will decide what happens to me in the next few days.

I have a friend named Dorothy. She's an old lady forty-five or so who brings me cookies.

I hope you are fine. I wish I could hear your voice. I love you Neena. I know that's hard to believe when I do the things I do like punch out your dad but I love you. I just need to learn some things to make me better.

> *Remember the time we walked the railroad trestle? You got scared that a train would come and squash you flat. I'm glad your mom never found out.*
> *I will love you for ever and ever. Love forever and ever, Will*
> *PS: Please write back.*

But he still had had no word from her.

36 | Will – Frederick County and Emmaus, Virginia
Fall 1951 – Spring 1959

The first week back to school, Will realized that he would have no contact with Neena, nor would he hear anything about her. On his first day there, Will cornered Neena's best friend, Betsy, and asked if she had any news. She said she had called and asked Neena's mother for her daughter's address but had been told that Neena was unable to receive mail. Betsy told Will that she would let him know if she found out anything new. Having acquired new friends, she seemed almost disinterested, but maybe he was reading more into it than was there.

Over the next few weeks, he asked everyone who might have information about Neena if they could tell him anything, but the only thing he learned was that she had left town shortly after he had and that she was off somewhere. That was the story, at least. He heard she was in Europe, in art school, perhaps at a relative's in another state. She might as well have been on the moon. It seemed so difficult to find anything about her.

During that first year Will hadn't forged any real friendships with his classmates or even his teammates beyond the camaraderie in the locker room. He ate lunch with his brother, Royce, unless Roycie's goober buddies were with him. He avoided his old pal, Peter, whom everyone from early childhood had called Peto. It hurt Will to ignore him, but he had to if he wasn't going to blow this chance to stay out of trouble. Instead Peto was in and out of trouble so much himself that he hardly attended school much, anyway.

* * * * *

Will avoided Teddy as Teddy did him, which wasn't all that hard since Teddy was two years ahead of him, had different classes, and went out for wrestling now, not football or track. He mostly saw him in the cafeteria and in the all-grade afternoon study hall. The few times he ran into Teddy, the look on the other boy's face told him not to ask any questions of him. Teddy seemed to despise him. But both school areas were large enough that they never had to speak to nor sit near one another.

By Christmas, 1951, Will had saved $17.25, which represented most of his allowance.

By his fifteenth birthday he had learned how to drive a tractor, how to plow, to rake hay, and to operate the hay baler.

By his sophomore year he had made quarterback.

By the second week of football in tenth grade, Josie Mahon started seeking him out, and he let her. A year younger than her classmates, she was dimpled and pudgy. Popular, she ran with a big crowd of friendly kids from good homes, or so Beulah said.

On Friday game nights and sometimes on Saturday nights, Beulah let him drive her old green Ford into town so that he could hang out with friends before coming home by curfew. Curfew had been extended to eleven p.m. If he returned Josie to her home by 10:30 p.m., he could make it out to the farm by eleven, sometimes arriving on the stroke of the hour.

Will was grateful to Beulah for letting him use her car. He was careful with it, usually washing and polishing it, even vacuuming it before he took it out.

Josie sat in the middle of the Ford's bench seat, seemingly proud to be seen in it and with him.

She taught him to dance. On Thursdays, if he had completed his homework and if his chores were caught up, he picked Josie up for the sock hop. She taught him a dance her mother had learned in England after the war called the jitterbug. He laughed a lot with her. It was unusual for the two of them to be alone except for a few minutes when he either picked her up or dropped her off, or on the twenty-five minute ride from the farm to town when she picked him up.

When he hadn't kissed her after two months of dating, she leaned into him one night at her front door and kissed him lightly on the lips. He kissed her back, his fondness for her showing. They kissed quite a bit after that, and once or twice he touched her ample breasts. But he was careful not to go beyond that. If she was disappointed, she never showed it.

They attended parties, drank some beer once in a while when they were at Frank Barco's family hunting camp, and danced. Slow dancing put him into a dreamy state and made him long for things he couldn't even name.

By the end of their junior year, his friends began discussing to which college they would go. Both his track coach and his football coach had assured him that one of the schools that had athletic programs would give him an athletic scholarship, but he didn't know which one so, while the others chattered about their favorite colleges, he kept quiet about his plans.

Josie planned to attend Westminster College, a small but academically prestigious school and the alma mater of both of her parents. She urged him to go there, too, but he didn't see them offering him a scholarship. He suspected they would drift apart once they left for school; he felt as if he had begun drifting a little already for some reason.

On June 6, 1955, McKinley High's graduation day, Beulah gave him his first and last hug from her. She seemed especially proud that he had been accepted by The Pennsylvania State University. The high school provided a boxed lunch on the lawn under the old oak trees. Parents brought blankets, spread them out, and settled in for a light lunch and friendly chats with their neighbors. Beulah and Bud Shaffer were especially proud, not only of his athletic accomplishments, but of his having won the language award and an honorable mention for his English composition. Although good enough to get by, his grades hadn't been the best in science.

As they nibbled their sugar cookies and sipped lemonade, Beulah handed him an envelope. Inside was a bankbook with weekly handwritten insertions. She had deposited varying amounts of money, in his name, every week for four years. The balance showed almost $500.00, more than he could even fathom.

Will was flabbergasted. He couldn't even speak for a second, but then he said, "I didn't expect this. Thank you."

"We worked you hard, boy," she said. "But you earned it. We wanted to give you a fresh start. You kept yourself out of trouble. You got good grades. You developed new friends. Now, do as well as you can in college. You can always come back to our house on breaks, on holidays, whenever. Remember that."

He thought she was going to tear up, but she abruptly started gathering the papers from their meals, stood up, motioned for them to do the same, and then began folding the blanket. On the excuse they had to get back to a calving cow, they left, allowing Will to go on to Josie's party.

Time passed quickly that summer with farm work, summer parties, picnics and outings. By early August, when his friends were beginning to collect what they would take to college, Will had already departed and begun football practice under Penn State University's Coach Rip Engle.

The University campus sat nestled against the foothills of the mountains. Brick walkways crisscrossed the lawns and ran among shade trees on the main common. He loved the pomp of the matriculation ceremony, the animated, yet detached, demeanors of the professors; he tolerated his well-worn dorm room and his smart-mouthed roommate, Dale.

His coach, old Rip himself, ticked him off daily and pushed him beyond what he thought he could endure. His freshman year he was benched a lot, which allowed for more study time. By his sophomore year he was backup quarterback. By the season's second half his junior year he played quarterback, continuing in that position until mid-season his senior year when a shoulder injury benched him for good.

By then Will really didn't mind so much not playing football. He was tired, had not done as well as he had hoped academically, and was awaiting his LSAT scores. He was hoping to go to Columbia or even back to Virginia.

When his scores came back, he had attained the lowest score possible for acceptance into New York's Columbia Law School. He was anxious to begin law school, to study harder than he had ever studied before, because he wanted to be successful at something.

But first the summer loomed before him. Earlier that year, the past fall really, he had met Allison Hunt who had quickly become his girlfriend, and was now his fiancé. She was a nice girl, older and more mature than he, which he thought he needed. She had been married, had two children, then divorced, and now was completing her studies at the university while her mother helped her with the children. Early that spring she had introduced him to her father, a senior partner in a prestigious Arlington, Virginia, law firm. He had offered Will a summer job. In June Allison and Will would be married. He didn't know whether to laugh or cry.

37 Neena, age – Selmer's Springs, North Carolina
November 1951

With six weeks to go in her pregnancy, Neena's Aunt Verina moved her across the state line into North Carolina to a home for unwed mothers. Verina said she wanted Neena to go where she could receive good care, including emotional counseling for when she had to give up the baby. Verina seemed to think that Neena was unstable. And she was, at times. Some days she couldn't wait to turn over the responsibility for that baby to someone else. Sometimes, though, she felt that the little thing was all she had in the world to love and maybe to love her. Her childish heart couldn't pick. Yet when Neena looked fairly at Aunt Verina, she realized that V probably wanted the best for her and her baby. Maybe V feared that Neena's child would come too quickly as Neena had or that Neena would need time to adjust. And maybe it was good that she would meet other girls in her same predicament.

That morning, as they shuffled her toward the waiting Packard, robins strolled across the lawn plucking breakfast worms. Flinging the *Grit* weekly newspaper toward the house, the paperboy, who lived down in the valley closer to Burl, waved at them, his bike wobbling precariously as he reached for the next newspaper.

Realizing she had forgotten the mystery book she had been reading, she trotted back into the house, past the wire-racked milk bottles with their little cardboard circle tops. Usually there was no milk delivery this far out in the country, but the dairy was only a half a mile away, so Mr. Gordon just dropped their order off on his way to town. The screen door slammed behind her. She stopped, returned to the porch, picked up the rack of milk, took it into the house, and, just like any other day, put the bottles into the refrigerator. When she stepped off the porch to return to the car, she cut across the grass. The sun highlighted little beads of dew; made them shimmer as they flew off the toes of her shoes.

She had no idea how long it would be before she returned to this house. People had a way of saying, "Off you go," when they sent her away. "Off you go," they'd say, never to return. Who knew? Who knew?

* * * *

Aunt V, Uncle Monroe, and Neena drove that day just before Thanksgiving, 1951, to Selmer's Springs, North Carolina. She moved her few belongings into the Ferguson Home, what she later learned was commonly known by the residents as the *Fergie House*. An old mansion donated by a benevolent and recently deceased widow, and endowed by a trust fund maintained by the deceased's executors, the home was managed by a board of directors made up of prominent women of Selmer's Springs, North Carolina. Most were solicitous, some very kindly, all of them bound to keep the little secrets of the residents. Neena's roommate, Teazie, called them *The Bored*.

The room Neena shared with three other girls who had also recently arrived was small yet held four single beds. Since she was the last of the four to move into the home, she was given the only unoccupied bed, one in the corner, by the closet. Because the room was over-crowded, Neena's dresser had been placed in a closet. Whenever she wanted to put something into it or take something out, she had to push back the hanging clothes and lean into them while she yanked her drawer open or rammed it shut.

The girls who lived at Fergie House had been sent by parents who could afford it or, in her case, she suspected, an aunt who could.

"There are no charity cases here," Tha, one of the roommates, informed her.

In the bed closest to Neena's lay Shinsie, a name Neena had never before heard; a nickname, Neena assumed. Shinsie seemed refined, guarded, and somewhat dismissive.

A chubby, rude and crude girl named Bertha slept in the bed closest to the window.

"Before we go any farther," Bertha said, "I'm named after my old hag of a grandmother. What a pig she was. I have been called Big Bertha by many people; people bigger than you, I might add, my whole life. So let's just cut the crap right in the beginning, and nobody even think about calling me Bertha. Now you know better. And don't call me Bert, either. My brother calls me Tha. I like that," she said, almost smiling. "My brother says that once you chip away all the nasty traits I inherited from my grandma – the Bert stuff - the good stuff that makes me special is what's left, the Tha part. Get it?"

Bertha looked at them like they were all too stupid to get anything.

"We get it, Tha," Teazie, the fourth girl, said.

"My mama named me Contessa," Teazie said to Neena. She divided her name into two parts so that it sounded like two names – Con Tessa. "Teachers told me I mispronounced my own name; that I didn't know how to spell it. My uncles called me *Girl* and *Snookums* so they wouldn't have to say my real name, or because they couldn't for the life of them remember it, or because they couldn't pronounce it either. Who knows? And then my little sister, when she was old enough to talk, she called me Teazie. And it fits, you know? It just fits."

Teazie seemed manic. She laughed a lot, and pontificated loudly and excitedly, as she moved around the room.

Teazie turned to Shinsie. "What kind of name is Shinsa, anyway? You a Buddhist or some odd religion like that?"

"I don't know. But the name is Shinsie, not Shinsa."

"You don't know if you are a Buddhist?"

"I don't know where my name came from. I'm as American as you are."

"You don't have to get all dithered, Shinsa," Teazie said, with derision. "I like it . . ., I like your name. I could pun your name to death." Then she winked and poked Tha with an elbow.

"Quit being a dumb jerk, Teazie," Tha said.

Teazie continued to pace the room, making comments and asking questions. But after sitting at a small vanity and examining herself in the mirror, Teazie began looking at Neena, as though studying her. The other girls lay back on their individual beds.

"You are innocent as can be, aren't you, Neena? You're like a little girl with those big eyes and pink cheeks. Do you even know how that baby got in there?"

"Shut up," Tha said. "Now you're just bein' mean."

"I wasn't talking to you," Teazie said, wincing as she plucked an eyebrow.

Neena feigned indifference yet listened intently, already embarrassed. Lying back on her bed, Shinsie seemed not to notice. Teazie had returned to filing her fingernails, but Neena could tell she continued to focus on her.

"There are many things I'll just bet you don't know," Teazie continued. "Like, for instance . . ."

She stopped when the pillow Tha had thrown hit her in the side of the head.

"You do that again, you little tramp," Teazie said, glaring at Tha, "and I'll show you what being mean really is." She tweezed another eyebrow.

* * * * *

Before many days had passed, Neena felt like she had fallen into a whole new world.

Their days were regimented. At 8:00 a.m. every morning a bell rang. The bell was a huge old church bell that had been hauled up to and mounted in a little cupola that sat atop the roof of the Ferguson Home. The bell rang again at noon and at dinner time. It could be heard up and down the street and anywhere in the house. Neena thought that the housekeeper, Dorothy, must be the bell ringer. The Bored had recently hired her, and she was in charge of cooking and supervising the cleaning, the laundry, and the endless miscellanea that arose. Neena heard through the grapevine that the previous housekeeper had insisted that the girls rise by 6:30 a.m., but too many people near the home complained about the bell ringing at that hour. So, to conform to the town's church bell-ringing schedules, the bell rang at eight o'clock a.m.

Upon hearing the first bell of the day, the girls bounded out of bed, brushed their teeth and their hair, used the restroom, and hurried down to breakfast in their bathrobes. Each girl fixed her own bowl of oatmeal or grits, toasted her own bread, and poured her own orange juice and coffee or tea. On

Saturdays they ate eggs, country ham, biscuits and hot chocolate, all prepared by Dorothy. On Sundays they enjoyed fresh cinnamon rolls.

After dinner on Tuesdays, Thursdays, and Saturdays they were permitted to take a bath. On Saturdays they washed and set their hair.

Each weekday morning, after dressing for the day, they adjourned to the library where several tables and chairs were spread about. Each girl was to work on independent study assigned every other Sunday during family visits.

In the forty-five minutes before lunch, they had a music class taught by Mum Clara, the house mother. She had come from England the year before Neena's arrival at the home, and the girls seemed fond of her. A childless old maid, she seemed to view the girls as oddities, yet she spoke with kindness to them. Not solicitous with them, she treated them merely as girls of assorted ages and varying belly size. Mum Clara lived like a nun in a room sparsely furnished and inordinately neat. She spent her days ostensibly shuffling correspondence or applications or poring over her ledgers.

In music class she explained how classical music was commonly commissioned by the church and that many masters' works – like Bach and Brahms – were still played on pipe organs in churches, even in the small town of Selmer's Springs. Music class consisted of listening to classical music and then being asked to identify the musical master. Neena learned to enjoy the class very much.

Lunch at noon consisted of a sandwich, an apple, and sweet iced tea.

After lunch the girls were permitted to rest for one hour. At two o'clock those girls who were not close to delivering went about their assigned tasks which consisted of dusting, folding laundry, or setting the table for the evening meal. After their chores were completed, they had leisure time for reading or additional study.

House Mum Clara, as she preferred to be called, spent her days in her office until dinner time when she presided over the dinner table. Her sometimes false assumption that the girls had never been taught the social graces by their parents required that she give detailed instruction, especially on table manners. At the dinner table, the girls were instructed that one hand must remain in their laps unless they were buttering, cutting, or passing, which never ceased to puzzle Neena since Mum Clara ate, without exception, with her knife in one hand and her fork in the other. Her knife aided her in sliding greens onto her fork, in smashing peas against the tines, and, of course, in cutting. But she rarely laid down the knife. And her idle hand remained in full sight most of the time; not fixed on her lap as she had instructed the girls.

Yet dinner was handled with equanimity. One night nine of the eighteen girls were those served. The next night they acted as servers.

"Serve to the left, take from the right," Mum Clara chanted as the girls placed or retrieved plates from the table. "If you enter and leave the kitchen on your right, we shall avoid collisions. The person leaving the kitchen must be the opener of the swinging door, otherwise we may experience some difficulty with rash consequences," she said. Each phrase of her instruction was enunciated like a proclamation.

"Why doesn't she just say we'll make a god-awful mess?" Tha whispered.

On Wednesdays a female physician came to examine the residents. On Thursdays a woman counselor came to talk with them collectively and, if asked, on a one-on-one basis.

"If you have questions," Teazie said, "just ask Tha. You don't have to talk to the head doctor. Tha knows what to do and what to expect. Don't you, Tha?"

"Shut up, Teazie. I'm warnin' ya. Shut up."

"C'mon, Tha. Take a deep breath. It's your second kid, and you know what to do. Why not share it with these girls?"

Tha stood and walked menacingly toward Teazie, reaching up as if to strike her. But then she stopped, turned, walked toward her bed and flopped down.

Neena saw tears on Tha's cheeks.

* * * * *

Time passed. Some girls left. V and Monroe visited on even Sundays, and Toot and Jimmy visited on odd ones. Thanksgiving, Christmas and New Years came and went. Some new girls arrived. But, since Neena was to be the first to deliver her baby, the four roommates remained together during Neena's entire stay at the Ferguson Home.

One night after Shinsie and Teazie had gone downstairs to listen to Groucho Marx's radio show, *You Bet Your Life*, Neena remained behind with Tha. Tha had seemed agitated since her Sunday visit with her mother. That afternoon Tha had cried and now looked close to tears. Neena pretended to be studying but couldn't concentrate.

"I did have a baby, before," Tha said. "A boy." She got up from her bed and walked over to the table and sat down. "Teazie's right. That's why I get so mad at her. She's savvy, like my mom says." She reached up and pulled the gum band from her pigtail and began combing her fingers down through her hair.

"I did have a baby. Two years ago. I hated that kid half the time I carried him but then it was like that little baby saw me through the tough times, through being homesick and sad that my boyfriend had just used me. That little baby was in there,

~ 146 ~

all the time. And then they took me to the hospital, and I had some pain, and then they just put me to sleep, and when I woke up, that little moving body was gone, and I never got to see him. I thought I was happy."

She got up and walked over to the window and then turned back to look at Neena.

Neena thought that Tha's eyes were the saddest she had ever seen.

"But I can't quit dreaming about him," she said, starting to cry. She swiped at her tears and continued. "I dream he's wrapped up in this blanket, and I take him everywhere with me. I hold him and carry him and put him down for a minute and then pick him right back up again. And then I realize he has been quiet for a long time and take him to someone, have someone look at him. I tell them he has been quiet, and I am worried, and they look at him and start yelling at me, telling me how stupid and terrible I am because I forgot to feed him. I forgot. How could I forget? And I start crying. Big tears fall out of my eyes onto his little face, and he reaches his tiny hand up and touches my face. It's like a caress, you know? It's like he says he forgives me."

Tha started sobbing then, unable to squeak out even one more word.

Finally, she spoke again. "I can't sleep without the dream coming. I'm so sorry," she said. "I'm so sorry, but sorry's not good enough, is it?"

She turned back, looking directly at Neena.

"And look at me. Just look at me. That's how sorry I am. I have up and done it all over again, all over again to some other little helpless baby. And they'll take this one, too, and I'll be dreaming double. She turned back toward the window. "I can't take it. I just can't."

Neena walked over to her and touched her shoulder.

When Tha turned, Neena put her arms around her and held on until Tha's sobbing subsided. "Have you talked to the counselor about this?" she asked, dropping her arms and moving away.

"Are you kidding? I can't believe I have even admitted it to you. Do you think some snooty-nosed blue-blood is going to understand a little tramp like me?"

"Yes. Yes, I do," Neena lied. She remembered all the people who had coursed into her father's study and who had left with relief on their faces. Yet she also remembered that her father had treated her with indifference and then sent her away. Still maybe this counselor was different; maybe she could help Tha.

"Please talk to her. She might be able to give you some coping method." *My father always says that*, she thought, *some coping method.*

When Tha left the room to go to the restroom to wash her face, Neena wondered how she would deal with someone taking her own baby. Would she miss it or be glad it was finally over.

Or, she wondered, would it never, really, ever be over.

38 Neena – Selmer's Springs, North Carolina
Memorial Hospital - January 1952

Neena's labor, lengthy and hard, lasted long enough for both of her aunts and their husbands to arrive in time for the delivery of a six-pound-thirteen ounce, pink and squealing baby girl. But by that time, the doctor had clapped a mask over Neena's face, administered ether, and sent her off into a sweet, dreamless sleep.

When she awakened, she was in a long hall, on a gurney, being taken to a ward room in the maternity wing of the old hospital. As she and the orderly neared her room, she saw V, Monroe and Jimmy standing outside the door with Toot pacing between them and the window at the end of the hall.

"Oh, she's back; she's back," Toot said, running to her and grabbing her hand. "You okay, Sweetheart?"

"She's fine," Jimmy said, grasping Toot's arm and pulling her back. "You are probably good and tired, aren't you, little girl?"

After the orderly and a nurse who magically appeared had settled her into her bed, a young woman, Ruthie, in the bed next to the door, introduced herself and the others in the room to Neena and her family.

The woman by the windows was Shirley, a forty-some-year-old, who seemed too tired to have had a baby, but she told them that she had just had her sixth boy. Evelyn, a prim woman, lay holding her husband's hand and smiled sweetly, mutely, as Ruthie introduced her.

Very talkative, Ruthie Norton appeared to be about eighteen or twenty.

"I had a girl, bless her little heart. I didn't have no name myself until I was three days old. Mama and Daddy kept fightin' over names. Daddy wanted a boy, so he called me Ralphie. I don't remember, of course. I was so little it's like I wasn't really there. But Mama wanted to name me Riata. That's a lasso, you know that? What a name, but Mama just liked the name ever since she read some story — can't remember the whole story. Anyway, the nurse at the hospital was a big colored lady, and she was so gentle, mama says. Her name was Ruth, and Mama made a compromise. 'We both want an R,' she says, 'so let's go with Ruthie,' she says to my Daddy. That old nurse was so pleased, mama said. Daddy never called me much of anything, but when he did, it was Ralphie."

She took a deep breath and then drank some water from a glass on the table beside her bed. "What'd you have?"

"A little girl," V quickly answered.

Ruthie looked at V and then back to Neena. "What's your name?"

"Neena, short for Christina."

"What'd you name your kid?"

"We haven't, yet; named her," Jimmy spoke up. "I don't mean to be rude, or anything, but I think Christina needs to settle in and rest a little bit. You two can chat later. Okay?" he asked, smiling charmingly.

When Neena's parents arrived later that evening, they announced that they were staying at a tourist home not far from the hospital, that they planned to take the baby and leave the next day, and that the pink-cheeked little child would be named Patrice Eleanor Teeple and that her nickname would be "Reecie."

* * * * *

The next morning, after Neena's parents left the hospital, taking with them baby Reecie, Neena cleared the doorway she had been stepping through for the past five or six months. Having stepped through, she now saw her life – and herself – from some distance, as though she were some clinical specimen that bore very little further examination. So she left her emotion back there, beyond that doorway, behind some line of demarcation, like some tossed-away possession she could no longer tolerate tending.

Lingering after the Teeple's departure, while waiting for V's arrival, Toot alternated between weeping into Jimmy's chest and peering out the window as though doing so would bring back baby Reecie. While Toot paced, Neena faked sleep so Toot would quit asking her if she were all right.

When V and Monroe arrived around noon to collect Neena, the two aunts and two uncles tripped over each other getting her from her hospital room, down to the curb, and into Monroe's car. Having pulled away from the curb and Toot's red-faced goodbyes, Monroe and V found Neena small and quiet there in the backseat of their roomy Packard. They had no idea that she was thinking of one thing: Returning to her studies.

For Neena, in that big backseat, had come to a realization: from her observations of the other girls at the Ferguson Home, and from her personal ponderings, she had sensed, and now knew, that education represented not only her one chance for survival but, perhaps, even a love that would not leave her barren and alone.

* * * * *

Neena kept the letters she received from her mother in an old cigar box Jimmy had given her. Brass hinges and a brass clasp with a C carved into the metal decorated the wooden box. On the inside of the box lid was stamped, *Twenty-five cigars* made from Cuban-grown tobaccos. Hand cut. The inside smelled sweet like the old tobacco barn behind Uncle Monroe's house.

Like clockwork, every Tuesday, with few exceptions, a letter from Mrs. Amos Teeple, Emmaus, Virginia was delivered to *Miss Christina Teeple, c/o V and Monroe Phillips, Rural Route 4, Burl, Virginia.* The letters varied little. In each letter Dessie inquired after Neena's health, she told some little thing about Teddy and his school studies, about Amos and his congregation or the latest church supper, what she cooked, that she had made a red cake for Mrs. Desmond, the old blind lady in one of Dessie's ladies' group meetings, and about Grandma, who had not been well the past few months. That explained why she had received fewer letters from Grandma in the past month than in previous months. Starting in January, after Reecie's birth, her mother's letters always included a small paragraph about baby Reecie and her progress:

> *Baby Reecie, your little sister, is doing fine. She is back up to her birth weight, eats with gusto, and sleeps sometimes four hours at a time.*

Or,

> *Your little sister is a joy. She smiles when she hears my voice. She smiles a lot.*

Or, later

> *Your little sister said her first word this morning at breakfast. She said, "Susu", the name of a character in one of the books I read to her, instead of the expected "Mama" or "Dada". She is a smart baby.*

Neena got so she barely read the letters and only answered when Uncle Monroe kindly asked her to do so.

After the first few months of letters, the cigar box got so full that Neena had to put a rubber band around it instead of using the clasp. Soon, she would ask V for a shoebox to put the letters into so she could keep something of more value in her little coveted cigar box.

Besides, she would rather read of the Greek Constantine who strode through the vast Roman Empire than hear of some Susu trudging through some children's book of which she had never even heard.

39 Neena, age 17 – Albemarle County, Virginia
1954

When she was seventeen, Neena applied to the University of Virginia. Her Uncle Jimmy, Aunt V, her mother, and Aunt Toot had all graduated from that institution but, surprisingly enough, Uncle Monroe had not. Nor had he graduated from any other college or university. In fact, he referred to himself as "self-taught in the Classics."

"That is the way many people were taught in the South, especially in the area from which I come. Many young people learned under tutors instead of being sent off to boarding school," he said, almost apologetically. "Of course, my family may have been the exception since I had so many siblings. My parents couldn't afford tutors for all of us. But I was a strong student, hungry for learning, so Mama literally used the egg money to pay for a tutor for me. Mr. Henry Lee, his name was," Monroe said, with a broad smile. "And not Light Horse Harry, either."

When she looked at him blankly, he asked, "You mean you don't remember? Light Horse Harry was Robert E. Lee's father, a Revolutionary War hero and Governor of Virginia."

His eyes twinkled, as though he had won a round in some trivia game.

That's what it was like, learning with Uncle Monroe. It was fun and challenging, like a game.

"After that I studied law with Judge Morehead," he continued. By the time I knew him he was no longer the senior judge and was able to slow his pace a bit to spend more time with me. He met with me three times a week and assigned piles of homework. I also shadowed him daily while he completed his bench duties, sitting in on court hearings, listening when his clerk synopsized appropriate case histories and briefs, and whenever I got a minute, scanning through the many law books on his shelves." He slid back in his chair and crossed his legs.

"Then I sat for the bar," he said.

So that was how Uncle Monroe became a lawyer. Yet, he was the best teacher Neena could ever have imagined. In fact, he was the best teacher she had in all of her years of study.

40

Will – New York City, New York
Columbia University Law School - 1955

Will could run. Still, he could run. He ran full-out, across the dorm parking lot. The rain pelted him, but he ran harder, sprinting at first, then with long strides that covered distance. As he rounded a corner onto a side street, he realized he had been running all of his life, or at least back as far as he could remember.

First, he ran from his daddy's fists, several times jumping through the upstairs window, skittering down the trellis, out into the snow sometimes, barefooted. He ran, grasping fruit stolen from the corner grocer. He ran from the police and then from the tackles as he carried the ball toward the end posts, dodging the big bruisers who aimed to knock him to the ground, grasping the ball tightly to his chest. He ran sometimes, still, for the pure joy of it, feeling the air evaporate the sweat beads on his face and neck while rivulets ran down his back. He ran from openness in his relationships into some dark cavernous place where his secrets lurked, coming at him like hungry dogs. He ran from having run in the first place, away from his daddy but away from his mama and the little ones, too.

Yet, still he ran, like some aboriginal on his quest for manhood. They all chased him, the hungry dogs of shame, the kingly beasts of recompense, the feared, the loved and neglected alike breathing hotly down his neck.

Worse yet, he was sure if he turned to really look at them, he would see, in their lead, his failed self.

41 — Neena, age 18 - Charlottesville, Virginia
University of Virginia- Fall 1955

Neena matriculated on September 6, 1955, a full-fledged member of the University of Virginia's Class of 1959. As the professors, deans and dignitaries of the institution filed in to take their places in the auditorium, she sat quietly but felt emotionally stirred by the pomp and circumstance of the affair. Clad in heavy robes of different colors and wearing tasseled caps, the professors and dignitaries appeared hot, bored, and even put-out by their required attendance. But a certain reverence had settled on Neena so that she barely felt the stifling heat generated by the unseasonably warm weather and the press of many bodies within the poorly vented structure.

After introductions, the president of the university spoke to the students, admonishing them to do their best in an institution populated by learned men and women, founded by Thomas Jefferson, a man dedicated to learning throughout his life. She was so infused with excitement that her mind wandered; she kept wondering which of the erudite men and women would be teaching her.

Following the ceremony, Neena caught up with Uncle Monroe and Aunt V who waited for her under an enormous evergreen tree just outside the main hall. Aunt V stood mopping her face with her embroidered hanky. Uncle Monroe moved forward, waving his hands in the air.

"Did you see that? Did you see the different caps and gowns and hoods worn by the professors? Did you see?"

"Yes. Yes, I saw."

"I just wanted you to realize what universities were represented here today." He cleared his throat and moved his hands, nervously pulling at his shirt button. "I told your aunt that Harvard was represented, and Yale, and, and William and Mary, and, I'm sure, even Oxford. I pointed out the various colors and stripes. Very prestigious. Very, very prestigious."

He seemed elated, and V acted pleased for him, even though he must have forgotten that V, herself, had attended the same university. Neena realized that Uncle Monroe had probably longed for such an opportunity, never got it, yet he wanted her to see how very lucky she was to be attending this university.

They walked around campus in the late summer heat, strolling in and out of buildings, peeking into classrooms, and reading plaques on walls.

At four p.m. they climbed back into Uncle Monroe's Pontiac Star Chief and headed back to Burl.

Sitting in the back seat, letting air from the open window blow across her face, Neena felt happy and relaxed. Uncle Monroe and Aunt V were taking her back home, back to Burl. They would not be delivering her to campus, saying, *Off you go*; would not be dropping her off, leaving her there with suitcases and boxes strewn around her feet. No, she would be a commuting student, driving the twelve miles each day to attend classes. She closed her eyes and silently thanked them for that, that above all else.

42 — Neena - Charlottesville, Virginia
University of Virginia — 1955 - 1957

Once Neena became established at the university, she and Teddy renewed and expanded their friendship.

A commuting student, Neena saw him only on occasion during her first term. A first term junior by then, Teddy had begun dating the girl of his dreams, Margot; he lived on campus, and had amassed a large circle of friends. Neena's acquaintances remained limited to the middle-aged woman who rode back and forth to Burl with her and a smattering of classmates.

By mid-October Neena and Teddy, sometimes joined by Margot, met for lunch on Wednesdays and Fridays. They discussed courses and people and, in doing so, learned much about the other's character, likes, dislikes, and interests. Neena seemed much too serious a student in Teddy's opinion so he teased her a lot, trying to lighten her moods a bit. On occasion Neena stayed with Margot on weekend nights to attend functions at the university.

By May of 1957 when Teddy graduated and went on to seminary, Neena and Margot had learned to trust each other, delighted in the other's company, and had accepted each other as dear friends.

But little was said of the past. Within the first month of their reunion, Teddy learned that the past remained a closed book to Neena, a book on which she had slammed the cover, and one she had returned to the shelf to gather dust. Or so it seemed.

43

Will - Arlington, Virginia
1955 - 1967

By the summer he married Allison, Will was drinking even then. He slogged through the courtship and the wedding like a tipsy sleepwalker, even though he hid it well. He seemed above the unfolding scene, or at least a step behind it, as though he merely observed. He remembered Allison walking down the church aisle toward him and recalled thinking over and over, it will be all right; she loves me, she loves me enough for both of us. And she did, it proved out, at least for a while.

There was the expected financial struggle in the first few years of their marriage while he established himself in the law practice. After a few years of long work hours plus considerable support from his father-in-law, he made partner.

Shortly after that Will got a lucky break when a young man came to his office with a proposal for a new business. He wanted Will to help him form a corporation, apply for some patents, and give him some direction on how to get started in running a business. He had little money but was sure that his idea and enthusiasm would pay off. Will proposed to his partners that they defray start-up expenses in return for stock ownership. The firm wanted no part of this incorporation nor the risky venture. Further, they insisted that Will sign a document saying that he was acting apart from the firm should he represent the young man because of the possible risk exposure.

Although the kid had no money, he convinced Will that his venture was worthwhile. Will did all the work and asked only that he be made a silent partner and that he receive a twelve percent share of the stock, should the company ever go public.

The kid turned his ideas and the business into a multi-million-dollar company within six years. Will got rich right along with him, so that, over the years, he provided handsomely for his wife and her children, but drank, caroused, and remained absent even when he was there.

After nine years of marriage, she asked him to leave. She didn't want a divorce. She just didn't want to witness close up his self-destruction.

44 — Neena - Charlottesville, Virginia
University of Virginia - Fall 1958

By her junior year at the University of Virginia, Neena had completed her base courses and could concentrate on her major, history. She had signed up for courses in both European and World History that term, but she preferred courses in American History. Her favorite that semester was an independent study of a course titled, *Early American Intellectual History from the Puritans through the Eighteenth Century Evangelists*. The course required a lot of library research.

So it was that on a beautiful fall day, the type of day that crops up in mid-November in the Piedmont of Virginia, Neena sauntered across campus on her way to the library. The university gardeners were planting some type of flowers – maybe pansies - re-fertilizing the shrubs, and mowing the grass. Smelling the pungent odor of manure and the fragrant smell of cut grass, she smiled. It felt like spring, her favorite time of year, but with a little nip in the air. The sky was clear except for impending clouds hovering over the western horizon.

She ambled along the sidewalk, the library in sight, when a young man several strides in front of her stumbled on a piece of broken concrete and fell headlong onto the lawn, his books scattering across the sidewalk and grass. Placing her stack of books on the ground, next to the walkway, she ran over to offer assistance. He had risen to a sitting position and was rubbing his ankle by the time she approached.

Dark, almost black, curly hair contrasted the bluest eyes she had ever seen. She had seen him around. His name was Herb, no, Kirb. No, Kirby. That was it. Kirby. But she didn't know his last name.

He moaned, shifting his leg to a new position and continuing to rub his ankle.

"Can I help you?" she asked, as she gathered his books into a pile, leaving them stacked on the grass.

She stood erect again and extended her hands, indicating she would try to help him to his feet.

He looked embarrassed, his face red. But perhaps he was in pain.

Leaving his injured leg extended on the grass, he drew his other leg up under his haunches so that he could rise a bit. Then he extended his hands toward her. She pulled him as hard as she could, and he came up on one leg while holding the other off to the side so as not to put weight on it.

"Thanks," he said, breathing hard. "I think I did a number on my ankle. You suppose you could help me over to the library until I figure out what to do?"

"Of course, but let's get you over to this tree first so you can support yourself. Then maybe the gardeners could run you over to the infirmary where the nurse can take a look at your ankle."

"Good idea," he said. "No sense getting stranded at the library." He attempted a smile.

As she moved into him, he draped his arm over her shoulders and, with her support, hopped over to the tree.

"Thank you for helping me."

"No problem."

Neena walked over to the nearest gardener, arranged for him to take the young man to the infirmary, went back over to where Kirby stood against the old oak tree, gathered his books, and waited.

Once the gardener had helped Kirby into his pickup truck, she handed Kirby his books.

Shutting the truck door, she asked, "Will you be okay? Do you need me to call anyone or send someone to go with you?"

"No, thank you so much. I'll be fine. If I need to call someone, they will do it over at the infirmary. Don't know what I would have done if you hadn't come along."

She waved as she picked up her own books and hustled off, her mind already on the paper due in two days.

This was the story they told when asked, over the years, of how they had met. Theirs was just a chance meeting on a sunny day. No stars. No long glimpses. No heart flutters. There was just one person being kindly to another who remembered with appreciation.

Cut and dried, pure and simple, not momentous but merely a moment. And, in the end, there was nothing cliché about it.

45 Will - Arlington, Virginia and Emmaus, Virginia
1963 - 1976

As he left his marriage, Will realized he had a reluctance to stay and work things out. But he just packed and left anyway. He had moved into a small apartment near his office and not far from his house. He had escaped once again. Having always thought of himself as a runner, he now realized he was a floater, after all.

Perched on some figurative hunk of driftwood, he let the course of whatever nameless current he was in just drag him along. Professionally and financially successful as he was, he now realized that lots of people lived their whole lives that way; went with the flow until they hit the bank one day and recognized that age was creeping up on them. They had just aimlessly floated past the life they could have lived.

In Will's case, Alcoholics Anonymous and its admonition to look to a Higher Power had helped him choose a course to take for the rest of his life. Anyone of importance, it seemed, had already been lost to him. So he gave up everything that held him back from complete surrender. He gave up booze, although drinking had been episodic, if excessive, women, carousing, even golf. He walked an inordinate amount of time. He followed the dictates of AA; he gave up any intimate relationship so he'd have no one but himself to blame for bad behavior. He went to so many AA meetings that he began to worry that he had become addicted to them. He meditated, he prayed, he studied God's word, and, when he felt stronger after three years, he began to help others who were struggling with addiction. And in the AA tradition which not only called for looking to a higher power, changing environments so that the temptation to resume old habits was lessened, he made a list of those whom his drinking had harmed. Then he apologized. He apologized to co-workers, sought forgiveness from friends whom he had influenced wrongly, and then began taking steps to redeem himself as a step-father. Beyond that he had four apologies left, four biggies, and they scared him to death.

46 — Neena – Albemarle County, Virginia
November 1959

"Hi Toot. Aunt V said you called. Is Grandma okay?"

"Hi, Christina. Yes, yes, as well as can be expected. Listen, I wondered if you are still coming over this weekend. You could come directly here from your last class of the day."

"That would be fine. Aunt V said the doctor went to see Grandma today."

"Yes, Doc Sonne came by today. She seems aware most of the time, but she asks for Daddy sometimes in the late evening. She gets a little confused then. Doc says she is strong and doing well, but she seems so frail. Flora's daughter can't take care of her on Tuesdays anymore, so her sister will be filling in. Land sakes, it takes three of them and a substitute to care for Mama. They are very kind to her, and Mama is spotless, no bed sores. I don't know what we would do without them. Doc says it's a miracle she can talk, poor dear. She sits up and listens to Arthur Godfrey with me, and we talk a lot until she gets tired. She likes it when I rub her hands."

"That's good, Toot. My last class is at 3:00 p.m. Tell Grandma and Uncle Jimmy I said 'hi.'"

As Neena hung up the telephone, she thought about all that had happened in the past six months. In January Neena had received the Hoyt award for academic excellence and in March had presented a paper on intellectual history at a conference held at William and Mary in Williamsburg. Then, in June, her father had a slight heart attack and, following that, in August, while Grandma Lowry was visiting with Aunt Toot, Grandma had a stroke, had remained in the hospital for a week or more, had been moved to rehabilitation, and then had finally been able to return to Aunt Toot's by the end of that month. Because of Grandma's condition and because of Neena's mother's many responsibilities, the sisters had decided that their mother would remain with Toot and Jimmy. And Toot was delighted to have her mother there with her. With round-the-clock help, Toot could have continued her usual daily activities, but she had resigned her various club positions, suspended her volunteer work, and now attended only Sunday worship and her weekly bridge club.

Since the end of August, Neena had been spending three weekends per month with Toot, Jimmy and Grandma. She could study there as easily as at V's, and she enjoyed spending time with Grandma Lowry.

Sometimes, in the afternoons after Grandma's nap, Neena and she chatted. Neena liked to ask her about her childhood days; what it was like in Emmaus back then.

"It was a beautiful little town. It felt large then because we really had little occasion to leave it. Everything you could want was available there. We knew our neighbors. For the most part, we lived beside some of the same people we came up with, grew up with. I remember when I was a very small child the spice man used to come through town. He had a horse drawn buckboard, much like a miniature Conestoga wagon. With a wooden framework and a white canvas top. He slept in there and everything. And the aroma, oh, it smelled so good. Mama would send me out with two little sacks. He'd put a couple of cinnamon sticks and some nutmeg pods in one. And I can't remember what he put into the other sack but I sniffed at it the whole way home."

She gazed out the window by her bed, seeming to fix on a bird swaying on a forsythia branch.

"And the German people, up on Dutch Hill, used to send their little kids down the hill to the brewery at creek side to get a small pail of beer for their dinner. Even the children were given a little of it at supper."

"Did you ever taste it; taste beer?"

"Oh, my, no. I was taught it was the drink of the Devil. You forget that my mama was a WCTU-er, you know, Women's Christian Temperance Union. They were appalled by the notion that children were taught to like beer. But Daddy told Mama to leave people different than we to their customs. What a silly thing for me to remember," she smiled, gathering the blanket in her lap.

She tired easily so Neena often sat in the rocker by her grandmother's bed and studied while her grandmother napped.

One afternoon, as Neena helped Grandma back into her bed, her grandmother hugged her and then held her at arm's length while she looked closely at her.

"I am so sorry for what happened to you. It just got so mixed up, first with their sending you to Verina's and then all the misunderstanding on both sides. And some things were misrepresented to you your whole life. I am so sorry for that. I truly apologize for any part I had in it. I have been beside myself with worry over you. Your parents love you, Christina. They have always loved you." She lay back in the bed. "Your mother . . .," she hesitated, "doesn't mean to appear, what should I say, cold, distant. She was always like that, I'm afraid. Some people never learn to relate to even the people they love. In your mother's case, I could never tell if it was lack of confidence or an effort to protect her heart from hurt."

"She has never had a problem with Reecie; she shows her plenty of affection," Neena said, trying to keep the edge out of her voice.

"Maybe she learned. I wish I could raise my children over again, knowing what I know now. I would do a better job. I wish I could do many things over again." She shifted in the bed as though growing agitated. Then she settled, looking earnestly at Neena.

"And your father; he takes great pride in you, in your scholastic accomplishments, in particular. He is proud of Teddy, too, I'm sure. But Amos, your father, is single-minded. He devotes himself so completely to his congregation that there is little of him left over for anyone else."

Neena hugged her grandmother and, wanting to change the subject, did. "I'm going to continue on with my schooling at the end of this year. Did you know that? I want to get my Master's Degree."

But her grandmother seemed to have nodded off.

"Love you, Grandma," she said, not knowing whether she heard or not.

Then Neena headed toward the kitchen to help Toot with dinner. After dinner she needed to read as much as possible before Monday.

She turned the corner from the hall into the kitchen looking for Toot. One great thing about Toot: She never mentioned Neena's parents. And that's exactly how Neena liked it.

47 — Will – Arlington, Virginia
1963 - 1975

After leaving his home, his wife, and his step-children, and while working to gain control of his life through Alcoholics Anonymous, Will often examined what he called critical moments in his life to see what had shaped or damaged him so that he could fix some things for his future.

He thought about the time he had stolen the dime from the teacher's desk and given it to his friend, thereby incriminating his friend when he had meant it merely as a gift. How strange that the dime and not the death of his beloved grandparents or the demise of some adored pet, would be the sort of thing that came often to the forefront of his mind.

Shame flushed him even now when he thought of the time he tattled on the twins in his class for throwing snowballs and then was made to watch them flogged with a razor strop. Or his stealthy habits, learned first in order to avoid his father's meanness, had escalated to stealing a piece of fruit from old Mr. Tedesca and then another and another until one day he stole innocence, hearts, and love without compunction. Those seemingly innocent childhood events to him, from this older adult perspective, now loomed as foreshadowing of a life of flawed character, of poor decisions that hurt others perhaps more than himself if that were at all possible, and of going beyond where some redemptive power could pull him back into a loving embrace.

As usual, he was working himself up from the little hiccups of character to those truly unforgivable belches of inflicting his bad character onto innocent others.

He thought of the first time his wife suspected his infidelity, the new pain he saw in her eyes and around her mouth, and how her hands moved without artifice first to her chest and then to the sides of her head as if someone slapped her. And the other woman, even before he was finished with her, wore a fine etching of old pain on her face, as though someone like him had been there before.

Recalling his indiscretions, he found it hard to face himself. Having sought forgiveness from the Father, he knew he must now seek forgiveness from those he had harmed. Pouring forth from his memory, the list seemed so long, so long that he fought the old desire to withdraw within himself, within a bottle full of forgetfulness. Will wanted memory to be some blissful, sleeping thing. But his memory, tamped down so long, lay there, just under the surface, ready to jar him back to reality.

So in the style he had used so many times in legal defense cases, he began organizing his thoughts as though jotting them on a legal pad, looking back, affixing blame, assessing damages, letting memories come at him at will, until he could deal with them once and for all, or perhaps wipe them from his brain forever.

In naming his five damage-inflicting critical moments, his father's face, swollen with drink, red with anger, loomed over him. Will could still feel his finger on the trigger, and hear the boom that echoed at ill-begotten times in his head. Still, he now saw that many of his actions had been reactions to his father's cruelty.

Conversely, many of the mistakes he, Will, had made were made as an adult, with full knowledge of what he was doing. So, in looking closer, he realized that the chronology of his life seemed straightforward enough, but, the pathology of his life needed a closer look. He could not look straight on it. It came at him, instead, in waves, in disjointed memories like dreams, some of it clear and touchable; some of it fogged over and far away, like it was happening to someone else.

Where to begin: With his dad, he knew that was important, and with his mother, of course. But he wasn't sure how much of his early life he misremembered, or how much he had added to temper his memory of it, to make ogres out of ordinary people or to make angels out of scoundrels.

He couldn't ask his siblings; they were younger and had their own stories, whole sections of which started long after Will's departure from the family house.

Perhaps Neena would remember. Still, even after the passage of years, no words came when he thought of Neena, except that he could be a better person, a person more deserving of her caring nature. She stealthily slipped into his mind randomly, nudging him back from joyful moments, ponderously trudging through his dreams, or tiptoeing around in that spot in his heart where she had taken up residence. Now, as a grown man who stood facing demons from his past, he realized that Neena represented a joyful moment in an otherwise turmoil-ridden existence. Yet, he had to remind himself that Neena represented merely a moment, a short span of time, less than two months, of his life. She had been like a lull between storms. After her, the storms had increased in intensity so that, now at least, he must pick his way through the rubble he had left in his swath of destruction.

Thus, just as he saw his life coming back together, and just when he was preparing to go to his wife, Allison, to beg her forgiveness, she called him.

48   Neena – Burl, Virginia
Summer 1962 and 1965

Neena received word through Aunt V that her father had died unexpectedly from heart failure the morning of April 30, 1962. Tragically enough, V, Monroe, Toot, Jimmy and Neena had sat vigil for three nights over Grandma, and Grandma Lowry had died that same day, April 30. Teddy and V managed to attend both funerals, literally passing each other on the road between Burl and Emmaus, but Neena had remained in Burl, and Dessie had remained in Emmaus.

In the prior week, Neena had reached the point where she felt selfish for wishing that her grandmother would linger on. Clearly in pain, Grandma Lowry recognized only Toot and then only sporadically. Neena said her goodbyes, hoping her dear grandmother could hear her but knowing that Grandma Lowry already knew how much Neena had always adored her.

Neena's communication with her father, however, over the past twelve years had been infrequent, stilted conversations. It seemed that Amos Teeple required the expiation of transgressions against God and Amos Teeple, sometimes confusing the line between the two. And any formal repentance from the daughter to her father, or even to her Lord, had never been forthcoming. Thus, the day Amos died, Neena had a similarly stilted telephone conversation with her mother in which she told her mother that she was sorry for Dessie's loss but made no mention of her own. Amos and Grandma had died on a Sunday. On Tuesday Neena defended her Master's Comp. On Wednesday she attended her Grandmother's funeral, spending a fleeting time with Teddy and introducing him to Kirby. On Thursday she drove to Arlington where she took a placement exam for a summer course at William and Mary. On Friday she bought a wedding dress.

Neena's marriage to Kirby had been scheduled for the second week in May of that year, but Neena feared it would be too much for V and Toot so postponed it.

Neena became Mrs. Kirby Shaw on June 10, 1962, a Saturday. The ceremony was a simple one held in Toot's garden with V's minister officiating. Toot's maid, Flora, served cucumber sandwiches, wedding cake, her specialty, punch, and homemade mints. Kirby's parents attended with their son, Norm, Kirby's brother. But Teddy was unable to attend because he had committed more than a year prior to Neena's wedding date to officiate at a wedding at his church in Emmaus. The newlyweds had intended to go on a weekend getaway, but Kirby's car broke down, and he spent the money he had earmarked for the weekend on a down-payment for a replacement car, a 1959 Corvair.

So went a day normally fit for a princess.

49

Neena – Burl, Virginia
Summer 1965

In June of 1965, Neena rushed up the stairs, struggled to hold sacks of groceries as she unlocked the door, and let herself into the apartment she and her husband had shared for the past three years. She liked the apartment, set on a side street, above a family of five, renters themselves. She relished the simplicity of their life, limited as they were financially. They played games, studied together, and took long walks. Their courtship had been brief. Lustful as she felt at that time, she wanted to be married before consummating this relationship.

She set the grocery bags on the red Formica-topped table that Kirby's brother, Norm, had given them as a wedding gift. She knew it was second-hand when Norm had bought it, but she liked it; liked especially the matching, thickly padded chairs with big red stripes dissecting the chair backs. They were like the ones from her childhood home, the ones her parents had bought when she was thirteen. In fact, the whole apartment felt like home, despite its hodge-podgey, sparse furnishings.

An old Frigidaire sat in the corner of the kitchen, clicking when it ran, as though it were ready to give up the ghost and call for extreme unction at any moment. The gas range that sat beside the refrigerator worked fine unless someone slammed the outside door too hard and blew out the pilots.

In typical fashion, she went about preparing the evening meal. Walking to the sink, she filled a pan with water, put it onto the range top, and turned the flame up high. She went into the living room, drew open the drapes, raised the sashes on both windows, and placed screens into them. Returning to the kitchen, she opened the small window over the table, placed a narrow screen into it, and returned to the counter. Opening a box of Kraft Dinner, she placed the macaroni into the now-boiling water, stirred it, lowered the flame, and then turned to set the table.

Once that task was completed, she took two pork chops from brown paper, coated them with a little flour, salt and pepper, drizzled some Crisco oil into an iron skillet, and added the chops. While everything simmered, she sliced a large tomato, placing it on a plate in the middle of the table. By the time she had strained the macaroni and stirred in the milk and sprinkle cheese, the chops were cooked and ready to go onto the table. She put two glasses of sweet tea onto the table, transferred the skillet onto a potholder in the center of the table, and then walked over to the screened door to watch for Kirb.

As if on cue, he pulled their 1959 Chevrolet Corvair up to the curb, jumped out, and slammed the door.

Grinning, he bounded up the stairs, two at a time, holding something behind his back. He flapped what looked like a brochure in the air, advanced toward her, and hugged her hard. Then he handed it to her.

It was blue with white edging. On the top, in large letters it read: *Cape May – Lewes Ferry.* Underneath that, in smaller print it read: *A ferry system that traverses a 17 mile crossing of the Delaware Bay to connect Cape May, New Jersey with Lewes, Delaware.*

"I checked it out," he said, grinning. "My uncle uses it when he has to travel up to the Jersey shore. He makes deliveries up there once a month and says it's much easier than going the long way around."

"But where would we be going?"

"To Cape May, New Jersey. That's the surprise. I had him stop by to make a hotel reservation for us when he went through last week. In Cape May. At this really old hotel. Built in the 1870's. It's only a short walk, three blocks or so, from the beach. We're staying two nights. We'll just do a walk-on. I mean, we'll park our car, walk onto the ferry, float over and then walk to our hotel and around the town for two days. Then we'll float back."

* * * * *

The drive to the Lewes Ferry took them all day.

They had started out early that morning, heading east, while dew still hung on the grass and the sun sneaked up in front of them. After an hour or so, leaving heavy traffic behind, they rode along a state road which meandered through fields of crops, only a few of which Neena could identify. She thought she saw tobacco, although she didn't think it grew this far north. She identified cabbage and sorghum and lots of tomatoes.

The air in the car grew hot, so they rolled down all four windows, let the breeze buffet them, and turned up the radio as loud as it would go. Dionne Warwick sang a song Neena hadn't heard in a while: *Don't Make Me Over*. Then the station played, *Make It Easy On Yourself*. Maybe it was Dionne Day. ?

Neena made them a peanut butter sandwich as they drove along. She cut it into quarters so that it would be easier for Kirby to eat as he drove. Then she popped the lid off a bottle of Hires Root Beer for them to share.

They made it to the ferry with only one bathroom break – a stop along the road in some tall grass – just in time to park the car, gather their few belongings, and run for all they were worth to the boat.

They stood at the railing the whole way across the channel, marveling at the jumping fish and even a few dolphins.

The hotel was old, the floors creaky, the bed well-used, and the tub so small Neena had to sit Indian-style in order to fit into it without her legs dangling over the sides.

The next morning they ate breakfast, included with their room, in a large dining room with white table cloths. Huge ceiling fans cooled the area as they ate eggs and ham and delectable homemade yeast biscuits with butter.

After leaving the hotel, they walked and walked, stopping at lunch time at a small grocery where they bought a tube of ham spread that they squeezed onto Wise Potato Chips and washed down with more Hires Root Beer. They finished every last bite of food and every last swallow of the soda-pop as they sat side-by-side looking out at the water waving up onto the shore.

They swam, they built sand castles, they listened to musicians in the park, they marveled at the Victorian architecture so reflective of the whole town, and they laughed.

But as the visit to Cape May neared an end, as the time wore down, Neena noticed a strange quietness between them, a prescient reserve that hovered over them like the slow formation of cumulonimbus clouds on an otherwise-sunny day.

50 — Reecie – Emmaus and University of Virginia
1969

Reecie had done most things prematurely in her short life. Her parents told her she began walking around furniture when she was barely seven months old. Her first word had been the name of a character in a book her grandmother and mother read to her daily, if Reecie could convince them to do so.

When Reecie was seven Grandma Lowry went to visit her daughter, Aunt Toot, had gotten sick there, and stayed down there in Burl, Virginia. Then, when Reecie was ten both her dad and grandmother had died on the same day. Teddy came when he could, but the deaths had dealt a devastating blow to their mother, Dessie. On top of that, since her father was no longer pastor of the church, Reecie and her mother had to move from the parsonage. Packing up a lifetime was difficult, but many of the congregation came over to help them and, later, to move them to their new home. Her mother must have inherited money from Grandma Lowry because she bought a small house not far from the parsonage so that the two of them moved literally five houses up the street.

After a few years Teddy and his wife moved back to Emmaus when he assumed the pastorate of his father's former church. Things improved after Teddy came back to town. Dessie seemed more upbeat; it was hard not to be happy around Teddy since he was always smiling and finding pleasure in living.

An observer, Reecie noticed that her mother (as had her father) and Teddy always chose the *appropriate* word when they spoke. In her opinion it made them appear ponderous. Maybe because of that, or for whatever reason, she was not careful at all with her speech. She just let the words tumble from her brain past her lips to fall wherever they may. Caring little about reading for the feelings the words evoked, or for the words, themselves, she sped read through books, caring only about plot, and forgetting a story shortly after she had read it. She saw herself instead as a numbers girl.

Reecie saw numbers everywhere: On license plates, in house addresses, and telephone numbers, of course. She counted bricks in the sidewalks, trying to figure how many fit into a three or four-foot-wide sidewalk, and then calculating how many bricks it would take on the transverse of one block. She loved numbers. Everything under the sun was solvable or explainable by using them. Math was cut and dried, not arbitrary as other areas of expertise. She wanted to be a mathematician, because she had to be something.

By the age of seventeen Reecie had completed high school, and was ready to head off to college in the fall. Her boyfriend, Danny, had gone to university the year before, had completed three semesters' worth of course work in two terms, and planned to graduate in three years instead of the usual four. Reecie planned to do the same. By her calculations she would be barely twenty when she graduated from college with a degree in math. She had no plans to use her degree. She would marry Danny and, within one year, be the mother of their first child. Then she would, thereafter, increase their family; even add to it exponentially, with twins and quadruplets, who knew? And later, as her children grew, she would grow dahlias as any proper English descendant must.

In March Reecie received word that she had been accepted by the University of Virginia, and could begin classes in the fall. She hated leaving her mother but made arrangements to live in a freshman dorm on campus, with trips planned to go home twice-a-month.

* * * * *

In September of 1969, Teddy and Margot drove Reecie to her dormitory where she could see the campus rotunda from her window. She liked her roommate, but spent little time socializing with her since she was so intent on her studies, and on spending every available free minute with Danny.

In her third semester she took a course from Professor Christina Shaw, her big sister. Reecie had always hated History, thinking how unnecessary it was to memorize dates and momentous occasions from the murky past. In a memoirs class, Neena made history come alive for Reecie. Surprisingly, for the first time she realized that history was all about perspective: Three people could be standing in front of Federal Hall on Wall Street in New York City in 1789 while George Washington was being sworn in as president, and those three persons could give three different versions of his appearance, his tone, and even his perceived sincerity or lack thereof. Neena's enthusiasm was catching so that Reecie studied hard for the course and must have made her sister proud when she attained an A plus for the class.

She started seeing more of Neena when they ate an occasional lunch together, or when Neena stayed late to have dinner with Reecie and Danny. The two women grew close over time, although Neena's whole person seemed closed, hesitant, as though every breath required thought, like well-chosen words and mindful steps.

51   Will – Arlington, Virginia
1972 - 1975

Will and Allison had never divorced, although they had been legally separated for four and one-half years. Even though they had remained polite to each other, and though he provided well for her, they could not communicate without rancor beyond an occasional telephone call. In the past year he had begun to feel strong and settled, so it surprised him that her call knocked him a bit off kilter.

"I need to talk with you, Will. Can we meet tomorrow at the house? 9:00 a.m.?"

"Yes, of course, Allison. Are you okay? What's wrong? Are Bruce and Molly okay?"

"We're okay, Will. We just need to talk."

He wondered why she wanted to speak with him and hoped that it wasn't to rehash what could have been different about their marriage. That Allison blamed him for most of the problems in their marriage seemed fair to him, but to blame him for everything was going too far. She had been sour for years, even back when he was still half-heartedly trying to make things work. Had he been a better husband, he still would not know if the marriage would have survived or if it was doomed with or without his misbehavior.

*   *   *   *   *

He arrived before 8:30 a.m. the next morning. She looked healthy, but her face looked a little drawn.

"Do you want coffee or some breakfast?"

"Sure, coffee sounds good and maybe some toast."

She brought two cups of coffee to the table, along with a plate on which she had arranged toast, butter, and jam.

"Will, I have accepted a position as head nurse at the oncology center in Baltimore. I know it's a two-and-one-half drive from here, but there are no opportunities here for me. We can make arrangements for Bruce and Molly to see you when they want."

Bruce was fifteen and Molly twelve.

As it turned out, Will spent time with them before they moved. But they treated him like an uncle they hardly knew.

After Allison and the children moved, he began the drive back and forth every other weekend, taking the children on outings, helping with homework, playing indoor and outdoor games, and accumulating frequent stay points at the Holiday Inn there.

The children began to warm to him a bit, especially Molly. Will saw more movies, played more board games, swam more, hiked more, and laughed more than he had in years. He began enjoying his step-children, and looked forward to his visits with them. Occasionally, during the school year, he attended evening school functions. Sometimes Allison joined them for a quick dinner before a function, but other than that he saw her only when he picked them up or dropped them off again.

The children's social life escalated as they matured, and once they began to drive he saw less of them, although he still spent two weekends a month in Baltimore. On occasion, over the years, they came to visit him or they traveled with him, but by the time they were ready for college, the visits had dropped off considerably.

Bruce went to an out-of-state trade school, and Molly entered his and Allison's alma mater. He visited her when she permitted it. He felt that he had forged a reasonably good relationship with his step-children, despite his early neglect.

By the time Will turned thirty-eight, Bruce had moved to Alaska where he worked in the oil fields, and Molly had completed one semester of college and had met the man of her dreams, Lockwood Hastings, a snob from Philadelphia. Will heard from Bruce every few months and from Molly about twice a month. He saw them when he could.

In 1975, Allison asked for a divorce, and he gladly granted it.

52 Neena – Thatcher, Albemarle County, Virginia
Spring 1975

Working on the daily crossword puzzle, Neena sat idling at the curb on a tree-lined street in Thatcher. A small town close to the university, it now boasted both a McDonalds and a root beer stand. She glanced up every few seconds to see if anyone had emerged from Apartment Number Three, the apartment she had been watching, yet she had only been there a few minutes. The apartment building was new, one of two, really, which had been built here in the past five years. The units were rented based on fixed income, she knew, because one of the graduate students she advised had lived there. Children's toys littered the yard. A barbeque grill stood like a potted plant beside each entrance door.

She reached down and turned on the radio. She only half-listened as the announcer listed the day's radio activities: Trading Post at nine o'clock; Decorating with Diane at one; Tips for Living with Naomi at three; and Candlelight and Silver at five. Sounds exciting, she jadedly thought.

At 7:20 a.m. she heard a loud voice as a teenage boy emerged from Apartment Number Three. He yelled something over his shoulder, slammed the door, kicked a Big Wheel toy out of his way and stomped toward the car. His long hair hung in his face, and he kept flicking it back, out of his eyes. As he opened the car door to get in, Neena noticed a woman emerge from the same apartment, stop to lock the door, then proceed down the sidewalk and steps to the same car.

She was short with big dark hair that had a light stripe angling across the front of her head like some big bird, traveling at high speed, had left its calling card. Despite having chubby legs and a paunchy belly, she wore hot pants, the type that had gone out five years before, and a tight t-shirt with printed words across her large breasts, words that Neena couldn't read from this distance.

Strutting toward the car, swaying her hips and teetering on wedgies, she glanced Neena's way, then continued on and got into the car. Neena was sure the woman hadn't seen her since the sun was wrong, casting Neena in shadow and because she had borrowed a friend's car, a little nondescript Chevy Vega.

The woman's car, an old Pontiac GTO, candy red with rusted rocker panels, listed to the driver's side. The boy in the passenger seat must have felt like he was riding high each morning on his way to school, elevated as he was. The car's tailpipe hung low, like it had loosened from its mooring clamp and, with each acceleration, quivered like some old hound dog begging to be let in out of a rain storm.

At the first stoplight the woman turned her rear view mirror toward her and then primped and fussed with her hair. Neena wanted to ram the old Pontiac, wanted to launch the woman right through the windshield, to mess her hair if nothing else. The light changed, the boy gestured something, and then the old car moved forward, belching smoke like the stacks down at the town dump incinerator.

After three blocks they arrived at the school where the old car dove into an open space along the curb, discharged its passenger, and then belched its way back onto the street. Neena merely hesitated as if waiting for a parking place and then moved on, again behind the old Pontiac. The woman zigzagged through town, going through the drive-thru at McDonalds, emerging back onto the street, and then drove to an apartment building on the edge of town. The apartment doors opened individually onto the sidewalk as the other apartments had. The woman crawled from the low-slung driver's seat, erected herself, reached back in to retrieve two cups of coffee, and then walked up to the door and, because her hands were occupied holding the cups, kicked the bottom of it instead of ringing the bell. A tall blonde with messy hair and a toddler clinging to her leg answered the door, and the woman entered.

Neena sat there a minute. Why had Kirby chosen this woman? Why this idle, out-of-shape woman? Was it just because she had big bouncy breasts? Then she wondered at herself. What did she intend to do? Idly follow this woman around while she whiled away her day until school let out and the woman picked up the boy again? Why had she, Neena, come here? Was it merely to compare herself to the competition? She felt ashamed and a little crazed. Then she thought of the insane things good people do during a divorce. How her colleague, bookish, sedate Tom Pennell, had peed onto the seat of his wife's new live-in boyfriend's open-topped convertible.

How he had hooked a chain to the bumper of his VW bus plastered with twenty-year-old peace stickers and *Save-the-Whales* decals and then looped the chain around the shrubs in her yard - once his yard, shrubs he had planted - and then yanked them out by the roots.

Tom had been stopped by the constable as those shrubs trailed him all the way down Beech Street, past the town hall and the new Safeway Market. Once they had phoned Tom's ex-wife and learned that she would not press charges and once he had disposed of the shrubs, they let him go. When he didn't come to the university that day, Neena had gone to his apartment looking for him. His door was ajar, and she called for him, but there was no answer. She entered, fear crawling on her skin. She found him sitting in a recliner in his otherwise bare living room. He was weeping, tears and snot running down his face, dripping off his chin, yet he seemed completely unaware of them.

"I don't know, Neena, I just don't know. I have valued everybody, everyone's contribution to the world; my students, my colleagues, certainly my wife, and even strangers on the street. But something has happened to me. To me this guy is nothing, nothing. He clears city sewers for heaven's sake. He mucks around in mud and crap and comes home to her and tracks that stuff all over the tile I laid in the kitchen. Yet I envy him."

Tom gasped for breath. When she offered him tissues, he looked at her dumbly, as though he didn't understand the gesture. Then he accepted them and slowly wiped his face and blew his nose.

"I never ran around on her, and I had opportunities, of course I had opportunities, but that's not what you do, is it? You go to work and then you go home to the warmth and comfort of the wife you adore. You shouldn't have to check up on her or watch her flirt with other men or feel that dread in the pit of your stomach when you realize she doesn't even see you anymore."

He bent over and put his head into his knee-propped hands.

"Sometimes I can't breathe. It's like my heart has swelled up into my throat until it cuts off my air. I can't explain it. I could feel when she was with someone else even before I found out. Feel it like some clairvoyant or something. See it in my mind's eye." He shook his head, back and forth, back and forth. "I don't know what to do, Neena, don't know how to be without her. I wish I could make you understand."

Oh, but she understood. She knew the smothering fear of first suspecting something, the gut-wrenching awareness that sets in when you can no longer lie to yourself that something is, indeed, going on behind your back – or, sometimes, right there, right under your very nose - and then the tears. She understood more than Tom Pennell had any idea. Because she knew the next stage – anger.

And not the almost-polite, dazed kind of anger that Tom expressed when he methodically pulled out his ex-wife's shrubs and calmly towed them down the street, or even when he left his mark on a convertible seat, but seething anger, anger so hot it sears your skin, steams your brain like coddled milk, dries up any hint of tears, and goes for your heart, to stomp it to death so that it will stop all that infernal feeling. She knew, dear, dear Tom Pennell, she knew. Oh, Lord above, she knew.

53   Will – Arlington and Emmaus, Virginia
1975 - 1977

After his divorce from Allison, Will continued working but only part-time. He didn't financially need to work so assumed a lower-key role as senior partner in his law firm, in consulting, deposing witnesses, and actively participating in only a handful of cases per year. He traveled. He volunteered. He started writing a legal thriller, and found that he could take that project with him wherever he traveled, to fill up his evenings. Besides that, travel enhanced his story as he placed his characters in different cities, in different parts of the country, or even in Europe.

He asked lady friends to dinner on occasion or to a movie, but he dated little.

After moving back to Emmaus, he decided to go across town one Sunday to Teddy Teeple's church, the one where Reverend Amos Teeple, Teddy's and Neena's father, had pastored.

That particular Sunday, Will sat in the back of the church but slipped out quickly after the service. He hadn't wanted to make Teddy feel uncomfortable and hadn't even known what to say to Teddy had he lingered.

Will knew he was there in large part because he wanted to learn something about Neena. At times he felt like some prepubescent boy, still love-struck and wanting to talk to her, to reclaim their friendship and, perhaps, more.

What path had her life taken?

54   Neena – Burl, Virginia
Summer 1975

Neena had completed her PhD, defended her thesis, and received what Teddy called her *colors* from him for her birthday in the spring of 1965. "Your doctor's robe and PhD hood," he had said, as he ceremoniously presented them to her. In the ensuing years she had eventually secured a tenured position on the University of Virginia faculty and wore the robe and hood proudly on each matriculation and graduation day.

By June of 1975, Kirby and Neena had been married thirteen years. By then, Kirby had exhausted a teaching assistanceship and was still doing course work for a second Master's Degree. He participated in as many sports as his schedule and the weather would permit, officiated at college basketball games, and taught Astronomy at a local community college twice a week. Their paths crossed on Thursday nights when they went to the local pizza parlor or broaster villa with faculty member friends. But the rest of the time they lived separate lives.

Neena still spent time with V, especially after Uncle Monroe's death in 1973. Uncle Monroe had contracted viral pneumonia while in declining health – he was 86, much older than V – and had died within days. Neena missed him yet still felt close to him when visiting the old homestead and V. With her usual vigor, V kept a garden, a smaller garden than in past years, still volunteered at the hospital and library in Burl, and lunched with Toot.

Neena would never forget the first-class education she had received from sweet Uncle Monroe. She strived to teach her students with the same fresh enthusiasm with which he had taught her those many years ago. That was how she honored him.

On September 4 of the previous year, 1974, she found the lump. She remembered because she was grading papers and kept reminding herself that she needed to call Toot, to wish her a happy birthday and to confirm their celebratory lunch for the following day.

While reading one particularly boring and inaccurate paper submitted by a floor-flushing nitwit in her class, she had noticed a lump on her neck. It felt like a swollen gland. She swallowed several times, testing to see if her throat felt scratchy. But she felt fine so ignored the lump until two weeks later when she noticed that the lump remained the same.

When her family doctor saw it he sent her to a surgeon he recommended. The surgeon asked if she could schedule surgery for the next day. He operated in mid-September, scheduled her for radiation and chemotherapy, and so began her cancer odyssey. She suffered setbacks during treatment so that, including interruptions, she visited the oncology center for six months and thirteen days.

She lost weight; her hair fell out in patches, her skin turned alternately gray and red where the radiation hit it. Cocoa butter became her ally as she slathered it all over her neck and chest to reduce her redness. And she continued to teach, although she had reduced her schedule to part-time.

By June she had regained some of her weight, and her hair had grown in to resemble a fashionable man-do. She scheduled a driving trip with Reecie and her son for August when summer school ended with a two-week break before fall semester. She hoped she was up to it.

On June 14, 1975, Neena heard her telephone ringing in the kitchen. Kirby said, "Hello. Oh, hi. Okay, just a minute."

He came to the doorway of the den where she worked at her desk.

"Neena, it's for you. It's Toot."

She finished typing the sentence she had just started. "I'll be right there."

She got up and walked out into the kitchen thinking again that they needed a phone extension in the den.

"Hello."

"Hi, Neena, dear. It's Toot."

"I recognized your voice, Toot. I always recognize your voice. What's up?"

"I have some bad news. Things just happen in bundles in our family. Oh, dear, anyway, anyway. It's V. She was down visiting Monroe's daughter, her step-daughter; oh, you know that, in Georgia, you know, Jeannie? She lives in the town where Monroe grew up, you remember? Well, anyway, she had been down there for a week. Well, you knew that. Anyway, she had been feeling fine, in fact, she drove down there herself, of course you knew that, too, but, but she's gone, Neena."

"What do you mean? Gone? Do you mean she died?"

"Yes, yes," Toot said with a little catch in her voice.

"Did she have an accident?"

"No, well, yes. Well — she drove over to the Piggly Wiggly. She was just in there, just shopping, and they said she just gracefully wilted down onto the floor. The coroner said she must have been gone before she ever hit the floor. I don't know how he'd know such a thing as that but that's what he said. They called me. I'm her only living relative, well, her closest one, you know what I mean. Actually they called Jeannie but then Jeannie went down there and then she called me."

Toot sniffed a little and then continued.

"I can just see her, Christina. I can just see that poor sad soul. She was probably standing there in the Piggly Wiggly by the turnips. She put those nasty turnips in everything. Rutabagas; she was probably buying rutabagas. She loved those things. Ate them raw. Well, you know that, too. Yuck. Can you just imagine her standing there pinching the fruit or sorting through the cucumbers and, poof, there you go? I just can't imagine. Well, I can imagine, that's the problem, I can. She never doctored that I ever heard of. She probably didn't even know her heart was bad. Of course, it could have been a stroke."

Toot was rambling now and sounding more and more upset. "I drove over to see her the day before she left. She was the same as ever," Toot continued. "You just never know. I just can't believe it. She was always so spry; I just thought she'd go on forever."

Toot's voice thickened with tears.

"Toot, Jimmy's still visiting his nephew; he won't be back until Monday. Why don't you come over here for at least the weekend? Kirby is going fishing with some friends. I'll come get you. I don't want you driving while you're upset."

Neena paced while she talked. "I would come over there to stay, but I'm working on a paper for a conference. It has to be submitted tomorrow."

She looked at her watch, noting that it was almost dinner time.

"I can be over there in twenty minutes. We can talk about arrangements when I get there. She probably had everything planned, but we'll talk about that when I get there. Just get packed up. If you forget something, we can always swing by and get it tomorrow."

"Why is Kirby going off on another fishing trip? Your Uncle Jimmy asks why he is never with you when you come over here. He fusses about it, he does. Oh, never mind. I'm just talking. I don't know what I'm saying. What was it *you* were saying? Oh, about my coming over. I don't know. Flora's daughter is coming by to catch up on some of the housework."

"She can get in like she always does when you aren't there. Just come ahead. We will both feel better if we are together. Just hang up the phone and pack a few things. I'll start right over."

"Okay, Honey. I'll be ready." Toot clicked off without a goodbye, something she never did.

As Neena drove across town she thought about Aunt V. She had wished so many times for a glimpse into V's heart. She speculated that something had happened to her. Maybe someone had broken her heart . . ..

She had cared for Neena so thoroughly. In fact she had taught her so many things, so much about efficiency, about tenacity. She had grown to love V. Yet she still had to wonder how you could love someone and want to be nothing like her.

55

Neena – Burl, Virginia
December 1975

Neena signed the divorce papers even though Kirby had insisted that she be named plaintiff and he be named defendant. He wanted to feel like the innocent and injured party. She just wanted it over with. She realized that he had been no happier in the marriage than she. Obviously neither of them had tried hard enough. Yet, she felt she had run the gamut, so to speak, cleared the hurdles, or bridged the chasm, any number of the clichés she might use in describing the tenure of her marriage and the effort she had put forth to preserve it. Despite her efforts, these divorce papers proved that she was no more successful at marriage than she had been as a daughter. Like most divorces, the blame came down in a 40-60% or 60-40% split. She moved back and forth, first assuming forty percent of the blame, and then, after looking closer, might be willing to assume sixty percent of it, but then she would vacillate back again.

Early in the marriage she had forgiven his indiscretions, or thought she had. Yet she wondered, now, who had come up with that milquetoast word, anyway? Indiscretion, like someone tripping or stumbling instead of consciously breaking a covenant they had made with another. In view of that, she couldn't forgive him, not really, despite rationalizing it until she felt like puking. The fact that he could sense her lack of tolerance, her lack of forgiveness, and felt the division between them widening, somehow, in his adolescent mind, at least, justified further indiscretion. What a muddled-up mess marriage could be, anyway.

Still, on the other hand, she had suspected before she married him that he didn't grasp the concept of real loving. So that ignored suspicion threw her back to assuming a bit more of the blame. And so it went. Despite her analysis, his infidelity had loosened something vital in her. His lying had shattered, really, that vital something; left it rattling around inside her as particles in a rain stick. Over time, although sometimes still tipped slightly off balance by his betrayal, she came to think of it merely as a soft pattering like light rain on window panes.

She tried not to fixate on that soft, steady sound, mesmerizing as it was, lest the pattering pick up speed and turn to a stop-you-in-your-tracks, pane-rattling roar.

56   Will – Emmaus, Virginia
January 1976

While out of the country taking depositions for an upcoming trial, Will received word that his mother had died. He had not seen her for years and could not accept her death as truth. He pretended he was dreaming and would waken to find that she was there, in their home on Bank Street, in that place he had last seen her, waiting for him to return. Mothers were not supposed to die at age fifty-six.

Vonnie said that she had had a heart attack, something she thought rare in such a young and trim woman.

"We were at a picnic and she just grabbed her chest and then slumped over in her chair. It was terrible. The only way I console myself is that she did not die alone. But, still, I was right there and couldn't do a thing. She seemed more relaxed in the past few years but I don't ever remember her happy, Will. Do you ever remember her giving a real belly laugh? Ever?"

He did remember her laughing but only while with her mother or one of her friends, when she was younger, never with Jake.

Will and Vonnie had talked for a while, promising each other that they would begin communicating on a regular basis. He meant to keep that promise. In fact, he was much better at things like that now than he ever used to be.

57 — Neena – Burl, Virginia
January 1976

While Toot, Neena, Teddy and Reecie lingered at graveside, Neena pondered the mutability of life. This week they had lost dear Jimmy. Tomorrow or next week they may celebrate an accomplishment or a joyful moment. Yet, it seemed that so much of one's life is documented by who died and when.

"He was so good to me. I can't do this; I can't leave him here, alone," Toot said, as she leaned on Teddy's arm.

Teddy softly talked to Toot in his ministerial voice while Neena and Reecie walked over to look at Jimmy's gravestone.

Reecie pointed to the information on the tombstone. "He was seventy-seven. I didn't know he was that old."

"I know. The poor guy seemed older than that these past few months. I couldn't understand how he could keep going."

"Why don't you and Toot move up to Emmaus? Give her a change of scenery, and you could teach up there at Shenandoah. The way everybody seems to die young in this family, maybe you better retire early. I would like to have you around more."

"I don't know, Reecie. That would be a big step for both of us. I'm not saying it's not a good idea. I think I'm ready for a change, but Toot would have to bring her former maid, Flora, and Flora's whole extended family with her. She wouldn't know how to function without them. I think they are more family to her than we are."

"I wish I knew Toot the way you do. She must be quite the character."

Neena reached out and traced the trees that had been carved into the granite of Jimmy's gravestone.

"Things seem to happen in pairs in our clan. Grandma and Daddy die the same day, and Jimmy dies a week after you have to put mom into a home. Does she ever know you or Danny?"

"Only on her good days, and they are far between."

* * * *

Neena lay on the sofa while the eleven o'clock newscaster droned on. The lights dimmed, she was growing sleepy. A thump on the deck made her jump, so she cautiously crept over to the outside light switch, flicked it on and swept the curtain back in one fluid motion. It was something she often did. She didn't know what she would do if someone looked back at her sometime. But there was nothing there, as usual.

She lay back down, wishing she had changed the channel.

Her heart felt heavy thinking of Uncle Jimmy and her mother.

She must have slept because she came awake abruptly, her heart pounding like it did whenever she had had a bad dream.

But it was no dream; it was The Dread, The Thing, The Fear.

The serpentine fear still sneaks up on her sometimes like the cancer did, like the hard lump in her neck, the tickle in her throat, the pallor of her skin, those signs she had so cavalierly ignored. The fear is sometimes worse than the Thing itself had been, or so it seems at this remove. It slithers around her, points at areas of her body as though it sees what she cannot. It wakens her sometimes from a sound sleep, bringing her upright to its encircling hold on her, its squeeze dashing all hope.

The scars on her body are nothing compared to the adhesions in her spirit, the nicks to the core of her. Those seven months of horror: Hearing the diagnosis, enduring the surgery, the radiation, the pain, the nausea coming at the same time each day, at the same spot along the same road. And hunger, hunger had nipped at her; the hunger for food that either would not go down or would not stay down; and the hunger for herself as she had been, so young, so carefree, so fearless, so physically free of pain and suffering.

She had hit her lowest point of despair the day she had given Kirby her blessing to go on a golf outing: "Go on your excursion. You can't do anything for me anyway. Go. Just go enjoy yourself."

And he had gone. He had loaded his clubs into his new pickup truck, waved indifferently as he walked out the sidewalk, and driven away from the curb and down the street. She had been flabbergasted that he would go; would leave her to fight this alone.

The nausea, the fear, the pain, the despair, the hunger — had chased her around the house for three days, stalked her, tackled her, and pummeled her until she ran into a closet, closed the door, and dissolved to the smallest form she could take. In the dark, dark corner of that closet and her being she had not known which desire was stronger: The will to live or the will to die.

58

Teddy - Emmaus, Virginia

Summer 1977

Teddy sat at his desk contemplating his Sunday sermon. He sorted through a pile on his desk and drew out two handwritten letters:

> *Hello my Sweatheart,*
> *I'm allowed to have a phonograph so my aunt sent me some records to use. Theresa Brewer sings 'Music, Music, Music', the Mills Brothers, 'Nevertheless I'm in Love With You'. Stuff like that.*
> *I think of you when I listen to them, especially the Mills Brothers. Try to listen to them and think of me, will you?*
> *If you could only know what I'm thinking about you, but I don't know how to write it. I love you. I know how to write the words but I can't think of words to show what I mean. Like when someone gets a new car and they drive up and it looks so polished and you look inside and it looks so shiny and smells so good. I know it's corny but that's how I think about you. I'm still feeling like my brain is stirred up. I don't mean to and you have to promise not to tell but I still cry a lot. Remember that time I was crying at your house and you came in the dark and just put your arms around me and we didn't even talk. I need that. I'm ashamed of myself. I'm still so scared. Please Neena please don't find another boyfriend. That would be more than I could take.*

> *Do me a favor. Put some lipstick on and kiss a piece of paper and send it to me. Please. Thanks. I would much rather have your lips on mine in person.*
>
> *Love, Will*

Teddy read the second letter:

> *August 11, 1951*
>
> *Dear Neena,*
>
> *I still haven't heard from you. My mother says she doesn't know anything about you. She can't ask my friends. She says they don't come around anymore.*
>
> *Oh how I miss you. I wish you could be around all the time. You always cheer me up. If I leave you with a guilty conscience please forgive me. I hope very much I don't have a hearing again tomorrow. I get so scared. Sometimes I wake up and can't believe I'm here. I wish it was over. I wish I was stronger and not afraid. I hope you love me.*
>
> *Love, Will*

The following Sunday Teddy stood at the pulpit for the reading of the Word.

> *This morning we will read selected verses from the King James' version of the Holy Bible. Turn with me now to the Fifth Chapter of Jeremiah's Book of Lamentations:*
> *'Remember, O Lord, what is come upon us;*
> *consider, and behold our reproach! . . .*
> *Our fathers sinned and are not; and we have borne their iniquities . . .*
> *The elders have ceased from the gate, the young*

men from their musick. . ..
The joy of our heart is ceased; our dance is
turned into mourning.
Wherefore dost thou forget us for ever,
and forsake us so long time? . . .
Restore us to thyself, O Lord, that we may be restored.
Renew our days as of old!'

And from Philippians 4:8:

'Finally, brethren, whatsoever things are true, whatsoever things are honest, whatsoever things are just, whatsoever things are pure, whatsoever things are lovely, whatsoever things are of good report, if there be any virtue, and if there be any praise, think on these things.'

After the opening prayer and while the choir sang the introit, Teddy worried as he often did about the connection between his thoughts and ideas - derived from yet another or two of Will's letters - and conveying the point of his sermon to his congregation. But, he reminded himself, Will's letters were just seeds, seeds which grew into ideas for sermons. The childish longing in fourteen-year-old Will's letters, the seemingly silly request for a paper kiss, and the adult-like love references or even physical and sexual overtones, seemed such an unlikely mix. And, likewise, Will's writing of pop songs and artists seemed incongruous with his grown-up expressions of longing and fear, and the reality of his circumstances. But that is how we sometimes mask fear, isn't it? Even as adults we hide our terror behind frenetic living, behind mundane talk, behind our efforts to amass fortunes. This morning Teddy wanted to address the fear he suspected lay in the hearts of his parishioners, using Jeremiah's laments and secretly inspired by Will's expressed plight.

In preparing his sermon, Teddy had thought of fear in its various forms; fear that each of us faces, and concluded that looking to God, living for God's approval, was one way to overcome fear. Sometimes, as trite as it may sound, overcoming fear meant telescoping, with God's help, beyond dire circumstances to hope for a positive outcome. How could he impart that to his congregation?

He bowed his head and prayed for guidance. Teddy stood, looked out over the congregation, paused, grasped the edges of the podium, and then began to speak:

I want to speak to you today about How We Look to God:

It seems the county road workers in some county, somewhere, put up a sign along a well-traveled road near a woman's house. The sign had the stencil of a running deer on it and below was printed: 'Deer Crossing'.

Upon arriving home that afternoon, the woman who lived in that house near where they had erected the sign, noticed it right away. It was there, right by her driveway, you see, so she couldn't help but notice it.

So the very next day the woman went into town, to the county commissioner's office, and told them she wanted the sign removed. When they asked why, she said, 'because I don't want any deer near my house!'

Now, from <u>her</u> perspective, at least, she made a reasonable request. But to that clerk there in the commissioner's office, she and her request may have looked pretty silly, indeed. I know many of us would have had to stifle a chuckle.

Teddy paused; looked out over the congregation and lowered his voice:

How silly we must look to others, at times; how foolish we must look to God.

In the early part of the sixteenth century when the martyr William Tyndale lived, a Scripture translation, based on available Greek and Hebrew manuscripts, was completed. And since Gutenberg's movable type method could make printing of these new translations possible, Tyndale while in Britain petitioned for approval of and support for printing these translations of God's Scripture. He made his petition, presumably, because he wanted more people to have access to God's Holy Word.

But some people, mostly clergy, in Britain didn't see things the way Tyndale did; they perhaps thought he was a bit silly making such a request. Why, what need did we have for printed Bibles when we had priests or ministers who could read the scripture to us and interpret it, as well, was possibly their question? Wasn't it dangerous to put a printed Bible in the hands of uneducated lay persons? Weren't we asking for unorthodox, skewed interpretations of God's Word if we allowed printed forms of it to end up in the hands of the average man? Besides, lots of people couldn't read!

So, not getting the support he needed in Britain, Tyndale went on to Cologne, Germany and, rebuffed there as well, he then fled Cologne. Despite that, eventually three thousand copies of the New Testament were printed because of his persistence. Unfortunately, the copies that were sent to England were seized and publicly burned because of the ban there. Over time, and because of his vision and perseverance, Tyndale completed several other translations and one of his revised translations of the New Testament became the basis for all later revisions and the main source of the authorized versions of the New Testament in English. Remarkably enough, much of his work was done while in captivity because he had defied those in authority. So, despite his persecution, we must suspect that William Tyndale cared only how God, God Himself, saw him. And in caring how God saw him, he could bear how others saw him, and what others did to him.

I can imagine that, in that prison cell, like Jeremiah, he would have lamented his captivity: 'Why, doest thou forget us forever; why doest thou so long forsake us?' Or he may have longed for the days when he was a free man, may have petitioned God as Jeremiah had: 'Renew our days as of old!' Or William Tyndale may have merely asked God that his work would not be in vain; that God's Holy Scripture may be distributed in the way he, Tyndale, had envisioned.

We can only speculate the discourse between God and his servant, William Tyndale. We don't know why God allowed Tyndale to be martyred, but become a martyr he did on October 6, 1536, in the castle Vilvoorde, where he was imprisoned, near Brussels, Belgium, when he was strangled and then his body burned. This, this ignominious end for a man who brought God's Word into the average home! But there is one thing of which I am sure: William Tyndale cared how God saw him. And God must have said, 'Well done, thou good and faithful servant.'

We also think of Paul before him who, while in captivity for furthering the teaching of God's Word, was stoned, flogged, beaten with rods, and left without food.

How frightened he must have been. Still, in the moments before his death, Paul sent letters of encouragement to Jesus' followers, to the pillars of the fledgling Church. And God must have said, 'Well done thou good and faithful servant.'

We think as well of Moses and of the broken-hearted prophet, Jeremiah, each of whom did God's bidding, not in some willful fashion, but obediently, in the way God instructed. How did they overcome their uncertainty, their fear? I think they were able to overcome fear and uncertainty, and in Jeremiah's case, rejection, because they had a purpose beyond their circumstances. They wished to serve God, to look good to Him.

How did these faithful servants look to God, you might ask? Remember, these men of God had lived most of their lives by the time they were imprisoned. They were not young men. They were mature, grounded in their beliefs and faith. But let's not discount the fear that even they must have felt in their darkest of moments.

As we sit here today I want you to look to your left, to your right. I want you to imagine the dungeons of despair in which those around you have, perhaps, dwelt sometimes through no fault of their own. Perhaps in those moments their fear obliterated any vision beyond their circumstances. But let us pray for our brothers and sisters that despite their real or figurative imprisonment that God will plant a seed of hope that will sustain them through their ordeals, and at some point when the bars of their imprisonment are spread wide that seed will lead them to and along the right path for their lives. With God's help it is never too late for hope. It is never too late to hear, 'Well done, thou good and faithful servant.'

And so it is. And the People said, 'Amen'.

59 | Will | 1951 - 1976

His first fornication had been one hundred years ago, five hundred stabbing confusions, one thousand love pangs, ten thousand recriminations ago. That one act, repeated to be sure over a short period of time, had dragged him into a category with his father, a muddler, a destroyer of lives. Yet, sometimes, in an effort to atone, he judged his actions too harshly, despite a sincere effort to go outside himself for rationale and objectivity. Just a boy when he had sex at too young an age to understand the commitment required by it, and when he raised a gun against his father, he had, while still a lad and then on into adulthood, allowed the effects of those two acts to compound, to gather speed like a downhill coaster.

With each ill-chosen act, he obliterated his path back to a better Will, a Will who gave, who enriched the lives of those he touched instead of tearing them down.

His first infidelity occurred two days before his wedding, with a woman twice his age. Occurred, he thought: What a laugh, like a pebble striking a windshield with no warning; he had *chosen* to be unfaithful two days before his wedding. But why would a man, once a boy who loved babies and bunnies and even old, worn out dogs, do such a thing?

He had tried blaming it on his drinking. It was true, drinking had been an escape. A fun drunk on those occasions when he tipped too much, he, unlike his father, didn't beat his wife, the kids, or the dog. When he drank, he dished out mirth like bar peanuts. But the truth was that he used drink or nothing at all as an excuse to be unfaithful.

Sometimes he wanted conquest, so he zeroed in on the most attractive woman in the room. At other times need drove him forward, not just his own but something he thought he saw in some woman's eyes, a sort of hollow longing. He wanted to ease her pain – and his – if only for a brief time.

So infidelity became a pattern for him. He had perfected his craft. Women noticed him, all right, but didn't really see him coming, like the second car behind the first, as you step off the curb. Then again, formal goodbyes had never worked for him. He just slipped back into the flow of traffic like the hit-n-run lover he was.

60 — Neena – Burl, Albemarle County, Virginia
1975

Neena entered her living room, closed the draperies, and walked over to the stereo cabinet. Sliding back the cabinet door, she ran her index finger along the record album spines until she found Della. This was definitely going to be a Della Reese night. She gently pulled the 33-1/3 LP from the album jacket, touching it only with her fingertips, only along its edges. She swung back the arm on the stereo, put the record onto the turntable, returned the arm, moved the needle over, and then flicked the switch.

Neena flopped down onto her old bean bag chair just as Della began *dimming the lights, sinking into her chair, and watching the smoke from her cigarette glide through the air*. Sophisticated and articulate, Della slid deep into her lover dream song.

But Neena merely sank deeper into the Naugahyde-covered beans, sweat already collecting on her back and butt from contact with the vinyl. She lay there passively while Della finished the song, letting the strings and the beautifully bronzed tones of Della's voice relax her, soothe her like balm for sore muscles. Then she listened to two more songs that barely registered before realizing that the stringed intro to her favorite Della song had begun. By the time Della began asking about her former fiancé; asking, *How did he look?* Neena could feel the longing that had no name building. As if right on cue, it crept up through Neena's chest to her eyes and spilt big drops onto her cheeks. Neena's reaction was always the same: Della plaintively asked the question, and Neena started to snivel.

On the occasion he had heard them, Teddy called these her pitiful songs. And, of course, they were. But she knew they had become an antidote to her ever-growing apathy or, at least, a test to see if she still felt anything at all.

By the time the first side of the album had finished, Neena crawled up from the bean bag, removed the record from the turntable, replaced it in the sleeve and then the album, and returned it to the cabinet. She hesitated a moment, toying with the idea of listening to Phyllis Diller complain about her husband, Fang, but that would ruin the moment, and Neena had work to do. So she wandered into the den to correct papers.

Relaxed and ready to work, she rolled up to the draftsman's table she used for a desk. She could really spread out here; this was her space.

Two hours later she had corrected all the papers but one. She always saved one girl's papers for last since reading hers before the other students' would have set Neena's expectations too high. The girl was a puzzle. Participating infrequently in class, she appeared distracted most of the time, yet her papers were insightful and showed a preparedness that was unmatched by any other student in any of Neena's classes. The girl made the connections Neena hoped for from her students; she cited passages from the readings that proved that she had read the assignment and pondered its significance. And even though she didn't often draw the same conclusions as well-known historians on a given subject, her insights were fresh and well-said.

And that's what kept Neena going sometimes, that one kid who said, "Hey, Teach, you reached me. I actually get it." That one student. And Della, of course. She could never forget Della. Della reached her. It was a chain reaction, really. Della reached her, and she reached maybe that one kid in all of her classes, and that kid touched someone else, and on down the line.

But for Neena at this moment, it started with Della. Because of Della she bruised when touched; she bled when pricked, and, on Della Night at least, she spilled tears.

61 — Neena – Aboard Ship
Fall 1977

In the dream her slender legs and hands thicken, shorten, and turn from flesh tones to gray, like snow on a television screen. From there, the dream takes variations. When she was a child, suffering from a fever, a Dick Tracy man with no face chased her. Her fat legs held her back, slowed her down, as they grew larger and larger until she could no longer even lift them. Still, he came closer and closer. Sometimes she made it to a phone booth, but her broad fingers could not fit into the holes of the rotary dial. Even her brain seemed thick, sluggish so that she could not remember the number anyway, no matter how desperately she tried to recall it. But at other times her thickened legs gradually slimmed and then worked like springs so that she could jump long distances, at first like a graceful, powerful dancer, then higher, farther still, like a gazelle. In those dreams she was beautiful.

The consistency of at least the early part of the dream, so familiar, had become a comfort. For one thing, she always woke to normal legs and hands. No Dick Tracy faceless man lurked there when she was awake. And on days when she was the beautiful gazelle, something strong and glowing stayed with her all day. So the dream itself was no longer something she continued to ponder at length to discover what message her psyche was trying to impart. It's timing, when it chose to come back, was what she looked at. It usually appeared after-the-fact, after some upset or conflicted decision. But when it came unexpectedly, she tamped it down, tried to strip it of power, not permitting it to serve as an omen, as some creaky, creepy foreboding.

Today she comes awake while her tingling hands are still filling out, before she can guess at the direction the dream will take, at its portent.

Neena peeks through her lashes and, in the early morning light, she sees Toot, birdlike, robe clad, hovering in the doorway to their sitting room.

"What are you doing? What in the world's wrong with you? You were making some yipping noise in your sleep."

But, wanting to ponder her dream a moment longer, Neena pretends to sleep.

"I know you're awake. I saw your eyelids flutter, my Dear."

Neena continues playing possum. And besides that, how can she, learned Professor Neena Teeple Shaw, admit to her aunt that she is perplexed by some adolescent dream; is sometimes, still, made uneasy by it? How can she admit that she had needed to come on this trip to be alone, to sort out her life, and to decide what to do with her anger? Her family had never even seen her little snits, her little temper tantrums, since she covered them so well and confined her expressions of lividity to her private sanctuary, whether it be a restroom stall, the ship deck, or her empty stateroom. She dare not admit that her anger threatened to consume her sometimes; that she was frightened of it. She knew, as well, she couldn't address her fear and anger with others distracting her. No one close to her seemed to understand that she needed solitude to come to some conclusions about herself. And then the dream, the dream always came back.

Toot turns, her breathing audible as though she has run three miles, and heads through the sitting area toward her stateroom.

"You do know we get off the ship in Madeira at nine?" she asks over her shoulder.

But Neena smiles at her retreating back, realizing again that Toot is a woman of many questions to which she somehow rarely requires response.

62	Neena – City of Funchal, Madeira Island
	(Off the coast of Portugal) Fall 1977

"Could you please tell us how to get to the gangway?" Toot asked the ship's mate.

"Certainly, Ma'am. Take the aft elevator and go down one flight of stairs to alpha. The gangway is there."

"Thank you," Toot said. After the man walked away she turned and asked Neena, "What floor is alpha?"

"Maybe deck A. It's probably the one below deck 1."

Toot, Reecie and Neena made their way down to deck A where there was a line into the gangway. Toot fussed about needing a jacket, about whether she had enough film for her camera, and asked again what time they had to be back on board ship. Occupied checking her own bag, Reecie ignored her.

So did Neena who had noticed Will just starting down the ramp to the dock. Alone, a camera slung over his shoulder, he held a guidebook. By the time the three women reached the ramp, he had neared a sidewalk at the end of the dock, and appeared to be heading into the town.

On the walk over to the town, Toot was all aflutter with excitement. "Look, we're just across a boulevard from what looks like shops and restaurants. We don't even need a taxi. The captain said it was twenty-six degrees Celsius. What is that in Fahrenheit, Neena Dear?"

"Seventy-five, no, seventy-eight, I think."

"Where's Teddy."

"He, Margot, Angie, and Twila went on that tour to Santa Cruz, a town on the far side of the island. In fact, I think they are going to tour the whole island. We won't see them until dinner," Reecie said.

"Oh, look," Toot said, pointing. "Look how the houses have been built right up the hillside, right on the edge of the ravines. There are palm trees everywhere! Hey, there's Will. Let's ask him to join us."

"No," Neena said, with finality. Both women glanced at her and continued following another group of people who jay-walked across the boulevard.

They zigzagged to their right, walking in the shadow of old buildings and crossing a little bridge, working their way toward the eastern end of the town, and the old fish market.

Once they got inside the building, Toot said, "Land sakes, it stinks in here."

"It's supposed to; it's a fish market," Reecie said, elbowing Toot.

"Oh, look. Look at all the little roosters. They have embroidered roosters on everything; on tea towels, on little bonnets and little dresses. Aren't they just unique?"

"They must be the island's mascot, or bring them good luck, or something. Neena, look that up in your little guidebook, there," Reecie said, smiling.

The three women wandered through the market, buying some souvenirs, tasting exotic fruits, and watching men cleaning fish on huge concrete slabs.

"Find us a restroom," Toot said. "I took my diuretic and drank about nine cups of coffee."

"You're kidding," Neena and Reecie said, in unison.

"I know, I know. You just wait. Your day is coming when you will know what it's like, but right now I don't need any disapproving looks. I just need me a commode, and in a hurry."

Directed to an upstairs lavatory, the three ascended the stairs and walked on, toward a short hallway.

Toot waddled ahead, duck-like, her legs held tightly together, holding it in.

"You look like a penguin, Toot."

"Don't you make me laugh. Don't you even think about it. I have enough troubles just getting there in time."

Toot rushed through the outer door to the restroom and into an individual stall, already unbuttoning her slacks. She closed the stall door, while Neena and Reecie went back out into the hall.

"This is no restroom," she said, loudly enough for them to hear her out in the hallway. "This is like a hole in the floor with a flusher. My land, and there's no toilet paper, either. Reecie! Christina! Are you girls out there?"

The women went back into the restroom and stood by the sinks.

"What's the problem, Tootie Babe? We can hear you clear out in the hall."

"Are all the restrooms like this? I mean, I'm going to wet on myself; my aim isn't that good. I just can't squat that far down without touching the wall for balance and, let me tell you, there's no way I'm touching this wall! And I only have one little tissue I brought with me. There's no tissue in this scary place. Oh, my soul. I did it. Oh, land sakes. I think I did it. I have wet on myself for sure."

"Here, Toot," Neena said as she stifled a laugh and shoved some tissue into the opening under the door. "Poor thing. And I can bet you she would rather fall into that hole than touch that wall."

They were both laughing so hard they went back into the hall so she couldn't hear them.

Finally, they heard a flush, then their names being called, and then banging sounds. "Help me! Help me!"

Neena went back in, followed by Reecie.

"What's wrong, Toot? Are you okay?" Neena peered under the door where Toot seemed to be on her feet, at least. "Maybe if you opened the door I could help you better."

"Open the door? I'm locked in here! I have been calling, banging, and crying out. Get someone, Dear. Please get me out of here."

"Listen just a moment, Toot. Are you pushing out or pulling in?"

"Pulling in, of course. The door's unlatched and I keep pulling and it just won't budge."

"Try pushing out."

After a big shove, Toot stumbled out and fell into Neena's arms, while Reecie looked on.

"You're laughing. Both of you are laughing. I could hear you, and I can see it in your eyes." Tears came into her eyes, then. "I don't do well in confined spaces."

"I'm sorry we laughed," Neena said, as she put her arms around Toot. "You okay now?"

"You're still laughing, both of you." She glared at Reecie, who was doubled over.

"Did you touch the wall, there, Tootie Babe?"

Toot pushed away from Neena and walked to the sink. "Where's the soap? Don't people wash their hands in this place?"

"That's why I tried to warn you when you ate that slice of fruit that vendor gave you, Tootie Babe. Remember, I said, don't you wonder where he last used that knife?"

"I thought you asked me if he had a wife," Toot said, as she winked at them. "If you can rough it, so can I." Then she strode through the door out into the hall.

* * * *

The trip up to Monte was fun. They walked some of the steep streets of the little village, went into the church, and looked out the window at the spectacular panorama below.

"There's our ship," Toot said, pointing down to the bay far below them.

They watched awhile as people rode sleds piloted by locals dressed in traditional garb down the steep city streets, a tradition brought back for the enjoyment of tourists. The ride back down the mountain evoked as much response from Toot as had the ride up.

"Oh, look. Look! People have leveled-off places in the hillside, not just for their houses but for gardens, too. And look at all the bananas. Gracious, that's a lot of bananas."

"I think Madeira is known for producing bananas."

"What are we known for, back there in Virginia? What is it we produce?" Toot asked.

"Presidents and tobacco," Reecie said, without hesitation.

"Well, good for us."

But Neena had tuned them out. She had spotted Will back in the fish market, and now she couldn't help but wonder where he was, what he was doing, whether he had really tried to contact her all those years ago, why he had horned in on their family trip, in fact, had been present at *every* dinner for the past six nights, and what kind of man he had turned out to be. But that was fanciful nonsense. She needed only to endure him through one more night, one more dinner and one more show, and then she was done with him, forever. Finished.

63 — Neena – Barcelona, Spain
Fall 1977

Toot disembarked the ship in Barcelona much more efficiently than she had boarded at the beginning of their journey.

"What a breeze," Toot said.

"We don't have our suitcases, yet, nor have we gone through customs," Reecie said, wishing she had kept her mouth shut.

"That might be interesting," Neena said.

The porter attending them found all of their bags except Toot's garment bag.

"What color was it, Toot?" Neena asked. "I can't remember."

"Green, Honey. It was green with a big, black name tag attached to the top handle."

"And you put it out with your other suitcases last night?"

"Yes, of course. I packed my small bag, and then I packed the big bag. Oh, land sakes," she said, shaking her head, "I remember now. I put the garment bag into that big leather suitcase that used to be Jimmy's. Land sakes, I don't know what I was thinking."

"No problem, Toot," Reecie said, winking. "You'll just have to up your tip to the porter to reward him for his patience."

They proceeded through customs without delay.

As the three women stood waiting at the curb for a taxi, Teddy, Margot, Angie and Twila came over to say goodbye one more time.

"Have you seen Will?" Teddy asked.

"We saw him last night, last night at dinner. We said our goodbyes then," Neena reminded him, coldly, but Teddy seemed not to notice her tone.

"I mean today. Did any of you see him today?"

"No, we haven't seen him."

"Well, this is goodbye for us. We have to scoot on to catch our bus to the airport. You were smart to stay over, Toot, Reecie. We'll see you soon. Let us hear from you, Nines."

A short time later the three women were assigned a taxi, the driver loaded their bags, and they were off to Hostal Fernando on Carrer Ferran, in the old part of the city, Barri Gotic.

Reecie strode purposefully up La Rambla, Barcelona's main pedestrian thoroughfare, past the chestnut vendor and a group of Asian tourists, Neena and Toot following closely behind. The palm trees stood like telephone poles.

"Wait up, Reecie Girl," Toot pled. "These shoes are pretty but not too sensible. Besides, I want to stop at one of these flower vendors."

"Why buy flowers, Toot?" Neena asked. "You're just going on a plane tomorrow."

"You can have them."

"I'm leaving on the train tomorrow."

"I could have them in my room tonight."

"Our room," Reecie said. "Besides, do you really want to carry them all the way up to that Goudi cathedral and back?"

"It's called Sagrada Familia," Neena said.

"What is? Oh, the cathedral," Toot said. "Well, then let me sit down for a minute."

Facing the Licieu Opera House, they sat and watched a group of children filing out of the building, walking single file.

"Isn't that wonderful?" Toot asked.

"What?" Reecie said.

"They must take small children to the opera. Isn't that wonderful?"

"Yes, it is, Toot. I think they expose children to more cultural events here than we do in the States," Neena said. "I wish we had time to go to the opera before we all leave."

"Aren't you scheduled to come back here, Neena?" Reecie asked.

"That's my plan, during my break between classes. I have a reservation at the same place we're staying tonight. I hope it all works out."

Reecie folded the map she had been studying. "Ready to go, Tootie Babe?"

"Yes. Yes. I'm raring to go. But after we leave the cathedral, I want to go over to the Mercado. It's off that way," she said, pointing to her left. "I saw a picture. They have these little smoked suckling piglets hanging from hooks, over there, in the market, the Mercado. Do you suppose you have to buy the whole thing; the whole piglet?"

"I think we go most of the way up this street," Reecie announced, ignoring Toot. "Then we bear off to the right. The cathedral, Sagrada Familia is over there, not too far. You doing okay, Tootie-Babe?"

"Oh, my. Oh, my, oh dear, dear me. Did you see that?" Toot asked, her hand in front of her mouth. "Quick, quickly, look behind you at that man we just passed."

"Which man?" both women asked in unison.

"The man with the bare behind. My gracious, he had no clothes on whatsoever, and every bit of him, and I mean every bit of him, was tattooed. My land, I have never seen anything like that before in my life. I thought he had clothes on, when I first saw him, but he's naked with tattoos." Snickering now, Toot turned half around and looked at the retreating man, and then turned back, facing up the street. "Can you just believe it?"

Reecie and Neena turned, stared and laughed.

"I think he winked at you, Tootie Babe. In fact, he's coming back. He's got his eye on you."

"Don't look; don't even look at him, you silly girls. Let's get out of here," Toot said, picking up her pace.

"Well, good, Toot. At least, at this pace, we might reach the cathedral before dark," Reecie said.

64

Neena – Barcelona, Spain
Hostal Fernando - Fall 1977

Neena lay in the narrow bed listening to the soft breathing of Reecie and Toot as they slept in their little beds in the small room they all shared. She couldn't sleep.

Since her divorce and cancer, she couldn't figure herself out. Over the past several months, what had been a slow burn had turned into a spiking anger. When she was alone, she wondered sometimes, rather bizarrely, if she had Tourrette's Syndrome the way foul words came out of her mouth unexpectedly, words she didn't know she knew.

She remembered that after completing her chemotherapy, her hair had started to re-grow. She covered the stubble with bandanas, ball caps, even sunbonnets. But one hot afternoon she stuck a bow in the middle of her cowlicky head, smack in front, just above her forehead, and stalked into her local supermarket. Adults glanced at her, did a double-take, and then quickly looked away. But children stared, pulling on their mother's sleeves, and even pointing and making comment. Neena preferred that, actually. Their staring seemed more honest than those who pretended not to notice.

She didn't buy much that day; she had just been making a statement, after all. But as she emerged onto the sidewalk a pigeon strutted in front of her, and she wanted to drop kick him, knock his head off, send him flying. She had to fight an inexplicable urge to do harm to some innocent thing perhaps since she couldn't attack the Thing, itself – her cancer. Cancer had brought her down to this level, had threatened her life, actually taken months out of her life, and, if recurring, could end it.

She felt ravaged, ugly, weak and alone. She found herself wanting to ram her old van into people who pulled in front of her, especially skinny little blondes driving sleek foreign sports cars.

Since the cancer, since the divorce, she increasingly despised the little breathless coeds who came into her office with their silly questions, their big hairdos, and their ever-widening headbands. Their fixed demeanors, their bored little voices suggested they were incapable of showing passion for anything, let alone a college course. She wanted to flunk their pampered little asses and tell them they hadn't had an original thought in their sorry little eighteen or twenty years of life. Instead – paid professor that she was – she offered venal awards - she put smiles in the margins of their papers.

Conversely, the truth was she preferred guys in her class who wore smelly clothes presumably dug from a heap in their dorm rooms, and who never darkened the doorway of her office. These same boys went out on Wednesday night, she supposed, got all drunked up, wrote the night before it was due a paper assigned ten days before. She recognized bluffing when she saw it, but at least they showed imagination.

She barely tolerated people who rudely answered telephones, who sloughed off responsibility, the shirkers who put her on hold in some power play.

And she withdrew or cut short her conversations before the person with whom she spoke could tick her off.

Why was she so angry? What had changed her?

She must have riled God one time or another, the way He kept throwing things at her.

Yet, many nights, she wept before God. She was afraid if she didn't quit railing against all who came at her, the erring, the lazy, the unkind, the inept, He would punish her more.

Ultimately, despite running around in this never-ending circle, she wished for some insight into her anger, some epiphany, really, a miracle, as she had seen in movies. But maybe awareness would be all she received.

So she began focusing more, trying to find the true origins of her anger. She knew it linked directly to recent events — cancer and divorce. But she had to consider that it had, instead, built up gradually, over time, despite its popping up, like a houseguest you weren't expecting. She couldn't be sure if it planned to stay a night or if it was a permanent live-in. And fear and resentment, her bedfellows for as long as she could remember, made her watchful that she would again be betrayed; that she would again lose those she loved. Watchfulness, then, had its broad, grimy hands around her throat, lest history did, indeed, repeat itself.

Consequently, as she had many nights lately, Neena mentally itemized possible sources.

She thought of her teenage pregnancy and all the repercussions of it. But that felt like ancient history.

She had experienced the deaths of some of those close to her: Her father, grandmother, Uncles Monroe and Jimmy, Aunt V, and her mother might as well be dead, the state she was in. But she felt she had lost her parents long before that, maybe even as long ago as when she had first moved south to Aunt Verina's.

On top of that, she had survived cancer but wasn't sure she had dealt with it. And she wasn't yet five years clear of it, of the possibility that it would recur.

Her husband, Kirby, had left her in 1974. They had divorced in 1975.

Today was December 16, 1977.

Needing desperately to get away and having attained eligibility for sabbatical leave, she had planned to sail to

Europe on a cruise ship. That Reecie and Aunt Toot had accompanied her had been Teddy's doing. Then Teddy had increased the size of the entourage, even including Will! She was still hot under the collar that Teddy had invited Will; Will of all people! She thought she would have some time to herself before arriving in Europe, but that had not happened.

Now, she was anxious to start the courses that she had prearranged, courses in French and European history at the Catholic Institute in Paris. The first course was to last for six weeks, after which she would have a three weeks' break. She planned to travel, taking long weekends, perhaps, but maintaining housing arrangements in Puteaux, just west of Paris.

The second course would last five weeks, after which she had planned to return home. She had already booked a TWA flight to New York City. Her ticket on Eastern Airlines would take her to Washington, DC, where Teddy would meet her, and drive her back to Burl.

So, she had made a conscious effort to come on this trip to be free of distractions so she would have solitude in which to sort out her life. She believed she was not running away. Yet sometimes she wondered if she were in shock. She felt more like an onlooker to than a participant in her own life. The anger she had felt for years had slowly dissipated for a time aboard ship. And now that she was about to say goodbye to her family, she felt calm. Yet she felt no joy, either. She experienced no peaks or valleys so that she felt like an emotional flat-liner.

65	Neena – To Madrid, Spain then to Italy
	(Naples, Sorrento, and Rome) Winter 1977

After saying goodbye to Toot and Reecie, in Barcelona, Neena boarded a train for Madrid. They had seen very little of the city, but Neena would be returning to Barcelona in the break between her classes and would have time then to explore the city further.

Leaving the province of Catalunya, the train followed the rails that lead southwest through the countryside and through tunnels that bored through hills and then broke out onto the plains where sheep grazed despite the dry-looking terrain. Old stone structures sat near the tracks, some of them presumably sheep herders' huts, some of them permanent residences. After a short stop in the provincial capital of Zaragoza, the train meandered through the Aragon countryside until it slowed as it entered the outskirts of Madrid.

After a seven-hour train ride, Neena was pleased to be on her feet again, walking. Pulling a collapsible aluminum cart with wobbly wheels on which her two suitcases were strapped, and carrying her briefcase, she walked three blocks, periodically consulting a map from the back of her guidebook. Readjusting a dragging suitcase back onto the cart, she proceeded in what she hoped was the right direction. Finally, after five blocks, she hailed a taxi.

Within minutes the taxi pulled up in front of an old pillared building with storefronts and cafés, across from a jail in the small Plaza de Santa Cruz. She stepped out of the taxi by the fountain in the center of the square, and followed the driver to the entrance to the hostal where she planned to stay. It was situated just one block from the Plaza Mayor, Madrid's most famous square.

After settling into her room, she hurried over to Plaza Mayor, a place she had read about first with her Uncle Monroe. Observing tourists or locals, perhaps, strolling through the plaza, it was hard to imagine heretics being burned to death in its center, or that the blood of bulls and Protestants alike had run red through this square for the entertainment or smug satisfaction of onlookers. Voices floated across the plaza, then across decades and centuries, a faint echo of a time, long past.

The narrow streets that led off the square like spokes of a wheel and the old buildings that stood up close to their curbs hinted, too, at a much different world at a much different time. She roamed the old streets, turning here, turning there until she feared she was lost and until she became tired and hungry. Realizing it was tapas time, the Spanish happy hour, she stopped when the proprietor of a small tascas, who stood out on the street, called to her. Despite the language barrier, she realized he was flirting with her and trying to entice her in for light fare and alcohol. He offered *mejillones*, little onion-topped mussels, paper-thin grilled eggplant, *cabrales*, an Asturian goat cheese, and the local staple, *tortilla española*, a potato-based omelet. Sitting at a sidewalk table, she ate with relish, lingering amid a growing crowd of happy voices.

After leaving the little café, it took her a while to find her way back to her hostal. She showered, read some guidebook entries, and then fell into an exhausted sleep.

She woke early the next morning, dressed, and emerged again out onto the little square her hostal faced. The morning was sunny but cold, so she pulled on both her hat and gloves and started down one of the streets off the plaza. Noticing a fur-clad lady walking briskly, she followed her. The woman went into a bar on a side street where other fur-clad ladies and some men in business suits stood dunking donut-like churros in thick, thick chocolate. She ordered some, feeling over-indulgent, and then she asked for American coffee which turned out to be espresso in a bigger cup.

By the second day, she had adjusted to the strong espresso; in fact, started to crave it.

Since she planned to be in Madrid for only two days, she walked for miles each day, wandering into as many parts of the city as possible. She regularly stopped at little chapels or large churches to rest and to pray. The city's main cathedral, located by the palace, was under construction, but she saw part of its interior anyway.

The next day Neena took the bus out to Barajas Airport and boarded a plane for Naples, Italy. Once she reached Naples, she had only two hours before her scheduled departure on a ferry bound for Sorrento, so she walked up to the fort, the Castel Nuovo, lugging her wobbly-wheeled suitcase cart behind her. When she finally reached the fort structure at the top of the hill, she wondered if it had been worth the long, strenuous walk up. Tired, she leaned against a stone wall, turned, and caught what little breath she had left as she looked out over the port. The bay was huge with boats of all sizes moored along several piers. The Mediterranean lay beyond, light shimmering off its swells with whole mysterious-looking sections lying in the shadow made by the gathering clouds overhead.

She walked around, stopping whenever she could to look out over the panorama of the bay and the city below. Finally, though, having stayed at the castel longer than she had intended, she had to hurry to make the ferry on time.

The boat ride to Sorrento was choppy. They passed by Pompeii and Herculeum, the ancient cities dug out of volcanic ash from Mount Vesuvius' eruption back in, what had Uncle

Monroe said, 79 A.D.? It was a long, long time ago in any event.

When the ferry approached Sorrento, she was surprised to see the city perched high up on a sheer-faced cliff. She hadn't remembered reading about that in any guidebook. After coming ashore, she noticed that taxis waited at the dock. She negotiated as well as she could with one of the drivers in a combination of French and English. If it were possible to go straight up to the city, the trip would cover a distance of a quarter of a mile; the taxi ride was four times that long, zigzagging back and forth on the switchbacks as the road wound up to the cliff's top.

Even though she liked the charming, narrow city streets here in Sorrento, this city felt more like an isolated village. It was one of the loveliest places she had ever seen. The innkeeper spoke passable English. The tiny elevator held her and her suitcases if she sucked in her breath and hugged to the wall tightly enough. The old lift labored up to the third floor. She found her room five steps from the elevator. Like most others she chose, this room was clean, spare, snug, and practical. Netting hung from the branches of olive trees visible from her window, in place to catch falling fruit. Lemon trees with fruit the size of large oranges or small grapefruit grew in the courtyard as well.

That night she went to a local operatic performance featuring musical selections representative of a traditional, small Italian fishing village with singers and dancers acting out stories of romance. She could not help noting how their stories differed from her own experience. For her, the highlight of the performance was the beautiful song, *Sorrento*.

As she came out onto the square after the performance, little Italian lights sparkled in the trees, their branches extending out over the street like a protective canopy. She ate a late dinner in a small café bursting with talkative people. In the Sorrento tradition, she chose lemon in or on everything: Sauce on her veal, a small lemon tart, and, after dinner, *limoncello*, liquor from the region. She walked late that night feeling safe yet very alone among small clusters of other walkers.

At one point she impulsively entered the lobby of a large hotel, much like an American hotel, all glitz and comfort. No one seemed to notice her, so she walked up the broad stairway to the first landing, paused to look out over the lobby, and then continued down a hallway toward the elevator. Looking down the hallway before her, she was reminded of a book her Uncle Monroe had given her for her tutored art class with him. She remembered in particular the lesson on perspective in painting and sketching. This hallway was a study in perspective sketching. With only the occasional wall-mounted light to break them up, the lines of the walls, the door bottoms and tops, even the carpet pattern continued into the distance toward some focal point somewhere beyond the far wall of the passageway. Where she was seemed broader than where she was going, farther along, down that long, almost interminable hallway. She paused, an interloper of sorts, contemplating a hallway which, in that moment, felt empty and lonely. Maybe that was what aging felt like: Life narrowed down more and more by limitations, life closing in and fizzling out. Like her mother's life — or her own one day.

The hallway seemed to be closing in on her so she ran for the elevator, ran from her narrowing focus. She heard the whir of the elevator and then the ding of its bell. She rushed forward, caught the door before it again closed, walked in, and pushed the button for the ground floor. When the doors again opened she rushed out as one trapped and now free.

Emerging back onto the twinkle-lighted street, she followed the sidewalk back to her hotel. Foregoing the elevator, she walked the stairs, reached her floor, and entered her room. Realizing she had developed blisters from all the walking, she treated them, showered, fell into bed and slept deeply despite the soft clanging of the heat pipes.

The next day she dragged her suitcases over to the train station and, after standing on the platform for only a few minutes, boarded, bound for Stazione Termini in Rome.

Enjoying the train ride, she watched the countryside go by, dozed a bit, and came awake again as they slowed entering the city.

Because of time limitations she had by-passed Pompeii, but she had no notion of missing Rome. She knew she must be efficient in touring the city so she had planned in advance what she would see, and how long to allow before going to the airport to catch her flight to Paris.

She put her luggage and cart into a locker at the train station, inserted coins, locked it, and tucked the key into her purse.

She headed first to Ancient Rome, walking quickly, cruising by the Campidoglio of the Capitol, the Forum, the Colosseum, and barely slowing for a look at the Palatine. At noon she grabbed a small slice of pizza at a standup bar, and hurried off to find the Pantheon. Almost getting lost in the winding streets, she finally found it. It had rained the night before and the floor inside was wet where the roof opened to the sky. Tourist map in hand, trying to find her way to the Spanish Steps, she happened upon the baroque Trevi Fountain. Digging through her purse she found a coin, tossed it into the fountain to insure her return to Rome, stared a moment longer at the sculpted wild steed fighting submission. She wanted to linger and give the complex masterpiece the scrutiny and appreciation it deserved but, running late, she knew she must move on.

Following yet another winding street, she felt some anxiety as her map seemed only occasionally to parallel her location. Nameless, curving streets surrounded by tall buildings blocked any daylight left to help her find her way. Sparse sign markers drove her to inquire of natives, "Piazza di Spagna?" which yielded her indecipherable Italian responses, accompanied by arm-waving and pointing. Soon she came into the piazza, the square at the foot of the Spanish Steps. Even at this time of year there were pots of hardy flowers on the first five tiers of steps leading up to the Trinita dei Monti, a sixteenth century church. The light was fading but she took pictures, made a note of which route to take back to the termini, and rushed off. The Vatican would have to wait for another visit to Rome. She felt almost ashamed that she had not allowed more time to tour the beautiful Eternal City. She would definitely return.

She arrived at the train station just in time to retrieve her belongings, and board the airport train. After a relaxing ride, she arrived at the Fiumicino Airport with time to spare. Leaving on schedule, her flight delivered her to the Roissy Airport on the outskirts of Paris later that evening.

66   Neena – Puteaux and Paris, France
Winter 1977

The airport, busy even for that time of the evening, felt inviting as she realized she was nearing the end of a long journey. Taking a airport bus to the west side of the city, she stepped out onto a well-lighted street, and gathered her luggage.

Having learned in Madrid that it was much easier to take a taxi than to drag her suitcases, she negotiated in passable French with a driver, asking him to take her to a suburb of Paris, to Puteaux. He took her to the address she had given him, unloaded her bags, and bade her goodnight. She had arranged for a walkup, a small functional flat, near the train station in Puteaux. Having arrived and carried her luggage up to the fourth floor, she walked around the apartment, grateful for a large bedroom with two armoires, a small sitting area with an ancient television, and a sunlit kitchen with an out-dated but usable stove with a double oven, and a little Formica table with two chairs. It would do. Clean and cheerful, it would do nicely. From the tiny window in her kitchen she could see the Eiffel Tower pointing skyward as though centered for a painting. It glowed, and even after she shut her eyes that night, it magically sparkled behind her closed lids.

Planning to be in Paris for eight weeks, she was scheduled to begin classes at the Catholic Institute in two days. On her first full day in Puteaux, she began the tradition that she would follow on her off-days, the days when she had no classes. She eagerly rose that first day upon wakening, bathed, fixed coffee, then went down to the street market to buy what she needed for her evening meal. The vendors chanted, each trying to entice her to buy from them. She tried to shop judiciously, buying some vegetables from one, blueberries from another. Before she had walked on down the block, she realized that she would not need more than the bare essentials, plus a little fruit, since she would be eating out at lunchtime. She chose a fruit-filled pastry at a little shop at the bottom of the hill, which she intended for her breakfast. The clerk looked at her and asked, "C'est tout?"

"C'est tout," she replied. "That's it."

On the second morning she bought another fruit tart that she parceled out, a slice for dinner, a slice for breakfast. It was expensive and too large for one person, so she began buying what she hoped were the ingredients, trying for the correct balance of taste until she had come pretty close. She made one each morning, small enough that she could have her morning and her evening piece, and then she would make another.

After her venture to the market it was her habit to take her purchases home, work for a couple of hours on her trip notes, the basis for her sabbatical paper, then walk somewhere for lunch. The old cobblestone streets wound through the suburb and the city like a maze. In little dead-end streets she often found Ma and Pa establishments, little cafés with four or five tables where the husband cooked and his wife served as waitress. Usually there were only two or three selections, the menus changing daily. In her experience, it was difficult to find bad food in Paris.

On Tuesday and Thursday mornings, the days she attended classes, when she exited the Métro and walked toward the Catholic Institute, the crêpe vendor greeted her at the corner. By the second week she knew that his name was Jacques, that he had two children, and that he had grown up in the small village of Chantilly. By the third week she learned that Jacques' father, as a young man, had also served crêpes in the streets of Paris. On each of those mornings she bought two espressos, one for him and one for her, and then ate the butter and sugar crêpe he gave her. He chuckled when butter dribbled down her hand so she had to slurp it off.

As she laughed with him, she realized that she had made her first friend in France, a humble crêpe maker who shared espresso and stories of his family with her, and who waved at her when she was still far up the street, as though he looked forward to her arrival.

67	Neena – Paris and Puteaux, France
	Early 1978

Life continued for Neena in France. She received both letters and telegrams from Teddy, an occasional note from Toot, and one card at Christmastime from Reecie. Once or twice Teddy phoned her.

She continued to view herself going about her daily schedule as though from some distance. She observed herself going to classes, exploring the streets, studying, greeting those she met with a warm hand on their arms and a quick bisoux to their cheeks. She, the calm American professor, anointed others with her well-pondered words. What they, and she, really, failed to notice was that she was an actress playing a role, seductively aloof, charmingly witty and oozing detached equanimity even while her core had begun to boil like Mount Vesuvius itself, a volcano about to erupt.

After feeling almost disembodied for months, after hovering above the circumstances surrounding her, the emotions she had swallowed whole started a steady crawl out of her, working their way into her extremities so that she felt almost tingly. Those sundry emotions edged up, threatening to burst forth in some onerous way.

Then they began manifesting themselves physically, like a cold coming on, or worse yet, like *febrile malaise*. She longingly watched couples sharing a meal, kissing on arriving and hugging as they left. She watched friends together, strolling along, talking, shopping or sharing a dessert. She had begun to wear her loneliness at times like an old, tattered coat – too ugly to keep but too familiar to discard.

Then emotion continued its stealthy creep up and out of her, as though peeking out to see if the coast were clear. But she beat it back, made it through the remainder of her classes. Each day after class she plodded up the stairs to her fourth floor apartment, entered her tiny kitchen, kicked aside the mail, ate too little or too much, and, usually never making it to her bed, dropped instead onto the sofa.

She stopped answering the telephone.

Each day she fell into a deep sleep, into some haunted, cavernous valley. When she wakened again around two a.m., she tried everything she could to sleep the remainder of the night. Nothing worked. So she paced, ironed, read, but mostly lay, unmotivated, on the sofa.

Most of all she would not let herself cry lest she never stop.

68   Teddy – Somewhere Over the Atlantic Ocean
Early Spring 1978

Teddy looked out of the window of the 747 as it barreled through the night. He hoped this proved to be a quick journey and that his fear for Neena proved unfounded. She had not answered her telephone in a week, had responded to neither his letters nor a telegram, yet when he called the Catholic Institute, the director there, after a thorough check, had assured him that she had been attending classes, as usual. When the director asked if Teddy wanted to forward a message to Neena, Teddy had told him that it was not necessary to do so. In truth, he wanted to see for himself, had made arrangements, and was now on his way to Paris.

He tipped back his seat.

In quiet moments such as these, Teddy seemed always to be preparing a sermon, searching his brain for a topic and then drawing forth examples he could use or scripture he could reference.

As he relaxed, his thoughts drifted to Will, his newly-found friend, and to how Will had matured beyond that scared boy to a man whom Teddy liked and respected. Thinking of Will as a boy and, then, as a man, made Teddy ponder his own metamorphosis.

As a youngster, sitting in the back of his father's church, sipping soda from a can on the floor through a series of strung-together straws, Teddy would never have guessed that he would follow in his father's footsteps and become a minister himself. In those days he had listened to only tidbits of his father's sermons, so busy was he trying to prove to his pals that he was nothing like his old man. Teddy had been cool and fun.

Then, in his senior year of high school and freshman year of college, he had discovered the scholar within himself. Questions, subjects to ponder, and age-old discussions drew him in. He found he was gifted in public speaking, excelled on the debate team, and, in his senior year at the university, followed his counselor's advice to apply to the Princeton Theological Seminary.

In early courses at the seminary, he studied Aristotle, Socrates, and even the natural philosopher, Gaius Plinius Secundus, or Pliny the Elder, who had died after the eruption of Mount Vesuvius. He liked to quote old Pliny: "True glory consists in doing what deserves to be written; in writing what deserves to be read." In later years, as Teddy typed his sermons, he remembered Pliny's words, laboring over worthy word choices. During seminary Teddy pored, as well, through various translations of the Bible, concordances, and memorized verses from A. B. Simpson's beautifully-worded, poignant hymns from an old hymnal he found in the attic of the parsonage. With all his accumulated knowledge, his acumen for public speaking and instant recall of things he had read, Teddy began envisioning himself as a great orator, and, with a little pulpit experience, a renowned preacher, replete with touching insight.

Once he had graduated seminary and assumed his first pastorate, the well-chosen words of his well-rehearsed sermons rattled around the sanctuary, skipping over, or falling short of those he intended to reach. And his first two congregations, having missed the point of Teddy's sermons altogether, had never risen to the inspiration of his words. They nodded off, fiddled in their pockets and purses, whispered to each other, or made notes that he suspected were grocery lists. Complimenting him on the mundane sections of his sermons, they seemed to ignore or miss altogether his lovely, alliterate phrases, his stunning observations, or his clever delivery.

Accordingly, he began resenting, almost despising, his congregation for their lack of taste and appreciation; for their lack of depth of thought. His sermons became a litany of his and, he projected, God's displeasure with them. He verbally pounded them with versions of the same lesson: There is no hierarchy of sin, if he, Teddy Teeple who possessed discerning insight, read his Bible correctly. And he, a Protestant seminarian, a learnèd scholar, most definitely read his Bible with much more authority than they. Sin was sin. Sins are equal in the sight of God, aren't they? Hadn't people, people like his father, decided that murder was worse than adultery, or that fornication was more punishable than pride? How could that be?

The petty things that recurred in congregations, he could no longer tolerate. He thought of eliminating the prayer chain altogether, seeing it as a way to gossip in the name of Christian concern. He lashed out at the Pharisees he saw in his congregation, not realizing his own resemblance to the very people a young Jesus had driven from the Temple.

Eventually, his fit of frustration and the sermons that sprang from it escalated when news of a parishioner couple's trial separation spread – and expanded like wildfire – through the congregation. He had planned to give the sermon-of-all-sermons and offer his resignation that very Sunday. And he would now be teaching college philosophy or something similar had his otherwise peace-loving wife not given him a Dutch uncle speech.

"Love them, Teddy," she had finally, simply pled with her face nose-to-nose with his.

Then, to his relief and that of the congregation, he had tendered his letter of resignation, sans a Bible-pounding sermon, and had moved on with a fresh start to, of all places, his father's old church – The Reformed Baptist Church of Emmaus, Virginia. Having started there, at that church in Emmaus, he had gone on to a Presbyterian seminary, had received first-rate training, and now had come full circle, back to his roots.

Even after many years of pastoring, Teddy still wanted the church's doors open to all who sought God. He still believed there was no hierarchy of sin. Those beliefs had not and never would change for him. Yet safely established there, in Emmaus, among some of the people he had known when he was a young man, among most he had never before met, he began closing his sermons with the same phrase, Sunday after Sunday: "Love one another as God loves us." That phrase became a mantra to him. Superfluous and perhaps unheard after a time by many, he nevertheless repeated the phrase every Sunday to his congregation, then every day, sometimes every hour, to himself, until he began practicing what he preached. There, in that church, or perhaps on his knees at bedside, he became a minister to God's people. At some point he began empathizing with them, feeling their pain of loss even though he had never really experienced much personal loss himself. It amazed him. The authority he had once derived from simply standing in the pulpit of this old structure where, before him, seasoned scholars had no doubt preached, his father among them, was now far-overshadowed by the authority of being merely, some would say, a mouthpiece of the Lord.

So he began loving his congregation.

He dearly loved the old ladies who sat in the front pews where individual speakers were available for the hard-of-hearing. Sight-impaired as they were, they looked, if not directly at him, in his general direction, at least. No fiddling among those old saints. After service and at social events, they told him he reminded them so much of his father, *that dear man*.

He adored the curly-haired lady, Edna, who trotted in late most Sundays, and who had missed the service altogether one spring when they moved the clocks ahead.

The two little widowed sisters who walked to church on Sundays, one trailing the other by half a block, a source of amusement to him, had won his affection, as well. One morning the elder sister, Liney, the pianist and the more reticent of the two, was reported by her sibling, Sissy, the spacey artist, to be constipated and unable to attend the Bible class one morning.

Hard-of-hearing, the sisters sat mid-church and commented loudly on the apparel choices of the girls and women attending on any given Sunday. But Liney and Sissy were faithful. Oh, they were faithful.

Even though some congregants looked around as Teddy spoke, even though some nodded off, and some snorted themselves awake again, they were there. They were there. They brought their tithes, their loved ones, their good intentions, and their erring love.

So the Great Orator, The Reverend Doctor Teddy Teeple, came to know the members of his congregation and to honor them each for his or her faithfulness, for his or her contributions, little quirks, and foibles, however distracting, however much they resembled his own. At this point in his metamorphosis, Teddy no longer sought to bask in the glow of his own glory but looked, instead, above and beyond himself for the Godly inspiration he sought and wished to impart.

So, now, as Teddy Teeple sat in coach on a 747 bound for Paris, France, and as he pondered the conundrum of how to deal with his grieving sister, both as a brother and as a counselor, he felt empty of answers but open to anything at all God might choose to impart before he arrived and found that he, the honorable Doctor Teeple, had nothing-at-all to say.

69	**Neena – Paris, France**
	Early Spring 1978

The last day of class she found her way home by rote. Having again ascended to the fourth floor, this time not stopping to eat, she walked through the kitchen of her apartment and, as had been her habit, fell onto the sofa, and dropped into a deep sleep so quickly she might have been sleep-deprived for months. At some point she thought she heard her name but assumed she had been dreaming. Again she heard it. It was off somehow. No French accent but an American one. She pulled herself up and stumbled out into her small kitchen.

"Nines." Teddy stood there, a look of grave concern on his face. "Oh, Nines," he said, holding his arms out to her.

She took another step and fell against him, feeling his warmth and soothing touch on her back.

Sobs broke from her mouth, then tears came, and she collapsed against him.

She cried and slept. She woke to find herself in her bedroom, in her bed. She cried and slept. Time passed; she wasn't sure if it was hours, days or weeks. Teddy woke her periodically and made her eat or drink.

At one point during one sobbing session, he came into her room. "Sit up, Nines," he commanded, softly, yet firmly.

She rose to a sitting position, confused but still crying.

"I want you to tell me why you are crying."

She looked at him incredulously, straining to see through her swollen eyes. "I want to sleep, Teddy," she said. "Leave me alone. In fact, just leave."

"You are going to answer me," he said as he grasped her arms. "I need you to answer me. Why are you crying?"

Finally, after struggling for words she said, "He left. They all leave."

"Who is he, Nines? Who? Tell me whom you mean. Say it."

"Kirby," she said through tears.

"When you were recovering from cancer?"

"No, before, years ago, when I caught him with a friend, with Nora. He left then. I mean he quit loving me. He was the one."

"The one, what?"

"He was the one who was supposed to love me more than I loved him."

"How did you love him? Put it into words."

"Desire, it was just desire at first," she sobbed. "Then like, like a puppy," she said, tears streaming down her face. "The desire, the respect; they left after Nora and the others."

"But I still cared," she continued. "I made excuses, like he couldn't help it. It's so hard to explain."

Despite her struggle, she finally found the words. She had questioned marrying him. He was so different from anyone in her family. She knew as she walked down the aisle that it was wrong. The proverbial warning bells were drowning out the *Wedding March*. She doubted her ability to love him or anyone else. Her willingness to commit seemed locked away somewhere inside her.

She had desires. She wanted intimacy within the moral bounds of marriage this time, but she feared that what she felt stopped short of passion.

As she walked toward him, he stared at her, rapt, like she was the only person in the sanctuary, on the globe. So she decided at that moment that he loved her and that what she felt must be love. It had to be, didn't it? It would be all right.

But it hadn't been. When she caught him with Nora she illogically blamed herself. She rationalized she hadn't loved him enough. Moreover, she reasoned that he probably intuited her lack of real love for him, so he turned to someone else. But then he begged her forgiveness, even falling down on his knees and crying real tears.

So even though her desire for him died when she learned of his infidelity, even though she had lost respect for his integrity, she consciously and ironically began really loving him then.

"It was odd, Teddy," she said. She realized she had quit crying. "I started to work at showing him love and understanding. But when I saw less and less to respect, even when he had subsequent affairs, I started caring for him like – not a puppy – like I would a child who needed me, who couldn't help his behavior."

She paused, smoothing her hair, readjusting her sweater. "But I struggle with that conclusion. It is so mixed with other things."

She resumed crying. "Everyone leaves me, Teddy."

"Who, Nines? Explain it to me."

"Mother and Daddy." She took a deep breath; let it out in a long sigh. "Will."

"Let's talk about Will first. You know differently now. He didn't leave you."

She became overly agitated. "What are you talking about? How can you believe such nonsense?"

Will had knocked her up and then he ran for the hills, his skinny little ass turned to her, his bulging arms hugging that coveted little football instead of her when she was so scared of what would happen to her. She could still picture his butt even now, when middle age spread threatened to crawl up her legs and settle into her own bottom.

Teddy touched her hair, bringing her back to attention. "That packet I sent you, before you left on the cruise. I keep waiting for you to mention it. Didn't you read the letters?"

"What packet, what letters? Oh, no." She put one hand up and stirred her hair. "I put the envelopes in the inside pocket of my suitcase, inside the lid. I never use that pocket so forgot I put them there. I forgot all about it."

"Once you read what I sent you, a lot of this will fall into place. About Will. We can talk about that later."

He sat down facing her with his knees against hers.

"Nines, do you see that you are sounding like a child sometimes, like an adult at other times when you answer me? You need to sit down, sort through, and organize your thoughts until they make sense to you before you can explain them to me. Then we'll talk about them, once you can articulate what you mean. You have kept things bottled up for too long. I suspect you keep dissecting the past, which perpetuates your pain. Once you have talked things out, I want you to do a mental exercise where you put the past and what happened in the past in some figurative place, where you can no longer visit them over and over, or at least less frequently." He gestured with his hands. "Maybe you can mentally write them down on paper and lock them in a strong box or something and just throw the key away. Refocus," he added gently.

She nodded somberly.

"Now let's talk about Mom and Dad," he said, resolution in his voice.

"You start, Teddy," she said. The tears had started again.

"You said they left you."

"Mother and Daddy sent me off, Teddy." There was anger and a palpable tone of despair in her voice. "Did they see me as an egregious reminder of my sin or of the fallibility of all of mankind? Or perhaps I was an embarrassment to the adulated Amos Teeple. Did they miss me, or did they merely exchange me for my baby? Did they transfer their feelings for me to Reecie? Did my sin truly earn my ostracism? Why didn't they explain why they sent me away? And, even if we put all of that aside, why didn't they bring me back?"

Was it possible to satisfy her many questions? Had she repeated to herself these questions so many times that she had invented her own specious argument, one that she could feed on?

She continued, "Daddy was a minister!" Her voice rose and began choking off again. "He could have relocated the whole family to a new pastorate. Or Mother and I could have gone to Aunt Verina's and then rejoined the family. Do you really think that anyone, anyone, anywhere, believed the lie about Reecie being theirs, about her being born to our mother?"

She got up and paced back and forth, stopping to flatten the curled edge of the rug.

"Do you think; do you really think anyone bought that? Why not invent a whole new lie, however unbelievable, that permitted me to remain in the family? A lie is a lie!"

She was crying again. She reached for a tissue and blew her nose loudly. She waved the tissue in her hand as she spoke. "Why stay in that pastorate? Or, why not explain to me their thinking, at least. They prayed for me. Oh, I'm sure they all prayed for me, but they didn't really talk to me!"

As soon as her words were uttered, it occurred to her that perhaps she had been complicit in allowing that silence to grow into an impenetrable wall separating her from her parents. She hadn't asked questions. She had never voiced real remorse. But she had been a scared kid.

"I was just a kid, Teddy. Just a stupid, ignorant kid."

Teddy took her hands and waited for her tears to subside.

"I don't have answers for you, Nines." He looked earnestly at her. "I have batted this around so many times myself, and I don't have any pat answers. I know society, and what it accepted was different in 1951 than it is now in 1978. That was twenty-seven years ago. That's why girls were shipped off when they became pregnant out-of-wedlock. That was the social perspective; the social mandate in some circles."

"But, as a parent myself, our parents puzzle me and they must you. I know that Mom and Dad never gave a worthy explanation for sending you away. I won't make excuses for them because I don't know what they intended. It's possible, given their generation and the sensibilities of that time, that they believed they were doing the right thing for both you and them. It's such a conundrum when you think about it. As a minister, I struggle with issues much like these all the time. Do we limit our actions as well as the actions of others, and hold to a standard that punishes everyone who sins in a particular way, who, for instance, has a baby out-of-wedlock? Do we take it further so that we hold congregations, or whole communities, or even whole societies to that standard? A minister must do that, you know. He must be the standard bearer; must be the example. What should he do? How far should he go in upholding some standard? Should he send his errant child away as an example to his congregation?"

"No, Teddy, in our father's case, he sent me away in secret, practically in the middle of the night, so that no one would ever find out, because if even one member of the congregation found out, it would reflect badly on him."

"You certainly have a point there."

Teddy removed his glasses, cleaned them with a cloth he drew from his pocket, put them back on, and continued. "Give me a minute, Neena. Let me go on with my little argument. So, do we as ministers, send our errant children away as an example? Or, in the name of love, compassion, empathy, do we relax the standard? Should Dad have relaxed the standard for you; should he have reached out to you because you were his daughter and not someone else's? Does he, the minister of his people, lead in that way? Does he extend a hand instead of a reprimand, instead of a sentence, to his child, and in doing so must he then extend a hand to the children of others? It's an erosive thing, you see, acceptance is. You accept divorce, and soon divorce becomes a casual thing. You accept out-of-wedlock conception and soon abortion becomes a morning-after remedy or single parent homes become commonplace."

"We are seeing it happen. I am not saying that there are not times when people should divorce; I'm not saying that some single-parent homes are not preferable to some two-parent ones. But I am talking about when we were kids. That is the real point of this conversation. When we were kids we knew one divorced lady who lived down the block. And she wasn't Catholic either because Roman Catholics made it nearly impossible to divorce. Back then, it was anathema to be divorced; there had to be one totally innocent party and one villain in a marriage that failed. But even the innocent party, if there is such a thing in a marriage, was avoided by the community as a whole. At least we have improved there. Back then it was thought that his or her sin or failure might rub off. The divorcee might lure your husband away. The divorced man might seduce your wife. But times have changed in thirty years. Now I can name thirty divorced people in my acquaintance. And we accept them."

"The truth is we pick our sins, because we all sin. Some people dig around in the Bible and find some little obscure passage, and that becomes the sin they condemn publicly, irately, to whomever will listen; almost like a politician who has established a platform on which to base his whole campaign. That's a safe way to rail against sin. Pick one that doesn't apply to too many people, and then you can speak out without stepping on too many toes. But while we are labeling another's actions a sin, we are often ignoring our own. What about pride? People have forgotten the sin of pride. Or we might condemn divorced people because our marriage is solid but, on the other hand, we might ogle women who are not our wives, essentially committing adultery in our hearts. Or we may condemn what we may see as sinful, whether it really is or not, and feel superior, and hateful, as can be while we are the biggest gossip in the church or in our whole community, or while we are gambling away the grocery money. Basically, we look down our prim little noses at what we see as someone else's sin while we sit plumb in the middle of our own."

"What is the right thing to do? Do you know, Nines, because I don't pretend to know? And I am a minister. I'm supposed to know. I have stuck to the rule that God is my judge; that man should extend a hand of love to his brother or sister as Jesus did, all the while being the best reflection he can be of the Lord, Himself. Who are we to sit around deciding what constitutes another's sin and who among us is the perpetrator of it? But some see that as too lenient. Some, while evoking the name of our Lord, disown their own children, shun loved ones, and treat them as dead when they have sinned, or when they have been perceived to have sinned. But usually the sins such people condemn and punish are ones that, if ignored, will reflect on the punisher in some adverse way. Other sins such people never see at all, especially if they are ones that they, themselves, practice on a daily basis."

"Enough with the preaching. In your case I suspect that our father made the decision to send you away, because, let's face it, he made the decisions in our household, and Mother went along. You remember Dad's sign: *As For Me and My House, We Will Serve the Lord.* That, in itself, seems like a great thing to display on the wall, don't you think? Yet, our father was the one who interpreted how it was we would serve the Lord. In the end, the rules were Amos Teeple's, not necessarily God's. Mother obeyed whatever Dad dictated. She was the biblical model of wife. Even in view of all that we have discussed, they weren't bad people. I want to believe that they always intended to bring you back. Is it possible that they felt that God was blessing them for their actions when it turned out that Uncle Monroe proved to be your superb teacher? And, based on that, they just left you there with V and Monroe, to blossom under his tutelage? Could it be that they hated to make you come back to face your classmates' questions? Could they have found you distant and unforgiving and, not intending to leave you there indefinitely, hesitated and thereby let weeks turn into months and then into years, until you had slipped away to the point where they didn't know how to remedy a bad choice? Do you think they were distracted by Grandma's illness and by Reecie's needs? I don't know. They weren't young when they had us; can you imagine how weary they must have been chasing that little live-wire, Reecie, around the house?"

Neena sat looking at him intently.

"But what is so hard to bear is that you will never know why they did what they did, what they intended, why they let you slip away. I can give you the tired clichés about how you must forgive, how being unforgiving is like acid that eats at the container in which it is stored, blah, blah, blah. Some believe that one can only forgive another if the other person asks for forgiveness. I don't even know if our parents considered what they did as wrong, so why would they seek forgiveness? Perhaps they thought they were being good and protective parents. Maybe they thought you should be asking them for forgiveness. Who can know?"

"I have chased this around like a puppy chasing his own tail. And, as a brother and a minister myself, my advice is that you forgive them. And even though I know you well enough to know that you have already addressed this, I must say that at some point during all your innocent confusion, in spite of your ignorance that what you were doing could make you pregnant, despite your youth, there had to be a moment when you knew what you were doing was wrong. You knew, little sister, as we all know when we beat back our consciences and do it anyway. Even kids who were not raised in the church as we were have been read stories with morals. We know about conscience, about when we push away that knowledge that we are doing wrong. But only you know if you have addressed that; if you have accepted the blame for that part of it, at least, and not tried to blame Mother and Dad, or even Will, for everything. Maybe you need to forgive yourself, foremost, utmost, and once and for all. I do not know; I am not your judge."

70   Neena and Teddy – Puteaux, France
Early Spring 1978

She stood and put her hands to the sides of her head, as though her head were about to burst open. Then she sat back down and stared into Teddy's eyes.

"Do you know what it was like, Teddy, living with Aunt Verina?" Neena leaned forward, and then drew back, sitting erect. "She was this morally superior wart!"

"Wart?" Teddy asked, smiling.

Neena smiled, too. "Sometimes when I'm emotional I can't think of the right word. I wonder how much I do things like that in front of my students." She shook her head.

She continued. "She was so smug with me, with her little anecdotal sermons. They were all about things I *should* have done, how I *could* have avoided my situation. She never called it what it was. It was always my *little problem*, or my *little difficulty*, or my *little predicament*. It was a pregnancy! It was a baby, and it could only have gotten there one way! What she said was one thing, but what she meant was sin, with a capital *S*. She could never look at it as a forgivable mistake. She seemed to me the last person to whom I should have been sent. She couldn't begin to understand."

"And she never told me how to cope after the fact. It was always what I *should* have done."

"But she loved me. Oh, she told me enough that she loved me. If I'm being fair, I have to admit that after Reecie was born, she never raised the subject again. I have to admit, too, that she wanted what was best for me. But sometimes, in the beginning at least, her wanting what was best for me was merely an excuse to sermonize. She provided me a home, cooked my meals, taught me to iron, to knit, to sew, and, eventually, to cook. But I rarely got the sense that she loved me enough to try to crawl into my skin, to see what it felt like to wear my sin, a sin so observable that there was no denying it. I think Uncle Monroe loved me just like I was. But he did not warm to me at first, at least in the very beginning."

She stood and began pacing while she talked.

"Aunt Toot and Uncle Jimmy tried to help. She'd drive all the way over to Aunt Verina's to ask if I could go shopping with her or to lunch, but V wouldn't let me go. I think Toot would have let me talk, would have answered some questions. You know how out-with-it she is."

They were both smiling now.

"Of course, after Reecie was born, I spent every other weekend with Toot and Uncle Jimmy. That kept me sane."

She stood and walked over to the window and looked down at the street. Umbrellas floated by as though maneuvered by remote control. She turned back away from the window.

She grew serious again. "When Aunt Verina died, when they died, Daddy, Uncle Monroe and Jimmy, it was like none of my questions would ever be answered. It made me feel like I had failed to be appreciative, like I had betrayed yet another person who loved me. I resented V so much I could taste it, sometimes. It made me pucker up, that taste, that acrid taste. It was like eating a green crab apple. The bitterness clings to your teeth, even after you free your tongue of it. Anyway, at some point I realized that I didn't resent her so much as I didn't remotely understand her. It made me angry that I would never know, never know the truth. Then it was like Death was hovering around, taking people who had been integral parts of my life. It hovered especially after I got cancer."

She shook her head, frustrated.

"The angry disease, they say. Like it's not bad enough to contract something so terrible, but then you got it because you were angry, like you intentionally brought it on yourself."

She walked back over and sat in front of Teddy.

"So there will never be any answers, will there?"

"Yes, you already have some answers in two manila envelopes that you tucked away in your suitcase. You need to spend some time with those after I leave. But, regarding Mom and Dad, I agree; we have no answers. And I think that anything Aunt Toot may have surmised and tried to share with you would have merely been speculation on her part. I know our parents well enough to guess that they talked to no one on the subject of your pregnancy, and probably not even to each other. Too embarrassing."

He stood and moved over by the window, looking out toward the Eiffel Tower. "It's beautiful here. So Old World."

"At least I got my education, my degrees," she said as she joined him at the window.

"I am grateful to them, to our parents, for that. I'm grateful to Uncle Monroe and even to Aunt Verina, as well. I received a classic education that made college easier. I had to work to support myself in college, but Mother and Daddy paid my tuition, at least," Neena said. "In fact, I have always suspected that Uncle Monroe and Aunt V helped as well. So tell me, how can I justifiably resent any of them?"

He turned, taking her into a warm embrace. "Maybe that's the only evidence you have that they wanted the best for you. And even though you had their financial help, you, Nines, you earned those degrees. Can that knowledge sustain you? Can you go on now? I want to see the sparkling Neena, not the sad and defeated one. From now on, don't let your frustration build, Nines. Talk! Talk to me if no one else suits. Talk, you little wart, you."

They both smiled, thinking their separate thoughts.

"Margot was so great to encourage me to come here," Teddy said. "I wanted to come but felt selfish leaving. I wanted to bring her, but we couldn't both leave Angie and, well, you know how it goes." He rubbed his head. "I was nuts to have a kid at age forty. What was I thinking?" He smiled, broadly. "She's such a precocious little twerp. We enjoy her so much."

"I am so grateful you came, Teddy. I know you are busy. I will thank Margot when I see her."

"You know I have to leave soon."

"I assumed so. I wish you could spend a little more time, but I understand."

"I have two more days and evenings. You are over your crying jag, aren't you?"

"Yes, Teddy, I think I have crawled out of an emotional pit, at least for the time being."

"Well, doll up because I want to explore this city, and I want to eat some of that good French food. You need to eat, too. You've lost weight despite my expert nursing. Get the lead out, little sister. Let's go."

As Neena walked toward the bedroom, Teddy added, "You can spend some time with the packets I sent after I leave. They will clear up some things and fog up some others. But overall they might help."

She nodded, turning again to enter the bedroom.

"He's a good guy, Nines; Will's a good guy, a guy who has worked hard to be the best version of him he could be. He holds no illusions regarding mistakes he has made in his life. He has made honest attempts to right wrongs. And after this discussion, you and I both know how important that is. He cares about what happened. I think, despite the years, that he still cares for you or at least a memory of you. You could be friends. He's interested. He has become my friend, reserved as he is. I like and respect him."

Skeptical, Neena lingered in the doorway for a moment, then entered her bedroom, and closed the door in preparation for dressing for their outing.

They talked at length for the rest of his visit, enjoying the city and each other. When he left for the airport, she hated seeing him go. But she felt stronger. She actually felt. And that in itself was an improvement.

Sally Kerr-Kelly

71 — Toot - Burl, Albemarle County, Virginia
Early Spring 1978

Toot still slept on her side of the bed, on the side she had occupied during all the years of her marriage. It felt right to stay there, as if Jimmy were up late, catching the end of a ballgame on television, or maybe in the bathroom brushing his teeth. Some nights, half-asleep, she found herself extending her toes slowly, gently across the mattress so as not to disturb him, searching, searching for his hairy shin. But now when her toes pushed past the edge of the sheet and beyond the edge of the mattress, they found empty, cool air instead.

How she missed him. Still, she missed him – not the new missing that knocks you to your knees in gulps of despair but random missing, the kind that just shows up like a shadow crossing your path, or a cool gust of air, or a sustained breeze that ever-so-gently stirs your hair. She didn't believe in ghosts. But his memory remained palpable, as though at any given moment she could reach out and feel warmth radiating from the spot where he should be, had he lived on.

Loneliness gnawed at her at times. Oh, she could fill the hours, could find companionship, but she remained only half of a couple. She found herself saving his seat at church. She often had to stop mid-turn when starting to lean to whisper something into his ear. She listened for his footsteps. She longed for his touch. She missed his smell, a combination of deodorant, soap, and what? She couldn't name it, but it lingered on his sweaters, ones he had worn once and put back into his bureau. His sport coats had retained his smell, his body's fragrance, for a time, but then they, too, began to smell merely like the closet in which they hung.

She tried accepting dinner invitations. She went out with Harry Weisman, the town undertaker who had graduated several years after she. But, as they ate their salads, she began noticing that his nose crinkled when he chewed, as if he had tasted something foul. Halfway into the steak and baked potato dinner she started counting the number of times he cleared his throat; got all the way to one hundred and twenty-six before dessert was served. And then, try as she might, she couldn't for the life of her remember anything of which he spoke. He must have found her vacant-headed.

When they arrived back at her house, he walked her to her door. She paused there on the step and, more out of gratitude than any heart-felt emotion, kissed him quickly on the cheek, thanking him for a wonderful dinner and good company. He told her they should do it again sometime, although she couldn't imagine how he could have enjoyed her at all, distracted as she had been.

When she got into the house, she was, at first, surprised to see that it was only eight p.m., and then amused that her hot date had lasted all of two hours.

She took off her coat, went into the den, and dialed Teddy.

"Hello. The Teeple residence." His voice sounded dull as though he had been sleeping or was about to fall asleep.

"Hi Teddy. You sound exhausted. When did you get in?"

"Oh, hi Toot. About two hours ago. Both flights were right on time."

Toot sat on the arm of her leather sofa. "How was Christina when you left? You think she's okay to be alone?"

"I would have liked to be able to stay a bit longer, but I think she is okay. She really needs time to sort through some things."

"I'm going over there, Teddy."

"Toot!"

"Now, don't interrupt me. Jimmy's niece, Nell, you met her once years ago. She's over there for a month. Has a flat right in Paris somewhere. She invited me to go stay there with her and her daughter."

"I don't know what I think about your going at all, and I surely don't like the idea of your flying over there alone. Can you go over with them?"

"Sure, I'm sure. I'll figure out something. Maybe I'll go with a friend. Don't worry about it. I won't go alone, I promise you that. In fact, I'll leave you a message giving you my arrangements once they have been made."

She walked over to look out the window. "Go to bed, Teddy. Sounds like you are done in. Goodnight."

"Nite, Toot. Call me, okay? Let me know what you are up to."

Toot clicked off, walked over to the desk, found the telephone book, looked up the number and dialed.

"Hello." He sounded expectant, alert, and maybe even hurried.

"Hello yourself," Toot said with a smile in her voice. "This is, well, it's Toot. You know. The wild one on the ship."

"Of course, of course. How are you?"

"I'm as fine as any middle-aged lady can be."

Smiling, she paced around a bit, going back over to look out of the window. "I'll make this short. I think Neena's in trouble."

She took a deep breath and continued before he could interrupt. "Teddy just got back from Paris as you may or may not know. She seems better but not good. I have a chance to go over to Paris, and an upstanding lady like me needs a chaperone. I'd like you to go because I feel that you really care for her. I can't offer you a place to stay since I am staying with my husband's niece and the apartment is small, but I'm still asking you to consider it. I'd like to go as soon as possible. I can get us the flight tickets if you'll agree to go."

"I do care about Neena. I feel I should explain some things to her, if I ever get the chance. I'm a little hesitant, though. She seems to be working through some things, if I read her right." Will grew silent, as though mulling it over.

He had been quiet way too long. Toot hated it when people did that, pondered things. Jimmy used to do that to her. She was in trouble, she knew she was. She was matchmaking, in large part, she feared because she missed Jimmy. Yet she saw something in Will, something that she had seen all those years ago in her Jimmy. He cared about Neena. If Neena would just relax and get over some things, like that namby-pamby Kirby, she could have a real peach in that McClure fellow. If not, Toot might think about going after him herself. She couldn't bear the silence any longer. "Listen, I can't go alone, and you always seem to be free as a bird, or so you said on the ship. Aren't you writing a book or something? You could get lots of fodder for your book over there in Pareee," she said, a smile in her voice.

"Okay, Toot. Even though I have misgivings about how Neena will receive me, I would love to accompany you, and I can find a place to stay, in fact, I have a place where I have stayed before."

"No, that won't work. She's in Puteaux, not Paris. It's a suburb. I'll get some information from Jimmy's niece about a hotel. I'll get back to you on that. How late do you stay up? I might call you yet tonight."

"I stay up until eleven or twelve. When do you want to go to France?"

"Tomorrow, the next day. I don't know. As soon as we can work it out. I just have this sense she needs someone right now. When we get over there, if you could check on her and keep me up-to-date, it would relieve me a great deal. Then I would be right there if I could be of help."

"I don't know that she would welcome my intrusion, but I could check on her and just let her know that we are there."

"Let's do it. Maybe you could, well, watch over her for me. No need to chat further. I'll get the tickets. I'll call you back tomorrow sometime."

"Toot, please let me buy the tickets. I'm an old hand at flight arrangements. I'll call you tomorrow with the information."

"How can a lady like me refuse?"

"Good night, Miss Toot."

"G'night, Will."

72   Neena– Puteaux, France
Late Winter - Early Spring 1978

Three days had passed since Teddy left.

Still, she couldn't quit her intermittent crying.

While he had still been there with her, she thought she had had an epiphany, had resolved issues just by recognizing they existed. Then she started missing him, his wisdom and his strength. Soon she resumed crying even though her ridiculous tears had subsided in his presence.

Her weeping reminded her of the spring rains when she was a kid. Up in the mountains, west of Emmaus, the rainfall seemed innocuous enough, but by the time it reached the bottomlands, what had been a sprinkling of water turned into a torrent, a real gulley washer.

She knew she was wading around in the boggy bottomlands, stepping over delicate forget-me-nots and plowing, instead, through muck, through pungent skunk cabbage to rehash past and recent, painful events. She could not stop lamenting her many losses. She realized, as well, that some of her reaction was typical and necessary, but she had gone beyond any normal reaction to events. Lack of resolution kept her there, her tears incapacitating her. She cried so much her face swelled so that her reflection in the mirror caught her off-guard.

As she stood at the kitchen sink or at the window in the sitting room, she envisioned great puddles of tears swirling around her feet and threatening to wash her away. Yet she couldn't stop, except momentarily. Then tears would flow again in great gulps, catching her unawares.

She thought she should get outside and walk, but she didn't want people staring at her. So she stayed in. She could eat only a few bites before the food seemed to lodge in her throat, trapped by a spasm that brought even more tears.

Disgusted, she thought that after these amounts of tears she would at least know what she was crying about, would know what, specifically, she could do to fix herself.

But loss, how do you go about getting back something lost to you forever, like childhood, the love of people now dead or gone, or even innocence? She wanted them back, and if she couldn't have them back, she at least wanted clarification. But how do you get either? How do you climb up from the bottomlands, down there where you have been mucking around? How do you climb all the way up to the mountaintop where the air is purportedly clearer, where the vista spreads out before you, when you don't even know if one is preferable to the other? Just how do you do that? If Teddy hadn't known how to, who in heaven's name would?

73 — Will and Toot – Transatlantic Flight
Spring 1978

Will had booked two first class seats on a TWA flight out of Washington National Airport to the Charles de Gaulle International Airport near Paris. Delighted that they would have first-class service and that she could sit by a window with Will on the aisle, Toot had settled in quickly and had ordered a coffee that she enjoyed in relative silence. She seemed tired or merely lost in thought.

Long after they were in the air, she shifted in her seat, accepted a soda from the stewardess, and said, "Okay, I think it is time to fill you in on ancient history. I'll try not to give you too much detail but, trust me, I can talk."

She brought her glass to her mouth and then lowered it again, sighing heavily. "Amos Teeple was a charismatic man. He was ten years older than I; twenty-four, actually, the first time my sister Dessie brought him to meet the family. I fell in love with him that moment and never, really, lost my infatuation for him, I suppose."

She took another sip. "Oh, I did, I did quit feeling that way. Yes, at some point I surely did."

She accepted one of the rolls the stewardess offered her, broke off a piece, buttered it, took a bite, and slowly chewed. After blotting her lips decorously with her napkin, she spoke. "That's what made him such a dynamic speaker, you know, his charisma. He could make you hang on his every word. He knew just when to add an amusing anecdote, when to lower his voice, when to raise it, and when to lower the boom, so to speak, when to make his point."

She buttered another section of her roll.

"And the King's English, he used the King's English so perfectly, so beautifully, really, that it was a pleasure to listen to him speak. Maybe you remember. I keep forgetting that you knew him."

"But they just get too big for their britches, you know? Charismatic people like that, you know? They've capitalized so long on personality that they don't develop other parts of their character. Or so it seems to me. But who knows? Who knows for sure? Yet pride does come before a fall, as my mother used to say. It's kind of understandable. I mean if you're a good speaker and you look out into the audience and see people taking notes on what you say, or you see these contemplative, almost rapt looks, it has to go to your head. And when he chose to, Amos could always find just the right thing to say, just the right retort, either to put people at ease or to say something funny to lighten a moment. He had a gift; that man did, he surely did."

She paused again when their dinners were served.

"Oh, I love salmon," she said, digging into her entrée.

They ate in silence. Realizing that Toot would speak again when she was ready, Will quietly ate his dinner.

Having finished her main course, Toot pushed her dessert back for later, accepted a cup of coffee, sipped at it, and continued. "But he never quit being that orator; that elevated man in the pulpit. He was formal, too formal, with his wife and children. He had this big sign in the foyer of the parsonage that read, *As For Me and My House, We Will Serve the Lord.* Based on that, I suppose, he ruled his house."

She smiled, as though remembering.

"Nothing like Jimmy. Now, there was a peach. He was so good to me. He put up with all my little quirks, although I never admitted to him that I had any."

She snickered then, but her face grew still as she continued. "In Amos and Dessie's house there was a hierarchy of sorts. First, were God's rules, or at least how Amos interpreted them, and then there were Amos' rules. And sometimes, I have to admit to you, they looked one and the same; you couldn't tell God's rules from Amos', which could be either good or bad, I guess, when I look at it now."

She screwed up her nose a bit. "And I watched my sister mold herself to his wishes. She became mindless, almost, as though she had to look at things just as old Amos looked at them. She must have bitten back any fresh perspective so often that she didn't even permit herself to think anymore."

"Could you hand me that blanket?" she asked, reaching for it and spreading it out across her lap. "Thank you, Dearie."

"Anyway, where was I? Oh, yes, yes. Well, as I was saying, he was the head of the household in the strictest interpretation of what the Bible says. He could wilt Dessie – and the children, or at least Christina – with a look."

She put her hand up to her forehead, smiled, brought it back down and said, "I know you call her Neena, but I just can't bring myself to call her that most of the time. She's Christina to me."

"Going back to Amos' ruling his household. Don't forget, he did it with charm. Don't forget that, because he didn't look like some tyrant. Not a tyrant at all, but like someone consistent, really consistent, who one day gets his dog to sit up and beg because he has been relentless in instructing the dog to do as he asks. You know, the dog is so devoted to him and it just can't please him enough. And that dog doesn't question. He has been consistently charmed, actually programmed, into doing his little trick, and he's so proud of himself, that little dog is. You know?"

"So malleable, that's the word I was looking for. So malleable, my sister was. She was a godly woman who looked to her husband for the major decisions of their lives. That's all I can come up with after studying it for so many years."

Toot reached for her dessert, ate a couple of small bites, seeming to relish it, and took a couple more sips of her coffee. "Ish," she said. "Coffee's stone cold."

Will motioned to get the stewardess' attention. Once the stewardess brought Toot another cup of coffee, she continued. "But you know, charismatic people, well, they get lifted up so high by the opinions that people have of them and then in their own minds, well, they have farther to fall. It only stands to reason. Those kinds of people have quick success, more often than not. And their heads swell." Toot gestured with her hands at the sides of her head as though her head were as large as a basketball. She even puffed out her cheeks.

"But then, just when their heads can't swell any bigger, that's when it all falls apart. Sister V, my sister Verina, bless her sad soul, did you ever meet her? She wouldn't say it was the Lord working in their lives, bringing their feet back to earth. No, she'd say it was the Devil working overtime, gets a hold of 'em. Pulls 'em down." Toot's voice was soft with just a hint of the south; a softening of her r's.

She paused for a moment, took a drink, nibbled at her pastry, and shifted in her seat so that she could look directly at Will. "Am I wearing your ears out, Willy Boy?"

"No, Toot, you are doing fine. I'm with you. I want to hear the story."

She took another sip of coffee, put down her cup, moved around until her legs were in a more comfortable position, and continued. "It's a good thing because it'll take awhile because I sure have some observations and opinions I have been wanting to share for a long time. And you're trapped."

"Anyway, that reminds me of an old joke. This woman spends too much money so her husband has a little talk with her, probably for the hundredth time. He says, now when you go shopping today and you are tempted to buy something, just say to the devil, 'Devil, get thee behind me.'"

"So she comes home that day wearing this luxurious full-length mink coat."

"He can't believe his eyes. So he says, 'Didn't you do what I told you to do?'"

"And she says, 'Yes, I did. I said, Devil, get thee behind me,' and he taps me on the shoulder and says, 'Hey, looks pretty good from back here, too.'"

They both laugh.

"Isn't that just a hoot? I have always loved that one."

"Anyway, I don't think it's the Devil gets a hold of a person, unless you're possessed, or something. Not at all. That's just a cop-out. It's more that you make a choice, clear and simple, between what's right and what's wrong. You hear it on the news all the time; they just can't wait to give you the dirt on public figures. You see yet another politician or religious leader caught in a lie, and all the wonderful things they have done for their country or state or county or community just fly right out the window."

She cleared her throat, as though her voice were giving out.

"We had a minister when I was a kid. He had the gift, all right. His sermons were wise and heartfelt. But he strayed once – and I believe it, too, *once* - and had a no-good rendezvous with some lady of questionable character. Just before he and his ministry came crashing down around his ankles, he even preached on temptation and fornication. I really think the darned fool was fighting it. But he lost the fight. Bottom line: He chose the wrong thing to do instead of the right thing to do."

Toot turned, raised her shade, lowered it again, shifted in her seat so that she was again facing Will, and lowered her voice. "But back then, in '51, just before old Amos sent Christina away, my brother-in-law was fighting some temptation of his own. I saw it plain as day; don't know what other people saw, but I saw it."

74 | Neena – Puteaux, France
Spring 1978

Neena stood looking out her window at the Eiffel Tower, thinking how incongruous it seemed towering over the baroque architecture surrounding it. She thought about Teddy, about his kindness to her and his wise counsel. Then she remembered! She had been wallowing around in tears and had forgotten! She spun in her bare feet and ran into her bedroom and knelt down on the floor beside her bed.

Within seconds she had pulled her suitcase out from under the bed, opened the lid, unzipped the lining pouch and took out its contents. There were two manila envelopes, one plain and one padded. Both had been addressed to her. She remembered receiving them while packing for her cruise even though she had only a vague recollection of having stuffed them into her suitcase. She remembered speculating that they contained some articles or something Teddy wanted her to read. So she saved them for the cruise and forgot all about them.

She chose the larger envelope. Curious why it was thicker than the other one, she figured there must be a lot to digest. While she pried up the metal prongs on the envelope flap, she absently slipped the thin, padded envelope back into the pocket of her suitcase. She thought she would look at that one later and didn't want to misplace it.

She put the suitcase back under the bed so she could spread the contents of the thick envelope on top of her bedspread. When she turned the envelope upside down, letters spilled out, and a small bound book, a ledger fell to the bed. She went for the letters first and realized that they were bundled chronologically with rubber bands.

Still kneeling with her elbows on the bed top, she looked at the envelopes, each addressed to her at the parsonage at 124 Elm Street, Emmaus. She scanned the letters, reading rapidly.

> *Dear Neena, I miss you. I always write to you just before I go to bed and then I dream about you. I pray every night that you are okay. I'm okay but I'm ashamed to say I'm scared. please write. I love you and always will.*
>
> *Forever, Will*

She read and then reread the letters frantically, as though she were being timed. She realized that tears were forming in her eyes, but these tears felt different somehow. They were not the tears of a wounded girl but a woman who felt shame washing over her like hot, hot water. She wilted into a sitting position, clutching some of the letters to her chest.

She gathered the letters, trying to put them back into chronological order. She wanted to reread them to see if she could piece together what Will had gone through while reaching out to her. Once she had them banded together, she noticed that the ledger still lay on the bed and she drew it down and opened it. There was a letter clipped onto the first page, addressed to Neena's father from Will. The ledger entries were in her father's handwriting. But it was the ledger heading that made Neena stare in disbelief.

75 — Toot and Will – Over the Atlantic Ocean
Spring 1978

"Her name was Carmella Somerville," Toot continued. "People called her Carnie, not Car*m*ie like you'd expect, but Carnie. Sounds like it derives from carnal, doesn't it? Anyway she wasn't all that much to look at. Her husband had died, and she was just the saddest, neediest thing you ever saw. Her heartbreak and the emotions from it dripped off her like sap leaks in a sugar bush."

Will peered at her blankly.

"Don't know what a sugar bush is? It's a stand of maple trees that produce maple sap that they collect in pails hanging from the side of a tree. Then they boil the sap down into maple syrup. My grandfather, Grandpap Townsend, moved to Pennsylvania when we were little. He had a stand of maple trees on his farm up there. We went up there once during boiling season. I remember snow piled high as the roof of that old black touring car Daddy drove. What a lot of work for a little bit of syrup. But it was yummy."

"Anyway, anyway. This Carnie person was the opposite of my sister, Dessie, Christina's mom, you know, just the polar opposite of Dessie."

"Dessie, so slim and ram-rod straight, and unapproachable. Warmer by far than sister V, but Dessie was always the picture of decorum. She was a walking advertisement for Miss Pratt's Social Skills School."

Toot cleared her throat. "We three all went there, you see, to Miss Pratt's Social Skills School, twice a week and on one Saturday per month. We learned everything from how to be civil, how to not say what we really felt, how to say no and make it feel like yes, how to entertain like the southern ladies we were bred to be, and, oh, I could go on and on. But the fun thing was we learned to ballroom dance. One time you got to be the boy, and the next time you got to be the girl. It was very confusing, to say the least. Then, twice a year, the boys from Delbert Dormer's class (now there's a name, how do you like that name, forgot all about that little nervous twerp) came over, and we would have a mixed dance. Boys and girls. It was really fun, but oh, so proper."

Toot laughed and shook her head a little as though she remembered some special moment that she did not wish to share. "I digress. Getting back to Dessie. You never really knew what was going on in there." Toot pointed first to her head and then to her heart. "She was shy, you know; most people didn't know that about her, and just so very proper, just right for a minister's wife, I always said. You could never accuse her of gossiping or causing trouble in the church. No way. The women of the church, the women she closely associated with in the weekly Bible studies still called her Mrs. Teeple, never Dessie, even ones she had known for years. Just one look at Dessie and you knew you were not to step one step closer."

Toot tapped her head. "I forget you knew her. You probably have your own opinions but you'll see I'm right."

"Anyway, this Carnie person was just the opposite of Dessie. This woman was soft and pink as a peach, friendly and needy as a one-legged, one-eyed beggar woman."

Toot chuckled and laid her hand on Will's arm.

"They don't call them that anymore, do they? Street person or something like that; that's what they call them now. You must think I'm a daft old lady. Well, that I am; that I am."

She took a deep breath and then let it out slowly.

"Anyway this Carnie cried at the drop of a hat; not that she didn't have something to cry about. It's terrible to lose a husband. Leaves a hole in your heart a truck could drive through. So she starts going to the church office for counseling — way too often. And people started talking. When the reverend brother-in-law got wind of the talk about him and her, he started making sure Dessie was in attendance at the counseling sessions. Boy, that brought the sessions to a screeching halt. Carnie didn't want Dessie there, hearing all her heartbreak. Next thing you know, Miss Carnie high-tails it to her daughter's place in Fauquier County. That's where she should have been in the first place."

"Yet even her departure didn't stop tongues from wagging about the reverend and Carnie. I still don't believe anything happened beyond Amos getting a swelled ego and being, maybe, a little too charming, a little too nice. Part of me honestly believes that he did nothing wrong at all. You know? He was supposed to be a man devoted to God and his congregation. But who knows; who even knows anything for sure."

"But those tongues kept a-wagging. I know because a childhood friend of mine kept me informed. This friend is the salt-of-the-earth type of person; honest, good and, believe me, no gossip. I believe every word she said. Even so, even after Carnie took to the hills, so to speak, the congregation didn't stop gossiping about her and Amos. But Christina's departure stopped the gossip. Well, it didn't stop the wagging tongues, but at least they switched from Carnie to Christina. Everyone started speculating. Of course, proper Dessie said that

Christina was studying abroad. At age fourteen! That was a stretch since she never went near Europe but, instead, went three hours south to my sister's. And since you, Will, got abruptly sent away and then, later, poof, so did she, the people found a lot to talk about. And the neighbors, if not the congregation, speculated about the whole scene when you punched poor Amos."

Will felt ashamed at the mention of his assault on Reverend Teeple.

"Oh, don't look so crestfallen, Will. Sometimes a person can take just so much, and then something has to give. Later on, I would have loved to give old Amos a good punch in the snout, but you saved me the trouble."

Toot looked disgusted but then she smiled and patted Will's arm.

"Amos must have thought he had a congregation full of idiots. Of course they had questions. And I honestly think that he wouldn't have sent Christina away if he weren't trying to save his own skinny neck, his own reputation. You know, we forget that ministers are really just men, just people, like you and me. And times were different then, don't you let anyone tell you otherwise. As I said, I have seen ministers fired for less. And he did a lot of good, Amos did. We mustn't forget that."

Toot seemed to be gesturing more and more with her hands.

"Did they visit her much?" Will asked, finally interrupting her narrative.

"No, not really. Well, maybe once before Reecie was born. But, no, not really, at least not consistently. Amos only went once; I'm sure, except for when they went to take Neecie. I was so disgusted. I went to see them. I begged; I cajoled; I threatened. Implacable, those two."

She sighed, like she was really tiring. "In my opinion they had more than one choice. They could have let her stay and just kept their chins up and dared anyone to find fault. But the rev would have been ousted, I'm sure. That was 1951, remember. We had rules, and we kept them."

"Or they could have made the decision to move to another church, another congregation. Or they could, at the very least, have sent her away until the baby was born and then brought her back."

She sighed again, as though the possibilities were endless. "And something that bothers me more than you can fathom: They sent her to live with Sister V instead of me! You know, sometimes the right choice is not always the best choice. Oh, dear me, I was beside myself. What a horrible choice. I know why. I know why. But my Sister V's house was the most somber place you could imagine. It was like a nunnery or a funeral parlor. Sister V, from her late twenties on at least, has been a saint with, what was that Jimmy used to say, oh, yes, a saint with a ramrod shoved up her woo-woo. Oh, that Jimmy was a pistol. But V was so driven to get her work done, to visit the sick, to provide for the needy. She did good, no, great, things. And Monroe was the sweetest man you could imagine. A little bookish, to be sure, but that's not a bad thing. But, ... Well, I might as well say it. V had a secret, and that secret and the guilt she carried took the joy right out of her. I'll spare you; I don't need to go into all of that right now."

76
Neena – Puteaux, France
Spring 1978

Neena stared at the ledger heading: *Willis McClure's Financial Contributions to the Support of Patrice Eleanor Teeple.*

Neena went back to the letter clipped to the ledger cover.

Dear Reverend Teeple,

I have just a little money I can earn but I feel a responsibility to my daughter. I understand that you call her Reecie. I am not asking for information about her.

I am sorry for all the wrong that I have done. Please take this money. I want to make things up to everybody I hurt. I will send more money. You can count on it.

Willis McClure

Neena looked closer at the ledger entries. On the third or fourth of each month starting February 1952 her father had entered the date and an amount varying between $3.50 and $4.25. This continued until June of 1955 when he entered a lump sum of $245.00. After that Will's job opportunities must have improved because the monthly amounts gradually increased until he was paying larger and larger amounts. The final notation read: *Trust for Patrice by McClure to include health care, education for herself and/or her children, and lump sums at age twenty-five, thirty, and thirty-five years of age.*

Her back against the bed, Neena sat staring at the Louis XVI-style armoire across the room, at the fine craftsmanship of the piece. She stared through it, finally, puzzling and piecing things together. So Will had tried for months and months to find her, to contact her. He had obviously learned somehow what he could about Reecie yet did not interfere in her life. And he supported her, meagerly at first, to the extent he was able, and then handsomely to the extent Reecie deserved. His adult-like assumption of responsibility at such a young age flabbergasted Neena.

How could she have been so wrong about another human being? How could she have just assumed that he immediately forgot her, their dilemma, and their daughter? Hadn't she seen how desperately he tried to get to her the day he came to the parsonage, crying, to talk with her and her father, to explain — but she should have recognized why he was so distraught. She knew him. He had invited her into his private, sorrowful soul. And her; Neena, Neena, just what kind of a person was she?

She got up, dropped the ledger and the letters onto the bed, and walked out into the kitchen. Looking out the window at the street below, she felt powerless. She realized that the bulk of her life now seemed pointless. The treachery she had railed against from her teen years on, had not existed, at least where Will was concerned. Will had not betrayed her nor had he abandoned her or their daughter.

She knew now that having been presented with the facts called for forgiveness on her part. But finding a path to forgiveness felt alien to her. She had gnawed on the bare bones of Will's rejection, and later, presumed indifference for so long she couldn't empty her mouth of the taste, however unsavory. She had to wonder just what she had missed while wasting her time on that part of her past. Then she had to wonder how wrong she had been about other parts of it, as well.

And Will, would he have made such a lasting impression on her had they not made a child together? Had her feelings for him represented some enduring love; the man against which she measured others; a first, much too early and, therefore, damaging sexual encounter; a commitment she couldn't renege upon, or an unrequited love, the subject of stalker stories? Did he represent one or all of these, or was he merely a target for blame for all that had proven painful to her over the years? Rather now she saw it as it truly was: This mixture of love and hate that she held for Will was merely an habituation.

Fittingly, then, like an adult thumb-sucker, she needed to sneak off to hide her habit, her little behind-the-door sucking resentment of someone she had last really spoken with over twenty-five years ago. What would she take to bed with her now? How, with what, would she replace that misshapen thumb of anger, that heat behind her eyes, that unwillingness to forgive?

And what manner of bed fellow had her memory been to him all these years?

77   Will and Toot – Over the Atlantic Ocean
Spring 1978

"I'll spare you how sour V became over the years. As far as V's little dirty secret, I'm not even sure it has any bearing on anything. But I will tell you so you can decide if Christina even needs to know. Lord knows Christina doesn't need anything more to digest and deal with right now."

Toot drew herself up in her seat, took a deep breath, and began again to speak. "In the spring of 1936 Monroe was called down to Panama, the Panama Canal, whatever it was called then. I forget. Some guy had been murdered. They knew who had murdered the man. It was just a dispute gone bad. The suspect needed representation. It was an international thing, in a sense. I never really was interested enough to get the details. I think Monroe donated his time. Oh, this all sounds so vague. I probably knew his reasoning, at the time but, not being directly involved, I have forgotten."

"V was fit to be tied. She thought it ridiculous that he would even go there, but he wanted the experience. There was something going on between them right then. I never really knew. But I suspected at the time that their marriage was a little rocky."

"Well, Monroe goes down there, gets in the thick of things doing his job, contracts malaria or some such ailment and became so sick they feared sending him home. All in all, he was there for twelve and one-half months."

"And, like most women then, V was a housewife, lived twenty minutes or so from me, and two hours or more from the rest of our family. Well, somehow she got involved with another man. She was never very forthcoming about any of it;

in fact, she never shared any of it with me at all. I can only guess that he was a married man, but I will never know the whole story. It was a very short involvement, it had to be, but V got pregnant. So, to make a long story short, Dessie took her in, kept her secret (except Mama told me, even though I never let on to V that I knew), and hired a mid-wife who was the most sealed-lipped woman you ever met. That's what Mama said, anyway."

"They lived in Warrenton, then. Amos pastured a little church down there, not that it makes any difference, now that I think about it." She waved her hand, as though dismissing the thought.

"V delivered a beautiful little girl on April 5, 1937. Christina. Dessie and Amos adopted her and, when Christina was three years old, moved to Emmaus so Amos could assume the pastorate there. As you can see, taking in Reecie was not their first experience with this type of thing. They were pretty well-practiced."

"So, by the time Christina got with child, V had become a woman who had repented of her sins and who had changed almost beyond recognition. The life had gone out of her. But because she was Neena's birth mother, she was first pick to take in Christina. And the truth was, sister Dessie saw over all those years the price V paid for her indiscretion. I suspect her heart ached for her. Dessie held back from Christina from the start, thinking, I'm sure, that she had taken from V the one thing nearest and dearest to V's heart, because V and Monroe never had children together. I don't know why. But please don't get me wrong. My sister Dessie loved Christina, but she held back. I think she even held back from Teddy in many ways."

"And Amos was Amos. He loved Christina, but it was two-thirds charm and one-third father-love. And while I was traveling to Emmaus for every holiday and occasion, in large part to see Mama, V kept her distance, feeling, I'm sure, that she had made a bargain and that she was going to keep it. I have always believed that her staying away had little to do with her marriage and the fear that Monroe would learn her secret and more to do with her wanting Christina to have a stable life, uncomplicated by her presence. So the one who formed a bond with Christina, the one whose heart wrapped thoroughly around Christina's, was Mama. Oh, how Mama loved her, and how Christina loved Mama."

"So I really do understand why they didn't choose me. I was a little zany, a little too pampered. Well, who cares now, right? This isn't about me. But, to continue, they chose V to take care of our darling Christina. As it turned out, after Reecie was born, Christina came to Burl to be with Jimmy and me every other weekend, at least. And once Mama came to be with us, Christina saw a lot of her until Mama's death. That was wonderful to be with Mama at the end. Mama's presence had a healing effect on my girl. But losing Mama devastated us all beyond words."

Toot's face softened; she looked near tears.

"Anyway, anyway. V softened after Christina arrived. She loved that girl more than life itself, but she just didn't know how, you know, just didn't know how to relax and show it. She worked her behind off all the time. That's how she said *I love you*. And Monroe believed the sun rose and set on that girl. Ah, how he loved Christina."

"But it felt like Amos and Dessie just pushed Christina away, and then when Reecie came along, they let her take Christina's place. I think that, unlike her reaction to Christina, Dessie let go and really allowed herself to bond with Reecie as she never had with my Christina."

Toot paused, frowning. "Of course, Mama got sick about then. Her health declined from the moment they took Christina away. Mama was never a meddler. But I'm sure she tried to reason with Dessie, tried to convince her not to send Christina away. In the end, though, Mama would acquiesce. I know she would. Mama was sick on and off a couple of years before I took her down to live with me. I hired a nurse. We took good care of her. And she rallied for a while. Then she went downhill again. Right up until the end, we took good care of her."

Toot yawned, covering her mouth with a hand.

"And another thing that Christina doesn't even know. At least I think she doesn't."

Toot paused; looked pensive. "Oh, I hate all these secrets. Secrets are destructive and usually unnecessary. After Christina was gone for about a month, Dessie started wearing baggy dresses and then, and then, she started stuffing her clothes with pillows, small ones at first, then bigger and bigger ones to make it look like her pregnancy was progressing. And she was in her forties at the time! I can't remember just exactly how old she was. Oh, I could figure it out. Let's see, Reecie was born — oh, what difference does it make now? It was ridiculous, any way you look at it. Of course, as off-putting as Dessie was, no one spoke to her about her pregnancy; I can almost guarantee you that one."

Toot drank some soda, ate a couple of pretzels and seemed to settle in so much so that Will thought she might even sleep a little before arriving in Europe. She was an old lady, after all, and would be exhausted when they got there. But she continued.

"So, as I said, I went to talk with them. Twice. Like talking to a wall. I told Dessie, old woman that she seemed, that stuffing pillows into her dresses was such a farce, and as I said, a bold-faced lie! But they continued the façade and then pretended the baby had just popped out when they were conveniently out-of-town. Blue blazes. How stupid do they think people are?"

"Whew," Toot said as she shook her head a little. "I'm wearing myself out talking so much. You must be desperately looking for some tape to shut my yap. I'll try to wrap this thing up. But first, I have to take a potty break."

78 — Neena – Puteaux, France
Spring 1978

Neena reread Will's August 28, 1951, letter:

Dear Neena,

I had my hearing. I wasn't allowed to go home. I'm with some farm family way out in the country on some dirt road.

I would run away and hitchhike into town to find you but my aunt says your gone. I can't believe it. No wonder you don't write. They took you away too. I feel so bad, Neena. I keep imagining what you are going through. Maybe when I'm allowed to start school again Betsy will know where you are.

I hate it here. I don't know what will happen to me maybe this is it. If I run away again I will go back to solitary. I just can't do that again it makes you feel like your going nuts.

I miss you.

Love Will

She put the letter back into the rubber-banded bunch, laid them with the ledger, gathered her things and went down the stairs and outside. She walked for a long time not really thinking anything at all. Then Will's words came back to her. *I hate it here. I don't know what will happen to me.*

She walked back as directly as possible to her apartment, rushed up the stairs, and dug through her desk until she found a note pad. She wanted to write a list of something, anything she could do to atone for being so wrong about another person. She wrote *expiate*, like one word could fix anything. She had never had much use for lists, anyway. She never followed them.

She wanted self-imposed exile to sort things out, to practice new habits before she could go back to those persons and circumstances that triggered her anger episodes. Or so she had thought. Now she knew she had been operating on false assumptions, at least as far as Will was concerned. And Will, oh, poor Will, he had suffered as she had.

She looked again at the pile of letters and the ledger lying there reproachfully on her bed. Settling on her chest, regret was such a heavy thing, its wide buttocks spreading out; its big belly distended from gorged mouthfuls of her version of events, events that had occurred so long ago they should have dimmed in her mind, not taken on a gross and bloated life of their own.

79 Toot and Will – Over the Atlantic Ocean
Spring 1978

"So they bring home this beautiful baby. I was there, of course, with Christina when little Reecie was born. I would not be anywhere else at a time like that. Anyway, anyway. What a doll that Reecie Mae was. Well, her name isn't Reecie Mae; it's Patrice Eleanor, of course. I just call her that. She had Christina's little ears and her long, slender, pianist's fingers. Well, you know. But she had your hair, at least then she did, and now I see that you both have some natural curl. You have a good girl there, Willy Boy," she said smiling, punching him lightly in the arm.

"And Reecie has always been the most laid-back child and adult you could ever imagine. She seemed the opposite of everyone around her. Nothing ruffled her feathers. She was pleasant, but if someone didn't deserve her good nature, she could be cool as a cucumber. Never rude but never too dependent upon what others thought. I like to think she's like me that way. Ha," she said as she laughed, a laugh more like a giggle.

"On the rare occasions they saw each other, Reecie took to Christina like a dog to … what is that expression, anyway? I tell you I'm daft. Oh, I remember, *like a duck to water*."

Toot kind of bent over as she chuckled. "That reminds me of my former maid, Flora. She worked for me for thirty-five years. She used to say, 'Miss Toot, you got you an audio discriminatory problem the way you mix things up when you say them.' Maybe she was right. I miss her coming to my house everyday, since she retired. We were always more friends than employer and employee. I go to lunch with her every once in a while, and she's as spry as ever."

Toot waved her hand again, a little swoosh past her ear, like she was waving a fly away. "Anyway. Anyway. I have always thought Christina studied history as a way of explaining her own somehow, as a way to find, what, maybe a better version of her own history? You know how people with emotional problems, they know, they know something's wrong, so they medicate themselves with drink or pills or worse, or else they study psychology to kind of understand their problems and to treat themselves and, heaven help us, others. It's a little scary when you think of cuckoos treating cuckoos, but it's true."

Toot shook her head. "I'm sorry. I'm sorry. I need a little button right here," she said, pointing to the side of her jaw. "A little retractor button to take back thoughtless comments. Or maybe I could hardwire my brain so there's a three-second delay between what pops into my head and what flows off my tongue. In any event, Miss Pratt would not be proud."

Toot yawned again, wider this time. "Anyway, Reecie takes to Christina, and Dessie discourages it big time. She wants to sit by Christina, and Dessie circumvents her every move. You get the picture."

"I never got to know Reecie until recently because there wasn't the opportunity you might think. But Christina is my special girl. We just have an affinity for each other. I can't even put it into words like I'd like. And my little girl is in trouble, I just feel it. She's had way too much piling up in her heart. And I'm so scared for her," she said as tears welled in her eyes.

Will reached over and took Toot's tiny, birdlike hand into his, and held it, stroking its top with his thumb. "And, Dear

Toot, we are going to do everything we can to watch over your girl, our girl," he said.

After a brief silence, Toot closed her eyes and put her head back against the seat. Before long her head had listed to the side until it rested against Will's upper arm. Even above the hum of the airplane, Will could hear a little steady buzz, the snore of a lady born of Miss Pratt's Social Skills School.

* * * * *

Will raised the blind by his window seat and angled his body so he could look to the east. He could see the sun coming up in the distance as they raced across the sky toward it.

He had switched seats with Toot after one of her many bathroom breaks and was now glad that he had. He liked looking out at the clouds and watching for holes in them, for momentary glimpses of maybe a dimly lit ship if they were over water, or a little hamlet if they were over land. His first view of Ireland had been just like that: A peek through the clouds.

That seemed an appropriate metaphor for his glimpses into Neena's life. He was merely peeking into her life through renditions of it by those who loved her or through his own inferences borne of observations of her now and in the past. But they were still just mere glimpses. He knew that only too well. Still, he wanted to touch her, not so much literally, but at least figuratively. He found himself wanting to dry her tears, laugh when she laughed, and, oddly enough, grab her hand and run, run until air whistled in their ears, until their hair riffled in a breeze and until sweat beaded their backs and foreheads. Running seemed to him a cathartic exercise, a cleansing experience where, at some point, at least, all he felt was the pumping of his arms, the striking of his feet against the path beneath him, and his breath coming in measured intervals until he reached that point, that point when breathing, mere breathing was all he could think about.

Despite his longing to be close to her, to really know her, he had to wonder if he could make the adjustment from knowing her from afar to knowing her again up close.

He felt reluctant, almost guilty, getting to know her again through others. He knew too well from his own experience that few people take the time or have the desire to know you as you really are. No one can know what boogey men nudge you over in your bed at night when sleep won't come, or what monsters come at you in your dreams. Or even what hopes for the future lift you above your sometimes ho-hum existence.

So being the efficient man he was, he made a mental to-do list to carry out his plans and Toot's wishes once his feet hit European soil: Get Toot delivered and settled, and that might be a huge task because he expected her to be totally exhausted when they arrived; then check into his hotel. If Toot's information was correct, that would place him directly across the street from Neena's apartment; linger nearby and watch over Neena, maybe even approach her, report back to Toot; he would have to play it by ear. He still was not comfortable with the idea, but Toot had been persuasive.

He had plenty to do while he sat around. Still working on his legal thriller, he had decided to write in a chapter or two about a small suburb of Paris, a place called Puteaux.

Beyond that he didn't know what to do. He did not want to look like a stalker. He wanted only to be near her, if possible, and to watch over her until he could one day approach her. He owed her that, at least. Perhaps they could be friends.

80 — Will – Puteaux, France
Spring 1978

Will deposited Toot with her husband's niece. They graciously invited him in for coffee, but he declined so he could be on his way. From there, he took a taxi to the metro station. Despite having to tote his luggage, the Métro seemed a quicker way to go this time of day.

He arrived at the Puteaux station on the outskirts of Paris a little before noon. He emerged onto a platform with his luggage, climbed a flight of stairs up to street level but discovered he was across the tracks from where he wanted to be. Dog-tired after the long flight, he wondered if he were making mistakes for lack of sleep. Too exhausted to analyze himself, he turned around, went back down the stairs, walked through an underground passageway, and proceeded up another flight of stairs on the other side, his luggage still in tow.

Walking down the platform he came to Boulevard Richard Wallace, followed it down a little hill until he came to la Rue Lucien Voilin, the street on which his hotel was supposedly located. Within half a block he found the entrance, crossed the marble foyer, went up a flight of stairs, and approached the front desk where a gentleman sat reading a newspaper.

"Bonjour, Monsieur," Will said, hesitantly, hoping the most rudimentary greeting would be understood in his poorly pronounced French.

"Bonjour, Monsieur," the man replied. Then, in Australian-accented English, he added, "Hello. Welcome. May I help you?"

Will was so relieved that the man spoke English that he hesitated in answering for a second.

Then he gave the clerk his reservation confirmation number and asked for a room facing Rue Lucien Voilin, the street on which Toot said Neena lived. He was immediately checked in and on his way up to the third floor. He lugged his bags up the many steps, reminded that in Europe the third floor was not the third floor at all but really the fourth floor. On the landing for his floor, he found three doors marked A, B and C. The brass key ring the clerk had given him marked 313 had three keys attached: One for the street-level door, one, presumably, for one of these doors, and another for his room within the A, B or C hallway. The door opened onto a hallway. He finally found his room at the end of a short hall.

The room was spare. The small bathroom included a shower so close to the commode that he could conceivably shower and do his business all at the same time. Still he was happy with the room. With sparkling tile floors, the room was spotless, the sheets crisp and clean. French doors opened out onto a very small balcony, large enough for a chair and a tiny table.

According to Toot, 36 Rue Lucien Voilin was Neena's apartment address, and it looked to be directly across the street from where he stood. With any luck at all, he was also on a level with her apartment, as well. Toot had certainly done her homework in picking this particular hotel and telling him to ask for a room facing Rue Lucien Voilin.

There appeared to be drawn drapes in the windows of what he assumed was Neena's apartment living room and no curtains at all in what appeared to be her kitchen. He hoped, come sundown, that her lights would be visible. The flat entrance opened out onto the street Will now faced so that he could see her comings and goings if he were diligent enough.

Maybe he could run into her tomorrow, talk with her, and be out of here the next day.

Now, he realized, he needed something to eat and drink. He unpacked some of his necessities and then went down to the street. It was a lovely narrow street, cobble-stoned, and winding down a hill to the main thoroughfare, Rue Jean Jaurès, where vendors bustled about, ostensibly closing for the day.

He found a small restaurant two doors down on his side of the street and took a seat at one of the tables on the sidewalk in front of the establishment. He noticed that all the chairs were oriented toward the street as though they were there for a parade or for the pleasure of people-watching. He asked for the *prix fixe* meal which, today, included: A bowl of soup, a piece of chicken in a lemon sauce, crusty bread, a small glass of house wine, water and an espresso, followed by a wedge of melon and two slices of cheese. Of course, being in AA, he didn't drink the wine.

His meal tasted delicious, and he relished the coffee, so weary he was of those instant versions offered in so many homes in the States. He sat there for at least an hour, huddling a bit in his jacket, warm except for an occasional gust of cool air. When a waiter appeared, asking if he wanted anything else, he readily requested a cappuccino. He knew he needed the caffeine in order to make it to bedtime, having slept less than an hour the night before.

Once his coffee was gone for the second time, he realized he could sit there no longer, so he got up and walked down the hill toward some little shops. He hoped Toot was correct that, at least on her free days, Neena usually went out in the morning to shop, ate lunch out and, after long walks, stayed in from late afternoon on. He knew she was not scheduled to go to Barcelona for two more days, if she went at all.

He went into a shop and bought two bottles of sparkling mineral water. After that he went into a cheese shop and bought some Camembert and some other kind he did not recognize. Then he walked over to a bakery and bought a baguette that the clerk unceremoniously rolled in paper, leaving the end sticking out. He had brought a canvas shopping bag with him that he had bought on a previous trip to Europe. He put his purchases into the bag, walked over to a newsstand where he bought an overpriced, abbreviated American newspaper, then proceeded to another sidewalk café, where he ordered a soda. He sat there and sipped it while he read old news.

He hadn't expected to see her his first day there, but when he looked up, there she was strolling up the hill carrying some sort of bag. Without using a key, she walked into the door leading to her apartment house. He assumed that there must be a foyer from which, perhaps, more than one apartment could be accessed.

Although it was still daylight, the street was in shadow enough so that he could see when she turned on the light in her kitchen.

The light was still on when, at 8:30 p.m., he went to bed and slept like he had not slept for weeks.

He followed the same pattern for two days. He marveled at how consistent she was in her leaving and returning. Mornings she went to the market, selected several items, and then returned to the apartment before continuing on. He followed her at a distance each day, enjoying the mere sight of her, of watching her eat and drink, of watching the movement of her hands as she pushed back her bangs or blotted her mouth with a napkin. She seemed thoughtful and absorbed, so absorbed that she didn't seem to notice anyone around her, including him.

She walked for hours each day, stopping for a lunch much like the one he had had his first day in France. She shopped but bought only bread or cheese, sometimes wine. She often stopped at churches, walking quietly in, sitting as though praying or perhaps resting before she went on. Each day she returned to her apartment between four and five and, to his knowledge, she remained in the apartment until morning.

She couldn't know that just across the street, keeping watch, stood Will, half holy valiant protector, half pathetic peeping tom.

81 — Will – Paris, France
Spring 1978

"Hi, Toot. I hoped I would catch you in. This is Will."

"I recognized you. I'm not dotty, yet. Is Christina all right?"

"She is fine from what I can tell. Has anyone spoken with her?"

"Teddy has. I finally spoke with him last night. He said she is okay but having some real moments, moments when she gets very upset. He's glad we are over here."

"You told him I'm here, too?"

"Yes. Why not?"

"Well, that's why I called. I called to report in and to tell you that Neena seems fine. She follows the same schedule every day. She shops, walks, dines, and spends the evenings in. But I just can't do this anymore. I feel like a creepy peeping tom. If she ever finds out I did this, she will hate me even more than she already does. I have decided to check out in the morning, and go on home. I had planned to talk with her but I suspect that she is working through some things from what you told me on the plane. I don't want to add any more drama to her life right now."

"Oh, please, please, Will, don't leave just yet. I agree you shouldn't approach her just yet, but please don't go home. Just pretend you are a private eye or something and keep an eye on her. Just until she goes to Barcelona. Oh, dear, I hope she doesn't go there. Then I *will* worry."

"Why don't I come on over there, pick you up, and you pay a surprise visit to Neena? Maybe her dear Aunt Toot is exactly what she needs. She wouldn't even have to know that I had been here."

"No, please, no; please stay just a few more days. Please, Will. Somehow I will make this up to you."

What could he say? He had already slunk around, noting what Neena ate, when she slept, practically what she put into her coffee. Why couldn't he say no to the old lady and just scram? When had he gone all soft, anyway?

"I'll stay a couple of more days. But that's it. I'm telling you, that's it." He was surprised at the firmness of his voice when he was usually such a puppy dog with this lady.

Sally Kerr-Kelly

82   Teddy – Emmaus, Virginia
Spring 1978

Teddy sat on the raised platform at the front of the church, his eyes and mind closed to anything that would distract him from the sermon he was about to give. Then he silently prayed as he always did before preaching to his congregation. After his prayer, he opened his eyes, gazing out over the people in their self-assigned seats. His glance rested on old Mr. Webber for a moment, taking in his quiet demeanor, his studied grace, his white hair. He seemed like an older version of Will. He missed Will; wondered how things were going for him over there in France. Toot had surely dragged poor Will into a mess. But Teddy was glad his friend was there, watching over his aunt and sister.

Teddy wondered, as well, if Will had seen himself in Teddy's sermons of late. He hoped not, but, on the other hand, he hoped all the people saw themselves in these sermons, and wished that the subject matter would touch their hearts as Will's letters had touched his.

He rose, offering the Scripture reading and continuing into his message:

> Our scripture reading is taken from the King James version of the Holy Bible. We'll start the reading with Verse 8, Genesis, Chapter 6:
>> 'Noah found grace in the eyes of the Lord. Noah was a just man and perfect . . ., and Noah walked with God . . .. And God said unto Noah . . ., the earth is filled with violence through them . . .(the unrighteous people) . . ., and, behold, I will destroy them with the

earth. Make thee an ark of gopher wood . . ., and of every living thing of all flesh, two of every sort shalt thou bring into the ark, to keep them alive with thee; they shall be male and female. You are to bring into the ark two of every living creature . . . . As God commanded him, so did he . . .. And God blessed Noah.'

And from The Book of Job, Chapter 1, Verse 1: 'There was a man in the land of Uz, whose name was Job; and that man was perfect and upright, and one that feared God, and eschewed evil . . ..'

But after receiving news of loss after loss, Job speaks, again in Verse 10 : 'My soul is weary of my life; I will leave my complaint upon myself; I will speak in the bitterness of my soul.'

Joseph, a young man of seventeen, was tending the flocks with his brothers.

These are three men who, in the course of their lives, faced adversity. We are well versed in their stories. Noah survives the flood and is blessed. The Lord made Job prosperous again and gave him twice as much as he had before. And Joseph survives the slavery to which his brothers sold him and becomes the ruler of all Egypt. Yet, what do these stories have to do with us today?

Yesterday, I read in the newspaper, 'Note for the day: Why didn't Noah swat those two mosquitoes?'

You might find that comical; I know I do. But the answer, of course, is that Noah was doing God's will. He had a direct dictate from God. He was gathering into the ark, two by two, the different species God told him to collect.

Yet, we have all been at the mercy of mosquitoes, their buzzing little bodies attacking us at picnics, on *hikes, or in the early hours of a morning. They are difficult to catch, to eliminate, those pestering little annoyances that complicate our lives. Sometimes it's the pea under the mattress or the pebble in the shoe or the sliver in the finger that gets us most, not the tumbling boulder or the falling tree. Those niggling little things that, when not dealt with over time, grow, take on a life of their own as they say, and then become big, overgrown obstructions to happiness and health.*

Some of us, unfortunately, have borne, are bearing, or must soon endure, adversity in our lives. For Job it was fire from the sky, locusts, and grief. Joseph had to endure the betrayal of jealous brothers. For Noah it was rain and rising floodwaters. Yet, unlike Noah, we do not always have a clear dictate from God on how to deal with our problems, and do not always have the promise of clear skies ahead in this life . . . .

Teddy droned on, finishing his sermon and feeling that he and it had fallen short of his and his congregation's expectations. He sat down after the benediction while the choir sang the closing canticle.

He was hung up on how to help Neena and couldn't get her out of his mind. Sure, Noah had a clear dictate from God. That seemed easier to Teddy than the dilemma his father, Amos, had faced. Teddy could not judge Amos but could not identify with him either; which made him think of Will and Neena. How could they have known how far-reaching their actions would prove to be? Their actions had not only affected them, but their extended families to some extent, their child, their marriages, and maybe even Neena's health. Nor had his father, Teddy was sure, foreseen the consequences of his actions, of his decision.

Thinking of his father, long deceased, and his mother who no longer even knew him, made him think of when he and Neena were kids, about their last innocent years, at least. It would have been just before Will came to their home.

The war had ended several years before but remained the topic of most male conversation. His Uncle Louie had returned from France or Germany or both. Teddy could never really remember which places he had been. He recalled some of the conversation down on the street corner on Friday nights when local men congregated to chat and, for a time, listen to Uncle Louie.

Louie had been a Screaming Eagle, a paratrooper with the 101st Airborne Division of the Army, dropped behind German lines in eastern France. Injured, he eluded capture when a French farm family took him in, cared for him, and hid him until he could be moved. He escaped and was shipped to England where he met and, at the end of the war, married a nurse who cared for him in a hospital there.

Uncle Louie's life depended, it seemed, not only on God's will but on the decisions others made or, perhaps, did not make: The French family could have turned him away; or someone in authority could have decided to keep him in France where he would not have met his wife. The possibilities were endless. So many lives, it seemed to Teddy at that moment, are shaped by decisions made by others, decisions that trickle down, sometimes through generations.

As a youngster, Teddy remembered parishioners coming to his father's office, talking for what seemed like hours, and then leaving with red, swollen eyes. As a pastor himself, he had heard the sad stories that evolved from one bad decision.

But when his sister needed his pastoral advice the most, he had none, really, to give. What kind of a pastor was he, anyway?

People forgot somehow that ministers were mere men; they had the same needs as others, farted in their sleep, ate too much, zipped their lips too little at times; mere mortals who needed God's advice on how to give good advice. And sometimes God seemed so silent.

He realized that the organ music had stopped, so he rose and went down the aisle to greet his people. Now *that* he could do.

83 — Will and Toot – Puteaux and Paris, France
Spring 1978

"Toot, so glad I caught you in. Will again. Teddy called; actually he called me in the middle of the night. I wasn't real sure what I was saying at first. But I wanted to fill you in."

"Why's he calling you in the middle of the night? Is he okay?"

"He miscalculated the difference in time from there to here, or just forgot there was a time difference. Not to worry. He just wanted to fill me in on Neena's plans. Teddy called her after he talked with me and just now left me a message with her travel arrangements."

"Travel? Is she going home? I thought she had another eight or nine weeks."

"She does. She has what's left of her three weeks' break and, after that, six more weeks of study. That gets her home in May. She had made plans to go to Barcelona sightseeing.

Teddy thought she might postpone the trip, but says that she has decided to go, after all. She leaves in two days."

"Oh, Will. Please, you must go. I'm just not able to go that quickly so I am relying on you to go. I spoke with Teddy yesterday and he is very worried about her. He said she keeps crying. I just want her to go home."

"Why don't you go to see her? I offered to take you."

"I really don't want her to know I'm here just yet. I will have to contact her before long because I have been here for days, and she will start to wonder why she hasn't heard from me. I didn't communicate that often but I had written a couple of times. She knows I would avoid making overseas calls, so she wouldn't expect that. I've been under-the-weather and didn't want to burden anyone with it. I'm just not able to go see her just yet. Can I count on you? Will you go?"

"Toot, I have to admit to you that I have stopped following Neena after the second day. I don't feel comfortable with it. I make sure I'm here when she leaves in the morning and when she returns in the afternoon. That way I know she is safely home each evening. But I can't keep following her. She deserves her own space. I am here in case either of you need me. I am just working on my novel, enjoying good food, walking, and that's all. What would you want me to do in Barcelona? I don't want to follow her."

"No, dear boy. What you are willing to do is fine. But please go there, just stay nearby, and make sure she gets in at night. Please, Will."

Will knew he was caving in, but he agreed to go. "Okay, I'll call Teddy to see if he can book me a room at her hostal there and get her travel arrangements. This is getting ridiculous; my spying on her. I must talk with her soon. I just don't know how she will react if she finds out I have been hanging around, following her. Maybe I can give her some time to settle in, and then I will just happen to *bump into* her and see how that goes."

"Sounds good. I was going home next week, but I really haven't felt well, and Nell wants me to stay on, so I might as well. Besides, you might need me. My wonderful neighbor is more than happy to keep an eye on my house, so I needn't worry. I want to see my Christina when she gets back from Barcelona."

"Well, good, Toot. I still don't have any pressing reason to go back to Emmaus, although I might go on home from Barcelona. Neena is scheduled to stay in Barcelona for four or five days so she, at least, will be returning here, for sure, within the next week. If she extends her stay, either Teddy or I will let you know."

"Great, Will. That sounds great."

"Okay. You have a good visit, and I'll talk with you soon. Bye for now."

"Goodbye, Dear Boy."

84

Neena – Barcelona, Spain
Spring 1978

In a pensione in the old city, Old Barcelona, Neena lay in the firm narrow bed, the crispy clean sheet and rough woolen blanket pulled up under her chin.

She had been awake for a while, how long she had no idea. There was no more sleeping, or even dozing, once the eight o'clock bells across the street at the old Sant Jaume church began to chime. She heard a *clop, clack, clop, clack* in the street. Getting out of bed and opening the shutters she expected to see a horse but saw instead two high-heeled women on their way to early Mass, their shoes slapping the cobblestones and the sound they made echoing off the old buildings on either side of the street.

Considering her Baptist background, she found it novel that Roman Catholic priests referred to their sermons as homilies. *Treat others the way you want to be treated. Give and you shall receive. Waste not, want not.* Good idea, so simple, so easy to understand, really.

Oh, the need to really understand. And yet, and yet . . . .

This pensione room, with its carved wood trim and the sun coming in on a slant reminded her of her childhood room, later Reecie's, she assumed. Neena's had albums on the bookshelf beside her Independence Hall money bank, a copy of Llewellyn's *How Green Was My Valley*, and the pompous little leather bound volume of *Julius Caesar* that she had always treasured. She had never understood William Shakespeare until she was much older, but she had pored through it anyway. And shoved up against the outer wall sat her single bed with a chenille spread that left a telltale pattern on her face when she fell asleep on top of it. But it was possible, of course, that her room had not been that way at all. It had been so long ago; now it seemed even longer. She could still bring forth images of her third grade sleepover friends, Carolyn and Judy, young faces that moved in and out of focus. And one of her well-loved third grade teacher. But, after thinking of them awhile, they faded like the picture on the televisions of the fifties when turned off. The full screen shrunk until it was just a lingering dot in the middle of a frame.

Walking back to the window, she looked down on the moving scene. The people who had been there just moments ago had now been replaced by others. How quickly one may move from one spot to another. How quickly we pass through this life. How quickly our memories, visual or otherwise, fade or become distorted. Still portraits of her parents posing for the camera and for the church directory flashed momentarily through her mind; unreadable, ascetic faces, theirs. And then Neena pulled up an image, a moment in time, the first of a montage, really, from a jerking eight-millimeter tape of her parents' wedding anniversary. Which anniversary had it been, twenty? They smile hugely yet silently as her mother says something funny to her father, as their amused relatives and church people surround them. And then a quick glimpse of herself at – what, thirteen – standing next to Teddy, the two of them laughing, their teeth sparkling in the sunlight? Had it really been that way, happy? Could one wrong choice, two, perhaps, yield a lifetime of impact? What had happened to her had happened to them all, she now realized.

Then, continuing the montage, snippets of her husband in his tuxedo and big bowtie, earnestly looking into her eyes, pledging undying love; or of his slender hips and broad shoulders outlined in the moonlight as he runs away from her, whooping as the waves move up his legs; or the tears in his eyes and those seeping from her soul when her grandmother died; or his rigid back turned to her as he walks through their doorway, his arms resolutely at his sides; hers too weary to reach for him one last time.

In the blink of an eye or a turn of the head, scenes fade or brighten unpredictably. He stops, having cleared the doorway; his curly head begins a turn. His nose comes into profile. But when he faces her full on, it's not his face at all, but Will's. Will, oh Will, looking at her with doleful eyes.

The old pain – or new, who could tell, who could tell - and despair come up into her mouth. Words form behind her lips wanting to force their way out, spewing forth in the old angry way, or irritatingly, staccato-like, as the drip of a faucet, or the tapping of fingers. But they dribble out, down her chin and onto the floor, like drool. Yet holding them in was like those hot fireballs that you roll around in your mouth. That's what censure tasted like – hot and rock-hard – rolling around in your mouth, never landing for any length of time in any one place, then ultimately nestling into your cheek now numb, and sucking on it, sucking on it until it diminishes in size and intensity. When it becomes bead-like, a manageable size, you either swallow it whole or crunch it up into a fine powder with no shards to scratch your throat on its way down.

Circles. Choices. Raging against Life or accepting it. She felt weighted down, as though a large hand kept pushing her under the surface so that breathing proved impossible.

Then, a flash of vision, clarity of thought, not so sage but elemental came to her. For that moment, at least, she understood that her parents were probably no different than she, after all. Going along paths parallel to hers, in many ways, separated by time and place, making choices that irrevocably affect the choices of others. We travel through life in a maze, after all, not on a straight, through street.

"Don't look back. Don't look back," a voice in her head stage-whispered, dramatically. "Don't sift through the dust of years for something lost too long ago. Limp on, trudge on, until you find your stride."

She lay back down. Tears trickled down into her ears. Alone. Alone, after all. We all are, you see. Oh, God is there of course, allowing us the free will to make our silly mistakes. But who, what other human being, can know another's heart at any moment, the extent of another's despair, another's longing? One can never fully know the heart of another. We can only speculate; merely speculate. Oh, but we are all so good at speculating.

She looked up at the intricate crown molding that edged the top of the walls. It reminded her that there is beauty everywhere, even in the drabbest of rooms.

And there had been beauty, even love, in her life. So what was love, after all, a word on a candy heart or a birthday card or in a touching song? Just a word, downright banal at times, overused, underused, addressed to lovers and desserts alike. Was love sending your daughter away to save her from the repercussions of a grievous mistake? Or was that love at all? Perhaps love was simpler, even, than that: A hand gently laid on a forearm; a tender stroke to a feverish brow; a patient attention to the voiced thoughts of another; or a lingering hug when you suspect that your arms, and your arms alone, at that moment keep the other on his feet.

How random are the beginnings of love - a mere moment in time. And sometimes to love is to continue for a time, at least, after the loved one has lost all taste for it.

How sad, how sad it is to lose love. How sad yet to never know it; but sadder still to never learn to give love even when you don't feel like it.

* * * * *

Exiting the pensione, Neena crossed Carrer Ferran and approached Sant Jaume, the church whose bells had wakened her that morning. Located in the Quarter Gotic of Barcelona, this Roman Catholic church, with spots of crumbling façade, had begun to show its age. In its slightly deteriorating state, it seemed humble and might go unnoticed, sandwiched as it was between two buildings built long after the aging church. But she found its imperfection and old-world charm to be just the things that attracted her to the structure.

Walking into the narthex, a nondescript area with wooden swinging entrance and exit doors, she chose the door to the left and entered the nave. Of cruciform construction, the interior of the church awed her with its high ceilings and its nave stretching before her and beyond the altar in the apse where the Christ hung high on the forward wall. The many lighted candles in crimson glass holders seemed to warm the sanctuary, bathing it in a flickering ruby glow.

She advanced up the aisle of the church and slipped into a pew. Sitting, she bowed her head and prayed for those she loved. She prayed as well for understanding and clarity of thought. As usual, she prayed – absurdly, she thought – that she be forgiven for being unforgiving.

She sat there a bit, listening to the creaking of the old structure, to the spitting of the many candles, and waited for a still, quiet voice of reason. Just then one of the entrance doors slammed against the back wall, and a group of tourists entered, one girl advancing forward into the nave. The girl stopped, took a series of pictures, and then retreated to rejoin the others who, speaking English, kept urging her to *hurry up*.

The girl slammed the door again as she exited the church.

When the sanctuary quieted again, Neena stood and moved forward into the chancel and facing the apse, all the while peering up at the beautiful, vaulted ceiling. Finally, she lowered her eyes to the Christ standing high above her, the quintessential Shepherd though crowned and regal. He appeared to be watching over his flock yet seemed somewhat detached or even distracted.

Moving counter-clockwise in the chancel, and entering the transept, Neena faced, first, the statue of the Conception, then, Sant Miguel outstretching his hand to the world, and then on to Santa Aguela who stood demurely with a garland of flowers on her head. As Neena reentered the nave, she stopped at the base of the statue of another Christ, a more protestant one in his rope-sashed peasant gown, a gown that seemed to drape him in humility. His feet were bare. A heart had been drawn over his own. Neena studied the statue at length and saw that His eyes were averted so that no matter where she stood she couldn't quite look into them.

As she continued moving along the outer wall, she saw the Lord depicted again in purple with a crown of thorns, and again standing with His mother who, inexplicably, held a golden scepter.

Farther along the wall toward the church entrance doors and behind iron bars, stood Sant Nicolau de Bari. At his feet was a tub full of little children. He looked down at them benevolently as though protecting them while they bathed. Wax hearts, hollow legs severed at the upper thigh, hands and torsos and little houses were tied to the gate surrounding Sant Nicolau, as though he had the power to bless, or perhaps even restore, the most personal of things.

And then Neena stopped before another statue, that of the slain Christ whose blood-stained body lay draped across his mother's legs. Except for the dried rivulets of blood still evident on his face, the agony he had suffered had softened in death. His mother looked down into his face, a look of love and pain seared into her dry eyes. Despite what she had seen, she remained the most regal of mothers in her gold embroidered gown, her crown-of-all-crowns, and her beatified demeanor.

Neena stood there a long time just peering into Mary's eyes. They seemed to look through Neena as though the Virgin Mother were in shock; had remained so for centuries.

Finally, Neena swiveled a quarter-turn and then a half-turn, looking back at the statues she had just viewed. They were on pedestals, of course, each of them had been there for hundreds of years.

Funny, but she had always thought of her parents that way – up high on their pedestals, above others, superior, at least morally, to those at their feet. Her father had always said that he was held to a higher standard; that he answered, not to man, but to God. As an adult Neena understood and agreed with what he had always said, at least to some extent. She believed that with each role we accept, whether Girl Scout, president of the church youth group, parent, teacher, minister, politician – oh, especially a politician! – we consent to be held to a higher standard if only because we have more people to whom we must answer! But how could she reconcile that belief with what they had done to her, their child, their only daughter? Perhaps that was what angered her the most, what *stuck in her craw*, as V used to say. Like royals of old, they laid down to their subject an edict, allowing her no say in her own fate. "Off you go," they pronounced. "Off you go." And so off she went, never, really, to return. At the heights from which they ruled, they had not deemed it necessary to even explain their decision, why they had arrived at it, or, heaven forbid, to deviate from it.

Her role had simply been that of the prelate's novice. She must bow, remain mute and, then at some point utter softly, "Yes, Your Grace. Whatever you say, Your Grace. I will accept without resentment, puzzlement, or question, Your Most Holy Grace."

She turned and walked back toward the transept, to Santa Aguela. She looked up into a face so fresh, so young, and so purely innocent. Had she, Neena, ever been that innocent? She could not remember.

She decided to leave the church.

Neena turned again, toward the back of the church and the exit. As she walked, she paused again before Mary holding her murdered son. The woman's eyes held her. Neena felt she was witnessing a private pain, one that no one should observe in another. Her impotence apparent, Mary had had to sit by while her son suffered unimaginable torture. Yet her sacrifice had, after all, been preordained. She had, perhaps quietly, even passively, relinquished her right to him but never her heart. And now Mary could hold her son, could once again cradle him in her arms, long after he had commended his spirit to his Father and had given up the Ghost in the company of thieves.

Unlike Mary's dry eyes, tears welled up in Neena's. Through her tears she looked again deeply into Mary's eyes. She realized with an imperceptible intake of breath that those eyes were Aunt V's eyes. And she saw with uncanny clarity that the impassivity Neena had seen time after time in Aunt V's eyes had, in fact, been pain, deep pain, old pain. What, oh what, had broken V's heart?

Then she knew; knew as surely as if someone had shouted the truth into her ear; she knew the source of V's pain. How could she not have seen it long before this? The realization struck her like a blow to the gut, and she began to crumple, found a seat in a nearby pew, lowered her head and, for the first time since V's death, Neena mourned her passing. She cried softly at first, and then harder. And, as with grief, she could not tell how much she cried for her aunt and how much she cried for herself. With her eyes closed Neena could clearly see V bustling about, readying one thing or another for one person or another. V was like Martha of the New Testament who served, served, served, some might say joylessly, but Neena now saw that her servitude to Neena and Uncle Mo had been single-minded love. She prayed for forgiveness for that immature assessment of V.

And then, for the first time since becoming an adult, she prayed for forgiveness for the past, for her mindful, wrong decisions, for her choices, for her bitterness and unwillingness to first understand and then forgive. The stark realization of her contribution to the mess that was her past stopped the flow of tears and left her dumb, almost mindless.

She rummaged through her purse until she found a tissue and, loudly it seemed in the quiet sanctuary, blew her nose. Her weeping had subsided to a child's dry heaves, the aftermath of heavy sobbing.

A hand gently touched her shoulder. She turned, startled.

A priest who appeared to be in his sixties looked down at her; his face lined, his eyes kindly.

"Buenos días, hija."

"Buenos días, Padre. No hablo español. Je parle français et anglais."

He smiled at her and in English, said, "I speak French and English, as well. In fact, I learned much of the American vernacular as a student while attending Princeton. I prefer to be called Padre René. I'm a priest here."

He motioned for her to slide over in the pew and, when she did, slid in beside her, turning his slim body slightly so he could look at her as he spoke. "I must admit I have been watching you for a few minutes. I had started to enter the apse and saw you studying the statues. You seemed so moved by the Virgin Mother and Son that I did not want to interrupt."

He turned his body farther until he was almost perpendicular with the pew and so he could better face her. Adjusting his long robe, he said, "I had turned back to reenter my office when I heard you weeping. You seem deeply troubled, and I hope I can be of some help."

85 Will – Barcelona, Spain
Hostal Fernando - Spring 1978

Still sitting on his little balcony, Will had read and reread the same page so many times he could recite it from memory. Distracted by the street pedestrian traffic, he gave up reading and continued to watch for Neena to emerge from the church across the street.

Lowering his feet from the railing, he went into his room, retrieved a banana bought from a street vendor, and went back out onto the balcony. He had just repositioned himself on the little chair and was peeling back the banana when Neena hied out the church and rushed across the street like she was being chased. He stood and leaned over the railing. She seemed to have disappeared, so he assumed she had entered the hotel.

Leaving the balcony, he walked to the door, opened it a crack so that he could peek out into the hall. Someone came bounding up the stairs, slammed through the outer hall door, and rushed down the hall past his room. He saw that it was Neena. She entered her room and let the door shut behind her.

Surely she hadn't found out he was here, in Barcelona, in the same hotel. She wouldn't like that; wouldn't like that at all.

86   Neena – Barcelona, Spain
Spring 1978

   Neena rushed across Carrer Ferran, looking both ways out of habit even though the street had been closed to all but pedestrian traffic. She slammed through the hostal door, hurried to the desk and asked for her room key. The clerk handed her the key, and she raced for the stairs, taking the marble steps two at a time.

   Upon entering her room, she took her suitcase from the armoire, threw it on the bed, unzipped the main compartment, and then pulled on the zipper of the small pouch on the lid of her suitcase. She pulled out the crumpled manila envelope and withdrew the sheets from it.

   She handled the sheets of old yellowed paper as though they were fragile and might shatter. She ran her fingers over the raised seal on the first sheet slowly, round and round as one ciphering and re-ciphering a line of Braille. It read:

CERTIFICATE OF BIRTH
COMMONWEALTH OF VIRGINIA

Date of Birth: *April 5, 1937*   **File No.** *0449238-1937*
County of Birth: *Adams*   **Date filed:** *April 10, 1937*
Date issued: *April 15, 1937*
Name: *Christina Mercer Phillips*
Sex: *Female*
Father: *No name given*
Mother: *Verina Lowry Phillips*

<u>**/s/ Cassius S. Kerr**</u>   <u>**/s/ Howard L. Knapp**</u>   **SEAL**
State Registrar   **Secretary of Health**

So her name had been Christina Mercer Phillips. She had been right; *right as rain*, as Toot liked to say.

She picked up the second document. It read:

COMMONWEALTH OF VIRGINIA
ADAMS COUNTY
CLERK OF COURTS

IN RE: ADOPTION OF CHRISTINA MERCER PHILLIPS

On this, the 27th day of June, in the year of our Lord, one thousand nine hundred and thirty-seven (1937), I hereby declare that Christina Mercer Phillips, who from this day forward shall be legally known as Christina Mercer Teeple, is now the legal daughter of Amos Teeple and Dessie Teeple, his wife, with all rights thereto.

/s/*William S. Jones*   Witness: /s/*Lance T. Kelly*
Senior Judge   **Clerk of Courts   SEAL**

Neena returned the documents to the envelope and put them into her suitcase compartment. She wished Toot were here right now. Toot *had* to know all about this; must have known about this! She would pick Toot's brain. She would nail her down until, once and for all, she had the answers she deserved.

Four Days Later

Neena exited Hostal Fernando and, once again, crossed Carrer Ferran as the bells of Sant Jaume Church began tolling in earnest. She planned to attend Mass, a relatively new experience for her.

As she pushed through the wooden swinging doors leading from the narthex into the nave, the smell of incense and burning candles again accosted her nostrils. Her eyes slowly adjusted to the low light. As she advanced forward in the center aisle, a young nun approached her, nodded her head silently, and extended what looked like a church bulletin with a typed sheet folded inside. In heavily accented English the young woman said, "This is from Padre René. Buenos días."

Then the nun nodded her head once again and turned to walk back into the alcove from which she had emerged. Neena smiled at the nun, accepted the papers, thanked her in halting Spanish, and then continued forward until she found a seat in one of the pews. She noticed others who had entered the church genuflected and made the sign of the cross before they seated themselves. But she merely bowed her head and slid into a pew. Settling back into the wooden seat, she opened the bulletin that was written in Spanish. Looking at the typed sheet of paper folded inside, she realized that Padre René had translated into English the format of the Mass, most of the readings, and the sermon or homily text.

He had attached a note, as well:

Christina,

    We are so happy that you are attending Mass this morning. I was able to practice my English in preparing this for you. God Bless You.

As a postscript he had added:

    Would you consider dinner with me this evening? There is an old town restaurant to which I would enjoy taking you. We can continue our talks, if you like, but perhaps you would merely enjoy my company as I would yours over a traditional Catalonian dinner. I will call at your hotel at 9:30 p.m. If you are unable to accompany me, please leave a note with the desk clerk. I suspect you did not anticipate an invitation from me, but I shall look forward to dining with you this evening if you so wish.

Your friend, Padre René.

Somewhat taken aback by the invitation, she smiled. He had been so kind to her. She had talked at length with him and, because he was an outsider, someone who had never known her parents, he had helped her gain a fresh perspective. Then she pulled down the kneeling rail, went to her knees, and began to silently pray. After a few minutes a pipe organ rumbled to life, and she rose and slid back into her seat. She recognized the introit selection as Bach's *Ode to Joy,* one of her favorites. She closed her eyes and felt the music.

When the organist segued into another, less familiar Bach number, she began reading the translated selections on the type-written sheet but quickly skipped ahead to the homily. The subject of the sermon and the choice of words seemed very Henri Nouwen-ish to her in its attempt to bring the reader (or listener) to the outstretched arms of God. Much like Father Nouwen, whom she had heard speak on two occasions, Padre René spoke of a universal brokenness of God's people, and of a universal longing for love, acceptance, unity, forgiveness and communion. Contemplative and earnest, Padre René's words strongly admonished his flock to move into the warm embrace of the Father. The sermon was sweet, touching and, while not necessarily tailored to her style of worship, nevertheless spoke to her heavy heart.

Abruptly, the organ music ceased, and there was a moment of silence where only the shuffling of feet and the occasional cough disturbed the stillness.

A priest – not Padre René – moved to the podium in the center of the apse and began reading. The people responded. Neena tried to follow the English translation of the readings but closed her eyes instead and listened. Her father had not believed in the Roman Catholic-style liturgy, the formal repetition of printed or memorized words. He had, in fact, preached against its use in his church, saying that, after a period of time, people no longer knew what they were saying, no longer understood the significance of the words. That was possibly true. But she found the liturgy comforting as she allowed the words to permeate her understanding.

Again there was a pause until she heard heavenly singing coming from the apse. She saw then that habit-clad nuns sat forward in the apse, six on a side. They sang in childlike voices, as if from much farther away, the melody floating back over the congregation and into the recesses of the church like a veiled blessing. The grouping on one side sang and then paused while the other side echoed a response; an antiphon. They paused in between verses almost as if they had no plans to continue, but then they resumed again. During one pause, a lyric soprano lifted her voice, sounding angelic as her strains wafted back toward Neena. And then the pattern began again.

Finally, and too soon in Neena's opinion, the singing ceased. Then the priest who had first spoken moved about on the platform, continuing the Mass.

Neena smiled at herself as she looked around the beautiful building. She had come a far distance to once again settle into her midway point, but she sat there anyway, halfway back, halfway forward, neither the backslider of the back pews nor the ultra-faithful of the front. "Good old Nines," as Teddy would say, "sitting smack-dab in the middle of the church, as usual."

She was surprised at that moment to find that she missed those practitioners of love in Teddy's church, once her father's church. The love of the faithful, some of whom she, as a youngster, at least, had summarily dismissed in overlooking their simple faith and the practice of it. She thought of Florence, the quiet, peaceful, now elderly, prayerful woman who came to church early and sat meditatively until the others started filing in. Or Beatrice with her loud entrances and lively affirmations of the preacher's words, who was first to hug her when, now an adult, Neena returned to the Emmaus church to hear one of Teddy's sermons. She missed, as well, her Aunt V, who had loved her in the way she knew. Who are we to tell others how to love? And Teddy himself, his sweet edification, his peaceful, playful, faithful devotion to his congregation, was and had been a positive constant in her life, in the lives of many others. And Christina Teeple Shaw, the resenter, the passive-aggressive fourteen-year-old in the forty-year-old body, how did others see her?

Neena sat while other worshipers filed up to receive the Eucharist, while they returned to their seats, even while they completed their final recitations, and long after they had exited the door. Still she sat.

She knew she was grieving; in fact, had been mired in her grief, but she kept having these nostalgic moments that her fellow-professors would call a classic, seventh-stage Erikson mid-life crisis. She had been thinking lately, back beyond V and her time there, beyond Will, back to when her family consisted of only her parents, Teddy, and her.

She thought often about Betsy, remembering their woven stick hideaway, constructed in the way of the Erie Indians they had read about in fourth grade. It had been their secret. Teddy didn't even know about it. They had tried to mud-chink it with genuine Virginia red clay, but the mud fell off the first time it rained. They had worked so hard, devoting every extra minute they had to their structure. Now she realized that the pleasure and satisfaction they had derived from their project was not from having a hideout at all but from constructing it together. Wasn't this the way friendship and marriage were supposed to work?

She missed those days when children played outside without real supervision until their mothers called them in for bath and bed. The only real threat they had had in their neighborhood was Peeping Pete, and Uncle Jimmy had broken the old peeping reprobate of his nasty habit when he caught him looking into the parsonage dining room window. Grandma had thought maybe old Pete was just lonely. But Teddy said that Jimmy wasn't confused about what old Pete was up to. He said that Jimmy lifted Pete right off his feet by the front of his shirt and told him to never set foot on that block again. He never did as far as anyone knew.

She remembered her mother and grandmother chatting with neighbor ladies while hanging out the Monday wash. In those days, back yards of whole streets sported white sheets flapping in a breeze, taking on a fresh outdoor scent that had never yet been duplicated by any laundry rinse.

She remembered Tuesdays, when her mother and grandmother faithfully listened to Arthur Godfrey on the radio as they ironed. And, Aunt V; Aunt V had followed the same regimen.

She could still see her grandmother, her mother, and later V, wandering across the yard, choosey in picking dandelion greens for dinner on any given summer evening. Grandma had always said, "I'll wilt the greens; Dessie, you cut up some eggs." Those greens were eaten at dinners where the whole family shared accounts of their days.

She could still see families walking to church on Sundays, fresh from their Saturday night baths, decked out in their best clothes. She remembered Sundays in her parents' home: Roast beef dinners, long afternoon naps, funny papers, and lively games of Sorry. She had always assumed her sheltered life had been representative of the times. Perhaps not. Possibly so.

She sighed. Ah, yes, they had been so innocent back then.

The quietness of the empty sanctuary brought her back from her reverie. She had been moved by the service, had felt God's presence, but wished for some epiphany, some lifting of her burden, miraculous, as she had seen in movies or read about in books. Maybe awareness was all she would receive. Even now, having fought disease, marriage failure, abandonment and betrayal, she was tired. It was time to surrender.

87 — Will – Barcelona, Spain
Hostal Fernando - Spring 1978

As he picked up his key, climbed the stairs, walked down the hall, entered his room, and opened the doors out onto his balcony, Will struggled with how he would approach Neena. He wasn't sure what to say or how to say that he had been stalking her for days and in two cities, to boot. He felt guilty and dishonest in spying on her. He also wondered if she might need more time to work things out for herself. Teddy had called last night and told Will that she had been meeting with a priest from the church across the street who had been counseling her. That was good.

Will had been listening for her this morning. In fact, he had just returned from fetching an early morning cup of coffee when he heard her leave her room. Watching from his balcony, he saw her enter the church just as the morning Mass bells tolled. He went across, as well, entered the church, and sat at the back, well behind her. She seemed to be praying and then reading something.

He felt comfortable in the church, having been raised in a church less ornate, perhaps, but similar in most other ways. The mass, given in Latin, was familiar. He was able to follow the service in much the same way he did back home. He enjoyed the music and the formality of the service. He was able to comprehend the Spanish portions of the service by using a mixture of his poorly spoken Spanish and his ability to read the language. The familiarity of the liturgy, a repertoire of words and ideals, touched him as they had in his youth, when repeating the same phrases over and over lent him deeper meaning and eventual understanding of what God wanted for his beloved people. The words, even though repeated so often over the years, still brought comfort to his heart and soul, as though God could not tell him often enough how much He loved him.

When people went forward for communion, he stayed in his seat. As they finished the service, he slipped out and across to his room so that he could see Neena emerge from the church.

He sat for a long time on a chair just inside his slightly ajar balcony door watching for her. When she didn't come out, he wondered if he had somehow missed her. Just when he was about to go back over and check on her, she emerged onto the street, walked down to the corner pastry shop, came back out onto the sidewalk holding a bag and a cup, and walked back toward the hostal. Within minutes he heard her enter her room and close the door.

He read all afternoon, working on background for his book, and listening for her to reenter the hall. Hungry beyond belief, he went down to a little café on Carrer Ferran and within sight of the hostal, sat in the window, and ordered an early dinner. Still she didn't emerge from the hostal. It grew dark, the street lights came on, and the shops reopened. He roamed the street, pausing to look into shop windows and entering some shops as long as he had a view of the hostal door. As the restaurants began reopening for dinner at nine o'clock, he entered another café and ordered another coffee and dessert. At 9:30 p.m. a man dressed in street clothes exited the church and walked across the street to enter the hostal. Shortly thereafter, Neena exited the hostal, accompanied by the man. Will wondered if the man was the priest who had counseled Neena. The couple walked up the street toward the main thoroughfare and turned right. By the time Will paid for his meal and walked to the alley they had taken, they were no longer in sight.

He didn't know what to do, so he walked across to Plaza Real, and then up La Rambla and back. He walked for an hour. Then he continued walking in the narrow side streets, enjoying the temperate night air. At eleven p.m. he decided to go back to his room. He bundled up in a blanket, then waited on his balcony for her return.

88   Neena – Barcelona, Spain
Spring 1978

Neena and Padre René left the hotel turning right onto Carrer Ferran and then right again onto Carrer Quintana, a narrow, cobblestoned alley, dimly lit at this time of the evening. Within half a block, René directed her into a restaurant. "This is Can Culleretes," he said. "It is the second-oldest restaurant in all of España."

The restaurant was cozy but noisy, the patrons laughing and talking. The ceiling was wood-beamed, and the walls were lined with pictures of past patrons. They were seated almost immediately in a little alcove situated a bit above the main floor so they looked down on other diners.

"They serve Catalan food here, a hearty regional cuisine. They have a delicious duck with prunes, but that may be an acquired taste," he said, with a smile. "I usually drink the house table wine which is mellow and very delicious. I hope you enjoy it as I do."

After wine was served, they ordered their food, limiting themselves to a small salad, some coarse bread, an assortment of olives, and a chicken dish for her, duck for him.

He talked about himself, this time, about his brothers and sisters, of his growing up in the old Moorish, walled city of Toledo, with its narrow, cobbled streets, and its view down onto the Tagus River. He spoke of his French-born mother and his Basque father as though they still lived in the old stone homestead despite their having been gone long years.

He spoke of his plan to leave the priesthood, although he made no mention of why he planned to do so. Neena thought of asking but decided that if he wanted her to know he would have shared that with her.

He asked how she was doing, and she told him, for the first time uttering words about her years-long resentment of Will, and about the letters from him, the ledger documenting how he had faithfully supported their daughter, and the sealed documents proving her parentage. "If I was so wrong about Will, perhaps I was wrong about everything I thought I remembered from my childhood, all those assumptions I made of people and their intentions."

"I'm sorry that there were secrets kept from you and that you must, now, deal with them. Dealing with a shadowy past is difficult. But it seems that the past must often be dealt with when we are in our middle years, after we slow down a bit in the midst of life or when some crisis halts us. It is often at that very time that the past catches up with us and demands to be examined."

At one point as they drank their coffee, he briefly placed his hand over hers, and looked intently at her with his dark brown eyes. "You are lovely and good. Don't ever marry again unless you find a man who loves you with a single-mindedness that permits him to learn everything about you and cherish you still. That's the kind of love I wish for you, Christina Shaw."

She blushed as tears came to her eyes. He was so kind.

"But," he added, lightly, "we shall keep in touch." With that he winked at her, and then asked for the check.

89 | Will – Barcelona, Spain
Spring 1978

On Tuesday Will decided he could wait no longer. He would approach Neena, pretending to bump into her by accident. He rehearsed what he would say. He would pretend that he was there, in the city, on business and just happened to be staying across the hall from her. What a surprise! Or he would say that he had regretted not touring Barcelona when they docked there in December and decided to come back.

But when the time came, he blurted out the truth.

90 Neena – Barcelona, Spain
Spring 1978

Will obviously thought she was blind. She had seen him walking toward the pastry shop early the day before. She would have recognized his walk anywhere, especially having just seen him in December. Then, late yesterday afternoon, she had seen movement on a second-story balcony directly across from the church entrance. Someone was moving from the balcony into a room in the same hostal in which she was staying. It was Will again. What was he doing, stalking her? But then she knew. Teddy, and possibly even Toot, had put him up to this. They must have done some fancy footwork to talk Will into this. They must think she had gone stark-raving-mad if they enlisted his help to this degree. She found it irritating yet amusing. She would continue the charade a little longer.

That morning at about the same time as she had seen him yesterday, she stood at her door listening for movement in the hall. She soon heard a door open and close and someone moving down the hall toward the stairway. She waited a minute and then left her room, went down to the hostal office to turn in her key, and proceeded out to the street. Will was walking up the street toward the pastry shop and a cup of morning coffee. She followed him. When she walked into the shop, he stood at the counter, choosing his breakfast roll. She moved up behind him. He paid for a roll and espresso, picked them up, and moved over to stand at the counter where he could enjoy his breakfast.

She moved up to the counter, pretending to search for something in her purse, and then concentrated on which roll she would choose. She felt his eyes on her. She chose a croissant and espresso, paid the cashier and moved over as though looking for a spot at the stand-up counter where he stood. Before she lifted her eyes to look at him, he blurted, "Neena!"

"Will," she said, as though surprised to see him.

"Okay, Neena. I'm just going to be straight with you. I have been following you for days, both here and in Puteaux. I have followed you on walks, I have watched your apartment door to see your comings and goings, I have eaten in the same restaurants as you while you ate and immersed yourself in a book. I have followed you here, am staying in the same hotel, and I even went to Mass when you did. I . . ."

"Did Teddy put you up to this," she asked, looking stern.

Red-faced, Will answered, "No, actually Toot did." She laughed then, unable to keep up the charade.

"What's going on? Do they think I have gone totally bonkers or something?"

"No, no, nothing like that, really. It's just that we have been worried about you. Teddy said you've been through a lot lately, but I didn't pry, really I didn't." Will seemed to be tripping over his own words; he appeared so intent on finishing what he had intended to say. His eyes were pleading. "I want to hear it from you, if you want to tell me, that is. Neena, I just want to be friends. And I want time to apologize."

She started to laugh then, thinking of Toot's persuasiveness in enlisting poor Will to keep an eye on her. Toot could talk anyone into anything. "It's okay, Will, really it is. I can't say no to Toot, either. And the truth is, Will, we need to talk."

They finished their breakfast, stopped by their separate rooms for a change of shoes, and began walking. They walked out Carrer Ferran to La Rambla, turned left, and walked down to the statue of Christopher Columbus. From there they continued down to the waterfront where there was a street festival in progress. They walked along the wharf, talking the entire time.

Neena apologized to Will, and he apologized to her. They talked about the past and each shared stories from their individual lives, as if they were at a class reunion and hadn't seen each other for twenty-seven years. They spoke matter-of-factly, hurriedly, as though they would run out of time before they got it all said. He commiserated with her, and she with him.

They bought some street food from a booth on the waterfront, found a bench and sat down to eat and rest.

"Have you seen Sagrada Familia?"

Looking sheepish, Will said, "I haven't really seen much of anything."

He was delighted when Neena laughed.

That afternoon they walked the full length of La Rambla, enjoying the street entertainment, the carnival-like atmosphere, especially the fat lady with huge, huggable bosoms created with balloons under her dress. They remarked on the mimes, the jugglers, and the street musicians.

By the time they had toured Sagrada Familia, the street lights had come on. They worked their way down into a different part of town and found a tascas. They went in, ordered a variety of tapas, drank seltzer water with fresh mango, then ate slowly for a full hour.

As they exited the café, Neena, very casually and naturally, took Will's arm as they sauntered along streets, winding through the city until they reached Gotic Barri and Carrer Ferran once again.

They reached their hostal at 10:45 p.m. Tired from all the walking and remembering that they had to be at the airport by noon the next day, they stood at Neena's door.

"Goodnight, Will."

"Goodnight, Neena. Would you like to have coffee in the morning, before we check out?"

"Sure. How about eight o'clock. Come knock on my door. Maybe we can get a table and enjoy our coffee in a more leisurely fashion than standing at the counter."

"Good plan."

They hugged, rather hurriedly and awkwardly. As Neena turned to enter her door, Will said, "Thank you, again, Neena. You can't imagine how many times I have wished I could talk with you again, like this, like old friends."

"Me, too," she said. "Me, too."

After she closed her door, he turned to walk down the hall to his room. It would have been so easy to tell her he loved her.

91   Neena and Will – Paris, France
Spring 1978

Once they reached the airport in the morning, Will was able to change his flight, to be on the same one as Neena. He was also able to arrange for them to sit together in first class.

They talked more on the flight, Neena sharing with Will what she had learned about her parentage. "I still can't quite believe that V was my mother. It amazes me how that could have been kept a secret all those years. I just don't know what to do with that information, Will. But I know one thing: Miss Toot and I are going to have a long talk when I get back home."

Will did not mention that Toot was in Paris and that Neena would be seeing her in the coming week.

They read, nodded off to sleep, and discussed their plans for the coming days.

"When do you leave for the States."

"I have no real deadline. I thought I would stay around for a few more days – my room is rented through the end of this week. I had hoped we could have dinner, and maybe I could see where you attend classes."

"That sounds great. I could show you around the neighborhood tomorrow, and then, maybe, we could have dinner somewhere?"

"That sounds wonderful. Perhaps the next day, if you are free, we could have lunch at a place I know in Paris proper, in the eighth arrondissement. I have a friend who would like to join us there. Will that work for you?"

She said she would look forward to it. "Is it Teddy? I haven't heard from him since I left Puteaux. He didn't tell me you were here. Has that bugger sneaked over here?"

"No, I don't think Teddy had any plans to come over to France. I talked with him two days ago. He was calling from home."

"Teddy told me last week that Toot is doing fine, but I haven't heard from her for a while either. She's kind of sporadic in sending letters."

* * * * *

Two days later Toot arrived by taxi at Chez Cochon. She approached the table where Will and Neena already sat. Will stood to greet her.

"Either my French is off, or I can't for the life of me figure out why they would name a restaurant, the House of Pig, or Pigs."

"I never knew what it meant, Toot. I thought it was some man's name. Neena asked me the same question."

Toot went around the table and hugged Neena hard. "I'm so happy to see you, Dear. Were you surprised to see Will?"

"Are we talking about Will-the-Stalker?"

They all laughed. "Don't forget how charming I can be," Toot said. "He was like butter in my hands." As she filled them in on her daily activities over the past week, they ordered lunch, ate, and then ordered coffee.

Will pushed back his chair and rose. "Take your time talking, Ladies. I have to make a few phone calls."

"Are you reporting in to Theodore," Neena asked?

"No, actually, he'll probably call me in the middle of the night again tonight. It's getting to be a habit."

Neena told Toot about the letters and ledger. Toot was as taken aback as she.

"So you didn't know he tried so hard to find me?"

"No, nor did I know about his support of Reecie. How did he know you were pregnant and that you gave birth to a girl? Did he say?"

"We have talked about everything under the sun, but I keep forgetting to ask that. I figure Grandma somehow got the information to him. I could see her doing that. I know Teddy would not have given him information at that point. It's not all that important, now. When I think of it, I'll ask him."

"I knew he was special, Christina. Just think how young he was when he began supporting his daughter."

"I hate that I was so wrong about him, Toot. I have apologized to him. I feel that we can be friends, and that has to benefit Reecie." Neena moved so that she could look into Toot's eyes, so that the older woman couldn't avoid her gaze. She smiled as she spoke.

"And there was another envelope, Toot. You might know something about it. It had a birth certificate in it, and we need to talk. I'm curious, Dearie, just how much did you know about the Lowry-Teeple family secrets?"

Toot's jaw dropped.

92 Will - Rural Frederick County, Virginia
Summer 1978

Will had traveled out Route 50 West and stopped at the post office in Hastings Corners to ask directions. By the time he was three miles farther along the highway he couldn't remember which way to turn so he pulled into a gas station. While the attendant, a sixty-or-so-years-old man pumped his gas, Will asked if he knew a man named Jake McClure who probably stopped by on occasion.

The man hitched up his jeans with his forearms, ostensibly so he wouldn't get grease or oil from his hands onto his pants.

"Big guy, but old, white beard? Has a limp? Smokes Pall Malls?"

Before Will could respond, the man said, "Yeah. Yeah. I remember, his name *is* Jake. He comes in here once or twice a month to pick up a few things. His son – looks just like Jake must have at a younger age - he comes in. Comes through a couple of times a month. Grabs some beers, some smokes, gas. Yep, I know who you mean."

He tips the hose up to get the last drops into the gas tank. "You a salesman?"

"No, no. I'm not selling anything."

"Just thought I should mention that Jake's durn mean, so go easy with him . . .." He shook his head. "No, on second thought I take that back, he's pretty much mean as a snake. I've seen him kick a cat clear across the parking lot. I wouldn't get in his way. You never know how drunked-up he might be."

Will walked into the building with the man, to pay him.

"Could you give me directions to his place?"

"Sure. It's pretty easy."

He tipped his hat back and scratched his head. After he put the hat back on he continued. "Continue on West here, and go to the second red dog road. It's called Stewart Road, but the sign fell off probably six years ago. Can't miss it. There's a sign for Mueller's Welding Shop at the end of the road. Turn right and go down to a fork where you bear to the left. You go on down a small hill until you think the road will peter out, and you'll see a narrow lane that goes back to a little walk-across bridge. Can't miss it. There's a chain across the driveway and a sign hanging from what's left of the mailbox. Sign's just danglin' there by one piece of wire. Anyways, you'll have to park there and walk in. Not too far."

"Thank you. I appreciate the help."

"Have a good one. Hope you find him."

Will got into his Wagoneer and merged back onto the highway. After a few miles he saw the welder's sign and turned onto the dirt road. The road was covered in some kind of slag, perhaps the red dog to which the gas station attendant had referred. After he came to the fork and bore to his left, the road narrowed and the trees arched over the road so he felt he was going through a tunnel. The branches were so thick with foliage the sun had to snake its way down through the leaves to reach the middle of the road. The grass along the road and even the lower branches of the trees were covered with a dull red dust, so heavy it brought them low to the ground.

As he started down the rutted hill the road narrowed more and he noticed that grass grew in the center. His window open, he could hear grackles chortling in the trees.

Rounding a bend in the road, he saw a mailbox that looked like it had been sledge-hammered a time or two. Sure enough, there was a chain over the driveway. A sign hung from it, low, almost touching the grass in the middle of the driveway. It read: *No Trespassing*. It was riddled with bullet holes.

He parked parallel to the chain over the driveway, making sure he was completely off the road.

He got out and, stepping over the chain, noticed that a beat-up old Dodge Power Wagon pickup truck sat parked off to his left in a little grove of pin oaks.

He started up the driveway even though he could not yet see a house. Rounding a curve in the dirt path he neared a bridge that hung so low it almost touched the swift-moving stream passing under it. When he reached the bridge, he saw that it was a hanging bridge, anchored on each side by big oak trees. Made of small diameter cables, the handrails looked burry and loose. He hesitated before stepping onto the first foot board, fearing that it would break loose as a dozen or so others seemed to have. While he was contemplating whether he even wanted to risk a crossing, he heard the baying of dogs, the sound coming closer. He expected to see slobbering coon hounds but saw instead two Basset hounds coming at him, their ears flowing behind them as they loped along.

They kept barking as they forded the creek. Their tails wagged as they circled him and sniffed at his shoes and pant legs.

Then they shook the water off of them and onto his khaki pants.

He reached down and stroked the white-muzzled one who ceased barking and nuzzled Will's hand.

He stepped onto the first board of the bridge, and then onto the second one, to see if they could hold him. They seemed sturdy enough so he continued crossing the bridge, almost on tip-toe as though to make himself lighter. He had to jump the last two feet in order to avoid the mud at the edge of the bank. He stood in buttercups to his knees.

There were still no living quarters in sight, but he continued walking along the path while the old dog trotted along beside him and the younger one circled back and forth around him, in front of him, behind him, like a cat vying for attention. He stopped and looked around him. He still couldn't see a house, but now that he was on the other side of the creek, he could see that there was a motorcycle parked in beside the old truck. It was shiny, well-cared for and looked out-of-place.

Will and the dogs rounded a curve in the path and there, in a clearing, sat a little travel trailer with a covered porch on which sat three rockers. Two of them were occupied by two men, one old, one young.

Will could hear a voice then, diminished to a raspy whisper over the noise of the stream.

"Jeb. Hoot. Hee-ya. Get back here," someone called to the dogs.

The dogs perked up their ears, gave him one last pass, and then they bounded ahead of him up the path.

"You lookin' for somebody?" the gravelly voice asked.

"Yes, I'm looking for Jake McClure. Do I have the right place?"

"Depends on who's askin'."

"I'm Will, Will McClure."

"Well, if it isn't the little son-of-a-bitch bastard."

Will recognized the voice and the familiarity of the words.

The old guy sat in one of the rockers with one foot propped up on a log stump. The younger man rose from his chair and walked to the edge of the porch.

"Hi, Will. Paul," he said, extending his hand as he stepped from the porch.

"Binky? I can't believe it. I guess I would have recognized you, but it has been quite a few years. I heard you moved away."

"Most people call me Paul, now. I moved to Roanoke but make it up here when I can." He pointed to a rocker on the far side of the porch. "Sit down."

"What do you want?" Jake asked.

"I just wanted to look you up. Maybe talk to you."

"Well, talk and then get the hell out of here," Jake said as he picked up a beer bottle and took a long drink.

"How have you been, Dad? You must be having your sixtieth birthday this month."

"Sixty, and I look eighty." He shifted in his chair, lowering his propped-up foot to the floor. "You shot off my damned kneecap; how'd you think I'd be? I walk around like a stiff-legged old cripple. I was only thirty-two when you maimed me. Do you know how tough it was making a living all bummed up like that?"

"I wanted to tell you that I'm sorry, Dad."

"Sorry doesn't bring me back the years you stole from me, Bigshot." He rose stiffly from his chair, hanging on to the porch post, bringing himself upright. "Now I can limp in there and get my shotgun and blow your kneecap off, or you can get your little bastard self outta here. Those are your choices. Now get goin'." His words were slurred as they squeezed through bared teeth and slithered past drawn-back lips.

Will rose from his chair, walked to the edge of the porch, and stepped off into the grass.

"Goodbye, Jake. Nice to see you, Binky, or Paul. I guess it's Paul now. Sorry, but I always think of you as that little tow-headed guy with the little kid nickname. I'll do better remembering after this."

He turned and started down the path the way he had come. The dogs didn't stir from their sunny spot but lifted their heads to watch him go.

I tried, he thought. I tried. I don't really know what I expected, but I tried.

As he neared the bridge, he heard at his back, "He doesn't mean the things he says, you know."

Will turned to look at Binky. "Oh, but he does, Binky. He always does. He always has."

The big hairy man stood there with a beer in one hand, his feet spread wide and his other hand on his opposite hip so his elbow stuck out to his side. He looked like a porcupine in defense mode who puffs up his quills to make him look bigger, more formidable. Will remained silent, studying Binky, thinking how much he looked like Jake had at that age.

"How's Ma?"

"She's dead," Will answered, cruelly. "She's been dead three years now," he added, his voice softening. "She asked for you at the end. No one could find you. You . . ., you should have stayed in touch with her, Binky." Will reached up and laid his hand on the big man's hairy arm. "I don't know." He shook his head. "Who am I to give advice?" Will said as he looked earnestly at his brother. "Just don't end up like him, Binky. It's a choice, you know. There's always a point where we make a choice that can affect us for the rest of our lives."

He half-turned so he faced back, toward the camper. Then he turned back to his brother.

"I'm sorry I maimed him for life, I really am. I made a choice that day, but it was a survival choice. He would have killed Mom, me or one of you little ones. I just picked up that gun — I didn't even aim. And, and the safety was not on; he meant to shoot someone that day. He intended to. That's how far he had let anger and hatred seep into him. And booze. Always the booze. Something was always chasing him or maybe drawing him toward that bottle. I wish I knew what."

The young dog trotted up to Binky, jumping at him as though he wanted to play.

He extended his hand toward Will, and they shook warmly.

"I'm glad to see you, Will."

Will stepped toward his little brother and took him into a warm embrace.

"Binky, Binky," he said, stepping back while tears flooded his eyes. "You were always such a cute little guy."

Will turned, putting his foot on the first board of the bridge. He turned back. "Look me up sometime. I came back to Emmaus. I'm in the book. Would sure love to see you again."

"I might do that," Binky said, turning away from Will and moving back up the path toward Jake.

93 | Neena and Toot – Burl and Emmaus, Virginia
Summer 1978

Moving Toot was like relocating the Vatican. She had friends who went back for years and years, to her early twenties, when she first married Jimmy and moved to Burl. Even her furniture and artwork went back beyond that, back across the pond to English ancestors on both sides of the family.

Over the years she had become well-established in Burl, Albemarle County, Virginia. She had been a member of the Burl Chapters of the Junior League, the Daughters of the American Revolution, Women's Club, Rotary International Wives, George Wythe Memorial Hospital Auxiliary, and the Lee Highway Women's Bridge Club.

Despite its impressive name, the bridge club consisted of Toot and three of her friends, all of whom, at one time or another, had lived within two miles of the well-known Lee Highway. Toot had inherited her seat in the club from an old southern matron, a contemporary of the other three members, so that Toot was the youngster of the quartet. The group had disbanded years before when one club member could no longer tell a club from a spade, and when dear old Honey Townsend, another member, kept nodding off during bidding. But right about that time, Toot's mother had come to Burl to live so that Toot was pleased when they disbanded the club.

Neena seemed surprised that Toot would even consider moving back to Emmaus. She had thrown the idea out to her aunt, testing the water, so to speak, but Toot showed instant enthusiasm for the change.

What she didn't know was that Toot had wearied of living in a house that had once been so filled with Jimmy's presence. She wandered around its empty expanses, feeling lonely and old. The fact was that for many years now, Toot had avoided both. She was outgoing and fun and youthful of spirit. Her old clubs, now governed and populated by youngsters, did not encourage her return, nor did she see herself back there. She was at a point in her life when she wanted to go to the birthday parties of extended family members and the graduations of relatives once, twice, even three times, removed. She wanted to eat the birthday and wedding cakes she had denied herself for all those many years when she was maintaining her girlish figure. She wanted to attend a Bible Study at Teddy's church, sing in the choir, and be the bird-like lady whom the locals discussed, who fluttered off to the library twice a week to return books that she had devoured instead of ones that had made her nod off in her chair. She wanted to be close enough so that Christina or Reecie or Teddy could call and suggest meeting for lunch. She wanted to babysit Reecie's little monsters and make them popcorn with Velveeta Cheese, if the little buggers liked it.

But Flora; Flora was the problem. The thing was that Toot and Flora had practically grown up together. Flora had been her maid when women still had live-in maids. But then, after living three years with Toot and Jimmy, on her twenty-eighth birthday, Flora had asked to speak with both Jimmy and Toot and told them that she was getting married, and wanted to continue working for them but as their day maid, if they wanted her. She went on to say that if she ever had children she could make arrangements for continuing on with them, despite contingencies. And she had stayed on until her poor old feet just couldn't take it anymore even though Toot had encouraged her for years to quit. Flora's granddaughter took over, then, although she never had the energy that dear Flora had.

But Toot and Flora had remained dear friends. Aware of that, both Christina and Reecie had promised to take Toot to see Flora monthly. They had promised and Toot would hold them to it.

Truth was, she wanted to be near her dear Christina; right down the street from her, if Christina would have it.

Things moved fast once Toot had made up her mind to move. She put her house on the market and a contract was put on it the next week. She bought a vacant lot six doors up the street from Teddy and the church, met with a builder, chose a house design that allowed for picture windows and lots of light, and put a rush on the construction. The contractor agreed to have her in the house in eight weeks. Fat chance for that, she knew, but in the meantime, she would live at Widow Howe's boarding house, even though Teddy had offered his spare room.

After signing both contracts and with the help of Flora's daughter and two granddaughters, Toot sorted through her house, discarding incidental items, donating others, and keeping the things most dear to her. The moving van came on a Friday. After packing all day, the movers pulled away from the curb at midnight. The movers must have had the weekend off because they arrived in Emmaus midday Monday and off-loaded half of her belongings into Teddy's garage and the other half into Reecie's garage, three blocks away.

Excited, Toot hadn't felt so young in years. She was starting a whole new life.

* * * * *

Having accepted a position at Shenandoah College in Winchester, Virginia, Neena resigned her position at the university. Giving up her tenured position at a prestigious university for a twenty-hour-week at a little-known college, she was, nevertheless, excited about the change. The Shenandoah Junior College and the well-respected Shenandoah Conservatory had, within the past several years, merged and now offered four-year degrees. And the administration of Shenandoah College looked, in the long-term, toward eventual university status, which goal Neena wanted to help facilitate, if possible.

Neena chose to live in Emmaus, commuting to Winchester on her teaching days. In keeping with her favorite subject, American History, she would teach one class in pre-revolutionary history and would assume, as well, the *Hugh D. and Virginia McCormick Chair in Civil War History*, a coveted position for her.

Packing up her apartment had been a relatively easy task. Two days after she packed the last of her possessions, Will and Teddy drove up with a rented U-Haul truck and loaded. The three of them drove back to Emmaus in a three-part caravan, Teddy in the lead with the van, Neena following him, and Will bringing up the rear

In Emmaus she had rented an apartment from Mr. Piazza's son, Mike, one of the little P's, planning to live there until she could find a house she wanted to buy.

So there she was, Neena Teeple Shaw, on her own road to Emmaus once again; this time following a van driven by her brother, Teddy, a truck with big red letters on its tailgate that read, "Rent Me".

How strange, she laughed to herself, how strange that she followed a dawdling van that weaved on the curves, did not no longer initiated hugs or kisses or touches despite being receptive to them.

But in these past few months, he had watched her sparkle slowly return. She had begun to chat with perfect strangers in supermarkets about fruit color and firmness, she sometimes worked at making grumpy people smile, and she touched. She touched old men with nose warts and hirsute ears and ancient women with chin hairs. She hugged little kids with jelly on their faces, and stuffed-toy pigs in department stores.

But then she would slip away again, somewhere alone and deep inside her, somewhere he was not welcome to go. Yet, in the past few months, at least, she slipped away less and less. As he studied her, he realized that she seemed to be slowly yet sporadically coming out of something unpleasant as when one's color returns after a long illness, or when one smiles again for the first time after losing a loved one. The truth was, she hadn't changed, not really; she was just coming back. And he was waiting there with arms and heart wide open, ready to welcome her.

signal when turning, and hogged the passing lane, yet she had no urge whatsoever, not even once, to ram it.

94   Will - Emmaus, Virginia
Summer 1978

Over the next few months, Will fell in love with Neena all over again. He didn't know how other men loved, but he loved, not blindly, but completely. She was pretty, yes, showing a little age at times when she was tired. She was fit but not skinny. She had developed little crinkles at the corners of her eyes that made her look impish. Having known her when she was a young and budding girl, he sometimes still saw her that way: Thin with coltish legs and eyes huge in her lean face. But it was more than that.

He watched her as they dated and got to know each other again. She arranged her spices alphabetically, left her dishes spread out on the countertop to air dry, even after drying them with a tea towel, before putting them away. She positioned items in her purse just right so that she could find them yet she still lost her keys. Over the past twenty-seven years he had experienced periods of time when he realized that Neena was slipping away from him; that her memory was dimming and eluding him, yet he had struggled to keep her alive in his memory. Then, when he had first seen her again after many years, he thought she had lost her sparkle, her warmth, and, he feared, her sense of humor. She still made people comfortable, but there were subtle changes, a slight difference in her, a diffidence, even anger. He speculated that perhaps that difference was just maturity, but she seemed to hold back; she

95 — Neena and Will - Emmaus, Virginia
Fall 1978

They were married in late November on a day when the wind swirls falling leaves into little whirling dervishes, and incident light touches around the edges of things.

Before the ceremony, as Neena approached the side entrance to the church in which she had spent so many of her childhood days, she watched the wind toying with the colorful leaves. It seemed so random in its selection of each leaf, one time letting a bright yellow one just be; oh, perhaps, ruffling it a moment but, in the end, just letting it be before moving on to pick up a red one, allowing the red one to hover there momentarily before wafting it far overhead and away. She paused there at the door, feeling the sun as it worked its way through the low-hanging clouds to warm her back. She turned and looked across the street at *the manse*, as her mother had called it, the Teeple residence, the parsonage. She remembered the swings on the veranda, her twin dolls, the French doors to her father's study, and the coziness of her grandmother's room and arms.

She had felt categorized in that house; over her whole life, in fact. She had not been just a girl, a daughter, a sister, but a PK, a preacher's kid, and then *that* preacher's kid, the one who . . .. She had always wanted to be more like others: More sure of herself, like Betsy; more fun, like Teddy. In the end, she had been just Neena. The truth was that all through her life she had spent, perhaps, too much thought on how others saw her. Some, she supposed, saw her now as a gifted teacher, somewhat absorbed, perhaps, like a mathematician who counts steps, or in the extreme, she feared, vapid or at least detached.

Or, more realistically and somewhat sadly, they did not see her at all.

Her own view of herself, however, had changed little over all those years between where she now stood and then, the PK on *the manse* veranda. So much of the time she was still, and merely, a child who had wandered from the pathway to pick flowers, those fragile purple violets she had gathered for her grandmother or, straying further, down to the boggy bottom where those wee forget-me-nots grew down at creek side. Maybe she had lingered too long, but it felt safer there, a little removed, down there among growing things, a gentle stir in the otherwise fetid air, as though a tiny hummingbird flew too close. She did not see herself as lost, as unable to find the pathway again. She was just off somewhere, viewing things, and herself, from some angle others could not understand. She lacked, at least at times, the momentum to rejoin the flow, a flow that had sometimes taken her places she had never meant to go.

Feeling a breeze lift her hair and cold migrating into her hand from the doorknob, she knew it was time to move up from that boggy bottom, time to labor up the sloped path from that place, to merge once again into the flow, looking ahead this time for choices she must make.

In early September of that year she had invited Will to her house for a home-cooked meal. They were inseparable by then, spending weekday evenings and weekend days and evenings together. That September evening she wanted to fix him a special meal, one she had learned to prepare while living in France. He seemed to relish the meal, complimenting her efforts, and thanking her. After dinner he helped her clear their plates, and dried the dishes she washed. When they were finished, he roamed the little house, picking up a figurine she kept on the entryway table, as if seeing it for the first time. He fingered the carved design of a bookend, touching random books on her bookshelf. Then he stood in the doorway to her bedroom, a door she normally kept closed, and asked, "Whose photographs are those, on your nightstands?"

"My grandparents, parents, one of my aunts and uncles on the left table; you, Reecie and family, and Teddy and family on the other," she said. "Go on in. You're welcome to look at them."

"When was this one of your grandparents taken?" he asked, picking up the framed photograph.

"The year I was born, 1937. I remember because my grandmother always told me that it was taken the day I was brought home from the hospital. At least that's what I was told," she said, shrugging her shoulders a bit, wondering again what was fact; what was fiction.

As she opened a drawer to put in some stockings she had just laundered, he walked over and took out a little packet from among her lingerie.

"Is this a sachet?"

When she told him it was, indeed, a sachet, he sniffed it, rolled it around in the palm of his hand, and said, "I thought only little old ladies kept these in their dresser drawers."

"How would you know?"

"Good question," he said with a smile as he put it back.

When she went into her walk-in closet to hang up a sweater, he followed her, lifting the sleeve of a blouse, or straightening a jacket on a hanger. Touching, touching, as was his habit.

"Why do you hang your dresses inside out? Did your mother do that, hang her clothes inside out?"

In fact, she had, Neena now realized although she had long forgotten such things. She never knew why Dessie, and now she, hung their clothes inside out. In truth it was, perhaps, merely to keep dust out of the shoulder seams.

"Quit snooping through my drawers and examining my clothes closet," she said, smiling, while nudging him backwards, toward the bedroom.

"Wait," he said. "Before we leave this inordinately orderly closet."

He took her hands, rubbing their tops with his thumbs.

"Please marry me. Tomorrow. The next day. As soon as possible. I don't want to live another day without you as my wife."

She had said, "Yes, of course."

* * * * *

Yet now she lingered, her hand on the church door, watching the wind play with leaves. This marriage, her second attempt at wedded bliss, frightened her whereas she had entered into the first one almost blithely. Now she knew some of the pitfalls of marriage. Still, she loved Will. They had given themselves time to know each other again, and as adults. He gave her much of the space to which she had grown accustomed. He listened when she talked of things general or near to her heart. He sought her companionship. He clearly desired her as she did him. They shared values, goals, tastes, hopes, and a child. They laughed together.

That day, standing in the chilled November wind, she wore, under her knobby tweed coat, her white Marilyn Monroe dress, Will's favorite. How bizarre, a proper southern girl wearing white in November at her second wedding, no less. How things had changed.

"Life is in flux," Uncle Monroe used to say. "Nothing stays still or remains the same for very long at a time." How trite that had seemed then, how pedestrian it seemed still, yet how timeless and true.

And life would change once she walked through that door. Feeling the breeze at her back, she turned the knob and entered.

* * * * *

Teddy married them on that chilly November day, using beautiful, traditional vows, adding a little humor, and prayed for God's blessing on their lives together.

That night they stayed in the Old American Hotel, where George Washington had purportedly once slept although it had not been completed until 1809, ten years after his death. They chose Room Seventeen for no particular reason.

They felt shy with each other, kissing, touching, tentative. Once they began making love, she felt virginal once again, opening herself to her lover, her first love, her last love. She threw wide the windows of her heart, and pitched fear through the openings, she hoped for the last time.

As he held her, possessed her, he made love to, love with, the woman he loved beyond all others, the person he loved sometimes more than he loved himself.

Their love-making was both tender and passionate, and in that moment there was only that moment.

Afterward, Will held Neena for a long time, her breath soft on his neck. He remembered holding her all those years before, much like this. Yet he recalled more poignantly how she had held him that first time, shortly after his arrival at the Teeple residence, while he had sobbed into her neck. Fear, embarrassment, regret, longing, bone-crushing need and grief had flowed from him that night. Later, as time passed, even though just a kid himself, when he took her into his arms for the first and subsequent times and looked into her eyes, he saw her, the lovely, loving, innocent girl she was. But that image blurred somehow, at times, the longer he looked into her eyes and into the eyes of others over the years. Sometimes he saw himself there, mirrored in her eyes, in their eyes, that poor, hungry-for-love child he had been and, sadly, had remained for years to come. Now, as he looked down onto her lovely face and into her knowing, blue eyes, he saw only Neena, the woman he cherished. And she looked back at him, into the depths of him, and ministered to the boy he had been and to the man he had become.

They finally slept that night, intertwined at first, but then moving, each to his or her side of the bed, facing each other, arms outstretched, still holding hands, her cold toes resting atop his warm ones.

96   Neena - Emmaus, Virginia
Summer 1979

"We're having a surprise visitor so I am fixing lunch," Will said as he kissed Neena on the cheek. "And I promise I won't fix instant rice and canned chicken," he added smiling.

"Who's coming? Is it Toot? Or Reecie? Who, Will? You know I can't stand not knowing."

"You don't have long to wonder. If you go out to sit on the porch you should see who it is right away, at least within ten minutes."

Neena poured a cup of coffee, went through the front screen door, and settled onto the swing, her favorite spot. She watched her neighbor across the street planting annuals, the man two doors down collecting his mail, and a stray dog sniffing her bushes. Within five minutes a long, maroon van eased up to the curb in front of her house, and parked, heading the wrong way, on the wrong side of the street. Neena thought it was a delivery because a tall woman got out of the van, walked around the front of it, and appeared to be opening a sliding door on the street side of the van. Soon, children of different sizes came around both ends of the van, some of them running, some of them holding the hands of smaller children. The woman carried an infant. So far, Neena had counted seven, no, eight children.

"Well, if it isn't," the woman said.

"Betsy? Betsy, is that you? I can't believe it; I just can't," Neena said as she searched for a place to put her cup.

Carrying a toddler, Betsy met her at the bottom of the steps. They embraced long and warmly.

"I want you to meet my brood. This is baby Lenore, those are the twins, Babs and Bonnie," she said as she pointed to two little carrot-topped girls. "This is Irving, my oldest boy, and David, Jr., and then, in descending order, Betty Jo, Polly, and Joey. I didn't leave one out, did I?" she asked as she counted on her fingers. "That's my brood. Don't worry; you won't be tested on their names. I have trouble remembering sometimes myself."

Neena invited them up onto the porch where all the smaller children either climbed on the railing or piled onto the swing. Neena and Betsy sat on the glider.

"Hi, little love," Neena said, bending down to look at the baby on Betsy's lap. "It looks like you have a new tooth, a brand new toofie."

"Where?" Betsy asked, bending down to look into the baby's mouth. "Where do you see a tooth?"

"Right there, in front, on the bottom," Neena said, pointing.

"Oh, my gosh, you're right! What kind of a mother is too busy to know her baby has a new tooth? Oh, well. Irving probably has pubic hair by now. I can't keep up."

Betsy gazed off, toward the side yard as though remembering. "Hey, Neena, look at this. Irving, come over here."

The older boy walked over, shyly.

"Look at his nose. Turn sideways, Irving. Is that my dad's nose or what? And Babs, she's the one over there shimmying up the porch post, look at her wild hair. Does that hair remind you of my hair at that age? Well, at this age. Nothing's improved; it's all gone the other way."

"I know the feeling. I know I'm going the other way."

"Okay, do tell. Are you pregnant? You look a little pregos, there," Betsy said, patting Neena's belly.

"I certainly am; can you believe it? I'm so excited I can hardly wait, although this time seems a little harder on my body than when I was a kid."

"Hold that thought and baby Lenore for a sec; I want to get the diaper bag out of the van," Betsy said as she plopped her baby onto Neena's lap, and headed toward her vehicle.

As Neena looked down at baby Lenore, watching her facial contortions and her moving legs and hands, she felt sheer gratitude that she would again be a mother. Her gynecologist had never given her a clear explanation why, after giving birth to Reecie, she never had more children. Of course, she would not have wanted to have a child with Kirby. They had never been a bonded team, living separately as they did. Still it had still stabbed at her rawly, at times; yet, on further reflection, the realization felt fair at other times. It seemed to be just one more question that was never answered to her satisfaction.

She drew baby Lenore up close against her distended belly, against her own child moving within her; her child — and Will's child. She bent and kissed baby Lenore.

Betsy trotted back up the steps and sat down beside Neena.

"Listen, being pregnant is the best. I went to a little private college up in northwestern Pennsylvania – that's where I met my husband. I majored in propagating. It won't take you long to realize I love bearing kids. I love it when they are in my tummy, when they are lying there breast feeding, and, especially, when they start with the wise cracks. By then, at least, I know they have a brain. David, Jr., can tell some jokes that would make your toes curl. It doesn't matter how many times I wash his mouth out with soap, he just keeps them coming."

The door opened, and Will stepped out onto the porch.

"Lord above," Betsy said, jumping to her feet. "Willis McClure, you are more handsome than ever. You look especially fetching in that apron," she said as she hugged him. "Thank you so much for inviting us. Did you tell Neena yet that we are moving back here? Back to Emmaus?"

"No, I was saving that as a surprise. You can fill her in. I came out here to tell you that lunch is served in the back yard at the picnic table. I hope you're hungry for man-food," he said, growling.

Seven of the eight kids started squealing, as they ran around the side of the house to the back yard. Baby Lenore just drooled.

Once they were seated at the table, Betsy asked Neena, "How are you, kiddo? I'm so sorry we didn't stay in touch. You don't even know who I married. His name is David Brewster. He's a nerd. He looks like Ichabod Crane, but who am I to complain when I look like Washington Irving?"

The women laughed, and began eating the potato salad, hot dogs, beans, and pickles Will served them.

"I told you it was man-food. Except for the pickles; Neena's big on pickles right now."

They ate while Will moved back and forth with iced tea and lemonade and a cake he had made. The women caught up on the past twenty-eight years, filling in the blanks, answering questions for each other.

"We're moving back in October," Betsy said, grinning. "Well, I'm moving back. The kids and Dave have only visited twice, so they are only moving here for me. We have been in Bagnoli, well, Naples, Italy, for the past four years. Dave is in army intelligence. We have lived in Germany twice, in England twice, and once in the Netherlands. It has been quite a life. My kids never met a stranger. I am so glad to be home.

We bought a house three streets up from you, up on snob knob. Ha."

Betsy and her clan spent the afternoon with Neena and Will. The kids climbed trees in the back yard, scaling even the holly tree.

"Aren't you afraid they'll get all scratched up on the holly leaves?" Neena asked.

"If they get scratched up enough, they'll move on to something else. No worries."

By four o'clock, Will had disappeared back into the house, and Betsy began gathering her kids and herding them back to the van. Taking a packet of some sort off the dash, she shut the van door, and walked back over to the porch. "We're leaving day after tomorrow, so I won't see you again until October. I am so excited to be back here where I can see something of you." She hugged Neena in a long embrace. "I'm so sorry I couldn't be there for you when you were going through so much. We heard nothing about you unless my grandmother slipped me some news now and again. But we never knew where you were or how to contact you. It drove everyone nuts. Teddy never told a soul." She hugged Neena once more. "Here," she said, as she handed Neena a slim envelope. "I saved these for some sam-hill reason. Thought maybe you'd like to read them. Take care, Pal," she said as she walked over and crawled into the van.

Neena continued waving until they had reached the corner and turned.

Curious, she went back up onto the porch and sat down on the swing. The envelope had one letter in it. It was addressed to Betsy Moran from Willis McClure. The other paper was a once-crumpled note, now smoothed out, ostensibly something passed at school.

Neena read the letter Betsy had given her:

Dear Betsy,

Thank you for answering. I know I wrote a lot of letters but I kept hoping you would write back. Are you sure Neena is pregnant? Is she okay? Does your grandma know for sure? I have written Neena a letter every day since I saw her but she doesn't answer. She must want nothing to do with me or it's possible she's not getting them. If you ever get a different address for her please let me know.

Willis McClure

Then Neena read the note:

Betsy,

So I'm a dad. Her name, Patrice Eleanor Teeple, is that a family name or did they just pick it? I like the nickname, Reecie. Did you see her? Did you see Neena or know anything about her? Is she okay? Will she come back? I gotta talk to her or something. Please tell me more.

Maybe I'll see you at the dance Friday night. You going?

Thank you,
Will

So Betsy had been Will's source. She should have guessed that Betsy would have dug around until she got some answers. Neena had wondered how Will knew she was pregnant, how he knew she had given birth to Reecie, but she had never thought to ask. He would have told her, she knew. She just never thought to ask. It made sense now; Betsy would have been relentless in finding what had happened to her.

Betsy had kept Will informed, had told him what had happened. That's how he knew that he was a father. Betsy. Neena thought her friend had faded into the woodwork the day after Neena left. She had been so wrong about so many things.

She gathered the letter and note and went in to find Will.

97 — Neena - Emmaus, Virginia
Late Summer 1981

She pulled back the covers and stole quietly out of their bed so as not to disturb Will who slept soundly at this time of morning. She felt like touching his face or his curly head but feared she would waken him. Instead, she slipped into a robe and walked out of the room on silent bare feet.

Their bedroom door latch made a click as she closed the door behind her, so she hesitated a moment, listening. Hearing no movement from Will, she continued down the hall.

She went into Jamie's room and looked down at him in the crib he would soon out-grow. At not quite two years old he had been crawling out of his crib for months, but now he slept soundly, his legs drawn up to his tummy under the blue blanket.

The room monitor remained on, but Neena left Jamie's door ajar anyway and then descended the stairs. She went to the kitchen, made herself an espresso from the tiny pot and poured it into a little cup she had brought back from her stay in France. It seemed like so long ago; so much had happened since then.

She took the cup and went out onto the porch at the front of the house, bent and wiped the dew from the swing seat, and then sat on it.

As Neena swung, Toot popped into her head for some reason, as she often did. She remembered her saying, "We are the sum total of our experiences."

Perhaps that was true, if a bit simplistic. Neena knew her experiences had shaped her.

Toot's little adages, where often unique to her, seemed alternately wise, mundane, or even inappropriate but endeared her to Neena. Toot had moved into a house beside Neena's and Will's two years ago. Toot could pass from her kitchen across the porch, through the gate, up the little walkway, and be in Neena's kitchen in twenty steps. She called at least five times a day but the calls were short and, while interruptive, usually made Neena smile. Neena cherished her; loved her more than she had ever loved Dessie, more than she had poor V. It's random, she thought, whom we love, how we love, when we love, and even why we love.

Neena pushed hard with her feet until the swing reached its full arc, then she drew her feet up, tucking her knees against her chest. The movement thrilled her as it had when she was just a child.

She sipped from her cup, pondering, realizing that she had grown accustomed to the vagaries of unhappiness, and now found it difficult to adjust to waking to one happy day after another. True, she experienced normalcy in her young life and even while living with both V and Toot, but there had long been an underlying unease, a niggling at her edges that kept her wary. Even now, on one glorious day after another, as she looked into the faces of her loving husband and her precious son, she hesitated in returning their smiles or their adoring gestures, as though she were caught off guard that they were, in fact, intended for her. Perhaps no one noticed her secret, that slight oscillation, that infinitesimal falter, but she remained acutely aware of it. She knew she had to work at this, this happiness, as one relearning to walk, with one measured, wobbly step after another.

She looked out across the lawn as the sun came up, the dew in the early morning light glistening like tears on eyelashes.

Will had said yesterday that the birds were calling for rain, and so they were. But not today; they would not get rain today, not with the heavy dew.

Everything seemed connected, after all: The dew to the rain; the rain to the earth; a man to his wife, to his children, to his God. It all trickled down somehow, although randomly it seemed at times, in spite of the artless prayers we utter over the cradles of our babies:

> *Let them be loved. Let them be safe.*
> *Let them take their pain and make of*
> *it something positive, for pain will*
> *come to them as it must to all of us.*

Perhaps her parents had prayed over her as she now prayed over little Jamie, and as she had, from afar, prayed over Reecie. Of course they would have. How absurd to think otherwise.

Perhaps her parents had prayed for guidance on just what specifically to do with their errant daughter all those many years ago.

Perhaps Aunt V had called when she found out about Neena's pregnancy and offered to let Neena come there and Neena's parents took it as a sign — or maybe Aunt Toot called a moment after Aunt V, a moment too late — or maybe Toot hadn't called at all, assuming that sending Neena away would never be an option . . ..

She sighed, trying to think of other possibilities. She didn't know why, after long periods of not even thinking of her parents, she would again begin mulling the same things over and over. At least, now, thanks to Toot, she knew why she had been given up for adoption. So, V had been a bad girl, just like her offspring. So many secrets.

Had her grandmother been complicit in rendering her yearly birthday recitation of how Neena had been born on the hard back pew? Had it happened that way only with a different mother than she, Neena, had assumed? Had it happened at all?

Had it been an oral history that her grandmother had given her to help her feel grounded? So many things she would never know.

That was done and over with. She would take Will's advice.

"I don't say this unkindly, Neena, but you are like one of those little windup toy cars. You crank it up, get the wheels spinning, put it down and it zips straight away. If a wall gets in its way, it just sits there and rams it over and over until it exhausts its power. Being unable to forgive is like that, my sweet, sweet Neena. Before you can forgive, you have to stop the futile repetition of ramming up against the past, rehashing what happened, what might have happened, what people's motives were... whether they loved you. Doesn't that just wear you out?"

He had taken her hands and rubbed their tops with his big thumbs.

"I suggest you visit the past one more time, as objectively as you can. Put the blame squarely where it belongs, if you can even objectively assign blame. The truth is you have spent enough time operating on the little evidence in front of you, but, as you have lamented many times, you don't have all the information. Try a different tack. Draw a different scenario that may be more fair – or not, who knows. Base it on what you know for certain, what you remember, what you wish had been the case, or even all of those mixed in together. What can it really hurt? The other way hasn't worked. Look at the good things that did happen. Then write your own endings, your own beginnings. You aren't really relinquishing anything of value either way. In any event, I suggest you forgive them even though they never asked for forgiveness."

He shook her hands gently until he was sure he had her attention.

"For your sake, my sweet Neena; forgive them for your sake."

He reached up and touched her cheek with his finger, lightly sliding it down until he reached the bottom of her chin.

"Then, once you have done that, you have to stop; just stop. Stop like you would if you were behind the wheel of that little toy car. Just stop. Draw your own scenarios and then write, *The End*.

* * * * *

So she would remember how Aunt Toot had always made an effort to be part of her life; how she had made her feel special. She would remember Aunt Verina bustling about on silent feet, cooking, cleaning, and making a home for her, with love, she now realized. She would remember her loving uncles. She would remember her dear grandmother, a woman who shaped her young years. She would remember her mother stroking her hair as she read to her, her little girl. She would remember her mother baking cookies with her in the middle of the night when Neena was sick and restless. She would remember her father resting his head on his hands as he held to the rail of her hospital bed when she was six and had her tonsils removed. Every time she had opened her eyes, he had been there, looking at her, or, if his eyes were closed, listening for her.

Her father hadn't come out to the car that mist-laden summer morning in 1951, the day they took her away.

She had always imagined that, after her departure that morning, he had finished his usual cup of coffee, and then had rushed, as was his custom, into his study to begin his day: Collecting ideas for sermons, reading, or checking to see who needed visiting that week.

Now, with her new-found vision, she could imagine, at least, that he had battled with himself over his decision for her, or that he had even, perhaps, run to the door too late to call her back.

Or perhaps – oh, perhaps, perhaps, he had stood and watched her go. Perhaps he had watched and watched until he could see her no longer.

The End.

About the Author

Sally Kerr-Kelly has always had a love of storytelling. She majored in English at the prestigious liberal arts institution of Allegheny College not far distant from her hometown of Titusville, Pennsylvania. She was the recipient of the Sandra Doane Turk Award for distinguished scholarship during her tenure there.

Sally has two grown sons, four step-children, and an abundance of grandchildren. She enjoys laughter with family and friends, likes to play games, appreciates nature's beauty, and travels extensively to experience other cultures in their particular environments.

Sally and her husband have lived in Virginia for the past sixteen years where she continues the quest of writing stories that will not only entertain, but will also provide insights that may help others find their way through their life struggles.

To direct comments to the author just send your emails to: SallyKerrKelly@PacohiPublishing.com.

Soon to be released...

BEYOND THE SCOPE OF REASON

By Sally Kerr-Kelly

A Rapport Books Novel
Pacohi Publishing

In her latest novel, *Beyond The Scope of Reason*, Sally Kerr-Kelly takes the reader on a journey of suspense rooted in a spur-of-the-moment, well-intentioned act.

Essie Caponetto is a quiet, unobtrusive person who has always been a model of dependability for those around her. When she witnesses a sordid deed, she reacts by taking matters into her own hands and flees without regard for the consequences.

In her rash departure, Essie betrays her rock-star cousin, Dregs, by taking something dear to him. Although they had always been close, he is hurt, angry, and seeks retaliation.

Essie escapes with the help of an acquaintance but is tracked by a hit man, her cousin's private investigator, and possibly others. She hides out moving from place to place.

Essie could never have guessed how much she would learn about herself and those close to her. Nor could she have known that her remorse for a well-intentioned act would push her to the brink, over the edge, *Beyond The Scope of Reason*.

Visit PacohiPublishing.com *for availability*